FAR NORTH
& OTHER DARK TALES
SARA MAITLAND

Published in 2008 by
The Maia Press Limited
82 Forest Road
London E8 3BH
www.maiapress.com

'Far North' (under the title 'True North'), 'Cassandra',
'Rapunzel Revisited' and 'The Tale of the Beautiful Princess
Kalito' were previously published in the UK in *Women Fly
When Men Aren't Watching* (1993); 'Siren Song' in *By the Light
of the Silvery Moon* (ed. Ruth Petrie, 1994); 'The Tale of the
Valiant Demoiselle' and 'Seal-self' in *A Book of Spells* (1987)

ISBN 978 1 904559 27 6

A CIP catalogue record for this book is available from the
British Library

Printed and bound in Great Britain by Thanet Press on
paper from sustainable managed forests

The Maia Press is supported by Arts Council England

CONTENTS

FAR NORTH

ar north, inside the ice circle, in the land of the long
night, lived two women. One was a young woman and
one was an old woman. The old woman must have
known how they came to be living there, on their own, so
far away from other people, but she never said. The young
woman did not know – she remembered no other view than
the long lifting of the snow banks and the chopped ragged
ice in the sea below their home.

Because there was no one else they did not need names
for each other and used none. Because they had no community they did not need to name their relationship either, and
they did not do so. They never used the words mother or
daughter or friend or sister or aunt, niece, cousin, lover.
They just lived there together. Because there was no one to
see they did not know that the young woman was very
beautiful and that the old woman was not. They knew that
the old woman was full of ancient knowledge and useful
skills, was wise in the ways of weather and seals, and knew
all the hundred words for snow. The young woman was
strong and tough and could run all day, a slow steady lope
across the snow, in pursuit of the moose herds, and she

could crawl and slither over the ice after seals and polar bears. And in the evenings the old woman could tell stories about the Seal Queen, and the lemmings maddened by each other and the winter fever who rushed into the sea; and her gums could chew, her hands could carve and her fingers could sew and plait and skin and braid. The young woman could sing and dance and let down her beautiful long hair and comb the thick dark mess until it glowed and sparkled with strange lights. And so they lived happily for a long time.

When spring comes inside the ice circle it is not with long rains and sweet emerging greenness. Instead there is the strange sound of the deep ice crashing and gonging as it breaks up – howling at night as it shifts and moves at last. The skeins of geese overhead break the stillness of the air with the powerful rush of their homecoming; and the she-seals are fat with promise and contentment. The light begins to seep back into the air; hardly noticed at first, the blubber lamp pales and the distant ice floes take on specific shapes. Where the winter freeze humped and pressured the sea into strange designs there is a new flatness smoothing itself back into water, but slowly.

And one year, with the spring, came something new. One morning when the young woman left the warmth of the ice house she saw, far away across the whiteness, a new shape she had never seen before and heard, borne on the motionless air, a new noise, a swish-swish. The shape was dark and tall and it was not silent. In fear she watched a while and the shape came nearer. She turned back into the ice house and told the old woman. And the old woman wrapped a polar fur around herself and came out. The shape had come nearer; it had a strange rising and falling gait, not the smoothness of an animal but rhythmic, lilting like the tune from a song. The shape was coming towards them directly and with purpose and both women were afraid, though for very different reasons: the young woman was afraid because she did not know what the shape was. The old woman was afraid because she did. It was a man.

He was a young man, tall and handsome. He was an ice traveller. He had spent the winter far from his village, all alone, because of a courageous but foolish error of judgement which had taken him too far to get back before the snow storms and the darkness had come. He had wintered far from his own people and was now on his way home. He was surprised to discover this ice house; he had not known that anyone could go away and live so far from the village. Now, swishing on his wide snow shoes, swinging each leg wide of the other, his pack on his back, he came across the snow plateau and, seeing the smoke, thought of singing and company and warm meals cooked by someone not himself and of a few days' rest before he went on with his endless ice travelling.

The two women stood at the door of their home. With the necessary courtesy of people who live in such cruel terrain it never occurred to them that they would not welcome him and feed him with whatever they had available and keep him in comfort until he was ready to travel again. In the pale light of the mid-morning he came towards them, slowly, swinging and swishing, and they stood there and waited for him. And when he came up they took him by the arms and led him into their home, and all three of them stood unwinding from their fur clothes in the light of the blubber oil lamp. And as she took off her seal-skin jacket and pulled back her fur-rimmed hood the young woman learned at last that she was beautiful, because his eyes told her so. And as she sunk to her haunches to tend the cooking the old woman knew that she was old and ugly, because his eyes did not even turn from the young woman.

Of course the young man loved the young woman; and the young woman loved the young man. Nothing else was possible with the spring crashing into life around them and both of them strangers to the other, and the young woman had never seen a man before and the young man was far from home on a courageous but foolish journey. Yes, they loved each other and the young man took the young woman to wife there in the ice house, on the fullness of the spring tides in front of the old woman and she said not a word, but squatted lower over the cooking pot and faded as the summer came. She could not hate the young woman because she had known and lived with her for far too long, and she could not hate the young man because she could see the rightness of this mating. But her sleep was disturbed by their loving and then by the dreams that came to her afterwards.

In some ways it was good to have the young man with them. With two hunters, both active and tireless and whose bodies know the curves and thoughts of each other's, there is hunting possible which cannot be done alone, and the piles of fur beside the house mounted and the young man talked of trading and possessions that the women knew nothing about – of drink that turned your head to fire and allowed you to meet the ancestors again and fight with the monsters; of fishing hooks and needles so fine and strong that they seemed magical; of colours and ribbons and beads and clothes that the women thought were parts of stories and not real though he told them over and over again. He took the old woman's skins in his hands and admired them and said that she had more skill with the knife than anyone, man or woman, he had ever seen and the skins that she handled would fetch higher prices. And he picked up the carvings she did, in bone and rock, marvelling how the walrus and the bear and the fish were revealed growing there. These too they could trade and he described the things that he and the young woman could have if they sold the carvings the old woman had made. And she who had carved for delight alone, through the long winter, wanted to snatch back her animals from his hands and hide them, but she did not. She did not because the muscles on his neck stood out like the sinews of the moose, and his legs were sturdy, strong and planted firmly in the ground, and his hands were driving into her heart and gut with their strength and beauty, and because the white horn of his nails made her think of the new moon. But she did not trust him.

And she was right. One day the young woman came to her and said that they were going away. She did not think about the old woman left alone in the ice house when winter came again; she did not think about the cold wind and the wildness to be endured alone. She said that he had made a sledge for her, each runner the rib of a great he-walrus that the young man had killed for her; he had worked on the sledge secretly when the old woman thought that he was hunting or walking or fishing. She said the sledge was the most beautiful thing she had ever seen; each runner was intricately carved; the seat was lined with pale fur; the seal sinews were so strong and taut that she would ride without a jolt across the frozen wastes. He would take her to his village and buy for her beads and jewels and garments worthy of her beauty. The young woman told the old woman that her husband was going to take her away from this dreary desolation, and this empty lonely life, and bring her to a place where her beauty would be appreciated and reflect credit on him. She told the old woman also that there was a child growing in her, that she hoped for a son as lithe and fine and strong as the young man, that she would have a son and a place where her beauty could be admired.

The old woman desired the beauty of the young woman; she desired the child of the young woman; she desired the husband of the young woman; and she had little enough to do all day except feed those desires. So that they ate into her, like the ice of the approaching autumn, creeping up the rivers of her blood. Soon the couple must be gone, because the courage and foolishness of the young man were diminished by the loveliness of his wife and his tenderness for her, and he wanted to be in his village safe and certain before the hard weather and the long night came. The time was approaching when the old woman could wait no longer. One day the young man was gone from the house, so the old woman said to the young woman that it was a long, long time since she had braided up that beautiful hair. She said that they should prepare a special feast for the young man and that the young woman must look her most beautiful. The young woman was pleased; she felt that the old woman had not entered into her joy and had withdrawn from her recently so she was happy to find that she had been mistaken. So she unpinned her long hair and sat cross-legged on the floor at the feet of the old woman. The old woman took the comb made from bone which she had carved many years ago for the young woman and began to comb her hair. And she combed and combed. She revelled for the last time in that living loveliness; the hair shone and shook in the light of the lamp and sparkled like the sea-deep does in midsummer when it is crazed by the lights of the underworld that float up and dance on the surface. The young woman told her to hurry, eager to see her beauty in the admiration of the young man. So then the old woman took the hair and began to twist and braid it into a fat rope, and she took the rope and wound it round the young woman's lovely cream-coloured neck and pulled and pulled, tighter and tighter, until the young woman was dead. Then she took her little hand knife, which she had made herself for skinning, down from the wall and, using all of her immense and practised skill, she skinned the young woman's face, not spoiling the hair which was both lovely and necessary, not pulling out one eyelash nor missing the soft curves of lip and cheek. And when the young woman was faceless and bloody she dragged her out of the house and buried her in the soft snow of a drift not far away. Then she took a broom and swept the house and the snow with great attention so that no blood and no drag lines and no mess could be seen. Then she took a soft sealskin shift that she had made herself for the young woman and put it on; its gentle folds caressed her skin and everything seemed possible for her. She washed in ice water, the coldness of it bracing her joyfully. After all that she took the skin from the face of the young woman and with the delicate practice of the years smoothed the young woman's face over her own. Its lovely pliability covered the wrinkles and jutting bones of her old, ugly face; she pulled the creamy skin of the neck down as far as it would go, securing it with an ivory pin to the top of the soft shift; she tugged the heavy mass of hair back over her own thinning greasy locks and shook her head so that it fell loose again covering the seam-lines. And then she lay on the bed that the young couple had made themselves, and covered herself with the furs and skins under which they lay night after night, leaving her outside. The thought of what she had done warmed her; the thought of what was coming heated her. She lay there waiting, reading and eager.

The young man came home. She heard the gentle rhythm of his snow shoes; she heard him banging off the spare snow and stomping about outside the house; she heard his muffled breath as he pulled his skin-jacket over his head; she heard the soft whistle that he always made when he was tired but pleased with himself. He came in. And seeing her lying on the bed all beautiful and waiting for him, he smiled. Where was the old one he asked. And she told him that she had gone to the beach to look for a special stone for a special carving, to be a present for them at their departure, a very special carving as a bride gift and a gift for the child. The young man said that that was good because such a carving by the old hag would fetch a good price from some white-skinned collector and he laughed. The old woman would be gone for hours on such a task. The young man tugged at his boots; then he pulled off his shift, his trousers. His chest was muscled and beautiful, his loins were leaping for his bride, he fell upon her and she, kicking back the blankets, received him in her eagerness. He plunged into her body and she responded with delight. He was so far into his joy and lust that he did not notice the changed body. He plunged and bucked like the melting of a river when the great chunks of ice are hurled suddenly into the sea; he melted into her like the full tide of spring; and she leaped up for him like a young seal taking to the water for the first time. He rode her like the porpoise schools, she held him like the ocean deep. There was a love and a knowing in them both.

He worked her like an old bull walrus and it was hot hard work and at last he was done and lifted his head and smiled down into her eyes. And the sweat from his joyful labour dripped from his forehead down the fringe of his black hair and fell on to her face. It shrivelled the skin, because the old woman had not had time for proper curing. The skin of the young woman shrank and curled away from the face of the old woman. Where it was secured at the neck with the ivory pin it tore away; from around her mouth the lips peeled back revealing her thin tired gums. The bones of her cheeks broke through the tenderness of the young woman's skin. The tears that sprang in her eyes rolled away the young woman's soft velvet and uncovered the harsh wrinkles. The hair-line parted under the strain – the thick hair falling backwards on to the pile of bed-skins, the forehead dissolving, shrinking, disappearing.

With his hands he completed the work his sweat had begun, scrabbling at her face, scratching her, making her bleed. She herself did not move. Still naked, still lying on her, his lower body still replete with joy, the horror came into his eyes. The young man screamed and leapt to his feet; he grabbed for his shift, his breeches and boots and rushed out into the gathering gloom. She heard him retching and gasping as he fumbled the straps of his snow shoes. She heard his heaves and moans as he gathered what was necessary from around him. At last she heard the swishing, swishing mixed with his horror, repulsion and guilt. The noises died away into the twilight, diminishing, fading and finally, after many many minutes, finally gone.

And then the old woman was alone.

THE SWANS

The Young Queen lies in her great bed and listens. In her own silence she has become attuned to the silence of the night, so she can hear the huge silent spinning of the stars and the soft footfalls of cats on the prowl. Her newborn boy-child in the carved and gilded cradle breathes silently through his first night.

The Young Queen has been silent long enough to hear properly. She hears the quiet malevolent steps of the Old Queen, her husband's mother, climbing the winding stair, and approaching the royal birth chamber along the cold passageway. The Young Queen closes her eyes so she cannot see, but she cannot close her ears. She hears the doorlatch lift and the candle flames shimmer in the new draught. She hears the Old Queen walk to the cradle and the whispered creak as the baby is lifted out. She hears the Old Queen's slippers turn on the stone floor and – nearly as silently as the cats – come towards the bed. She knows the Old Queen is standing beside her, the child on one arm and the small bowl of goat's blood in her other hand.

'I know you are awake,' says the Old Queen, very softly.

The Young Queen opens her eyes and the two of them look straight at each other. Almost, perhaps, nearly, they smile.

The Young Queen respects the Old Queen; she even admires her. The Young Queen knows that she herself would not rest easy if her son, if any of her three sons, came home one day with a half-naked but beautiful woman-child who would not speak. A woman whose eyes proved her understanding and her feeling, but who never spoke, never laughed, never sang. 'Witchcraft', she would have feared, 'magic things'; and the Old Queen fears them too. Sometimes, as the Old Queen does always, the Young Queen despises the King, her husband, because he loves a woman about whom he knows nothing – a woman who never speaks, never laughs, never sings, never cries out in joy or pain, even in the night in the great royal bed.

'I know you are awake,' says the Old Queen into the Young Queen's silence.

'Look,' says the Old Queen, 'Look at me. Once again, I am going to steal this child away. I am going to smear your mouth with goat's blood and tell them you have eaten him. This will be the third time. This time they will believe me. You will be burned for a witch.'

The Young Queen closes her eyes.

'Call, go on, call out,' says the Old Queen, 'shout, just once, and they'll come running. I have the baby and the bowl of blood. Proof. They'll burn me instead.'

And I will have won, says her silence, which the Young Queen can hear, I will have defeated you and your everlasting silence.

The Old Queen places the bowl on the table beside the

bed and dabbles her fingers in it. The Young Queen feels the Old Queen's hand warm on her mouth and chin; she can smell the salt sweet goat's blood. Then she feels the air stretch between her lips and the heavy ringed fingers, hears the Old Queen shift the child on her arm, pick up the bowl, turn and leave the room.

The Young Queen lies quite still. There is blood on her mouth and blood between her legs but she does not attempt to wipe either away. Silently the night turns, turns towards the morning and the Young Queen waits until there is light enough to get up and continue her sewing.

High on the shoulder, in the pass between the mountains, the tarn holds the water from the steep hills above in its peaceful arms. This plateau is the watershed; two tiny streams flow out at either end of the tarn, but it itself is perfectly still. The dawn comes slowly. The stars fade and the black sky turns indigo. Details emerge colourless out of the darkness. The sky changes: indigo, grey, cream. The view opens away mysteriously: far, far below, southwards, the river twists and loops silver down to the bay; far, far below, northwards, the forest stretches dark and dense into the distance.

The sky changes: grey, cream, peach. The higher mountains to the west catch the first sun, a splash of brightness like blood. Over the eastern cliff two buzzards float. The moth-markings of their under-wings are lit suddenly by the new sun, tawny gold as they ride the air.

The sky changes: cream, peach, pale, palest blue. There is no wind. The tarn is milky white. But when the seven swans lumber up out of the reed bed and lurch clumsy, bulky, awkward on their stubby feet to the pebble shore, then the surface of the tarn is not white but silver because the swans are white. They take to the water and are changed, graceful, wild and silent. Whiter than dreams, their beaks red-orange, with black knobbed nostrils and eyes, they drift so, not rippling the shining silver. The sun rises. A sudden shocking gold stabs on to the water. The swans swim together, a raft of white, heads curving forward. They turn together, facing northwards, the sun bright on their right flanks.

There is a huge bashing, crashing, splashing din as they lumber, beat their way down the tarn, wings labouring, feet running, kicking on the water. Faster, louder. Then on a breath they are airborne, majestic, powerful, circling as the water falls back into stillness. Above the tarn they form themselves into a wedge, an arrowhead. Together as a single flight they turn north. As they settle into their steady drive, the throbbing music of their wingbeats breaks the silence over the hills and forest.

The Young Queen sits near the window to catch the first light. As soon as she can see what she is doing she picks up her sewing. Her stitches are tiny, delicate and placed with exquisite care. The middle finger of her right hand is roughened and calloused from the pricks and pins of her long task. Even after all her years of practice it is still difficult to sew the dry white starwort petals with the short threads of yellow sepal. She cannot hurry this work. She does not hurry even though she is fairly certain that she will not have time now to complete the last of the shirts.

The sky changes: grey, cream, peach. She does not wipe

the blood from her lips. As the sky brightens she hears the King come up the stairs. There is a knock on her door but no pause before the latch is lifted. She lowers her head over her sewing. The King and his close council come into the room, standing solemn, stern, strangely calm. The King crosses the floor and glances into the empty cradle. He looks at her and she raises her head to meet his eyes. She sees his horror and sadness. He sees how beautiful she is, and how serene. Tears spring in both their eyes, spill over the lashes, run down their cheeks, but they say nothing. For once he has joined her in her silence. They look at each other for a long moment. Then he turns, and all the court with him, and blunders from the room.

The sky changes: cream, peach, pale palest blue. At last she rises and looks out the window southward over the enormous forest. She is not frightened of the forest though many people are. She has wandered there by moonlight from April through to June gathering starwort, the white flowers nodding on their tall straggling stems. Today there is nothing to be seen but the dark of the forest and the pale blue sky. She leans forward over the casement and looks down on the courtyard where there are men busy building a pile of tarred wood around a stake, a bonfire to burn the witch. The tower is high so they look foreshortened, unreal, like insects scuttling. She walks to a chest on the far side of the room, and opens it and takes out the six shirts she has finished. She goes back to her seat, lays the shirts in a tidy pile beside her and picks up the unfinished shirt. She starts sewing again; stitching carefully, patiently, while she waits.

It is clear that she cannot walk down the spiral staircase.

Only yesterday she had a child. One of the guards carries her. His arms are strong and her head lies on his shoulder. She has one arm round his neck and on the other she carries the seven starwort shirts, even the last, the unfinished one which has no left sleeve, because there is no more time. They have a strange old-fashioned scent, a smell of summer and hops and mown grass, that soothes her.

At the foot of the tower the young guard puts her down, but she sways and falls against him. He picks her up again and slowly and solemnly carries her across the great courtyard to the pyre they have built for her. She is so beautiful he thinks his heart will break, but when she raises her head he sees the blood still on her mouth and his gorge rises and he puts her down abruptly. She turns away from him and by herself, freely, she clambers up the log pile. At the top she pauses. Now she uses one of the shirts to wipe her face, to wipe away the blood. Then she turns to face the crowd and she is so beautiful that there is silence.

The silence is broken by a pompous lawyer reading a long and pointless document. You cannot kill a Queen or a witch in silence. There has to be some legal process to go through. The law is about words so it is no concern of hers. She wants for him to be done and, while she waits, she thinks. She is sad because she does not want to die. She is sad because she loves the King. She is sad because she has held each of her three children for only a few moments. She is sad because she has not rescued her seven brothers from their enchantment, although she has tried so hard.

The reading finishes. They ask her formally if she has any defence, but they know now she will not speak and so there is a slight blurring of the protocol. Let what must be done be done quickly now. No one likes it and no one will turn back. The Old Queen is as silent now as the Young Queen. A trumpet is blown. A brand is lit. The smoke rises thick and black against the white walls of the palace; then thinner and whiter against the pale blue sky. Everyone's eyes follow it upwards, then squint into the morning sun. The bearer of the flaming brand starts to march up the courtyard towards the Young Queen on her high pyre.

There is a throbbing song, a dark music in the air and, through the smoke, fast, faster than dreams, there is an arrow-head, a white drive of power and air and wind and the great beating music of the swans' wings and a high shrill cry. And the Young Queen takes the shirts from her left arm with her right hand and tosses them high into the air and each swan, without a break in its onrushing flight, without shifting its place in the wedge, catches up a shirt in its red-orange bill. Sssssssssssssshshshshshs. Is it the hiss of angry swans or of swords swift-drawn from their scabbards as the seven brothers surround their sister? They are swans no more, but the Young Queen's brothers, now set free from their long enchantment. Then there is a peal of laughter like a bell and it is the Young Queen laughing in the arms of the King.

They all live happily ever after. Even the three lost children are found, hidden in the Old Queen's Dower House. The two older ones are happy to meet their happy father and their beautiful mother; the new, tiny one gurgles joyful on her breast. They have learned something from her silence; they never ask why she preferred her brothers to her sons.

The brothers and the King become friends. They hunt and drink and sing together. They all love the Young Queen and are grateful to her. Though the youngest brother walks strangely, lopsided, and grows wild and silent. He has no left arm and from his left shoulder springs a great white wing of power and beauty. But even the youngest brother in a fairy story cannot fly with only one wing.

CASSANDRA

ection of the interhemispheric tracts (commissurotomy) to control epilepsy has been found to eliminate much of the normal integration of sensory
information. . . . For instance commissurotomised
subjects cannot put words to music, or music to words.
Subjects could identify by pointing to stimuli seen in the
left field and by naming stimuli simultaneously seen in the
right field. They could not explain the discrepancy and
they gave no indication that they had seen either stimulus
as other than complete and regular. The recognition and
memory of faces – a skill of the 'minor' (right) hemisphere – cannot be articulated in language – a skill of the
'major' (left) hemisphere. Catastrophic reactions and
feelings of guilt and depression were common after left-
hemisphere anaesthetisation; while feelings of euphoria
often followed right-side anaesthetisation. Commissurotomised patients reacted strongly with blushing and
giggling to the presentation of pictures of nudes in
the left visual field, even when the 'major' hemisphere
showed by its verbalisations that it had no idea why this
was happening. The right hemisphere outperformed the
left in accurate perception and memory of stimuli that
have no verbal label or are too complex or too similar to

express the words, but only the left hemisphere can give language to these memories.

There is a gap and she knows there is a gap between what she sees and what she says. She cannot, she cannot leap the gap. It is lonely. It is cold. There are too many feelings of depression and guilt and euphoria. She feels entirely alone, and the horizon still glows with the burning of the towers of Ilium.

> The severing of the *corpus callosum*, the hard bond of nerves that connects the left and right hemispheres of the brain, has been found to eliminate the normal integration of sensory information.

He watches her unhappily as she stands in the prow of the boat; she looks huddled and cold. The usual scars, bruises and scratches on her face seem to stand out. She seems small and frail. Her beauty is not diminished, indeed it is undeniable, overwhelming, but suddenly it is the beauty of a child, not of a woman. A child, and a sad lost child at that. He draws in a breath, racked with a new pain. He, Agamemnon, King of Argos, commander of the victorious forces of Greece, is in pain; and the pain is inflicted on him by a little hunched child who rides the prow of his boat with an unreadable expression. It is called compassion, that is the name of his pain, and he is not used to feeling it. They say, the Greek warriors, that he struck a poor bargain in the taking of the spoils; that he chose the mad woman, the crazy one, when he could have chosen the voluptuous courtesans of Troy, any of the women of the city who flocked in defeat about his feet and begged to be his portion. He knows, fretfully, that he made the best bargain of his life, that just to have her, have her here, untouchable and untouched, to have her ride the prow of his ship and gaze at the sea with her dark eyes, that this is enough. And if he is gentle, gentle and patient as a fisherman, strong and unmoving as the sea, she will come to him and tell him, tell him what it is, what happens in her head, what happened in the beginning to make her so different from other women, so alone, so powerful, so frail. But the pain of patience irks him and he paces the boat half-irritated.

He is wrong. She will not tell him. She will not tell him any of it. At one moment she is riding the ship, mourning the city of her childhood, mourning the bright princes who were her brothers, mourning the gallant stupidity with which they died. 'Hector,' she murmurs, but even as she says his name his face disappears from her mind, and when she finds the face again she does not know whose face it is. She likes Agamemnon. She has a knowing that he will not . . . that he will wait . . . that he will . . . she does not know the word for what it is she fears, for what it is she knows he will not do. Then the next minute it is gone, it is all gone; there is a clear, familiar, strange sensation which begins in the middle finger of her left hand and spreads through her body, a feeling of intense stillness and power that reaches out from inside her to the whole sea; and the bright islands of the Aegean dance on the water, totally vital, totally still. A transparent moment, turning from gold to green. Everything is green. Green. She feels quite clearly the spittle forming on her lips, she hears her own mouth open with a strange birdlike noise, she feels her whole body lurch forward, her shoulders smashing down, the heel of the God forcing her face into the wooden deck.

He runs along the ship, suddenly shaken into movement. He feels immediately the compassion of the crew, but his fear is that she will fall into the sea. He forces her mouth open, inserts the leather scabbard of his dagger between her teeth, wipes the foam from the side of her mouth, tries to hold her firmly but gently, and is amazed at the extraordinary strength of her convulsions. It does not last long; as suddenly as it started she flops against him, limp, washed out like a soft cloth. She opens her eyes and smiles at him.

'She will kill you,' she says, 'in water. Not in the sea, which can wash away the blood. She will kill you. There will be a lot of blood. I can see it.'

'It's all right,' he says, 'it's all right, don't worry. I'm here, I won't let anyone hurt you.'

'Not me. You. It's the swan's eggs; there was too much blood, there in the laying of the eggs, too much blood and yours will be there.'

'Don't worry,' he says again desperately. Is the look in her eyes consent or despair? Quite suddenly she seems very sleepy. He gathers her up in his arms and carries her like a little child below decks and there on his own bunk, surrounded by the outward signs of his military prestige – sword, helmet, trophies from Troy – she sleeps, curled round; the scab of blood on her lip looking like the traces of a child's sweetmeat. She seems innocent and open, but she is closed off from him. Asleep, this feels forgivable, although with a sigh he knows he would forgive her anyway. He tries to focus on what she said. He had killed his own daughter for a prophecy; he believes in prophecy. 'She will kill you.' The first time she had said it it had been with urgency, with commitment. It was only the repetition that had sounded crazed. As he tries to concentrate he sees the speckled foam from her mouth still clinging to his left sleeve, he remembers the power of her body racked by the convulsions. She was raving. He shrugs his shoulders. Of course she was raving, he tells himself. Standing up he feels his tunic wet against his stomach. She had lost control of her bladder and he had carried her closely: he does not know why he is touched instead of revolted. Checking surreptitiously that she is truly asleep he strips and changes. He wants to promise the world to her; he wants, against his own self-knowledge, to swear that he will never use his power against her, that he will keep her safe, that he will never do anything she does not like. But she is asleep, uninterested in his professions, in his promises.

She dreams. But even she does not know what she dreams.

Troy burns. The flames are high and hot. She has fled from the broken city to a sanctuary. But the Greeks come there and all women are spoils of war. She is spoiled, despoiled, raped. There is no end to it; the flames in her eyes and in her belly. Her vagina broken, the secret places smashed into. She could have suffered this in the beginning, and then all would have been well.

Hector's body is dragged around the walls of the city. She sees Helen smile faintly, uncaring. She sees the eyes of Paris, her favourite brother, light up with jealousy relieved. Paris has hated Hector for years. Hector, the bravest of the Trojans, the hero without blemish, is dragged round the walls of Troy and her sad, old father has to beg his enemies for the return of the battered flesh.

Agamemnon who has rescued her is chopped up with an axe. Undignified, struggling to pull on a tunic whose armholes have been sewn together. An infantile prank turned deadly. And everything she sees, she sees over and over and over again. Again and again in the still, pure moment before the God stamps on her shoulders and flattens her to the ground, she sees. She sees what will happen and she tells it and no one can believe her. She cannot believe herself; in each bitter instant Cassandra hears her own truths as spittle and crazed foaming. There is a gap and she knows there is a gap between what she sees and what she says. She cannot, she cannot leap that gap. She cannot fit the words to music, nor music to words. She cannot remember faces and names at the same time. It is very lonely.

> Commissurotomy – the severing of the *corpus callosum*, the tissue which provides the connection between the two functionally asymmetric hemispheres of the brain – has been found to eliminate the normal integration of sensory information. The left hemisphere thus receives detailed information about visual stimuli only if they fall in the right visual half-field and about some aesthetic stimuli only if they contact the right side of the body. The same is obviously true for the right hemisphere. The two hemispheres process information differently; the left hemisphere being superior in terms of language function while the right is superior when required to perform a spatial transformation on sensory input. Moreover, there is competition between the left and right hemispheres of commissurotomised patients for control of motor output;

and this leads to further, complicated distortions in motor-dependent communication.

She is a very beautiful woman. No one ever questioned this, even with the inevitable cuts and bruises to her face and hands; and her frequently bizarre and inappropriate expressions. She had been, though, a radiant child. Loving, laughing, lovely. Cassandra. Now there is, inside her own ears, a hissing and a writhing in her name; but then there had been a musical giggle.

Apollo had desired her. No, Apollo had loved her. But this she does not remember. She remembers nothing about this at all. It is all burned away. She sees the future, but she does not see the past. She does not remember, recall, recollect.

But Apollo, the burning sun-god, the most beautiful, most vital of the Olympians, loved her. Before there was time for confusion, before there was time for anyone else, he came to her. Just post-menarche, still joyful in her own power, still untried, untouched. Too much love for one so simple. His desire left him insensitive to his love. He would not be stayed. The horses of the sun champed on their bits while he spoke with her; she was blinded, confused by his brightness. Perhaps she did not even know what he was talking about. It was the first time. The first time that every inch of her flesh reached out greedy, greedy and needy. There was no past, no future; no family, no friends. He offered her anything, anything that she wanted; he was a god and his godliness rose up between his legs just to watch her considering the offer, halfway between greedy spoiled child and greedy sexy woman. He felt his power and prepared to produce for her castles made of ice that would not melt although the sun shone day and night upon them. He prepared to unsling his own lute from his shoulders and give her authority over all the music in the world. He prepared to summon Pegasus so that she might ride on the great winged horse and bestride the mountains and the oceans to the stabling place of the golden sun chariot and the eight great stallions that pulled it. His power to give her what she wanted delighted him. And she asked him for a spiral shell that was pink inside and without a chip missing. She and her sisters had a collection of shells; they would walk with their handmaids beside the sea and gather up beautiful shells from the beautiful beaches of Ilium and carry them home; but none of them had ever found an unflawed, perfect, spiralled horn with the silvery pink lining. The request struck his pride, and in his anger he laughed at her and she was humiliated. She spoke as a child and was exposed as a child, and in the shadow of his mockery she became a woman, a woman who knew her power over men and gods. She said, 'Give me the power to tell the future, give me the power to know what will happen. Make me a prophetess and a seer and a soothsayer and an oracle. If you can.'

There was a flicker, a flicker in the sunlight by the river. There are things that are not permitted, even to the most golden and potent of young gods. The sunlight flickered, and the flickering was the shadow of his doubt. She sat, not caring, as happy to dabble her toes in the river and smile as she was to be given this thing. But she clearly sensed her own desirability, and she pulled in her cheeks and pouted and looked little and cross and his heart melted with . . .

with what? With lust, with amusement, with tenderness, with the desire to show off? She was old enough to seduce and not old enough to know what it meant. He knew then that he did not have the right; that he could give her presents and affection, and love, but he did not have the right to take her, to own her, to possess her whole lovely sweet virginal body. And he was ashamed, and angry and greedy. So he did not restrain himself from using all his power.

'If I do that for you, what will you do for me?'

'What do you want?'

She became sly, the slyness of curiosity, because she wanted to know, wanted to know what this feeling was, both the feeling of power and the feeling of reaching towards, wanting, wanting, wanting.

'I want you to be my lover.'

She laughed. It seemed so little a thing, of course she would love someone who gave her what she wanted; and the words brought a feeling to her arms and her high hard little breasts; the tickling rising feeling in her nipples and the soft sinking feeling in the pit of her belly, and she wanted suddenly to cover his golden body with honey all over and lick it off slowly, slowly in the sunshine. She wanted to spread her legs and . . . and she knew not what, but she consented to the bargain.

And now he was haughty and calm. He spat neatly on his finger, and crouched down beside her on the grass. He touched quite gently her lips, and then her eyes, and last her ears, and when he touched her ears she saw the first high flames leap above the topless towers of Troy and felt the great grief of loss and pain and the great chasm of fear, but before she could think about it he took his finger and laid it on her right nipple and the darkness vanished and she reached up with the innocence of a child and the passion of a woman and put her arms around him and gave his neck a long kiss. They stayed there a minute and her desire mounted. Then he took his hand away from her breast and placed it under her chin and compelled her mouth towards his. The sun shone and she was full of joy and curiosity and excitement.

Then he kissed her.

She responded to his kiss with an eagerness, a voluptuous enthusiasm, receiving his tongue deep in her mouth and working her own with happy little wriggles along the inside of his lip. And he pushed her gently backwards and kissed her deeper, harder, more demandingly, reaching with his free hand for her white thigh. And suddenly she could not.

It was too much, too much feeling, too much closeness, there was no Cassandra, no princess there, but only flesh and burning flesh and she could not. She was frightened. He did not feel her fear, he could not give her space, he was not willing to wait. She pushed at him and there was no escape, and she hit out at his face with her hands, and she bent her head back strangely and banged it, banged it on a rock. She was outside herself and unable to think, unable to breathe, and there was too much feeling and he was too close and she would not survive it, and she could not bear it, and she could not, she could not, she could not. Her whole self went cold, because it was too much. Too much feeling, and she would be lost in it, lost if she let him nearer to her own darkness and let him illuminate it with light. And she beat at him and herself, fluttering like a bird, not like a little chicken bird but like a trapped eagle.

'I can't,' she cried. 'Stop it, let me go. I can't.'

'You must,' he said. 'You like it.'

'I know. Yes. No. No I don't like it. I won't. I can't.' And she scratched at him, and at herself, her nails tearing her own face and his. He thought at first it was her passion and he was excited, but she beat and fought, lost, lost, lost, in a strange place and insanely she muttered and banged and struggled.

He could not speak to her, she had gone away. He was almost frightened, but more angry. He could not for some time get her back to him, get her conscious. She was shaking and deranged. She was mute and broken.

'You have to,' he said, 'you promised. We made a bargain.'

'I don't care. I cannot.' Now she was sulking like a baby, her face turned away. She knew only that it would kill her if she did, that the explosion in her would kill her if she let him bring that golden pleasure any nearer. He could kill her by some other means if he wanted to, she was not going there. She was shaking with fear.

'I don't want it. I don't want your present. I don't want to know the future. I was only joking.'

He has made love to mortals before and they have delighted in him; who is she, this child, to make mock of a god's desire? Who is she to shame him and despise him? And seeing her as a child, he is more ashamed than ever. And like white heat his anger rises, rises to replace the rising of his genitals, which are withered by her rejection.

'We gods don't take back our gifts. But I will punish you.'

'Yes,' she sighs, 'yes, do that.' The punishment will obliterate the dangerous joy; she will not go to that perilous place, the punishment will take away the memory of the pleasure. 'Please.'

He is vengeful because he is baffled and embarrassed. He is vengeful because he is ashamed. She does not look radiant now, but little and shrivelled.

'I won't take back my gift,' he tells her, 'but I shall make it so that you will always know the future but no credit or reliance will ever be placed on anything you say. Ever. Even by you. Since you make a gap between me and my desire I shall make one between your seeing and your saying. You can never leap that gap. You will never leap that gap. It will be a very lonely place.'

He stood her up. He held her by the shoulders and he looked at her. She felt the desire rise again and with it the fear. The desire, the fear, the pain. She cannot. But now he does not let her go. His hands are very hard; they shift from her shoulders to her upper arms, which he grips tightly.

'You're hurting me,' she says, trying to wriggle free.

'I know,' he says, without compassion. He puts his tongue on her lips, but now there is no desire, his tongue is like a knife, he runs it up the narrow crevice above her upper lip, very slowly, very coldly. She feels his saliva on her like a snail's trail; straight up the middle of her nose and forehead. With the force of his chin he bows her head and runs his hard cutting tongue right across the centre of her crown, and she feels the sharp blade cut into her cranium, and into the depths of her brain, a single even slicing and there is intolerable pain, intolerable confusion. Her mind is severed. She is severed. There is a gap between her seeing and her saying. It is a very lonely place. It is very cold. The words and the music separate: she feels them pulling apart, stretching out, out, till the song collapses into chaos and she will never sing again. She feels catastrophic reactions of guilt and depression and euphoria. She remembers faces and names but she cannot associate them with each other. The normal integration of sensory knowledge is destroyed. She faints.

When she becomes conscious, she does not remember. They do not understand the long scratches on her face, nor the bruising on her head until she starts having fits. In her fits she murmurs dreadful and dangerous things, lost perceptions that make no sense but are discouraging and not to be encouraged. Although she is very beautiful they conclude that she is mad. She is often placed under restraint, because of the complicated distortions in all her forms of communication. She likes men still, but she will not let anyone touch her. She will never let anyone touch her, although she is not able to say why.

She says over and over again that Troy will be destroyed.

The city will burn, she tells them. The flames will be high and bright. As bright as a god, she says. But she also says as bright as lentils, or as bright as three days ago, or as bright as stag's antlers, so they do not understand. They place no credit or reliance on anything she ever says, and she does not know why.

When she wakes up in Agamemnon's bunk she does not remember what has happened. He comes down again into the cabin and smiles at her. She smiles back, warm and sleepy. He is overwhelmed again with tenderness. He will not hurry, he must not hurry, he will be patient, patient and kind, because she moves him so, as no woman has ever done.

'Feeling better?' He fills the hatchway and for a moment cuts off the light. They rock together in the dark movement of the ship's belly.

'I feel fine,' she replies, then as he moves the light floods back into the small space, she smiles radiantly and says, 'She'll kill you. With an axe. So don't change your tunic. In the bath.'

He thinks it is a joke; that perhaps she was awake when he changed his tunic before, and is teasing him.

'All right,' he says, 'that's all right.'

'I know,' she says, giggling because his smile in the half-light is so sweet. 'By the way, she'll kill me too.' They both laugh and the ship sails gently on towards Argos and Clytemnestra who will indeed kill both of them.

Despite its effectiveness in the control of certain forms of epilepsy, commissurotomy (section of the *corpus callosum* – the interhemispheric tract) is no longer used as a surgical treatment. Since the discovery of multiple functional asymmetries favouring the right as well as the left hemisphere, it is generally recognised that the therapeutic value of this intervention is outweighed by the fact that it has been found to eliminate much of the normal integration of sensory information.

The information on hemispheric section comes principally from Robert Nebes's article in Marcel Kinsbourne, ed., *Assymetrical Function of the Brain* (CUP, 1978), to whom thanks.

RAPUNZEL REVISITED

There is a story — no hardly that, there is a ghost, a legend of a story that when her king had died and her children were grown, Rapunzel returned to her tower, for she had found, despite the delights of Court, that she had come to miss the sounds of silence, the wind swinging in from the sea and the birds singing before the day's dawn. And she lived there until she was old.

Nothing changes.
Nothing has changed. Still the river spreads out into the sand and the tide rises and falls; still the shore is half-hidden by the standing grasses in which the wind moves softly; still the village is half-hidden in the trees and the little path comes winding out towards me. Still the sea is a soft grey smudge half a mile away and the estuary drifts down towards it. The first morning I saw what I took to be a curlew on flight against the soft morning clouds, bubbling its loud musical song as it flew; and then I realised I could not see its feet trailing behind it and knew it was a whimbrel. And when I knew I remembered how the whimbrel in the air moves its wings faster, less like a lumbering gull, and

I was happy. I have not seen a whimbrel singing on the wing as it passes for a long, long time.

Nothing has changed. The windows stand as they always did; deep-bayed curving round with the round walls. The room was ready, waiting. The mirror hangs where the mirror hung and the little brass bed which was too small for the two of us is now too small for me alone.

My embroidery frame is still, is again, on the little marquetrie table by the western window so that the last of the evening light will shine and, as it grows too dark to set my stitches, I can still, or again, watch the distant lights in the village come on and prickle the dusk. Now on the road beyond the village I can see the bright tiger eyes of cars as they swoop round the long bend and descend the hill into the valley; I can see the red glow of their backward glances too; of their passing out of the village and away to the big wide world which I have left behind. But I climbed and descended that curved path so often in my childhood dreams that it does not seem strange to see the animals of the night do it now.

My writing table stands once more where it always stood in front of the eastern window so that I can record my dreams in the pale wash of dawn, before the sun comes up spreading the brightness that dries them away and turns my thoughts to the day ahead and the hopes of the future. My dream notebook is covered now in a highly wrought pattern of pinks and greens but, to tell the truth, I write little in it because I do not have many dreams. Perhaps I do not dream because I have no desires, or perhaps because I have no conflicts. I have not yet decided. Instead, in a different, more chastely designed notebook, I keep detailed records of the birds I see and the cloud patterns over the estuary and the maze of molehills nightly renewed on the green salt sward below the window. No botany, of course, because that needs close-up viewing, would require me to go down and out and scrabble in the fields and woods; I prefer ornithology now because the birds come to me, or rather pass by about their own business, as I watch them.

The blue velvet chair in which the princess curls up to read romances, and looks out from in her romantic daydreams, is still beside the south-facing window, with its lower sill and its enormous view over the reed marsh and the sand dunes. Of course I never was a princess; my parents were humble and slightly criminal members of the agricultural working class, although my dear husband kept this a well-guarded secret. But every small girl who curls up in a blue velvet winged armchair with silk cushions and reads romances is a princess – and so, since nothing changes, is every middle-aged woman; especially one who was brought up by a Witch.

And the northern window. Can I truly say that nothing changes, that nothing has changed? The wide sill is there still, the casement fitted to the inner wall, not the outer one as the others are; the darker view of the winding path from the village, approaching through the pine trees; the bramble bushes still grow round about if I lean out far enough to look down. That has not changed. Yesterday I looked up from my reading and saw there were three butterflies dancing in the embrasure, as they used to dance, dark red against the pale grey stone. But . . . But . . . I have let them put in a wrought-iron ladder; we did our best, my architect and I; it is a beautiful ladder designed like a vine, so that you can climb up to the window, or I suppose I could climb down to the ground, treading leaves and bunches of grapes. They call it a fire-escape and are happy for my safety, but I know that is not why I did it. I cheated. For although my hair is still long, indeed it will still tumble the twenty ells to the ground – and I know this because practically the first thing I did when I returned here was to unwind it and test it – in the last few years it has started to feel brittle. I do not think it has the bouncy toughness of youth, and I am afraid it might snap; I do not want to be reminded of Him falling, falling and crying out like a bird in pain, a baby bird falling from its nest squawking – that is no way to remember one's hero.

Or perhaps it is just vanity, my one gesture of regret for my departing youth, that I should not have, daily, to test my one claim to fame and immortality: I was the woman up whose pure golden hair her lover could climb to a secret chamber of delight. And to be honest there is another reason, not disconnected with this vanity: I have the most agonising arthritis in my neck and shoulders. My doctor cannot understand it. Osteoporosis, he mutters, a common symptom of women of a certain age, that is my age; eat more bananas and take replacement hormones. But why your neck, he asks, as such complaints usually affect joints which have been overused. Like most doctors, he is not really asking me so I do not have to tell him; and this amuses me. The ladder is the price I pay for my amusement, for my vanity and for my ineradicable female concern for the safety and comfort of others. In any order that feels appropriate. But it is not quite true to say that nothing has changed.

The Witch has changed too, although not very much, not as much as I expected.

When I first planned to come back here I was worried about the Witch. I did not want a servant at my beck and call, for then nothing would be the same. My Witch was never my servant – she was not my servant, nor my mother. She came and went of her own choosing and yet she chose, each morning, to bring me porridge in a little red bowl, to bring it so swiftly through the pine forest that it was still steaming hot when she arrived at the tower, the brown sugar on the top only beginning to melt into golden pools, still crispy in the middle, and the thick cream still floating in the middle of the porridge and erupting up round the inner rim of the bowl. She came and went of her own choosing, and yet she chose each evening to take up the whalebone comb which still sits on the shelf below the mirror and comb out my hair. The songs of the whales, who call their lovers across the grey-green oceans of the earth, sang through each golden strand of my golden hair, and she would comb, comb, comb the twenty ells of gold and singing, like the whales, would braid it up again.

> *Over and under, in and out,*
> *under and over, out and in,*
> *Rapunzel, Rapunzel,*
> *I'm combing your hair.*

But she had gone, long years ago, to wherever it is that witches go after their work is done and I was worried.

I did need a Witch and I did not want a servant. One of the problems with witches, the useful sort as much as the wicked ones, is that even if you are a queen and a princess, you cannot require their services. That much I have learned from life. Desire may conjure up a lover, or a child, or a quest; but witches come and go about their own business and not even dire need and the exhaustion of your own resources will compel them. It is as chancy as the behaviour of a single particle in a sunbeam and many of the most deserving women have had to manage without, while Cinderella, for example, who never lifted a finger to help herself, had no difficulties. I had treated my Witch brutally and ungratefully, and had assumed it my duty to do so. And now I needed one badly, even though I was well past the usual age, so of course I was worried.

I need not have been, of course. There is a tendency to assume that witches have to be older than their Princesses, but my new Witch is as young as my daughter. She does not know she is a Witch, she thinks she is a health visitor and she bounces up the ladder with youthful enthusiasm, radiant good health and a mild excess of jollity which might irritate me if it did not so remind me of my first Witch bustling through the forest at dawn. She brings me my shopping and my post and massages my poor neck and shoulders for me and she brushes my hair because it becomes harder and harder for me to get my arms up to do the job. She waxes it too to protect it against its own brittleness, rubbing in the wax down all twenty ells and then wrapping it up in hot towels that she heats in her microwave. I know she is a Witch because she protects my privacy and does not believe in replacement hormones, but in hot wax and warm towels.

I know she is a Witch for another reason too: I have seen her fly. When I came back I brought a telescope with me so that I could watch the stars and the birds feeding on the water line. Because of the pain in my neck I brought a refracting telescope. A refracting telescope has a lens with a mirror inside that turns the thing you are looking at at right angles to the sight-tube so that you can look without having to sit on the floor and bend your head back. One summer morning I scanned the telescope along the distant bays where the white, bright water was meeting the bright, white sky – not at anything but for my own pleasure, randomly, asking the world what it would give me as gift, for the brightness of the sunshine and the glory of the silence – and I saw my young Witch, flying in the air, cavorting naked, splashing sunlight from her wild dance, skimming low along the water line. I stared amazed and delighted, knowing why she protected my privacy – because it matched her own secrecy. I had forgotten, in my delight, that a refracting telescope reverses the image, left to right and top to bottom like a magic mirror: she was running and dancing on the beach really, but it was a magic moment and I knew she was a Witch and believe still that had I not been looking she might indeed have been flying as the whimbrel flies, not slow and lumbering like a gull, but swift and true in the sunshine.

Refraction distorts the image, but does not thereby make it less true. I chose to come back here because it was the only place I had direct experience of. It has been my story to see the world only through refractors, and never to experience it directly. When I was a child I sat in my blue velvet chair and learned everything through images, through books, through stories. Only out of the windows could I see the world; only through the climbings up and down of the Witch and of the Prince could I have contact with the outside world. But here, I thought, here there was my real experience: here, untramelled by the refractions, I could hear the sounds of silence, the wind swinging in from the sea and the birds singing before the day's dawn.

I came because there were questions that I wanted to answer.

Did I love my Witch or hate her?

Did she imprison me or protect me?

Did she love me or hate me?

Was she a good Witch or a wicked one?

Why did my parents give me away so lightly when they had, so they say, wanted me for so long?

Did they love me or hate me?

Did I love the Prince for himself or for the love he gave me?

Did I ever make a choice, or did I move with the tides, as the reeds and the river do? As the reeds and river must?

As all the stories must?

But it does not work. I find that I do not, as I had planned, brood obsessively on my past, but rather that my past comes creeping in to shape my present. My past demands a Witch; and I peer through my telescope and find one.

The stories still come between me and my seeing, me and my hearing. Long ago I read that in a country far away to the south they believe that the Milky Way is a river of stars that connects in the deep sea with the rivers of the land, and that the two nourish each other. Now I cannot look at the estuary under the light of the moon without joining it, far away out there with the river in the sky. The story has fixed my seeing.

Long ago I read that in the cold icelands in the north where the geese go for the summer they believe that twins are salmon-babies; their souls are the souls of the great fish and their hearts have the same playfulness and the longing to be travelling that the salmon have. Now I cannot watch the fishermen go out to their nets at low tide and carry in their catch without my heart being caught in anxiety for my own twins, and I fear that they have slipped back into their true bodies and have been caught in the nets themselves. The story has fixed my seeing.

So it is impossible for me to shape my future, although that is what I came to do. I have been the child, and the beloved and the queen and the widow. I have come to a place where I need a new story, a new way of seeing and I am so entangled in the old ones, unbrushed and unbraided, that I cannot let down my hair and haul up a future.

The world is refracted through the lens of my life and I cannot see it natural and undistorted. Perhaps instead of coming back here I would have done better to go travelling. I have read that in the jungle you can see dancing clouds of tiny yellow and white butterflies. They hover over the places where turtles come out of the water to sun themselves on fallen logs; the butterflies gather, like confetti in a breeze, to sip the tears from the turtles' eyes. I would have liked to have seen that: and as the pain of my past joys bends my neck forward and I retreat into my tower like a shell, I wonder if this is the story for my old age when my cheerful Witch dances up the ladder to comfort me?

So, in a way, it is true that nothing has changed. But I have changed.

It is, and you were fairly warned, not a story, only the ghost, the legend of a story. There is no plot, no narrative. Nothing happens. But still the wind swings in from the sea and the birds sing before the day's dawn; and still she listens to the sounds of silence which she had missed, despite the delights of the Court. Still she finds witches and whimbrels to enchant her days and still she looks through the refracting lens of all the stories to try and find her own truth, her own story: the story of the woman who has been child and beloved and queen and has finished with all those tasks and must now try to learn to be herself.

AFTER LIFE

Cuthbert of Lindisfarne, bishop-monk, hermit, friend, missionary, thaumaturge, great saint of the North, was born in 634 and trained as a monk at Melrose. After the Synod of Whitby in 663/4 he spent much of his energy restabilising the church that had been seriously disrupted by the success of the universalist party led by Wilfred. Colman, Abbot of Lindisfarne, and many of the monks from this centre of northern Christianity felt unable to accept the changes and departed to Ireland. Cuthbert, who was at Whitby, accepted the King's decisions and worked to restore and expand harmony in the North-East. From 676 he was a hermit in the Farne Islands for nine years, then a Bishop for two, and finally returned to his island hermitage to die in 687.

This is the beginning of the story. After that . . . after that there is no story. The silence of eternity has no narrative. The wind blows and the tides wax and wane under the moon. The interfolded, intwining, intricate lines maze round and over and under and through. They *do not end, they come back to the beginning and the end is the beginning is the end.*

His posthumous fame grew. Eleven years after he died the Lindisfarne community decided, as was normal practice, to elevate his bones to a more public shrine. But on opening the coffin his body was found to be incorrupt: rust and moth had not consumed nor time like a thief broken in and stolen. His body was not decomposed, rotted, putrescent, desiccated nor in any way decayed.

This miracle inspired a profound devotion to the saint. For nearly 200 years he was enshrined at Lindisfarne in great honour. In 875 however Lindisfarne was threatened by a Viking attack. Not for the first time – ten years before Lindisfarne had been devastated by the Norsemen, many of its treasures stolen, and many members of the community killed. They could not face it again and decided to escape, taking Cuthbert with them. They opened the coffin and placed other important relics in it with Cuthbert's body, and took to the hills. For seven years the coffin and its bearers roamed northern England and South-West Scotland, seeking a safe asylum. Eventually they settled in Chester-le-Street for nearly a century, before further Viking raids sent them on their travels again.

In 995 they finally reached Durham. After the conquest a new Norman cathedral was built for Durham and in 1104 Cuthbert's remains were translated into it. Once again his coffin was opened and his body examined and found to be unaffected by four hundred years and much journeying. At the Reformation the shrine was dismantled, with a view to burning the saint's

bones, according to Reformation practice. However, the
commissioners were so shaken by discovering that the
body was still unaffected that, after writing to London
for special instructions, they reburied the bones under the
now dismantled shrine.

In 1828 the grave was reopened. The bones were
found bare and dry as might have been expected, the
treasures removed to a museum and the saint buried
again and, so far or finally, left in peace.

In heaven he rejoices to be with the hermits. They sit back-to-back, leaning against and so supporting each other. They shift slightly so that the nobbly protuberances of their spiritual spines fit into each other like the pieces of a jigsaw puzzle, their thin hard souls in perfect, silent companionship. He never has to be with priests, monks, abbots or bishops because in heaven, thank heaven, those things neither matter nor count. But sometimes, except that here there is no time, he finds himself with the other members of the Sea Green Society and, despite the name, which ought to please him, he grows as near to irritability and dislike as is possible for a blessed saint. The other members are, to his harsh and disciplined heart, too often neurasthenic Italian girls with a tendency to giggle. He feels slightly embarrassed, and then ashamed of himself. To be truthful he finds incorruptibility vulgar – it offends his fierce purity.

He died quietly in the arms of his friend Herefrith. Outside his monks were keeping vigil for him, singing the fifty-ninth psalm. As was proper. Then the trouble started and it was his own fault. Never give in to the demands of love. He should have known better but he had been weary, in pain, alone for too long, wrestling with the enemy, pleading with his God. His resistance worn down, he rescinded his demand to be buried here in his own place, on the island at the edge of the void.

His soul went home. In the dark morning hours, on the turning of the tide.

But they take his body back to Lindisfarne, to the Holy Island. They bury it with honour. Treasure it. Beg for miracles. And God of course hears their need and does not consult his. Incorruptibility is a faith-enhancing, joy-giving, powerful miracle. God *would*.

> The sublimity of the saint's earthly life was well attested by his numerous miracles. Almighty God in his providence now chose to give further proof of Cuthbert's glory in heaven by putting into the mind of the brothers to dig up his bones. They expected to find the bones quite bare (as is usual with the dead), the rest of the body having dwindled to dust. . . . On opening the coffin they found the body completely intact, looking as though still alive, and the joints of the limbs still flexible. It seemed not dead but sleeping.

Still the wind comes in, harsh, unrelenting, from the East across the huge grey sea. It carries flotsam from Nordic wrecks; great flights of geese from the ice circle; and the sharp acrid stench of blood and grease that comes on the tide, swelling under the bows of the square-sailed Viking ships.

He is caught, like a fly in a web, a web of love and need and tenderness.

At least the love, which bound him to them, is useful to them. The community grows rich in his prestige. But in the end his love is not enough, not enough to cast out their fear, to set them free or to make them indifferent to material possessions – the funny mossy-soft thing that is his useless but incorrupt body. When they hear the Viking ships are in the Tyne estuary again terror strikes deep and sharp. Foolish panic, rat-like scuffling in the church, sharper breaths, hoarse cries and tears.

He does not want to go. On the storm wind, in the strong tide pushing the longships up on to the mud flats, in the screams and smoke of their approaching rampage, he hears the song of the Storm Woman coming in to set him free.

They are concerned that the Norsemen will burn and destroy his shrine, his body, their treasure. It doesn't matter. 'It doesn't matter,' he wants to shout out, but cannot. They love him too much and not enough. He cannot leave them. His spirit grunted, cross and weary.

In their panic they open his coffin, shove in their other great treasures. They have to tip him over on to his side so he can no longer even look up at the huge blue sky and the wild clouds. He is wedged in by King Oswald's skull. This makes him smile.

Through the night, carrying him far too carefully, they flee into the hills. From there they can look down and see the orange shadow of the flames, which smudge the darkness; smell the sharp tang, which is smoke and flesh together; congratulate themselves on their wisdom and promptness. All night there is fierce burning, stripping away riches, beauty, serenity, rootedness. Above them the moon still shines, ducking in and out of silver clouds and high, cold, unmoved, the stars sing their ancient silent song. The wind runs over the grasses of the hills, the heather stirs and the many waters slip over the edge heading with rattling determination towards the sea and their own dissolution. None of them notices those things, none of them looks up or around. They look down in terror at the looting, and at his coffin with a desperate self-seeking love. He cannot leave them.

It is better on the long journey. Under his shoulder is the hard round skull of the noble Oswald, Aidan's friend. Stripped bare and bold. It forces him to lie on his side, as he would never have let his novices lie. The monks, his children, carry him on their shoulders as they climb high into the hills, with the long views of nothing, the cold wind, and the slow drift of gulls. They settle nowhere. They grow lean and hard and hardy. Sowing but not gathering and free as the foxes, which sniff around at night.

They think they will follow Colman home to Ireland and so they trek their slow way across the rough mountains, and down to the Western coast. Ireland is so full of God's servants and relics and miracles that he thinks they will not need him there and he might be set free. They take ship, secretly, on those brackish seas, but – as the land vanished into the grey rain – he hears the cry of his people, a great wailing of childish need and despair. The people he was called to love. And he hears the dark voice of the storm woman far to the East, riding the longer swell of her fiercer sea. So they have to go back. A storm drives them back.

Still the rivers come down, tumultuous, laughing, from the high moors to the West. They curl, curve, carve across the low lands. They hurl themselves against all the long waves. Fresh and salt mixing; pushing against each other. Only Farne is free of it all. Free of direction thrust purpose; free of cities ambitions power time greed and longing. The tide rises and falls. The wind comes and goes. The long swells give storm or silence in a rhythm that rocks his prayers and sets him free.

He should have stayed. He should not have given in. He should have insisted, been buried there, stayed a few seasons and been washed away. They were always the great betrayals – the betrayals in love and tenderness. With a kiss.

Sometimes he wishes he had committed some nice juicy sin. A real sin of the flesh, a stinking sin of corruption. The trouble was that women have never really much interested him, at least not in that way. He hears those sins, sees how they shake his brothers. He listens attentively but without understanding. He can only feel a wide compassion and tolerance, which is never the response they want.

There are only two women in his life.

Hild, old enough to be his mother, who shares with him a sort of distance, a detached hilarity through the long synod meetings at Whitby. He holds by instinct, by training and by love to Columba's rule, Columba's Easter, Aidan's gentle holiness. But . . . once he looks away from Colman's grief, avoids looking at Wilfred's determination. Instead, suddenly, he catches Hild's glance, her deep smile. Games, foolish games. Hild who teaches him there, without words, in a silent smile, that although it is all genuinely, terribly important, it really does not matter very much. She gives him freedom; and one long evening the two of them listen to Caedmon singing the huge ancient stories of the faith in his own, their own, language, a gift to the poor, regardless of the date of Easter or the shape of the tonsure. He smiles whenever he thinks of Hild.

And there is the storm woman.

There are other sins of course, juicier than seeking a little comfort in the arms of another against the cold nights of the soul. There is love of wealth; blasphemy; discourtesy to the poor – or indeed to kings, to one's own brothers, to any created thing. There is violence, arrogance of office and of mind; self-serving anger; withholding consolation; impenitence; apostasy. There is always pride. And the mysterious sin against the Holy Spirit, which can never be forgiven, whatever it may be. It is not that he has not sinned, but he has failed to sin with enough energy or commitment. Cursed are the pure in heart, they are doomed to incorruptibility. He cannot abandon the people, and the harsh habits of love.

He has never seen the storm woman, but she comes. She comes straight as the wind from the cold lands of dawn, and she rides the long grey swell in from the long grey sea. She is without pity, ruthless. She is not bound by love and compassion. She is free. Her fierce freedom strikes a chord in him, low and unsettling. She stands before the mast and the wind blows her hair towards him, plaited, interwoven as the pages of his lovely book, but alive and wild. She treads on the lion and the dragon; the young lion and dragon she tramples under her feet. She is clothed not with the sun but with the storm, and the sword and the wild.

The longship surfs in fast on a white roll of fume and spray, swoops into the bay and they drop the square sail. She does not waver. She spreads her arms out in greeting. She is black and blood-red and she brings the brands for the burning – for the stripping down, the purging, the looting, the making of deserts. He sees her even in the dark. He sees her arms stretched out, the mast and boom behind her is her cross. She is a wild Christ to him, from a heroic people, crucified, harrowing hell, rejoicing on the far side of destruction. He wants her; he wants to go out to her across the breaking waves. To walk to her on the water and share her bloodstained laughter. He understands her dark joy. Here we have no abiding city, he thinks, here we have only wooden longships with their dragon prows, storming heaven with a fierce bloodlust.

To us otters he was otter.

He was otter in the economy of his movement. Humans fidget. But he was an otter.

Silent and still when he was not moving. Swift and sleek when he moved. He slid into the water like an otter, swam so quietly; stood all night while stars wheeled overhead, and the night waves lapped at his shoulders. He was otter: defenceless, innocent, playful. He laughed as an otter laughs, deep inside and silently. He was otter, weightless, graceful and free in the water and the cold did not reach into the depths of his belly. He stayed in the sea all night.

He was otter but he had no fur. When he came out of the water we could see he was cold. We warmed him and he blessed us. Why be surprised? That is no miracle, not as otters think.

The heavy weight of Durham Cathedral pins him down.

He makes a terrible mistake. For over a hundred years they settle in Chester-le-Street and he tries to settle with them and enjoy prosperity, to offer his support to a new-style Bishop who lives like a King. But he hears the storm woman calling, and smells the Viking smell and they are on the road again. He wants to go back to Farne, to the wind and the sea. He wants his body to disintegrate gently the way other bodies do. Dust to dust, to dissolve into the water, his bones powdered into the fine sand. They travel northward again, and he hears a curlew in the mist, sees a river curl, curl around a standing rock. He thinks it is an island. He thinks he can be free there. The mist is dense; they are lost and longing for supper.

'Mmmmoooooo, ooooo,' calls the dun cow out of the mist. 'Moooo,' she lows, longing to let down, to have the warm milk pulled out of her gently and to feel the milkmaid's forehead pressed against her flank in the warm byre. He sees an island, hears a dun cow longing to go home. He yearns towards the standing rock with the water all around it. His soft flesh sinks towards his island – towards a silence that will let his flesh flow out of him like milk. He is cow. God is his milkmaid, pulling the soft flesh out of him. Soft, warm, milky as a child. He will travel no further. Here is his resting place.

He is wrong. It is not an island. The tight loop of the river leaves a neck of land – like Lindisfarne, not Farne. The desire of his incorrupt body and the tenderness of his heart betray him again.

But they take him to Durham, which is not island but

fortress. Its heavy weight, and the weight of people's love and need pin him down. The cathedral is heavy over him. He wants to be free of it, and charity demands that he is not. Actually he never liked Wilfred. Hild is right and the date of Easter does not matter, because Christ is risen, alleluia, and running wild and free in the dark night. Hild is right because someone was going to be hurt. Colman's hurt is sad but Wilfred's hurt would be dangerous. None of these things matters, but stone churches matter. They pin him down, Wilfred's stone churches.

Here we have no abiding city. The clear line of hill or horizon abides. It is constant and it holds the silence. The line that divides earth and sky, clear and clean, also unites them. And it abides. It emerges out of the dark in the first dawn light and is swallowed back into the dark at nightfall. Above the line, infinity; below the line, mortality. But the line itself is both, and holds them both and the wind blows along hill or sea, fresh and free like the passage of the spirit. That is where he wants to be, dust to dust, blown along the edge of the wild. Not pinned here in a splendid tomb, weighed down by a stone church.

They spend over one hundred years building a stone church grand enough for their idea of him.

> The Abbot of Seez, unwrapping with the aid of the local brethren, the covering of the venerable head, raised it a little in both his hands in the sight of everyone, and bending it about in different directions, found it adhering to the rest of the body, with all the neck joints perfect. Then taking hold of an ear he waggled it backwards and forwards with some degree of force. He found the whole body with its nerves and bones solid and covered with

soft flesh. He also shook it and raised it so high that it almost appeared to sit in its quiet abode. Moreover he also took care to examine into the perfect state of its feet and legs. But there were some who now exclaimed that he had carried proof of the truth further than was required. So raising his voice he announced: 'Behold, brothers, this body lies here, lifeless indeed but as sound and entire as on that day on which the soul left it to wing its flight to heaven.'

No escape. He is lumbered with incorruptibility.

And then at last the blessed commissioners come. He loves their harsh commitment, their untiring zeal for their Lord. He loathes their theology of course, but Hild's deep smile had taught him that although theology was all genuinely, terribly important, it really did not matter very much. They are like the Norsemen, set upon freedom and ferocity. They have a savage contempt for his body that he shares with them. Carelessly they break his leg with a hammer. 'Chuck the bones down,' they shout.

Before the Crown took possession of the Church and monastery of Durham the royal commissioners had defaced the shrine of St Cuthbert. The Commissioners were Dr Ley, Dr Henley and Mr Blythman. After the spoil of his ornaments and jewels, and finding the chest he lay in very strongly bound with iron, the goldsmith took a great fore-hammer and did break the said chest. When they opened the chest they found him lying whole, incorrupt, with his face bare and his beard as if it had been a fortnight's growth.

Then when the goldsmith saw that he had smashed one of his legs when he broke into the chest, he was very sorry for it and cried out, 'Alas I have broken one of his legs.'

Dr Henley called up to him and told him to throw down the bones. The goldsmith answered that he could not get them asunder for the sinews and skin held them. Dr Ley climbed up to see if this was true and then called back to Dr Henley that Cuthbert was lying whole.

Dr Henley would give this no credit and again called out, 'Chuck down the bones.'

Dr Ley replied, 'If you don't believe me come up and see for yourself.'

Finally Dr Henley stepped up and handled the body and saw that he was whole and uncorrupt. So they ordered him to be carried to the vestry and kept securely there until they could find out what the King wanted done with him. When they heard from the King the Prior and monks buried him in the ground underneath where his shrine had been.

Dear Dr Henley, sweet, kind, merciful Dr Henley and all his ilk. No excessive respect, no childlike, clinging love that holds the flesh in bondage and will not let it go back to the source and be forgotten. Burn the bones, Dr Henley, as you burned Thomas's and Edmund's – ashes to ashes. Why him? The great saints, the true saints were not held captive. Aidan's body was not incorrupt. The great apostle Peter's body was not incorrupt. Wilfred's – he hardly hesitates; he knows that Wilfred was a very great saint; that is quite different from liking him – Wilfred's body was not incorrupt. This is so unfair, Wilfred would have loved incorruptibility. Another excuse for another stonking great stone church. There had been a plan once to enshrine him with

Wilfred at Ripon. Wilfred would not have liked that. Nor would he.

The commissioners have set him free. They shove his body back into an ordinary grave and dismantle the shrine and laugh. They do not need him. They do not love him. They do not want him. He laughs at their impertinent indifference. He can go now. Deep below his new grave he can hear the waters rushing, curling round the peninsula, washing away at hard rock and sanctuary and tomb.

Pulling, pulling him towards the sea. At last.

His body dissolves.

Dust to dust.

His body dissolves into the great nothing – of cloud formations, of curlews and terns, and of winds. The nothing pulls him in. The arms of the storm woman hold him. There is silence.

The line of the moor holds the silence.

There is no narrative in silence. The interfolded, intwining, intricate lines of life maze round and over and under and through. They do not end, they come back to the beginning and the end is the beginning is the end. The sea deep is the spume of the waves is the foam in the wind is the billow of the clouds is the rain on the crops is the stillness of the well is spilled on the ground is flowing back into the depths of the sea.

The words drop away

into the ocean

of silence

SLICING THE GINGERBREAD

How old were we when we went into the forest and got lost?

The first time we were tiny – three perhaps. The little pink toes on our bare feet were still half-furled. We held each other's chubby hands and toddled down through the orchard, over the duck-cropped grass. My pigtails had not grown then, so we both wore the same neat bowl of silver-gilt hair. 'How sweet,' they would have said, if anyone had seen us go. We were not secret, but we were never lonely either, so we did not need the attention of adults.

We did not go into the real forest then, although we thought we did. We just explored the scrub beyond the fence and stream – the fringes of the forest. Here, close against the orchard and the vegetable patch and the flowerbeds, were birch, rowan and coppiced hazel and wild roses and honeysuckle hot-scented in the summer sun. We pulled down the heads of the ox-eye daisies and threw handfuls of buttercups at each other and peered up into the spotted velvet bells of huge purple foxgloves. From below, each poppy petal seemed translucent and each head of cow parsley was both a vaulted cathedral roof and a white cloud against the blue sky. We crawled into the bracken jungle, sniffing the crumbly gold-brown floor for the acrid scent of fox. We were surrounded by the waxy bracken trunks that seemed to soar away above us, and we looked up through the green ferny canopy that seemed far above our heads and was speckled in hot shards of sunshine.

That was forest enough for two so small. We fell asleep there in the tender warmth, weary from our bold adventure, coiled round each other like kittens. We did not hear them calling, so we were lost in the forest for an hour or two although we did not know it. They found us in the long evening shadows and gathered us up and carried us home still drowsy and drunken on sunshine and freedom. Within their angry reprimands we could hear their anxiety; and beneath their anxiety we could feel their love. They tucked us up in our little cot and we curled together like spoons in a drawer and barely noticed them. That day became a repeated page in the family storybook, a tale of sweet naughtiness and courage. I cannot, truly, remember any of this although I think I can.

And as we grew bigger we went to and fro along the edges of the forest, looking both ways – in towards the shadows and out towards the daylight. Sometimes, slightly self-conscious, watching each other to see whose nerve would break first, we went deeper in and sometimes we got lost for a little while, and then found our way home again, a little scared perhaps, but holding hands and feeling safe enough together.

We were twelve when we went into the forest and got lost the last time, the time you think you know about. By then we had been told of all the dangers. Our mother had died and our father had brought home a town woman who was frightened of the forest. Her terrors were well founded, but often children are freer on false confidence than on true fears, so we did not like her and tried to ignore her. But we could not help but learn: the forest was full of wolves; in the depths of winter they would come down to the villages and howl at night, waiting, watching. Worse, there were wolverine whose ferocity is unparalleled, whose scavenging jaws once they have latched on cannot be separated by anything less than death. There were bogs, which gave out a vile stench and a thin eerie mist; they sucked you in and never let you out. There were giants: the trunks of the great firs were the legs of giants who came alive in the full moon. The winds in the trees were the cries of babies who had died unbaptised. There were ghosts in the forest, and spirits of evil intent. The forest stretched away, eastward and eastward for ever and ever. There was no end to it, not ever. Row upon row of trees marching solemnly to the end of the world. There were, though, occasional clearings and in them lived heroic hermits and wicked witches. The hermits turned silent backs on noisy children, too taken up with God to offer help or guidance. The witches, however, were on the prowl: they seduced naughty children and then ate them. Of course there were witches – deceitful, greedy and mean. Old and ugly, and yet somehow . . . somehow alluring. We sniggered.

We were twelve. We were still together, but there was a new tension. We were together but we were no longer the same. We needed time to be with our own kind. Girls with girls for giggling and caressing and using those few precious years when we are bigger and cleverer and more powerful than the boys are. Boys with boys for whatever it is that boys need from boys and girls will never understand.

But nice little girls were not allowed to walk up the lane in the evening, to play on even the fringe-iest outermost edges of the forest. Their mothers kept them home, seducing them with women's secrets and promises, beguiling them with ribbons and gingerbread, so I was alone.

The boys came, though, swaggering, superior, taunting. He yearned for them – to be gone with them, away into whatever worlds they are that boys make for themselves and come home from filthy, scab-kneed and contented. This is a difficult time, when the boys cling wisely to childhood while we girls are lured away from it. He needed them so much. He could not risk including me. I know that now, but I did not know it then.

'Gretel is a girlie. We hate girls.' Chanted and then spoken peremptorily, 'Get rid of her, Hansel.'

He did love me. He did, but in the back of their throats he knew the dread words waited, 'Hansel is a girlie.' Twins are naturally suspect – too potent, too close to the mysterious otherness of the other. Besides, he wanted them, he needed them.

'Go away, Gretel,' he said. 'Go away.' He turned his back on them, faced me directly. 'Please.' He mouthed the last word; he could not let them hear him.

I was ashamed of him and of myself. 'Shan't,' I said and, 'You can't make me.' I said it loudly: a challenge.

So they ran off into the forest. I followed them – sulky, spying, desperate. The trees were huge. The trunks ran up, ribbed and muscular. The roots gnarled the ground into humps and hags of moss and lichen and the canopy was so far overhead that the clouds looked as though they floated for another universe. It was dark and cool in the forest, and I stomped after the boys, aggressively flaunting my nonchalance. I could see him divided and unhappy, on the edge of his own gang, but I could not give him his freedom. I was too young and had none of my own.

They tried to escape, to hide from me, to get away. I pounded after them, hands cut on rough branches, my face scratched and bleeding, my frock torn and grubby, hot tears smearing my cheeks. Their laughter was loud and angry. Deeper and deeper into the forest we all went, not caring.

Finally, as hunted animals will, they turned at bay. I saw them pause and group in a clearing ahead of me. A single vast tree had fallen sideways letting in the light and here there was underbrush – grass and flowers. I came up to them victorious.

'Huh!'

'OK,' they said. 'You can play. We are playing witches and you are the witch.'

'First,' said Hansel, too loudly, 'first we must prick her for a witch. Just to be certain.'

'Course she's a witch. She's a girl.'

'You still have to prick them.'

They broke off twigs of dead pine, sharpened them on penknives and pricked my arms and legs. They were raucous, jeering, uneasy. They tore at my clothes, pushed my skirt up and pricked my thighs and tummy. They were not gentle and it hurt.

'This is silly,' I said, still stubborn. 'It's babyish.'

'See, she must be a witch; if she wasn't a witch she'd be grateful we're checking her out.'

The pricking got out of hand – they started pinching and slapping. And saying *things*. They pulled my hair, stamping the ribbons into the pine needles. My plaits uncoiled.

'Straggly rats' tails!' they shrieked with mounting glee. 'Let's chuck the rat in the river and see if it floats.'

There was no river; they made do with a stagnant pool, shoving my head in, holding it a little too long, laughing when I came up with green algae on my cheeks.

'It's not funny,' I sobbed. But they thought it was.

'And now,' said Hansel, 'let's burn her.' There were two bright red patches on his cheeks, but he was dogged.

They tied me to a tree. They gathered fallen sticks to stack around my feet; they discussed solemnly whether moss could make good kindling. I was blubbering now, begging for mercy, scared, about to wet my panties, but they had gone into that earnest busy abstraction that makes youthful cruelty so possible.

Mercifully, they had no matches. The game ran out of steam. They milled about, uncertain, then took to some new enterprise, cheered up, ran off. Somehow no one remembered to untie me.

I was there for hours. The wind dropped at sunset, as it does, and as the light faded the silence grew. It grew huge and menacing. My ears strained for something, for anything, but all I could hear was nothing. Then after a long while there was a distant, strange purr that came out of the heart of the forest. It was the sound of silence itself, the hum of pure terror.

It got cooler as it grew dark. A little wind got up and then it was night. The forest is not silent at night. There were noises, noises without names. Strange little patterings, tappings, creakings; the forest moved very quietly all around me. I could hear the trees growing. I was scared.

A shape moved across the clearing – white against the dark, slow, vigilant. An owl; it was an owl I tried to tell myself but I knew it was a spirit of the dead come from hell to find me. Later there was an eldritch shriek, far away in the darkness – a long dying scream of something that had been alive and, in the silence after the scream, was dead. I was very scared.

Time passed. As I grew tired and cramped I could not fight off the fear. The forest was dense with terror: with wolves, wolverine and weasels. With long invisible strands of poisonous fungi creeping towards my feet in the dark. With giants, ghosts and witches. Witches, whose glamour would ensnare me, bind me, make me one of them. I would never go home. I would die here in the forest. I deserved to die because I was a witch. As the night wore out my fear drew in the whispers, swelled, grew darkly in the dark. I was very, very frightened.

I heard new sounds, and saw, patchily through the trees, the lantern light. I knew that She was coming and her cold eyes, her bony fingers would hold me forever. There was nowhere else to go but into her sweet sticky embrace.

It was Hansel, shamefaced, hasty. He untied my arms. I knew he was sorry because he was rough and silent, but it was too late. I had gone so far into my own terror that the only way back was on the wings of rage. The boys had shown me my witch power and now I claimed it. I built my witch's house of gingerbread and ribbons there in the night clearing. I built it out of fear and fury.

As soon as my hands were free, I flew at him, fierce as the screech owl. Talons out and with no warning I pounced – I scratched and bit – his blood was in my mouth, sweet and hot. Unprepared, he had no resistance. He shrieked once and covered his face with his arms. I struck out, felled him, laughed at him: eager, greedy, and cruel.

He was on the ground. I raked his face with my nails and mocked him.

'You're a skinny little morsel,' I giggled, pinching, prodding, hurting him gleefully. 'You're not worth the eating of.'

He moaned – my fear flew into him – I was witch for him too now. 'I shall feed you fat and cook you in my oven and eat you up.' Witches cackle. I cackled.

My rage overpowered him. He was whimpering, blubbering, begging. I laughed. I scrabbled on the forest floor and rammed handfuls of dead needles, fungus, and earth mould into his mouth.

'Gingerbread,' I shrieked. 'Is it good?'

He was gagging, choking on dead forest. 'Is it good?' I yelled, slapping his face. He could not speak. His eyes were shut. He could not see, but he saw that I was the witch and he nodded.

I pinched him again, letting my nails break through his skin. 'You'll never be big enough,' I shouted, 'You're too puny, too weak. You're pathetic. You're a *girlie*. I'll just have to cook you now.'

I grabbed his hair to drag him across the clearing, but it was too short. My fingers slipped through it suddenly and I stumbled, fell. Lying on my side in the dark, I saw the huddled, terrified, shaking mound of him. Abruptly it was over. Finished. Suddenly it was *Hansel*. I loved him.

There was a long silence.

'Hansel?' I said.

There was a longer silence. Then he moved his hands and opened his eyes. I saw them in the dark, still dark with fear. He reached an arm towards me.

'Gretel,' he said.

Then we were both weeping, weeping. We groped towards each other, curled up together like spoons in a drawer and no longer noticed the terror of the night.

In the morning we walked, holding hands, until we found our way home. His face was serrated with long scabby wounds. My arms and legs were covered with bruises and punctures. They put it all down to walking in the forest at night. He got a bollocking for not looking after his little sister, though I am a whole half-hour older than he is, and at that time taller as well. I felt both smug and lonely. After that we always slept each in our own bed.

Now we go into the forest every summer, riding two trains, one from each side, because the forest does not go on forever. We never get lost now. We meet for a picnic – he, his nice wife and their sweet children; me, my man and my golden twins. We chat, eat, take a small walk. Hansel knows the names – Latin and local – of all the flowers. He enjoys telling us. Every year, all the time, I watch him very carefully, but I still don't know if he remembers.

MOTHER OF THE PROMISE

Sarah is old, old and very tired. She dwells now in Hebron and waits under the oaks of Mamre to find out what will happen next.

Sarah is old, old and very tired. Her mind wanders, sometimes she laughs and sometimes she weeps and those who love her do not know why. Her mind wanders across all her long life and she struggles to make it into a story: the story of her life, the story of Sarah.

It is hard to make sense of sometimes.

Sarah's household, who love her, although not without a touch of that fear which the very old age of a beloved and respected woman makes sweet, bring her bread soaked in milk and sweetened with honey. They worry that she does not eat enough. She mumbles the soft mush in her toothless mouth and occasionally the sweet milk dribbles down her chin. It is hard for her household not to find this pathetic and to add pity to the love and fear they already feel. But when she wipes her chin and returns the bowl with an imperious gesture of her long hand, honey-coloured but sprinkled now with dark patches like the sheep themselves, and sits up straight in the shade of the ancient oak trees, then they remember that she is, as she always was, a beautiful woman, and a hard gritty woman who has travelled all her life and that pity is not an appropriate emotion.

Sometimes when Sarah mumbles and drools on the slops they bring her she is resentful of her own body, and that resentment becomes a memory and she is fretful. But sometimes when she tastes the honey in the milk she is filled with joy and knows there is nothing better in old age than to be brought sweetness in a bowl and to sit looking down the long pathway and watch and learn if her son will come up from Beersheba today to visit her.

Sometimes Sarah sits and dreams of the past, and sometimes she forces her memory where it does not want to go with the harsh desert strength that those memories themselves give back to her. She has learned many things in her long life and most of them are useless now, but they do not leave her, and indeed form way-markers for the last journey she is making, the journey across the great desert of her own life, which has brought her at last and for a second time to sit under the oaks of Mamre.

Once, long ago, so long ago, she had lived in Ur of the Chaldees; a proud city with a huge pyramid, arranged in tiers like a mountain. Ur was a city of princes and priests. It was a city of temples and palaces and pools, a beautiful city rising above the flood plain of the land between the two rivers. A rich city with a great market and a high tower where the priests watched the stars and ordered their well-trained gods to deliver the rains and the river's risings that made the flood plain fertile. And those gods, grown fat on sacrifices and obedient, did indeed deliver the rains and the city prospered and the slaves built the ziggurats and the palaces and the gardens, and life was very good for the noble families.

Once long ago, so long ago, she had been a beautiful princess. Sarai, the beautiful princess. Smooth, she could remember that, her skin had been as smooth as the silks that the merchant caravans from the east had brought in. Her skin had been smooth; her toenails painted; her hands oiled each morning until they glowed like honey, sweet honey from the honeycomb; her hair had been brushed and braided in complex elaborate arrangements.

Once, long ago, so long ago, when she was still beautiful, she had married a mad man. She had set out, light-hearted and simple-minded, still smooth and giggling, she had set out on a journey with a mad man: a wonderful exciting mad man who dreamed dreams and saw visions; a fierce, dark, laughing mad man who was her husband and her lover; whose laugh was so deep and full and free that he laughed even at God, and God laughed back; whose strong laughter had pulled the rope of a bell in her and she laughed with him, a golden glorious laugh in perfect harmony with his rich deep laughter.

In Ur of the Chaldees she had been a pampered princess. She had not laughed then because she had not known there was anything to laugh about. She had giggled of course as princesses do; she had giggled in the women's palace, giggled and tittered and smirked, but she had not laughed. She had smiled of course, as young wives do, smiled and beguiled and flirted. When they had left Ur of the Chaldees and begun the long journey north, first to

Babylon and then beyond, out, out into the great desert, the sea of sand, the ocean of dryness and heat, she had not laughed. She had smiled – silent, diligent, sweet, obedient. A good wife.

Out in the desert it was different. It was harsh. It was not smooth. She had wept in her tent, wept because her hands were not oiled and her hair was not brushed and her toenails were not painted. She had lamented and complained and been frightened. And it soon became clear that she was not a good wife.

She was not a good wife. A good wife has children. Sarah did not have children. Therefore she was not a good wife. Because she was not a good wife, she did not have to be silent, diligent, sweet or obedient and so, once she had stopped complaining and lamenting and being frightened, she could learn to laugh. That was what Abraham taught her.

In Ur of the Chaldees it had been easy to be good. Everything had been easy. But in the desert it was not easy. It was fierce, burning, dangerous and wild. The days were hot and hot winds pressed gritty sand into her hair, her eyes, her ears, her skin; those winds turned her from a sweet smooth woman into a tough gritty one. The nights were cold and the cold glare of the enormous stars broke the good little gods of Ur and scattered the dust of them across the sands and they had to dream out a God big enough for this enormous place.

Sarah learned to laugh. And she learned to love Abraham as only a woman who laughs can love a man. A love that is not sweet or good or obedient, but is courageous and high-handed and free and very, very sexy.

They were in the desert for a long time and it was harsh. Many of the sheep, many of the camels and too many of the people died in the desert and the rest of them had to travel on and leave their kindred's bones unburied on the wide dunes or in the stony wadis where they fell. There were no graves, no altars, no memorials. But they survived the desert, just. The whole troop and tribe of them limped in to Haran exhausted. Although they had set out from Ur meaning to travel until they came to a place where there was no city, they somehow ran out of energy and hope and settled in Haran, half-merchants, half-farmers. They sold the camels and bought land.

Sarah had left Ur of the Chaldees as a good wife, but she arrived in Haran as a free woman. Moreover, since she had no children, there was nothing to hold her. Children teach their mothers to behave like mothers; Sarah had no one to teach her so she did not learn. It is the duty of children to tame their mothers; and of mothers to tame the fathers, so that the fathers can tame the gods. Sarah and Abraham and the God they had met in the desert did not get tamed. They laughed.

Sarah and Abraham did stay in Haran for a while. It had been very perilous in the desert and they had only just survived. But while the others settled they only rested. In the night they heard many things – the soft noises their gritty skin made against the other's, the songs of the huge desert stars and the voice of their God.

Go from your country and your kindred and your father's house to the land that I will show you. And I will make you a great nation, and I will bless you and make your

name great, so that you will be a blessing. I will bless
those that bless you and those that curse I will curse, and
by you all the families of the earth will bless themselves.

Once they had rested, they became restless. They heard
the voice of God in the night and they laughed uproari-
ously together and packed up all their possessions and set
out again. They travelled southwards now, south and east.
They were not in a hurry because they did not know where
they were going, but they travelled for the great delight of
travelling, in a spirit of adventure. They came with their
sheep straggling out behind them, down the eastern side of
a great lake and crossed the river at its foot; then they
turned south again. And all the time they laughed and
teased each other and their God laughed with them, but
prodded them on.

Southwards they travelled, into a new land, a richer
land, the land of Canaanites, where fat nanny goats
pumped rich creamy milk into the mouths of their growing
kids and the flowers blossomed in the fields more colour-
fully than in the gardens of Ur, and the beehives were
overflowing with sweetness.

When the hot weather came, they went up into the hill
country and made a summer camp high in rocky meadows
that they found there, and it was a time of great delight and
joy in each other and in their travelling lives. One morning,
while it was still dark, they woke sticky and gritty from the
night before, and dressed in the tent excited as children are
by the hope of an adventure. Together they went out, and
in the darkness they could hear the sheep chomping,
dozing, warm, fat, contented. There was a huge but gentle

waiting and they walked into the waiting and into the last of the night. The moon set and the great constellations were dancing, swinging through the sky over the land they had left far away to the east and over this new to which they had come. The stars, the stars alone were the same, the same in Ur of the Chaldees and in the desert and in this rich strange land.

They were hushed with excitement, though they did not know why. As they walked up over a rocky meadow, the stars faded and the light came, the colour of apricots ripening, ripening, full deep orange, gold, flame, fire, heart of light and life and joy. The birds were singing. A covey of couched quail sprang up from almost under their feet, startling them. They walked on. They sang together, a quiet joyful song as they walked – a song for each other, for the morning, for the sun that would rise and for the God they had met in the desert and who went before them always and now hovered, they knew it, waiting in the mountain heights as they climbed up.

They came out on a high place, with a long wide view. Over towards the river, south and towards the sunrise they could see a mountain, a mountain with a flat crown, well protected, a citadel still awaiting its city, with wide valleys running up to it. Behind them westwards and northwards they could see the great sweeping pasturelands, the way the green hills sank gently down into greener valleys, where there were streams and pools of still waters. And as she looked, as she gazed, Sarah had the sure and certain knowledge that it was for this, for this morning, this view, this land, that they had come out from Ur of the Chaldees, from safety and from comfort. For this.

The sun rose.

God, their God, their untamed God of the desert, their God who was not walled and bound to a place, their God who travels, their God who was god-without-a-name, their God who dwells in the high places, was with them. They did not know the way of God's coming. God is there. El Shaddai, the Almighty. God came to them, appeared with them on that prominence, looking towards the mountain where one day there would be a city and across the wide lands where one day there would be a people, God appeared to them and was with them and said, absolutely and forever, 'I will give this land to your descendants.'

They laughed. In the shining morning and laughing they built an altar to God, to their God who was with them. Then they went back down to the camp. Before long they had packed up and travelled on, south still, south to Bethel, where now in her old age she has returned; south to Beersheba where Abraham now lived; south into the Negeb, where famine found them; south into Egypt where they had grown rich, and whence they had turned north again to war and grief.

But still there is that morning, that joyful dawn, that wide view, that moment when God was with them in the glory of the rising sun and the three of them had laughed together. Still there is a citadel waiting for its city and still the lands where the shepherds can tend their sheep. Still there is the promise, 'I will give this land to your descendants. I will make you a great nation.' Still, bright as the stars at night is the memory of the three of them, Sarah, Abraham and their God laughing in the dawn, singing to the sunrise.

Sarah is old, old and very tired. Sometimes she remembers things out of order, out of sequence. Sometimes she cannot stiffen herself to remember some things at all. She remembers only the sweet things, and looks sour because she knows she is too weak. Sometimes she weakens further and remembers Abraham, young and mad and energetic and beautiful and sexy. She forgets all the anger and the betrayal and remembers only that there was once a man who knew her too well, and used his knowledge well because he loved her in his knowing.

She remembers when Isaac was born.

She had been of course too old; too old to have the child. Not too old just in the sense that she had made other arrangements, although she had. Living with Abraham she had learned that although their God was faithful, he was not straightforward. Their God's early promise to make her a mother of many nations; to make her descendants as the stars of the heavens and the sands of the desert had seemed clear enough, but by the time she sent Hagar in to Abraham to get a child by him she had been willing to accept that in making Hagar her daughter, she could make Hagar's child the first of those descendants. She had worked it out, slowly and carefully in her mind, she had spoken of it to Abraham and to their enigmatic God and it had seemed sensible – had seemed that this might have been what he meant – that there should be a new thing – that the promise of the child might be to the man not to the woman, from a laughing God not from Great Mother as in Ur of the Chaldees. This they thought was what God had meant, what he had planned and promised all along. She had no problem with that; she, sophisticated, witty, complex herself, liked to know that she had a complex, crafty, subtle God. Although afterwards it had always niggled away in her mind the thought that God had kept faith, she herself had lacked it – that she should have trusted to a simpler meaning and just waited. Too late for that when the strangers had sat down to eat her hastily baked bread, and swiftly killed calf. They had sat down and eaten and told her that she would get pregnant, now after all these years, now after her flow had stopped, now after her breasts had withered. She had laughed in the folds of the tent hanging then, because it was ridiculous, because the twists and loops of their dealings with God were pre-posterous. They were funny. Their God made them laugh unlike other Gods.

But it was not in that sense that she had been too old. In a far more basic sense she was too old. Her body had been too worn, too used, too aged. She had been too old.

When Hagar had been pregnant with Ishmael she had blossomed, her cheeks full and soft. Always lovely, she had become radiant. Most of the young women did. Sometimes Sarah knew they were pregnant even before they knew themselves, because with the eyes of experience she could see the richness flower in their faces.

But she had not become lovely, she had become sick. Far from blooming like the springtime she had become haggard, exhausted, plain and harsh-tempered. She had taken to her tent, anxious, nervous, demanding and cross. She had scarcely known herself. Who was this woman, she would ask herself, this woman who languished and grumbled like an old lady? This was not her. She was Sarah, a travelling woman. She was Sarah who had crossed

the desert laughing; who had come out of Ur of the
Chaldees a princess, and had arrived in Haran a strong
woman. She was the woman who had gone down into
Egypt pinched with famine and had come back through the
Negeb rich in cattle and silver and gold because her beauty
had beguiled the Pharaoh and he had given her gifts
worthy of a queen. She came to fear, even to hate, the child
who was stealing her from herself, who was inside her like
a thief in the sheepfold, like a rat in the meal sacks, growing
fat at her expense.

And if her body was too old for pregnancy then it was
much too old for childbirth. She had attended many births;
it was her duty and her joy as the head woman in the camp.
She had buried a dead baby in the desert six months out of
Ur; but it would not have died if she had known then what
she has learned since. Later, even in prosperity, she would
rise in the night at the sound of a woman's first moan and
would stay with her; the woman crouched between Sarah's
knees, Sarah's strong arms under her armpits and Sarah
singing, gentle and firm, close in her ears. The women of
the camp want Sarah with them when their labour is on
them. They know she will not lose a child who could be
saved, nor a mother who will stay with her on that long
journey. And afterwards Sarah's hands, untiring, loving,
would wash the new mother with a soft cloth, washing tenderly and happily, all over, hands like cool honey, all over.

The women knew what they had been given but they
could not give it back. Sarah was too old. Sarah was old
and cross and had gone away from them all into herself.
Sarah was the one who gave and they were all used
to receiving. There was something unnatural about her

bloated ugly old body. It takes a simple love to help a woman birth her child in the tents.

Because Sarah had always been the wise woman who stayed with the mothers who birthed their children in the camp, there was no one to do that for her. And she did not have an easy labour. Her body was too old.

Towards sunset her waters broke, warm against her thighs and she knew she was already too tired, too old for this terrible work. And she turned away and hid in her bed coverings and waited mute, like a lamb before the shearer, numb with misery and exhaustion.

And there was a long cold night, and long hot day; and another long night and another hot day. Towards the end of the third night, when the moon was riding westwards, Hagar went to Abraham. All the men were waiting, all the camp was waiting, even the sheep it seemed, huddled close in their night-folds, were waiting.

'We are going to lose her,' Hagar told him, 'her and the child.'

Abraham looked startled. It was not a thing he had even thought of.

'She'll be all right,' he said. Their God was not straight-forward, but he was not treacherous. Abraham said, 'She'll be all right,' gruffly because he wanted reassurance even if he had to make it up for himself.

'I don't know,' said Hagar. 'I don't think so. She won't travel with us. She says she is too tired.'

'Sarah?' He said bemused, unhinged by this news.

'She won't even try,' said Hagar.

Abraham concentrated suddenly. His eyes narrowed and he looked up at the sinking moon and the enormous fierce stars. Then he smiled. A crooked smile and one of deep knowing. He knew Sarah, he knew her so well because years ago when they were young they had set out together on a long, long journey which had brought them to this place.

He put his arm round Hagar, still smiling. 'I'd better come,' he said.

Abraham came to the women's tent; he stood in the entrance and all the women there were shocked. Men did not come where women were birthing. It was not lucky. It was perilous.

But Abraham did not care. He stood in the entrance, one arm hooked casually round the tent pole, and looked at her. Even in the disturbance of his arrival she did not turn her head.

'You're a soft woman, Sarah,' he said, 'a pampered idle bitch. I should have left you in Ur where all the women are soft.' He strode over to the chest where she kept her jewels; the jewels the Pharaoh had given her, her silks and perfumes, her hair combs from Egypt. He snatched it up and tipped it all out. There was a crashing and tinkling as her treasures tumbled to the ground and spread across the tent floor. 'You're a soft woman,' he said again, 'a soft cowardly woman.'

She was furious. She turned in her anger. She sat up. 'How dare you, you bastard?' She shouted at him. 'Get out of here. Get out of my tent. Can't you see there is women's work to be done here?'

He looked at her with disdain. 'There's not much work being done here at all as far as I can see. Do you think we've got all month to be about this business? We're travelling people, Sarah, we don't have time for this soft rubbish.'

'Get out,' she yelled, tucking her chin down, deepening her voice, 'get out.'

He stood there mocking; a long wrought-gold chain dangling in his hand. 'You can't make me,' he said insolently.

She got to her feet; she rushed at him, her arm swinging for a slap. The pain of her son shifting inside her was convulsive. She screamed once and fell towards him. He caught her under her armpits, strong and solid. He held her. Her body heaved usefully now. He held her – unmoving, tough, present. He held her and he did not let her go. Her contractions wrenched her, she was screaming and he held her. The pain seized her and she bit hard into the side of his neck, fierce as an animal, and he was bleeding and he held her.

There was a pause. Sarah was panting. She threw back her head seeking for air and looked straight into his eyes.

'Soft,' he said softly, 'you're a soft woman, Sarah.' And he smiled.

She knew she had been tricked, she knew that he had tricked her; she was furious and she laughed. They both laughed. They laughed together, deep full laughter, and on the wave of her anger and laughter their child was born.

They called him Isaac – God's laughter.

God laughed; God their God their untamed God of the desert, their God who travels with them, their God who was god-without-a-name, their faithful tricky complex God, El Shaddai the Almighty laughed with them. Their God who likes there to be not despair and corruption, but life and laughter in the tents, in all the holy places, laughed with them.

And when Sarah, now even older, remembers this she laughs although those who love her do not know why.

But even in the laughter she knows that it is not all laughter. Some days it seems important, necessary, that she should remember the moment when they had changed. There had to be a moment of changing; a moment so subtle that she had not noticed it at the time, but a moment so absolute that they had all lived in the shadow of it forever. There had to have been a moment when everything changed, so that what was unimaginable before became normal and, in some crooked way, straightforward; a moment that made what happened later inevitable. Somewhere, on some day, at some well-side, by some oasis, under some fierce moon, everything had changed and some days it seems important to her that she should find that moment, mark it and learn from it.

They had gone into the Negeb as travelling people; but they had come back laden with riches, unable to travel lightly; they had lived for years as guests, but when they came back to the land their God had given them they were a tribe with three hundred trained warriors in the camp. She thinks perhaps it follows from that, but she cannot remember.

On other days it does not matter at all. On other days she remembers only and in perfect detail that place, slightly to the left of Hagar's full upper lip, a patch of smooth on which soft hairs, as fine as peach bloom in Ur of the Chaldees, lie golden. Some days, some nights, especially some nights, she can even count the pores on that patch of skin: the patch of skin which she kissed before she sent her friend out into the desert to die.

And now she cannot even remember why. She only knows that she will not forgive Abraham, because she cannot forgive herself. That what he did to Isaac she did to Ishmael. And now she does not even know why. There were no excuses.

She summons up excuses.

There are no excuses.

Hagar had treated her with contempt. Hagar had flaunted her pregnant belly in Sarah's barren face, and all the camp knew it, because Hagar and Abraham had been without discretion or care. They had laughed in her face.

There are no excuses.

Abraham had been unfaithful to her and she deserved better. Unfaithful not in sleeping with Hagar, but in sharing with her; in the little glances of intimacy and the huge desert laughter. She had done nothing – Abraham had sent Hagar into the desert. He did not have to give way to her every crotchet, and mostly did not. Yes, she had asked him, but he did not have to obey her.

There are no excuses.

Isaac, she had done it for Isaac. Isaac was the child of the promise. It was not right that her son should have to share his inheritance with the child of a slave girl. A woman has a right, has a duty, to protect the interests of her own child.

There are no excuses.

And in the end it did not matter. Nowadays she hears that Ishmael swaggers into the camp down at Beersheba, a lordly man, a chieftain in Paran with his lovely Egyptian wife and his trail of children. So he did not die in the desert and nor did Hagar so it does not really matter. He comes and goes, a desert ranger, his hand against all men, still Abraham's son. He and Isaac, she hears, content, easy with each other, cuffing each other's shoulders as men do. He does not come up to Hebron to visit her, but she would not wish him to. It did not really matter.

It mattered.

There are no excuses.

Because even if all these things were true, and she no longer knows if they were true, but even if they were true there is something truer – that no woman ever, for whatever reason, may kiss another woman on the cheek, just to the left of her mouth, and send her and her child out into the desert to die.

It mattered because betrayal matters. She had kissed Hagar and smiled.

It mattered. God, their God, their untamed God, their God who was not walled or bound to a place, their God who travels, their God who was god-without-a-name, El Shaddai the Almighty went out with Hagar into the desert. They should have known their God would do so.

They had stopped laughing. They had become rich. They had laid claim to a land flowing with milk and honey. They had formed a war band; they had made treaties, alliances and blood-strewn sacrifices to their own advantage with people who had tame gods. They had bargained with El Shaddai the Almighty, offering their god-without-a-name petty gifts in exchange for petty gifts – a foreskin for your name, oh God; a dead child on a windswept sand dune, a tiny pile of bones bleached on miles of gritty sand for a true inheritance, oh Lord.

On some days Sarah saw Hagar in the desert. She saw the woman she had known and loved, the woman whose labour pains were painfully engraved on her own now ancient wrists, the woman she had kissed when she sent her out to die for no excuses that were good enough because there are no such excuses. Sarah saw her in the desert walking with God. She saw the God who had appeared to Abraham and her at Bethel and laughed with them, walking now with Hagar, walking slowly so that the shadow of the Almighty fell over her and protected her from the heat of the midday sun. She saw their God opening the sand to find water for Hagar and comforting her and promising her that she would be the mother of many nations.

Sarah knew that God did not do this to punish her, nor Abraham, but simply because that was how God was. God walks with the traveller.

And when Sarah remembers this she weeps although those who love her do not know why. But even in the weeping she knows that it is not all tears.

Sarah is old, old and very tired. Her mind wanders, sometimes she laughs and sometimes she weeps and those who love her do not know why. Her mind wanders across all her long life and she struggles to make much sense of it.

It is hard to make sense of sometimes. There are gaps. She does not know what happened between Abraham and Isaac in the land of Moriah. She does not speak to Abraham any more and she knows that Isaac will never tell her. Now he is grown he will toss his head and speak of women with contempt. He will take an advantageous wife from a distant people, a woman he has never met and into whose eyes he has not looked deep to see if they share a laughter that will sustain them even in the desert.

Abraham came back from the land of Moriah smug, contented, smooth and sleek. Isaac came back from the land of Moriah like a wild animal, bound but not tamed. There was a look in his eyes still, evasive, distant, the look of a man who uses pride to cover betrayal.

She does not know what happened. Once Abraham rose early in the morning, saddled his ass and took two of his young men with him and his son Isaac and went out of the camp. And seven days later, at the setting of the sun, he came back looking sleek and contented. Isaac looked glazed with fear and would not let his father touch him. That is all she knows.

It is not all she knows. When she lets herself know it, although in her mind she dodges and weaves around her memories, she knows that that morning Abraham would not look at her. Abraham who even then, even though they had grown old and had betrayed each other and themselves too often, had a wide open gaze for her, full of respect and sharing. He would not look at her, he did not tell her where he was going. And she had not asked him.

'Where are you going?' she asked Isaac when he came for his mother's travelling blessing.

'With the men,' he said and there was pride in his eyes, the pride of an eight-year-old who was counted that morning with the men and is going where the women do not go. He laughed, wriggling with excitement because he is going with the men and even his mother, who knows everything, has to ask him where he is going. So she laughed with him in the golden dawn and let him go out with his father.

She sent him off with a laugh and after that he did not laugh, she did not laugh and God, the untamed God who travelled with them, did not laugh any more. It was not her fault. It was not her fault; she had not known.

But she had watched Abraham cut the wood for a burnt offering and load it on the ass. She had watched him take down the sacrificial knife from its peg on the tent pole and slide it into his belt. He had not taken a kid, a sheep, an ox, not even a cockerel or dove, but he had loaded the wood for a burnt offering and taken his son by the hand.

Seven days. She will never see her son again. She will never see Hagar again. The laughter of God is a treacherous laughter.

Then burning in her is the knowledge that God, their God, their untamed God of the desert, their God who was not walled and bound to a place, their God who travels, their God who was god-without-a-name, their God who dwells in the high places, El Shaddai the Almighty, the God who laughs with the people, does not order the murder of children, does not deceive and hoodwink young boys in joy and excitement. Their God, who is contented to eat bread and wine and tease her in the shade of a terebinth tree, their God, the God who travelled with them in the desert, does not act so. And if this is true, and she knows that it is true, then Abraham is not only wrong, he is monstrous. He has remade God in his own mad image and she had failed to notice. She too was monstrous; she had sent Hagar out into the desert to die and tried to find excuses.

What had they both wanted? They had wanted to turn their God into a monster, so that nothing, nothing, would be their fault. A God who travelled with them, who had eaten and laughed with them, was too vast and too sweet for them. She could remember the awful gods of her childhood in Ur of the Chaldees, gods greedy for blood, who withheld rain or sent floods only for a high price paid in death and misery. She knew they had not left them behind, those gods. They wanted a God as petty and tyrannical as those had been, a God not of the free but of the slave, because slaves were not guilty, were not responsible, were not heirs but property. They had tamed their God because they wanted to be tamed themselves and could not bear the demands of a God who loved freedom and friendship.

Abraham could believe that God wanted him to take his son, his only son, and make a sacrifice of him; that God would treat as a son a man who would destroy his own son, his laughter, for some future personal gain. And she could believe that their laughing God would be pleased to watch Ishmael die whimpering under a bush in the hot, cruel desert. They had been offered a gift and they had not been strong enough to accept it.

Knowing all this she wept. She wept bitterly, forgetting all laughter. Deep inside the tears was a terrible anger, a rage of grief and loss and despair. For the long week she stayed in her tent mourning for the child she would not see again; mourning for the man who had become so monstrous that he would deceive his own son, leading him out through the golden dawn as though for a game, to slit his throat on a high mountain and who would believe that God would be pleased; mourning for the woman who had become such a good and obedient wife that she did nothing to stop this cruelty, who had changed without noticing the moment into a woman who could do such a thing. And she swore an unbreakable oath that she would never speak to Abraham again. There could be no comfort between them any more, because he had taken something that was not his. No man, no God and no woman has the right to claim the life of a child. There are no excuses.

And on the seventh day, in the evening, still weeping, she comes to sit at the door of her tent, so the westering sun can warm her. The air is golden from the long hot day; the trees around the well-head cast long blue shadows across the grass. She can see the ranged tents and hear the rustling of the sheep. The young men and the maidens, work over for the day, are singing around a fire, and women nurse their babies and rock their weans towards sleep.

Round the base of the small hill comes an old man, with a donkey, two young men and a boy. They are travelling light, walking with the long loping stride of people who are well used to travelling on foot in rough country.

Isaac. Isaac. Her heart sings. The camp dogs, which should have barked sooner in warning, start to bark. She stands up, unbelieving, great bubbles of joy like frothed foam on a waterfall spray up in her. She stands up. She flings open her arms.

'Isaac,' she calls to her son, 'Isaac.' He is eight years old, sturdy, the colour of dried grass and tough as a goat. He tugs his hand from his father's and runs. He runs towards her and she waits for him, smiling.

'Isaac,' she calls. 'Come, my laughter.' This is the child

conceived in her laughter and in God's. He runs up the slight slope, around the trees, he runs towards her waiting arms. And then, almost within reach, he sheers away, stops, panting, and looks at her with wild eyes; eyes that have a terrible knowing in them; eyes that sneer at her. Eyes that sneer from a depth of fear that no child should have to know.

'Shalom. The blessing of El Shaddai be upon you, my mother,' he says formally as soon as he can catch breath to speak. Then, wild as an untamed foal, he runs through the grass, up on to the top of hillock, where he turns away, spreads his arms as wide as she had spread hers and laughs a harsh laughter that flows down over the camp. Distant. Unreachable.

With dignity, but under the shadow of that mocking laughter, Abraham came up through the camp and stood in front of her.

'What happened?' she asked abruptly, 'what has happened?'

He would not meet her look. His eyes were fixed on a point behind her left shoulder. She saw that he looked contented and smug. He sounded complacent.

'El Shaddai, the Almighty, has given me a great blessing, a reward for my great faith.'

She looked at him in silence. It was not enough, he was determined that she should congratulate him, embrace him, admire his courage and resolution.

'Sarah,' he said, 'our God has blessed us.'

'Your God, not mine,' she said, and bowed formally and turned and went into the tent.

After that she never spoke to him again. She stayed in

Kiriath-arba by Hebron and he camped at Beersheba. It was not that she could not forgive him or even that she could not forgive herself. It was that she had nothing to say to a man who believed that God had blessed him for being willing to kill her child.

Sarah is old now, old and very tired. She is not always certain what she remembers and what she invents. But she knows with a certainty that does not waver that tears and laughter belong together. She wishes that Isaac would marry so that she could have a daughter-in-law. She knows that he will not do so while she lives. Sometimes she even regrets that she does not have Abraham with her, to help her remember, to help her invent and to remind themselves of their courage, of their failure and of the untameable, unnameable God they met in the desert, the God who travels, El Shaddai the Almighty. But it is too late to do anything about that now.

On her best days she believes that their God is big enough to cope even with this treachery, this spoiling of a huge and beautiful thing. Some other days she cannot bring herself to believe this and thinks that sometime, somewhere, another little people will have to set off from another great city and burn in the desert as they burned and dance in a new country as they had danced, and learn all over again that God is not to be tamed but to be laughed with.

Sarah is old and very tired. On many days she sits in the sun and her mind wanders. Sometimes she laughs and sometimes she weeps and she does not know which or why.

Her mind wanders across all her long life and she struggles to make it into a story: the story of her life, the story of Sarah.

HOW DO I KNOW WHO I AM IF I KEEP CHANGING?

(In honour of Lewis Carroll)

arly, early spring and the sky pale grey with a sheen of
pearls. Outside the air will be cool and dawn-damp. In
here it is warm (good) but dry (less good). Less good
for her anyway – she cannot breathe freely and her skin is
itchy and flaking. They say it is old age, but she thinks it
is because the ward is too hot and too dry, and too many
people have breathed the air in and out all through the
night.

'I want to go home,' she sobs silently, exactly as she
sobbed when she was sent away to boarding school. Suddenly she had not been Daddy's 'Tweedles', nor Mummy's
'Dearest' any more. She was changed into 'Mabel'. Once
they were kind and loving parents, and now they changed
into monsters – monsters who would send her away, and
monsters from before that when they had given her a name
so stupid that everyone laughed at her.

She struggles to sit up and reaches out for her watch and
for her box. There is a good deal of clutter on her bedside
table, but her hand manages to grope its way through it and
find them both without knocking anything on to the floor
and making a nuisance of herself. The watch tells her it will

be more than an hour before They come. The box tells her nothing at first, even though she shifts it around on her lap and peers very closely at the delicate shrivelled pod. 'Soon,' she thinks, but then wonders whether the hot dry air will slow things down or speed them up or make no difference at all. She must ask Pobble when he comes, except she must not call him Pobble but David, because now there is a new tiny Pobble and she is a great-grandmother.

'And that's another one,' she thinks. Then it all starts slipping again: Dearest, Tweedles, Mabel, Miss Ferguson, Darling, Mrs Dalston, Mummy, Mother, Gran and now a great-grandmother, though not yet with a new name for that new person. Having so many names, being so many people: baby, girl, student, scientist (wartime only), fiancée, bride, wife, mother, assistant (to a proper scientist), grandmother, widow, stupid old bag. 'Great-grandmother,' she thinks, 'that's another one.' She is fully aware of names she has not claimed, but some things are too secret even to think about.

She looks into the box again. It is easy to look into because it has glass sides. Is the pod . . . ? Is it swelling, quivering, changing, or is it just her hands shaking? It had been fun watching the caterpillar, stomping about on all those legs, gobbling down the leaves, sitting up to look at her with an apparently wise expression, munching, grow-ing. Then it changed and was not a caterpillar, but a chrysalis. The long silent waiting was less interesting but more exciting. Perhaps it is on the move again. She is uncertain.

Soon They will come. They bring a cup of tea (good) and ask their daily questions (less good). They ask which day of the week it is and she tells them, because she really does know, at least usually and if not then it is worth a good guess; the poor things have their work to do after all. Next They ask, with various degrees of subtlety, what her name is. Then it depends. It depends partly on what is slipping and partly on who is doing the asking.

If it is Lynn she is a little girl, a child again, though in a warm sort of way. She giggles and pretends she doesn't know and Lynn teases her like her big brothers used to tease her when she was Tweedles and smaller than they were. She likes Lynn.

If it is Taz, who is tiny and too conscientious and solemn for her own good, she will be a helpful grown-up, a mother who gives motherly helpful answers. 'Mabel Dalston,' she says, if things aren't slipping too much. She loves Taz.

Some of Them she neither likes nor loves, and knows very well that this is entirely mutual. Then she will be a sulking snappy adolescent, or act as though she does not understand. Serves them right. They have to mess around and try to extract an answer from her, their hands hovering over their report sheets and their faces trying to hide their exasperation. Or not. Some of Them are better at this than others – she cannot quite decide which she admires least.

But more and more often now when they ask her who she is she wants to cry, 'How can I tell when I keep changing?'

When she was little and skinny everyone said, 'Eat this, and you'll grow into a big girl.' So she did and she did. Then they said, 'Eat this so you will grow smaller.' So she did and indeed she did and Harry put his arms round her and said, 'You are as slender as a wave, my darling.' Then she married him and got bigger and bigger and then there was a baby and she got smaller and then there was another baby and after that she didn't get quite so much smaller, and it was back to the eat this and eat this business. Not just Them but her own head as well, on and on about it. Then, about when she stopped caring, she started getting smaller again. 'There's nothing to her,' they say, 'skin and bones.' Then they cut bits off her and out of her, though how on earth that was supposed to make her bigger . . . And still they want her to know who she is all the time.

'I am . . . who am I?' But no one would tell her. It all starts slipping again: Darling, Gran, Tweedles, Mrs Dalston, Mummy, Dearest, Mabel Elizabeth Ferguson, Mabel Elizabeth Dalston. It is too chancy. If it hadn't been for the doodlebug and his pride in his clean uniform so he didn't lie down on the wet pavement when they heard the warning whine, she might well have been Mrs Mallin Montgomery III and lived in Arizona not Andover and then she would be someone else now – not Darling but Honey; not Mummy but Mom, and perhaps not a widow at all. She had lain down quick as thinking and laddered the new nylons he had brought her – and then he was too dead to give her another pair. But even without stockings Harry put his arms round her and said, 'You are as slender as a wave, my darling,' and she changed again.

They seem to think that you are who you are. That those torn stockings and Mal's sweet vanity, and her getting smaller and slimmer so that Harry's wounded arm could go round her comfortably, and all those other things, they think they do not matter. She thought that too, once:

thought that somewhere inside is a cherry stone, a kernel, and that was who you are and it couldn't change. But now she thinks: it does change. Big and little changes, chancy and chosen changes; wilful, playful, mournful; loss and gain, but change and change and what you want and what you know, and even what you remember changes, slipping off sideways, unstable.

'How do I know who I am when I keep changing?' she asks.

Lynn laughs and says, 'Give us a break, Mrs D.'

Taz looks startled and says, 'Oh dear.' Then she smiles and says, 'Look, Mrs Dalston, your tulips. They've come out.' She wants to ask if they were tulips before they came out, but she does not want Taz to be worried.

Harry frowns and says, 'You are my wife.' She cannot tell him that this is exactly why she feels muddled, especially as he has been dead for fifteen years – as dead as Mal, really, though with a lot less blood.

Susie, who is her daughter-in-law and Pobble's mother, wrinkles her face and says, 'Oh don't be silly, Mother.'

The Chaplain, who certainly means well, looks embarrassed and says, 'I think . . . I believe that your soul doesn't change. Whatever you do God loves the real you, you see.'

But she did not see.

One of Them shrugs and says, over her shoulder to someone else, 'I really do think we should move her on to geriatrics.'

Pobble says, 'That's interesting. I'll get you a caterpillar.'

Which is what is in the box, she remembers now, and looks again. Now it is not a caterpillar any longer. It hasn't been for some time. It was a caterpillar but now it is a chrysalis. Some people think that the caterpillar is inside the chrysalis, but it isn't; it isn't in there making its antennae longer and its body slimmer. She knows. Inside the chrysalis there is a horror of nothingness, a dark smear of disintegration, organic ooze. When Pobble was still Pobble, before he became David, he played in her garden and they collected caterpillars together and learned about them. They kept the chrysalises in the airing cupboard. Usually they forgot about them, or Pobble was off being somebody else. And in the spring she would find dead butterflies, lighter than feathers among the pillowcases.

'This time,' says Pobble, 'you have more time. You may get to see it change. Keep a sharp eye out.' And this time she is trying to.

She cannot see too clearly. Perhaps it is changing.

Yesterday the tiny new Pobble, her first great-granddaughter, was born. She was feeling very small. A child again, a baby. She had . . . she hates it. She did ring but no one came, so why is it her fault? And Lynn, who can make her laugh even about this, was not on duty. Babies are allowed to dirty themselves, so if she is blamed she is not a baby, but they talk to her and treat her like a baby and she changes into a baby. Small, shrinking, vanishing.

Then Pobble came, except that he was suddenly David and Father – though he wasn't very good at that yet, still looking both smug and awed, more like a small boy with a new puppy. He needs more practice, she thought.

'Handy you're right here in the same hospital,' he said, 'I can show her off without waiting for you to come.' One of Them hovered, disapproving, but he didn't care. 'Nell's sleeping,' he said, 'So I've brought Pobble Junior down to meet you.' He put the baby on to her lap. Suddenly she changes again, grows tall and weighty, because the baby is so tiny; and she stretches out a whole past and an enormous future. She is big and old and happy. She looks at the tiny scrunched-up red baby, touches its head and sees her own hands are huge and strong.

'Isn't she beautiful?' says her Father, and under the paternal gaze the red wrinkly bundle changes and is, magically, a beautiful baby.

'Has she got all her toes?' she asks, smiling now. 'Will Nell give her lots of lavender water tinged with pink?' 'Of course,' he says, 'For everyone knows there's nothing so good for a Pobble's toes.' A very old joke, and they both laugh, so not everything changes.

'You had to be first,' he said, 'but I must take her away now for when Mum gets here. And Nell's mother. Oh Lord.'

Now, watching her box with hope, she is striding a new mountain, finding in herself a new thing, a great-grand-mother, an ancestral goddess, a giantess looking down on the world through the tree tops, tall and strong. Things slip suddenly and she is a little old woman again who wants her morning tea. 'How do I know who I am when I keep changing?' she thinks, but the question has changed too and gives her no anxiety.

By the time the tea comes, she has changed her mind and no longer wants it. It is not her hands; it is the chrysalis that is quivering. She watches it all day. It is feathering the air. She needs to keep a sharp eye on it. Sometimes things slip and she cannot remember quite what she is watching.

Then it comes back. The chrysalis is changing: swelling, pulsating. Taz comes and sits by her, to see it change perhaps, or perhaps not.

Things are slipping again, faster now: Dearest, Tweedles, Mabel, Miss Ferguson, Honey, Darling, Mrs Dalston, Mummy, Mother, Gran and now a new name the new baby has not found yet. Baby, girl, student, scientist, fiancée, bride, wife, mother, grandmother, widow, stupid old bag, great-grandmother. Bigger, smaller. Egg, caterpillar, chrysalis, butterfly. How can I know who I am if I keep changing? And if I'm not the same, who in the world am I?

Late in the afternoon, when the sun is pouring through the ward windows, the butterfly pushes through and flops out of the chrysalis. It hangs there, dazed, its folded wings pulsing, gathering its new self.

David is here now. He says, 'Look.' The butterfly opens its wings, wide and lovely. It crawls on to her hand, and sits there gaining warmth. Then it takes off – across the ward towards the window.

David sounds as if he is crying. She doesn't know why. Nothing is slipping now but something is changing. David says, 'Oh Gran.' And then, his arms round her, he asks urgently, 'How does the caterpillar learn to consent? Learn to dare to change?'

'Practice makes perfect,' she wants to say but it is too late.

THE TALE OF
THE BEAUTIFUL
PRINCESS KALITO

Once upon a time, long, long ago and far, far away – if that makes it any easier – there lived The Beautiful Princess Kalito.

The Beautiful Princess Kalito really was very beautiful: she had skin the colour of pure strained honey waiting warm and soft in the sunshine – golden with hints of darkness, but smooth and cool and glowing like the skin of a ripe cherry. She had soft black eyes, painted smoothly on to her cheeks with a disciplined, apparently casual brushstroke and her mouth was little and round and pink. Her fringe of hair lay on her forehead like mulberry silk, dyed black with all the skills of the northern dyers. She had a little round soft body. She had very tiny feet and no name. None of this is surprising.

She had always been beautiful, even as a little child; moreover she had then had feet which, while pretty of course, had been of a perfectly ordinary and uninteresting size, suitable in every way for a pretty, active and rich little princess. She had also had a name then, although she was now not always able to remember what it had been. She had abandoned it on marriage. The Beautiful Princess Kalito, understandably, was not her name, but a title indicating that she was her husband's wife.

The Beautiful Princess Kalito, as well as having a very important and highly placed husband, had also had an extensive palace: at least she understood that it was extensive, because an extensive palace is one of the things that The Beautiful Princess Kalito had every right to expect, along with not having a name and having very tiny feet. She had not of course seen much of it, but what she had seen was, like herself, precious and beautiful. There were gardens of intricate delicacy, where water-wheels turned musically and lotus flowers – blood-red and milk-white – flowered immaculate, and waterlilies floated serenely on ponds deep with golden fish. And the gardens changed magically, gently, into pagodas and terraces of wrought wood, where birds in cages sang tunes of entrancing loveliness. And the terraces, too, dissolved through trellises and archways into rooms where more lotus flowers – redder than blood and whiter than milk – flowered on the walls with an even finer perfection than those in the gardens; where golden fishes swam forever across walls of waterlilies; where at every turn huntsmen on horses, with long spears and dogs, chased deer of slenderness and grace around pagodas more intricate and refined than those in the garden – and did so without the noise and the sweat and the disturbance that her husband complained of on those few occasions when he could bring himself to leave those disagreeable pursuits and spend an evening of perfect joy, 'in heaven, beloved, in heaven' with her.

The Beautiful Princess Kalito also had three sons, who had once been golden tumbling bundles of delight with little thatched lids of black hair, and shiny black eyes who had played and giggled around her feet when their nurses brought them in to her. They had once climbed on to her lap and stood with their arms round her neck and gazed levelly into her eyes with glorious smiles of pure devotion, but who now had gone away and when they appeared at all it was to look at her with nervous scorn through hard black lenses. The Beautiful Princess Kalito did not have any daughters; but she did have piles of silk cushions which exuded a warm rich smell, and cases of jewels which glowed and stabbed at the darkness when her maidservant opened the caskets and selected the appropriate items for The Beautiful Princess Kalito to wear. And she had porcelain bowls so fine that the light filtered through them in colours strange and rich – blues and crimson and flame. And she had horses of bronze and clay which stood with a military stiffness and an interesting greenish tinge. And she had jade palanquins carved far away and so fragile in their perfection that breath could shatter them. And she had gold ornaments so fine as to need no purpose, or use, or explanation. And she had a carved wall of pink stone and white stone with plants growing from it here and there, which kept her and all her husband's other treasures safe from all eyes. What more could any beautiful princess wish for?

The Beautiful Princess Kalito had, moreover, memories. She could remember when her sons were a delight and a refuge for her. She could remember before that, when her servants looked at her with admiration and envy. She could remember when her husband spent time with her in joy. On golden sunlit evenings when the blossom of her trees cast a special light in the garden, she could

even remember how it was when she could run and dance
and live without pain. And in the late watches of the night,
when the huge fierce stars gaped coldly at her, she could,
just sometimes, remember the day when all simplicity of
joy had ended.

Although The Beautiful Princess Kalito had little to do
all day and nothing to do most nights, three times a week,
at the very least, she had an important and private engagement. Then they would bring to her very inner and most
private room great bowls of warm scented water and herbs
and unguents and oils, all strongly redolent and heady in
their sweetness like overblown hyacinths. The richness of
their savour would creep up her little curved nostrils and
weave about in her brain until she nearly fainted with the
excess of their beauty. And there, alone and unattended,
The Beautiful Princess Kalito would ceremoniously take
off her clean-every-morning knitted white cotton oversocks and start to unwrap and clean her feet. As she ritually
unbound the bandages a new smell would start to contend
with the giddy scents of her room. They were at war with
each other: the perfumes of the master perfumers of the
Great Empire and the stink of the rotting, unaired, dead
flesh of The Beautiful Princess Kalito's tiny feet.

When the last bandage was off and the nakedness of her
feet exposed, the stench from them would overwhelm the
room. Then taking the dead flesh in her hands, The Beautiful Princess Kalito would lower the inanimate hunks into
the warm scented water. She would prize the hooked claw
of the big toe with its soft spongy nail away from the petal-
like mass of where her other toes had once been and scoop
out the new white dead matter from the space. She would

tenderly scrape the freshly putrefied gunge from around her heels and pry into the crevasses of the rounded slug which made up the middle part of that glob. Each object was only four inches long and still it would take her over an hour to wash and re-perfume them. Then, finally satisfied, taking up the new pile of white bandages, the new pots of sweet scented oils and creams, she would re-bandage them. There was a point at the centre of this process when she would be tempted to despair; when it seemed impossible that even the softest bleached wool, even the incense of the whole world, would be able to cover over that stink of putrefaction. But always, by the end, she would have won, would have ordered all things aright, and pulling on the delicately knitted oversocks, she would toddle back into her world; her feet, the lotus flowers of her husband's heart, restored, perfect.

Her husband too, incidentally, had fine feet; long and straight with a high delicate arch. Each toe, to her early amusement and delighted fascination, was separated and could be flexed individually. When she was first married she had very much wanted to touch them as he did hers. 'Ah, my love,' he would say, 'ah, my beautiful princess.' He would hold those tiny, tender, white as mountain snows little socks, each in the palm of his hand, squeezing them, caressing them; leaning over her, folding her soft little body almost in half, he would place each immaculate little cotton bundle against the soft golden skin above his brown nipples, just where the secret hiddenness of his underarm met the bold openness of his chest and seem almost to swoon with joy. Recovering physically, he would press down on her, now almost out of his mind with passion, so that the weight on her never-exercised muscles hurt – but what was the hurt compared with the pleasure that she could give him, the amount that he loved her? 'Ah, my lotus flower, ah, pearl of all my riches, ah, see these perfect . . .' he could scarcely even speak for his entrancement, 'for me, for me. Oh I will love you always and always, because my precious can never run away. See each little mouse, hiding in its scented hole, that is what my beautiful little princess is for me. See these feet, so tiny, so perfect, that my love could dance on a lotus flower and not bend or crush one petal of it.' But as, in fact, The Beautiful Princess Kalito could not dance at all, he would have to call in dancing girls to inspire his erotic imagination further and they would lie together watching the dancing girls disrobe, while she tried neither to giggle nor to weep and he fondled and turned and twisted and hurt The Beautiful Princess Kalito's beautiful little lotus-flower feet.

And after all it was precisely for this that her mother, weeping, had called her in from her games with her brothers one day when she was seven years old. Weeping, laughing, she had told her daughter that she was now old enough to become a woman. Tickling, teasing, she had wrapped the first soft bandages, sung the first binding songs, trying through her tears to tell her daughter the old stories. How the Emperor had bound the feet of his favourite dancing girl, long, long ago and far, far away, so that she could dance for him on a lotus flower and not bend nor crush one petal of it. How, despite the pain, one day, when her little daughter lay so soft and sweet with her tiny feet against the chest of her lover and her lord, just where the secret hiddenness of his armpit met the bold openness of his chest, she would sing and praise the tiny feet which bound her lover to her with a tighter binding than any which might now seem to hurt her. And together they laughed and the bandages were made tighter and tighter. But The Beautiful Princess Kalito – although then of course she was no such thing, but a pretty little girl who played in the rich acres of her noble father's cherry trees – The Beautiful Princess Kalito was allowed to sit with her mother and her aunts and her grandmother all day and be counted by them as a grown-up, as a woman. So that it was not until some days later that she discovered that she could no longer run down to the stream and dabble her toes in its icy coldness until each individually they wriggled up, rearing away from the water until she laughed and had pity on them.

That night when the little girl was unable to settle down to sleep because of the unaccustomed tightness – too extreme yet to call it pain, although there would be nights and nights to come when pain would be a gentle and kindly word for what that child was to endure – she was surprised to hear her mother sobbing and sobbing in the next room. Her mother, who was a great lady and the wife of a great warrior prince, sobbing so loudly, so inelegantly. Then she heard her aunt come toddling in on her tiny feet and sit beside her sister and mutter sweetly, softly as women do with each other when there is great grief and nothing to be done about it. The child heard one remark only with any clarity; the aunt said to the mother, 'Sweet, you know what they say, if we love our daughters we cannot love their feet.' A pause, and then moving from the old proverb to her own sharp merry tone, the aunt laughed loudly, though not very happily, and said, 'We love the daughters, the men love their feet . . . it all works out I suppose.'

And indeed her aunt was right, because her husband did love her feet. As described earlier and so on and so on. She loved his feet too, as it happened, but once she had tried to take them in her hands – or rather to take one of them, for her sweet little hands could not encompass even one of his fine-boned feet. At the time, which was quite soon after they were married, he was lying back in that joyful exhaustion she could never understand. The silk cushions were piled around him and he was beautiful and he loved her and he had given her a palace and he spent every evening with her. She was filled with a new and restless feeling which she did not recognise, growing perhaps from somewhere near the base of her smooth golden belly. She sat up giggling with her legs crossed under her, and she did of course look sweet and enchanting and very young and innocent, as well as beautiful. She picked up one of his feet and, bending forward, inserted her little tongue into the space between his largest toe and the one next to it. They had a strong flavour of salt and a smell of grass and goats. She turned the foot back at the ankle and her tongue went exploring the stiff firm arc of his instep, while her fingers felt the powerful tension in his tendon, running up from heel to leg and then, perhaps, on upwards. He lay back sighing and she let her mouth wander on in the enchanted valleys and the mountain ranges and the forests of his foot. And the restless feeling ran up from the base of her stomach to her tongue and back again like a silk cord that tightened and tightened and also somehow spread outwards so that her fingers and her back too were caught in the cord, were part of the cord, and she toppled forward and lay out beside him, her fine silk shift rumpled up on her soft honey-coloured thighs which were unable any longer to remain still, and she sucked and groped at his feet and knew that something was going to happen.

And something did. He changed from liquid delight into iron. He sat up. He said, 'That's quite enough.' He pulled his foot away. He got up and left the room, his back expressing displeasure.

And after that, although she never repeated the experiment; although she never asked, not even herself, what the purpose and meaning of that strange tight cord might be; although his sons grew in her body and were born with little round bodies and flabby squashed feet just like hers; although they grew up with straight fine bodies and tough strong feet just like his; although she was beautiful and sat in her beautiful palace; although she allowed him, whenever he wanted, to take her little lotus-flower cotton socks in his hands and croon to them; although she was as good as the gold she both resembled and was adorned with – still he came less and less often to her part of the extensive palace and from the pitying looks and half-heard gossip of her servants she knew that he was keeping concubines – neither as well-born nor as beautiful as she, but able to please him without challenge, without questions.

So there she was, The Beautiful Princess Kalito, and time went by. And what with dressing up in the morning and again in the evening, and washing her feet three times a week, and wondering if her husband would come and visit her in the evenings, she probably had as much to do as was good for any beautiful princess in a story.

But one day something new happened. She was

toddling around the extensive palace and quite by chance she found a new room. It was a pretty little room, high up in the palace and hung with the most exquisite silk paintings. It had obviously been the favourite room of some other Beautiful Princess Kalito before her and the idea of this tenuous link appealed to her somehow and she took to sitting there sometimes on her silken cushions to sip her tea. And after another little while she discovered that her pretty little room had a little window and that the windows looked out over the filigree wall of pink and white stone and into an orchard of fruit trees very like the one she had played in with her brothers many, many years before. And she grew to like to look out of the window at the orchard and, with a caution quite unbecoming to a beautiful princess, she never mentioned to her husband that she sometimes sat in this little room, and sometimes looked out of the window. But then, he really did not come very often, and when he did they really had far more important things to be doing and thinking of than in which of her many rooms the princess liked to sit and drink her tea.

So, gradually, as she heard that her sons had married in their turns beautiful princesses with soft painted eyes, tiny feet and no names either; and as she met these younger women and was forced to know that she was no longer quite as beautiful as she had been; and as she discovered again the joy of plump babies in her grandsons and discovered again that they grew up and vanished; as time passed she spent more and more of it in this pretty little room. And more and more of the time she spent there she used looking out of the window at the orchard and remembering how it was when she was a little girl.

One year, spring came again as usual, and the white frothy flowers leapt on to the branches of the orchard trees and were suddenly, surprisingly much more lovely than the perfect blossoms painted on the silk on the walls of the little room. By this spring The Beautiful Princess Kalito was spending so much time in her little room that she could not fail to notice the peasant women who came to work in the orchard. Tall young women with dirty yellow faces, not little and beautiful at all, with eyes heavy and dark as though their craftsman had used his thumb instead of a paintbrush. The young women came to the orchard on long strong legs with hard bare feet. Some of them carried their babies on their backs and laughed and sang to them while they cut the bright spring grass which was sprouting energetically around the trunks of the trees in the orchard. As they worked they sang – sometimes loud rough songs and sometimes sad songs, or one of them would cry or shout and the others would tease or comfort her according to rules which The Beautiful Princess Kalito could not understand. Sometimes their roughness and abuse, or the anger with which they slapped at their babies' fat legs, appalled her, and sometimes their energetic cruelty made her giggle. But whether or not she could understand, whether or not she liked what she saw, she still hung against the window of the little room and watched and watched them. And when she saw their strong muddy feet with proud straight toes moving naked across the grass; when she saw one of them wrap a strong arm round another or heard them break into song again, she would feel that strange cord which she had almost forgotten tighten again, not in her stomach now but round her throat and her heart, but gradually as strong and tight as ever before. And as though the cord were pulling her together she started thinking new thoughts – about poverty and luxury and herself and the other women, thoughts that she hardly knew how to think. One day she went to her jewel chests and reaching in with her fist drew out a handful of gems. The cord was tight and almost hurting her and she scuttled and toddled as fast as she could and threw the jewels out of the window to the women below. But the singing stopped abruptly and they looked up askance, fearful, mute. The jewels were still lying there, bright and beautiful, when the women went silently home. Then The Beautiful Princess Kalito realised that it would have been better, safer, wiser, to have thrown them down food, bread and fruit, which would need no explanation, but she found she had none to throw and she did not dare to ask for any. And the cord in her throat grew tighter.

The blossoms fell from the trees and instead they were green with a sweeter, more translucent green than any of the paints on the walls of the palace: a green that was never flat and smooth like the green jade bijouterie in the beautiful rooms, but soft and musical in its changes. And then from where the blossom had fallen the cherries sprang – first green too, then the colour of cream and finally turning to a richer red than the mouth of The Beautiful Princess Kalito had ever been, even in the first days of her marriage when it had been stung to fire by the passion of her husband's teeth. Then the women came back for the harvest and worked all through the day and into the night, when they would light lanterns that glowed like benign stars. Though the women shouted of their tiredness and moved sometimes with a slow weariness that hurt, they still worked on their long feet and they still sang and joked to one another. And the cord tightened and tightened again inside The Beautiful Princess Kalito until she knew that something was going to happen.

And something did. Afterwards of course they said it was the Woman Madness, the lost craziness that comes to women when their blood is no longer drawn off once a month but stays inside them to rot and fester their minds. They said that seeing herself old and wrinkled was too much for her to bear. They said that her sons' wives had not always been kind. They said there had always been bad air in that little room and that she should have been warned. They said her maids had not been loyal to their master, her husband. They said that it just went to show. One day as The Beautiful Princess Kalito watched the women and their beautiful feet busy at the cherry harvest she could stand it no longer. She left the window and tottered back to the silk cushions. She sank down on them. She looked at her tiny white feet with loathing, and tore off the white knitted oversocks. Then she ripped away at the bandages. And although the stench was as strong as ever and the room had not been filled in advance with unguents and the sweet smell of herbs, The Beautiful Princess Kalito did not even notice the evil rottenness – from the orchard came the odour of sunshine, of ripe cherries and of women's sweat. She threw the bandages behind her without even looking and as the women outside began to sing a bright brave song The Beautiful Princess Kalito, a child again, clambered to her feet to run in a renewed freedom back to her window.

When she had taken perhaps two paces the pain began.

There was always some pain in walking – a dull ache which she had grown so used to over the years that she did not even know it was pain. But this was totally different: her unbound feet were exposed to a pressure which they had never experienced before; the rotted flesh, the ruined muscles, the distorted tendons could not carry even the delicate weight of the shrivelled old Beautiful Princess Kalito. After four paces she knew she would never reach the window even though the room was a small one and softly carpeted. After five paces she began to scream. She could not see the women in the orchard and she could not stop the screams. There, halfway between the memories of sunlit orchards with the tough reality of the women who worked there and the pile of putrefied bandages The Beautiful Princess Kalito was suspended, screaming, screaming, screaming.

The screams detached themselves from her captured body and took embodiment from the air. They arrested the women in the orchard, swooping around their ears, careening out above the trees and preventing the work from continuing. The screams smashed down the corridors and spaces of the extensive palace, reverberating against the delicate jade, staining the painted walls, dumbing the musical gardens. Even when The Beautiful Princess Kalito fell to the ground in her pretty little room the screams did not cease; even when they rushed in and found her there, broken, unconscious, the screams did not finish . . . and they have not finished yet. I told you it was long, long ago and far, far away, but that might not make it any easier.

SIREN SONG

Come, sailor, I am your dreaming;
long voyaging on icy seas
leads to the white haven of my arms.

It is never silent on the sea coast. There is always, even
in a flat calm, the whispered sound of the smallest waves
licking the silvered sand of the beach, tonguing the face
of the rocks, and the soft sigh of the sand as each wave
retreats and a few grains are carried down with it, reluctantly, inexorably.

It is never silent on the sea coast, but sometimes, at
night, in the summer months, there can be a fleeting
moment of something sweeter than silence; a magical hush.
The soft irregular rhythms of that continuous rise and fall,
rise and fall, rise and fall, rise and fall, become so monotonous, so expected, and so gentle, that they fit perfectly to
heartbeat and to breathing; out on the seaway there is a
slow roll of water, a gentle heave, and a flowing gleam of
phosphorescence, and we know a porpoise is passing on its
long travels.

In that moment, just occasionally, but worth the long expectancy, the moon rises, full, round, silver, and lays her swathe of white light across the barely shifting waters, and the twin points of light on the facing slope of each slow lift of water dance in delight. The moon at her full puts out the stars around her, but in compensation lays these dancing stars on the sea itself. The air is balmy, heavy, scented with summer and with seaweed. And if on such nights as these, we lay our hands or bare arms so that the moonbeams fall on them, we can feel – attenuated, fragile, delicate – the warmth of the sun, kissing his virgin sister, and letting the last reverberation of his power refracted from her across the wide spaces caress us in the darkness of the night.

When the white lady rides her pathway on the sea, when all else is still, when the waves have sunk to this sparkling, dancing murmur, then we rise from our nest and preen ourselves, preparing ourselves as the young bride does for her beloved and with an excitement that is not altogether different although we wish that it were.

We wait.

It is our destiny to wait, but we chose that destiny and so our waiting is not the anxious wonderings of the sailor's beloved in the noisy harbours north of us. Will he come? will he come on this light breeze, bending his back to the drumbeat and pulling wearily? or on another, on the shoulder of a storm? or out of the sunset boldly with the sails set filled with a home wind and a golden light? Will he come today? Tomorrow? Will he ever come again?

Our waiting is not like that. It is a long calm waiting and we are always ready when he comes.

We wait.

And so, when those other three sisters, the Fates, have spun a sailor's life-thread so thin and taut that it can be spun no further, then far away a new rhythm begins, so gentle and distant, that it is hard to be certain, although we are certain. More a movement on the surface of the water than a sound, but the feathers, the hairs – both – on our necks rise sensitive to his coming and we smile a little at each other and preen.

And carried on the calm night the sound of his coming takes shape. The slow drumbeat counts out the strokes. The cry of the helmsman in the stern is borne across the surface of the water to our longing ears. 'In,' he cries, '. . . and out. In – two, three; out – two, three.' The oars hit the surface together as he calls them; the drum and the oars and the strong rich voice of the helmsman. 'In . . . out . . . In . . . out.'

They are freemen who row such a ship, for we do not hear the harsh sound of the lash; a dark arhythmic note, joyless and painful, with which we have no business, no concern. As soon as we hear the coming of the ship clearly we draw breath and we strike the chord and we sing, so that our singing runs out along the pathway that the moon is making, towards the approaching ship. And the sweetness of our singing in the moonlight is what all men dream of.

The sound of our music comes to them first so gentle and distant that it is hard to be certain. Perhaps it is just the wishes of tired men rowing southwards through a calm night. We sing and the sound of our music swelling in the darkness becomes unmistakable, mysterious, desirable. The sweetness of our singing makes it so that each man believes we sing to him, for him alone. He does not see the rapt face of his companion on the rowing bench; he does not notice that he too has raised his head from the low easy slouch of the practised rower and has thrown it back, harkening to the music that is coming across the moonlight as his mother used to come when he cried in the night.

> *Come sailor, I am your dreaming,*
> *long voyaging on icy seas*
> *leads to the white haven of my arms.*
> *Come, sailor.*
> *At home your mother weeps for you;*
> *She begs Athene, lover of brave men,*
> *to bring her boy-child home to her.*
> *The candle she has lit for you*
> *dims in the twin flames of my eyes.*
> *Put out her candle, sailor,*
> *and I will give you a place for each strong limb.*

We sing to each man alone and what we sing is what he dreams.

If he dreams of his mother, he will hear her voice in our song, he will see her sad patient waiting and her joy at his coming.

If he dreams of power and glory, swords will flash in the moonlight, like hot day, and chariot wheels will throw up the spray of the sea like dust, and the crown of laurel will glimmer on his brow.

If he dreams of wealth, Hera, Queen of Olympus, will descend and give him the jewels from her peacocks' tails and the golden apples from the islands beyond the uttermost west.

If he dreams of poetry, the moon herself, Artemis the pure, will offer to teach him the music of the spheres, and he will hear the roar of applause in the amphitheatre, taste the pride of his city, and the immortality of his name.

If he dreams of the gods, Poseidon will rise glorious on the wave crest and greet him as lover and as friend; and the dark voice of the sibyl will speak of the great mysteries in the cave and he will understand her as though she were his own chattering child.

Mostly however their dreams are not so high. Mostly they dream, as most men dream, of long white thighs, and full breasts and the dark place between women's legs. Some dream of it soft and welcoming; some dream of it proud and to be fought for. Some dream pleasure for their beloved and some dream pain for their paid whore, for their defeated enemy, for their chaste neighbour. Some dream women too young with frail fine bodies, long legs like colts and high tight little breasts with icy, frightened nipples; and some dream women too high and noble who would not look at them save with scorn, and dream them humbled and begging.

And to each of them, our song is the promise of the fulfilment of their dream. Just beyond the bowsprit, just beyond the pale light of the moon, there, there, almost within reach, there waiting to be taken, there, here, now, at once and easily, here, here their dream is waiting and will be given to them.

> *Come, sailor; make me a bride gift of your soul*
> *and I will give you the pearls*
> *and salt blood of my mouth.*

'Come, sailor.' We sing and they come.

The drumbeat wavers. The drummer lets his palms go soft, they beat little, desperate, plaintive tattoos that cannot command the muscled backs. The helmsman whimpers; his 'ins' and his 'outs' are no longer orders to be obeyed, but the sobs of each man's longing. The rhythm of the oars breaks down into chaos, and the ship turning a little even in the calm begins to drift towards the shallows.

There is a sudden splash. One has dropped his oar and hurled himself over the gunwale; we hear his arms beating the water and the heavier breathing as he starts to swim. Now there are shouts form the ship. Not shouts of fear – except for those of course whose fear is the kernel of their lust – but shouts of desire, of longing, of greeting, of joy. There are more splashes, more heavy bodies entering the water, more shouts and anger and laughter and tears.

More are so perplexed and foolish in their lust that they drown long before they reach our shore. Some are killed by their colleagues as each man fears that the next – who at sunset only a few hours ago was his brother on the row-ing bench, his comrade-in-arms, his dearest friend – may steal the object of his lust, his chosen victim, from him. Those that do not drown, or die at their comrade's hand, come wet and panting to the rocks at our feet and when they have had time to realise the empty hollowness of all they have ever dreamed of, we rend them with our long talons, sear them with our sharp beaks, destroy them with our bright eyes and devour them for our amusement and nourishment.

Then, with the moon high above us, white and harsh on the jagged rocks, we laugh; and for a few moments our pain is softened, our grief is comforted, our anger is slaked, our desire is fulfilled.

This is how it is. This is what we do, because this is what Sirens do and we are Sirens. Sirens, by the deceptive sweetness of their voices, lure brave travellers to their doom.

Down southwards, along the coasts of Sicily, of Demeter's own island, there are many dangers and pitfalls to trap the unwary and unlucky, to snare the bold high-hearted men who bend to the oars and plough the seaway's furrow into the bright future. But of all the perils the peril of the Sirens is the most perilous, not just to life but to men's souls, because the Sirens break a man on the snares and delusions of his own heart. There is blood and death and malevolence lurking under all desire and the desire for women is the darkest. A woman will take a man from his noble path for her own amusement, for no better motive than spite, for no higher gain than the satisfaction of her own foul lusts and greeds. There is vicious malice always beneath those fair appearances and Sirens are monsters who prove the evil that comes always with female beauty.

They tell the stories of Sirens, so that men may be warned not just when heaving on the rowing bench, or running before a following wind along the rocky, lovely coast of Sicily; but everywhere and always to beware, to beware of sweetness and rest and dreams. To beware of women and of womanly doings.

They tell the end of the story, they do not tell the beginning. They do not tell why we sing and why men must die from our song. They do not tell why we seek for revenge, why we need it and take it and only in taking it can we find any peace.

We will tell you.

She was our duty and our joy. Persephone – our care and our delight. When she had hardly grown into the woman months, into the turnings of the moon, while her cheeks were still smooth and round and her eyes too big for the precious face that carried them, before she was fully grown her mother gave her into our keeping.

Her mother, Demeter, the mother of all living things, Goddess of hill and valley, of flower and fern, of root and bud, tree and leaf, giver of fertility and growth and grace. Just to walk behind Demeter, just to see even the passing of the hem of her skirt as she moved through the fields touching grain stalk and fruit blossom into ripeness, is to have known joy. To look full into her generous face as we did, to help her with her strong labour, to receive as gift the warm smile that makes all plants grow, as we did – we, her chosen nymphs – is to drink deep of the nectar of the earth, to know the music of the world's spiralled dancing, and to live in the richness of springtime.

She gave us her daughter, the most precious of the many things she loved; she gave us her daughter, the beautiful Persephone, daughter of the gods and heir to all loveliness. She gave us Persephone to play with and take care of, while she, Demeter, mother of growth, of seed-time and harvest, was busy about her world-task.

We danced the hills and shores, the bright meadows of Sicily, most pleasing of all the islands, place of vine and olive and corn and wildflowers. We taught the child the music of mountain streams and the song of slow rivers; we taught her the harmony of bird wing and bat flight and the tune the clouds make by day and the stars make by night as they journey across the sky. It is hard to find words for that time, for our joy and our industry. We left nothing undone that we ought to have done and the doing of it was always a pleasure. We loved Persephone, we loved her because we loved her mother and we loved her because she was lovable, loveworthy.

She was innocent and we were careful.

It made no difference.

He came sudden, dark, fierce. He did not speak. He did not try to woo her or charm her or comfort her. He came in the dark sullen cold of the dead lands where he is King; and she had never known anything but life and warmth. He came with power. With strength. He raped her. It was not enough that he violated her, that he broke her and her dark private blood flowed out on the grass staining it and her. He hurt her. She cried not with authority, but with weakness in a whimpering pain. He raped her and the sun shone unmoved.

We tried to defend her and there was nothing we could do.

Our little white hands beat his back uselessly, so we have grown talons.

Our slim white legs ran to seek help but not swiftly enough, so we have grown wings.

The cold wind of his coming carried our little weak voices into nothingness, so we learned to sing.

His hand smashed against our complaining mouths, blood and saliva on our white little teeth and so now we have beaks of iron.

There is no pain in our drowning sailors that can compare with the pain he inflicted on her.

There is no sadness in men's faces when they see us that can compare with the sadness of Demeter when we told her.

There is no shock in their dying that can compare with the shock when we learned she had consented; had eaten, had taken the six black pomegranate seeds from their sticky luscious red nest. Now that we have watched enough men die we understand better, but then, in our naivety, we thought that to consent, to eat, to live rather than to die, meant that she had chosen. Now we know that sometimes, when there is no choice, when there is nothing that will change how the humiliation is then it is sometimes necessary to consent because that is the one, the only, thing that you can do; that you must do to be other than victim, to be yourself. That is a real thing and the worst thing.

We searched for her, with her mother, high and low, in heaven and on earth, and Demeter never reproached us. She did not reproach us. Her sadness became madness; became long days of weeping and long nights of wailing. She left the buds to rot on the tree, the grapes to stay unripened on the vine, the standing corn un-eared un-loved. She howled the dark moors and cursed the birds on the wing, but she did not reproach us.

We asked Zeus himself to return her to us. We humbled ourselves to ask him, as a favour, to give us back what was ours in the first place. And he laughed.

He laughed and told us that he thought it did not matter. He told us that the Dark Lord, his brother, was an honorable mate for Persephone, was a fitting lover for that sweet child. He told us that Hell, the place of shadows, could be a fine home for someone born and brought up in the sunshine. He told her mother not to be so foolish. He said that now she was deflowered there was nothing better she could hope for. And he laughed.

In the end, irritated by Demeter's insistence rather than moved by her grief, he allowed Persephone to come home for half the year: he made a gift out of what was her right. He felt generous and thought we should be grateful.

We are teaching him gratitude now. Are the sailors who drown grateful? Does the flesh we eat give thanks? Our seductions are sweeter than his was, and we kill our lovers rather than make them drag out long years in the darkness.

Sometimes, at the moon's setting, we wonder; we wonder if our vengeance has hurt us as much as it hurts them. We cannot dance in the sunlit fields any more, we cannot accompany Demeter on her joyful wandering. We cannot comb Persephone's hair or dance with her in the springtime. Instead we must wait here.

We wait; we wait, we sing, and we destroy.

This is what Sirens do. We wait for the coming of strong men and by the deceptive sweetness of our voices we lure them to their doom. We are Sirens, this is what we do.

We break a man on the snares and delusions of his own heart. For our own amusement, for no better motive than spite, for no higher gain than the satisfaction of our own foul lusts and greeds.

There is vicious malice always beneath those fair appearances and we are monsters who prove the evil that comes always with female beauty. But our malice is not without cause; our cruelty is small payment for men's lust.

She was defenceless and he raped her. He raped her and went unpunished.

When they die, the sailors, when they drown or kill each other or are eaten while the moon shines high above us, white and harsh on the jagged rocks, we laugh; and for a few moments our pain is softened, our grief is comforted, our anger is slaked, our desire is fulfilled.

It will not last forever, our waiting. The priestess of the oracle has spoken: when a man comes, a single man, who does not respond to our singing, who passes by unmoved, whose desires are pure, without greed, without lust, then our waiting will be over and we will be free again.

We know that one day he will come. Odysseus, the shrewd one, red-headed, limping, pitching his sly good sense against the power of all the songs: the one who looked on Helen and was not moved, the one whose desire is simply to be home with his own woman, so that we have nothing to offer him.

We know he will come. We do not know if we will be glad or sorry. We do not know if we will be able to rest; we do not know if she, her despairing cries, wild against the shock and pain, will let us rest; we do not know if we want to rest.

And until he comes, whenever there is, in the summer months, a fleeting moment of something sweeter than silence – a magical hush; whenever the soft irregular rhythms of the calm sea's rise and fall, rise and fall, rise and fall, rise and fall, become so monotonous, so expected, and so gentle, that they fit perfectly to heartbeat and to breathing; whenever out on the seaway there is a slow roll of water, a gentle heave, and a flowing gleam of phosphorescence, and we know a porpoise is passing on its long

travels; whenever these nights are upon us, we will be waiting, waiting and singing.

In the name of all the gods, we are justified when we
seek vengeance; for our malice is not without cause; our
cruelty is small payment for men's lust.

WATU

'There is death in the pot for the living's food.'

Watu is in the jungle.
Watu is in the jungle, alone.
It is strange in the jungle.

Despite the humming of life, the music of energy, power, growth, greed, the jungle is fragile. There is no depth or richness to the soil. Each dead leaf is stripped of its goodness by new growth so quickly that nothing sinks down into the earth.

Because it is fragile, it is competitive and cruel. The strangler vine entwines itself around the huge ficus trees and squeezes them to death in its desire to reach up through the canopy to the sun. Then insects devour the dead wood and the vine is left, a vertical spiral with an empty core. Down on the floor young trees grow to about the height of one of us and then they wait; they wait with infinite patience; they wait for years. They wait for a larger tree near them to die and make a hole in the green roof. Then the small trees make a wild dash upwards, growing twice their own height in the time it takes the moon to come back

159

to the full, fast, faster than the other trees around them, for there is only space for one in the sun. The jungle is stirring with energy, with life and power; if we can get it, if we can win.

In the jungle it is hot and sweaty. In the jungle there are insects, so many biting feeding insects. They cling closer than a lover by night and by day. They need our blood to live on. In the jungle there is a deathly intimacy of need and desire. In the dark the jaguar carries his silken beauty, his great heavy tail and flaming eyes, to the killing grounds and the night is alive with the screams of death.

In the jungle it is beautiful and deadly.

Watu is in the jungle. Alone.

Watu is always alone in the jungle – and now is an especially perilous moment. This morning we moved on. Every so often we move on – we dismantle the village, load up the dug-outs and move on. We paddle upriver chanting the rhythm, or drift downstream languorous, telling stories, enjoying the changes, except there are no changes. Always there is the yellow river and beside the yellow river are the green trees and above the yellow river is the blue sky and there is nothing else. It goes on and on and there is no distance, no depth, no inside nor outside; there is only the jungle and it is beautiful and deadly. We need points of discrimination; we need to draw boundaries, set up markers, create clear definitions; we make them and we drive them home with the rhythms of the stories, and the beating of the drums. And we draw them on our bodies in the Rituals of the Skin.

When we move on, we come, after a day or a week, to a sandbar or a beach that makes a small clear space between the river and the trees. We have been here before but now it is new. We stop and resettle. We take the fire from the fire pot and hearth it; we feed it tenderly and then victoriously. We gather around it for the Ritual of Welcome and we tell the children the stories so that they may be safe. Pat, pat patter like raindrops on the drums to mark the rhythm of the story, and the Teller works through the tales. The children raise their hands to their cheeks and feel the edges of the yellow circles, the sign of the Turtle Father, pricked in at birth so He will know His own. We are His People.

But Watu cannot come in the boats, because there is no place, no place for Watu. We do not know if Watu is drummer, or paddler, or baggage. We do not know if Watu is teller or tale. We do not know if Watu should be in the women's boat or the men's boat. We do not know, not for certain, if Watu is animal or spirit or one of the People. So Watu has to follow as best as maybe. Always, before, before this time, Watu has arrived in the end. A few days, a week, once nearly a whole moon later, Watu will creep out of the jungle, and sit at the very margin of the village, at the very edge of the jungle, in the place between. We are glad when Watu comes, but it is a dark gladness. We are frightened, we are endangered and we are guilty. Watu is the shadow.

In the jungle, under the canopy, there is always shadow, a strange darkness even at midday. The spirits like the darkness, but the People do not. Watu is in the jungle, alone, under the canopy. Watu is our shadow, our strange darkness.

Watu came in a hard time. This is no excuse. We are guilty. But it was a hard time.

Here is one of the stories that we tell at the Ritual of Welcome. The story of the Waters of Separation.

Once upon a time there was no difference between the People and the spirits.

Dub . . . dub . . . dub . . .

We and they moved in their world and in our world and in the space between, and we talked and laughed and sang together. There was no difference, then, between the yellow river and the blue sky and they were both green like the jungle. And this time went on for a long, long time, longer than the river, except that then there was no time because there was no difference.

Dub . . . dub . . . dub

Then the flood came. It came as rain from the sky, coming down; it came as waves from the river, rising up. All the yellow from the green sky fell down into the river and all the blue from the green river was tossed up to the sky. And when morning came and the waters were calm again the sky was blue and the river was yellow and they were separated. The jungle between them, sharing both, was still green, and so it has remained, but now there is shadow and darkness in it because the sky and the river, the blue and the yellow are struggling always to be together again.

Dub . . . dub . . . dub on the drums

The spirits did not like this new situation – they did not like the clear lines, the boundaries, the differences. They wanted to leave our world and live only and forever in the spirit world. They asked the People to come with them.

Dub . . . dub . . . dub

But there was a girl and a boy – and who can know when the young are foolish and when they are wise – and they would not come. In the rain on the water, and the rain on the broad leaves, and the lapping of the waves beside the river they had heard the drums, the music of the People. In the forest, on the river and in the place between they went tapping, tapping, listening, asking, seeking and finding – finding the trees and the stones and the sand that made the music, the way of tapping it out from the root and the branch, the ways to make the rhythm. They were so busy looking for the sound of the waters, the way to make the drums that marked difference and time, that marked the clear lines of the stories and boundaries of river and jungle and sky. They would not come.

Dub . . . dub . . . dub

In the end the spirits were angry and went away to the spirit world and would not tell the People how to travel there. So to this day the spirits can come to the People as they wish but the People cannot go to them.

Dub . . . dub . . . dub

Only the Turtle Father, the oldest of us all, stayed. He said he was too old to move on; but we think he stayed because he loved us. He became our Father, and every child of the People carries on their cheeks the yellow marks that he carries on his, so that the spirits do not treat us with malice and so that we are not altogether alone.

Dub . . . dub . . . dub

So, when new members of the People, new children of the Turtle Father, come to us, when they make the long hard journey from the spirit world down the two rivers – the yellow river of the jungle and the red river from our bellies, and the waters of the two rivers mingle and stain them orange-gold – we must rejoice and make them welcome, we must laugh and sing for them. But some come only to visit. They are not People, they are spirits on a different journey who have perhaps taken a wrong turning, got lost, or weary and come to us only in passing. We cannot tell, we can only wait and see. So the Turtle Father taught us to build birth huts at the very margin of the village, at the very edge of the jungle, in the place between, where the turtles also lay their eggs. And we wait, very quietly, the mother and birthed thing in the dark hut, and the rest of us about our daily business, because if it is a spirit we do not want it to feel too much at home, we do not want it to stay. Then if it remains with us through seven nights and seven dawns we know it is truly one of the People, and we hold the Ritual of Outdooring. One of the Old Ones goes into the birth hut and takes the child from its mother and brings it out into the sunshine and we laugh and sing to the drums and make the child welcome. And we prick into its cheeks the yellow circles of the Turtle Father, so that he will know that it is His and other greedy spirits will know it is His, one of the People, and leave it with us.

And around the child's belly button we prick in the rays of
the sun, because it has come out of the darkness as we all
have. The child screams and we laugh because spirits do
not suffer pain, and the child's pain joins it to us for the
whole time of its life, short or long. We share with the
Turtle Father the task of making the People. We bathe the
child in the water from the river and wrap it in the leaves
from the jungle, and place a butterfly on its breast and we
know the child is one of us, one of the People, not a spirit
who leaves when it feels like it.

Here is another of the stories that we tell at the Ritual
of Welcome. The story of the Foolish Monkeys.

Tap . . . tap . . . tap

Once upon another time, after the world had separated into river and sky and jungle, there was no
difference between the People and the animals. We
and they moved in their world and in our world and
in the space between, and we talked and laughed and
sang together. There was no difference, then.

Tap . . . tap . . . tap on the drums

In those times when the river rose too high and
the children were cold and wet the Jaguar would
come out of the darkness of the jungle and hold the
children against her fur to warm them and lullaby
them in her deep purring. In those times the giant
otters would teach the People to swim in the *cochas*
and the mosquitoes fed on dew; and only the wisest
of the Old Ones could tell who was of the People
and who was a monkey. The monkeys too were children of the Turtle Father and told their stories from

the treetops while we told ours beside the river, and there was no misunderstanding.

Tap . . . tap . . . tap

But the monkeys were foolish; they would not teach their children. The monkey children were restless and chattering like all children, but the monkeys would not make them stay still and learn the stories. The monkeys thought that it was too difficult for the little ones to learn the stories properly and they petted them and gave them nuts even when they just chattered and did not keep to the rhythms of the drums, and the words of the chants and the shape and boundaries of the tales so the children grew up without rhythm and without sense, chattering of nothing until their chatter made no sense.

Tap . . . tap . . . tap

The foolish monkeys were too soft with the monkey children, because their cries hurt the parents also. When the little monkeys cried out in pain at the Outdooring and the Pricking, the monkeys stopped pricking them: the monkeys stopped marking the sun on their bellies, and the yellow circles on their cheeks in honour of the Turtle Father. So the Turtle Father said, 'Since they have no tales I will give them tails instead,' and the monkeys grew tails and fur on their faces and chattered senselessly. So the Turtle Father could not recognise them as his children. But he said to the People, 'I know you. You are mine.'

Tap . . . tap . . . tap

The monkeys were jealous then and gathered the other animals into their villages and made a distance and a difference between themselves and the People, and from that time to this time there has been war between the animals and the People.

Tap . . . tap . . . tap

So, when new members of the People, new children of the Turtle Father, come to us we mark them. We prick them with the yellow circles of the Turtle Father so that he will know they are not little monkeys, and we prick them also on the forehead with the five marks, which have no meaning. They are senseless so that they will make sense to the foolish monkeys. They are there to tell the animals that this is one of us – this is not another animal but one of the People, one of the children of the Turtle Father and so worthy of respect.

Here is another of the stories that we tell at the Ritual of Welcome. The story of the Lazy Child.

Putta . . . putta . . . putta

Once upon another time, after the world had separated into river and sky and jungle, after the monkeys had swung away to their senseless chatter in the treetops, there was no difference between the women and the men among the People. We all did the work and cooked the food and nursed the babies and sang the songs. And in those times the children did not come to us down the Red River, but hatched from eggs like turtle babies, along the river edge, and whoever found one newly hatched would take it into a hut and care for it.

Putta . . . putta . . . putta on the drums

Then after a long time, a time of great peace and happiness, a child came to us who was lazy. This child was very lazy. This child would do no work – would not cook the food or nurse the babies or sing the songs. Ay-yay, this child was lazy – it would do no work at all and lay in the sunshine growing fat and sleek and cunning. Wo-wo-wo. That lazy, lazy child.

Putta . . . putta . . . putta

The Old Ones came to the child and said that it must work.

Tend the fire, one said. *Putta putta*

Go with the hunters, one said. *Putta putta*

Feed the babies, one said. *Put-put-putta*

Catch some fish, one said. *Putta-putta-putta*

Stir the cook-pot, one said. *Put-put*

Yes and yes and yes, said the lazy child – and slipped away into the green jungle and did nothing.

And when the Old Ones spoke together each thought the Lazy Child was doing a different kind of work. There were too many different tasks and no one to watch the Lazy Child do them, so he played in the sunshine and grew fatter and fatter.

Put . . . Put . . . putta

And soon the other children would not work either. They said, as children say, it was not fair. They all tumbled and laughed in the sunshine and bathed in the yellow river and sang songs without meaning.

Putta . . . putta . . . putta

Then one day, as the Lazy Child lay all fat in the

sunshine, the Jaguar came down to the place in between the river and the jungle and looked at the child through its great green eyes.

I am the Jaguar, said the Jaguar. You should run away or else I will eat you, because you are fat and sleek and tasty.

Yes, yes, said the Lazy Child, not even standing up.

Pppp . . . pppp . . . put

And that was that. The Jaguar ate up the Lazy Child.

The other children came to the Old Ones and said, Let us work with the grown people, because we do not want to be eaten. And the Old Ones said, Yes. But the Turtle Father said, No. The Turtle Father said it was the People's fault, because they had not properly considered how children were. The tasks should be divided, so that they were done in groups and not alone all mixed and muddled. The People needed to know where each child should be and what its tasks were and who was looking to it and who its fellows were at the work. There would be men's work and women's work and they would be divided fairly, but every one must be one or the other so that the children could learn well and not be eaten.

And then the Turtle Father changed things so that the People could have the joy of making their own babies: a man and a woman together – the joyful shared work.

Putta . . . putta . . . putta
Put . . . put . . . putt

This is a funny story and we all laugh, and the children giggle and look at each other with promises for the future and shame for the tasks they have left undone. But so, when new members of the People, new children of the Turtle Father, come to us we look at them with care and attention and decide which half of the People they are. And when they have been with us for two whole moons, we prick them with the sign of the men's huts, or the house of the women. A long curved line down the boys' backs, so that even from behind and in silence we can tell them in the hunt. A circle above the left breast of each woman, so that the babies will know where to feed. Thus each child has a belonging in both its work and in its joy. And the jaguar needs must go hungry.

We tell the stories and the children learn the stories and take pride in their pricking and know they are neither spirits nor animals but members of the People. They know who they are and what songs they must learn and what work they must do and how they should do it and with whom, so that the People may flourish and live in harmony and joy.

This is one part of the Ritual of Welcome, when we move on to a new place, which is also always an old place and we hearth the fire and sing the songs and tell the stories so that we know and our children know and under the blue sky through the green jungle the yellow river flows on.

But even as we do these things we look slantwise along the beach, along the side of the river and at the edge of the jungle, and we disguise our looking from each other. We look to see if Watu has followed on, has arrived.

Watu came in a hard time. We have no story for that coming.

Perhaps Watu's mother died even as the child struggled down the red river.

Perhaps a snake came into the birth hut and bit the birth friend. The birth hut is a secret place.

Perhaps Watu's father was killed hunting.

Perhaps we did not know the child had come so we could not count the days.

Perhaps we were moving on.

Perhaps there was a sickness. There was a flood perhaps.

Perhaps one of the Old Ones took Watu, but perhaps she was very old and had gone back to the time before and chattered like the monkeys.

Perhaps that moving on went awry. Sometimes in the moving on the boats get separated and it takes some moons for the People to re-gather.

Someone took Watu. Then . . . this is our shame . . . we do not know . . . there is no story, there is no song, no rhythm for the drums.

After the passing of some moons, after some space too long to turn back and pretend, there was Watu, lively, healthy, crawling in the village, holding up little hands and laughing at the butterflies.

Not pricked.

One of us noticed she was not pricked. The beat of the drum faltered, the rhythm of the day was broken. There was a silence.

There are no yellow circles on Watu's cheeks.

There are no coloured marks on Watu's forehead.

We cannot know if Watu is a spirit or an animal or one of the People.

Watu is the space between.

Watu sits at the very edge of the village, between the river and the jungle, in the place between. We feed Watu. We are not cruel. But Watu cannot come in the boats. Cannot sing the songs. Cannot join the Rituals. Cannot touch the drums, or the spears, or the fire pot, or any of the People. That is too perilous.

Watu is our shadow, our strange darkness. And although no one wants to, even as we sing the songs in the Ritual of Welcome we glance, secretly, towards the place between to see if Watu has arrived. We are glad when Watu comes, but it is a dark gladness. We are frightened, we are endangered and we are guilty. Watu is our shadow. We are glad that Watu comes but we will be glad when Watu does not come. One day Watu will not come, the jungle will have taken Watu and we will be free.

In the dawn of the morning after the Ritual of Welcome there is the Ritual of First Hunting. This is the boys' hunting. Because we are a wise people and not like the monkeys we never move on without good supplies so need does not drive this hunt. The new and growing power of our young warriors needs freedom, needs its moments of wildness and they swagger out on the First Hunting unguided and undirected. If they bring home meat we will feast for them and if they bring home nothing we will laugh with them.

We are proud of the First Hunters. At dawn they gather by the side of the river to oil and paint each other and they skip with glee, dancing little dances and flourishing their bows and pipes. They stamp their feet like drums and slap each other and pin feathers in their hair. The girls, watching closely, pretend not to notice, and the men and the women laugh together to see so much beauty and promise and power.

We can never ask questions about the First Hunting – it is the boys' secret as the Ritual of Blood is the girls' secret. It is not our business. The young ones are our promise and are worthy of our respect.

So we do not have any story. We do not know what happened. We do not want to know what happened. The boys of that First Hunting stayed out in the jungle a long time, too long. It was fully dark before they came back to the village. They came with a good-sized peccary, but they slung it down by the fireside without pride or pleasure. They were sullen and shamefaced. There was a great deal of blood on their faces – both the line of the kill, running from hair line to nose tip, and the mark of the Turtle, the mark of initiation and spirit travel running from cheek bone to ear, but messy, part obliterated or half-hearted. Perhaps they were just the daubs of blood that get smeared on any hunter in a clumsy group killing. We do not know. We cannot ask. There were nightmares in the huts that night, cries of anguish and of horror; there were blundering sounds of half-sleeping young men lurching out of their huts to vomit by the river. Next day there were gaggles of them, avoiding the elders, low-voiced and tense in the space between the village and the jungle, the jungle and the river.

Watu never came again.

But time passed and the smoothness returned – the songs are sung, the babies birthed, the People thrive. And the Turtle Father crawls out of the yellow river to sun himself on a fallen log.

The yellow-spotted side-necked turtle is an ancient species. They are very ancient, these turtles. When the continents had not yet divided but still clung together, their crafty treacherous roots still acting out stability and security, when dinosaurs roamed the flood plains that have since grown into mountains and the mosasaurs were the most rapacious predators of the seas, already these small turtles swam and laid their eggs and crept out of the dangerous waters to sun themselves on the dangerous shores. They look old. They look very old. Their eyes are small and lost in wrinkles of skin and they drag themselves on battered flippers like the arthritic feet of the aged.

In the jungle they crawl out of the yellow river to sun themselves on fallen logs. You cannot know what they are dreaming of, but tears form in their rheumy eyes and slide down their wrinkled faces. Their hard, resistant shells are green-grey, the same colour as the logs on which they lie. They ought to be nearly impossible to see. But in fact they are easy to spot. Because when the turtles come out to weep in the sunshine a dancing cloud of tiny yellow and white butterflies gathers around their heads, like confetti in a breeze, to sip the tears from the turtles' eyes.

Listen, listen through the dark music of the jungle, listen very carefully and you may hear the drumming of impatient butterfly feet and the tiny kisses of greedy delicate butterfly tongues as they come, windblown and dancing, to drink the tears that flow from all our eyes.

IN THE RED BREAD OVEN

For the first weeks after the test, after she knew for certain, after she got used to knowing, she felt sleek and feline. Smug. She stretched and dozed and prowled like a cat. She felt creamy – as though her hip sockets were full of whipped cream. As though each of the tiny joints that held her back ribs to her spine were soaked in oil – in extra-virgin olive oil. Extra virgin? She laughed at herself – how virgin can you be? Very virgin? More virgin? Supercalifragilisticexpially-virgin? Not a chance. Her hands fluttered, caressing the skin below her navel. The cat had got the cream. She smiled secretly. Not at all virgin, to tell the happy truth. Pregnant.

Once upon a time there was a beautiful queen. She lived in a white palace and wore a gold crown. She was tall and slim and lovely, and all the people said, 'How lucky we are, how fortunate we are, to have such a beautiful queen.'

It was her secret, hugged in the night, hidden in the light. She loved her body, which had given her this secret; a secret worth keeping. Her very own. Sleek, smooth, contented, alone . . . like a cat, purring, head swaying, undulating, coiled, sleek, creamy, secret, feline. Smug – filled full and convinced of her own cleverness, creativity, power.

But if they had known the truth, the people would not have thought, 'how lucky we are', because the queen was really a wicked witch. Inside all that white and gold she had a cold and selfish heart, and although she liked it when all the people loved her, she never loved them.

Then, pop! Suddenly, the bubble burst.

'Y'know, Anna, you're putting on weight,' Stella said, only a little complacently.

'Jealous,' Anna thought, rather more complacently; and looked down and saw the ugly cross-wrinkle below her waist where her skirt was too tight. She felt a shudder of revulsion. She was not fat, she was never fat, she . . . She looked up, irritated, and saw the knowing looks and soppy smiles. Her secret was out, and no one seemed overly impressed. Suddenly she was thirty-eight years old, single and pregnant. Their eyes all said she had got her come-uppance. The oil drained out of her joints; the cream curdled and turned sour. She felt the baby move deep inside her, fluttering with laughter. Laughing at her.

During the daytime she looked like a beautiful queen and danced and sang like a good queen should; but at night she went secretly out of the white palace into the black forest and ran with the wild beasts.

Later Colin stopped by her desk. She kept her head down, forcing her eyes across the surface of a sheet of paper.

He put his hands on the desk, leant over, quiet, intimate, 'Is it mine?' he asked.

'No,' she said, 'no, it's mine.' She owed him more, but she did not want to pay. 'It's not yours.'

She looked up then and he was not laughing. He was looking concerned, curious, not angry, almost . . . almost greedy. He wanted to share her baby. Well, he couldn't. 'I'm not due until the middle of October. Count, Colin, count. It's not yours.' She got up and walked away, trying to look elegant and contemptuous, feeling only fury. He hadn't loved her, but he would love to love the baby. She hadn't loved him, but that was not the point.

A few days later she overheard them in the ladies' loo, the coffee klatch, her colleagues. They weren't saying 'poor Anna' which would have been bad enough; they were saying 'poor brat'. After the lunch break, Hazel came up to her, offered her an illustrated brochure. She assumed it was work, took it, glanced down and it was a knitting pattern – little jerseys, cardigans, things called matinée jackets. They were pretty. She could see that they would be a lot of work. Did she want the one with buttons or this one?

'What?' she asked.

'I thought I'd make something for the baby,' Hazel said. Hazel, who had been too busy to help Anna out on a rush job ten days ago.

Sometimes on the darkest nights she went down the narrow winding paths of the forest searching for poisonous herbs and noxious berries and the toadstools of midnight which turn out their ruffled edges and glow with a deathly green-cream light.

Then she did not feel like a cat, purring. She felt like a prisoner, a victim. Everyone was on the side of her torturer. Even her own mother, who grinned inanely, patted Anna's stomach in a way that seemed both intrusive and impersonal, said she had always so longed to be a grandmother and made an appointment with a solicitor to change her will. 'How's my baby?' she would ask on the phone.

The queen would gather these wicked things into her basket and carry them back to a little room, high up in one of the towers of the palace. She would use them to mix potent poisons in her black iron cauldron and bake evil food in her red bread oven.

It wasn't fair. Her body, her home, her life had been invaded by a stranger – a mean, attention-seeking alien. Instead of sympathy or admiration, instead of lavishing themselves on her, instead of envying and cosseting her, everyone seemed to be in love with this illegal immigrant. The few people who did not fall in love with the baby appeared to think that Anna had been not clever, not beautiful, not creative, but simply stupid. And everyone, whichever side they were on, seemed to think they had the right to tell her what to think, what to feel, what to be.

The baby was the meanest of all. The baby did not sympathise, admire, lavish, envy or cosset. It was not grateful, affectionate, generous or loving. It demanded and it took. It told her in no uncertain terms what she was allowed to do; what she was supposed to feel; who she was meant to be. Not herself any more, but its mother and its slave, for always and for ever. She nourished it, but it gave nothing back. Nothing. It was separate from her. It lay sullen against her ribs, demanding more blood, more iron, more time, more space. It took more space, pushing, scrambling inside her. She was powerless. It stretched, kicked now, somersaulted, beat its feet and fists against her. It kept her awake at night; it swelled her breasts; it wore her out. Not like that early serene doziness, but a grinding weariness, in her legs and in her back and in her heart. Me, she wanted to shout. Me. Me. Me. My baby not theirs; my body not its. It's stealing my life and I hate it. I hate it. I hate it. I want it dead.

But it was too late. She knew it was too late. They were bound together now, for the duration. There was no escape.

One night as she was walking she found a tiny baby, as beautiful as a princess and as small as your thumb, lying beside the pathway. She did not think, 'Oh, this poor baby has got no mother, and I must try and find her one.' Oh no. 'Mine,' she thought to herself, 'mine.' She put the baby in her basket and carried it home.

She dragged herself to the clinic. I'm too tired, she thought, I'm too tired, and my back aches, and my ankles ache and I feel sick and it is too heavy. I will tell the doctor, I will tell the doctor that I cannot, that someone else must, that I hate this baby. She could barely remember how the first richness had felt. She had felt it and now she could not touch the feeling. It wasn't fair. She had felt full of oil, and now she felt greasy. She had felt full of cream and now she felt rancid.

The midwives all smiled, not at the mothers but at the lumps that stuck out of the front of the mothers. They looked dewy-eyed as well as bossy. Midwives love babies and are none too keen on mothers. If she told them how she felt they would be angry; they would tell her not to be so selfish; they would tell her how many women longed to be where she was now. They would all be on the baby's side. It was her baby, hers. But no one believed that. She could not believe it herself. The baby was theirs, because they loved it and she didn't. Why didn't they take care of it then, and let her off, let her out, let her go? If they wanted it, they could have it. And she could have her body, her space, her own life back.

The wicked queen climbed the narrow stairs and took out her secret key and let herself into her secret chamber and unpacked her little basket, and looked at the tiny princess. 'Mine,' she thought to herself, 'mine. I will rub her with yeast and put her to rise in the red bread oven and when she is grown – then if she is sweet she will love me and if she is strong she will serve me.' So she rubbed the baby in yeast and put her to rise in the red bread oven.

Someone took her blood pressure, wrapping the band too tight. She felt the blood being forced through her wrist, pounding, drumming. The baby was not drumming now, but lying inert, sulking on her pubic bones. There was a fluster, something she did not understand was happening.

They told her to lie on this trolley; one of the midwives produced her little trumpet. They were prodding at the huge lump, which was the baby; it hurt her. They did not care. They only cared about the baby. Something was wrong. She could not understand. They pushed the trolley down a long passage. She lay on the trolley and the baby lay heavily on top of her.

The yeast worked well and the little princess grew. At first she was as small as your thumb, but she grew; then she was as small as a just-born kitten, but she grew. Soon she was nearly as big as a baby.

Someone was saying something about a scan. Then they ran the scanner across her belly as though they were doing the ironing.

'There it is,' someone said. 'Oh, look, Anna.'

She wanted someone to look at her, not at the baby. She did not want to look, but she looked. She could see the hard shape of its round head, like the moon. The baby was curled up. It had its hands over its face. She did not want to count, but she counted – eight fingers, and two tiny thumbs. The baby looked even wearier than she felt, and more secret. She could not stop looking.

'OK,' said a voice, 'we've got a heartbeat. See?'

She felt her own heart lurch suddenly, in tune with the baby's. She felt oil flowing into her joints.

Someone said 'thank God' and someone else said, 'hush.'

There was some talking going on that she couldn't hear

properly or understand at all and then the doctor's face loomed above her. 'Anna,' he said, 'I think we need to get the little one out of there.'

She felt something new. She felt sorry for the baby in there and uncomfortable.

The doctor was talking, 'It's earlier than we'd like but . . . we don't think your baby's at all happy in there.'

'No,' said Anna. She felt guilty. She didn't ask, 'Have I killed it, starved it, poisoned it with my hatred?' But she knew she hoped not.

Then she felt frightened. Not for herself, but for the little trapped child. 'Will it die?' she asked. And she knew she hoped not.

'We hope not,' said the doctor. He produced a syringe, squeezed her arm, found a vein, 'Go to sleep now,' he said, 'trust us, we'll do everything we can.' A nurse held her hand, gently.

'Poor Anna,' said the nurse, and she felt safe and loved again. The nurse stroked her hair and she felt smooth and sleek, like a cat. She held tightly to the nurse with one hand but with her other hand she stroked the baby, like a cat with a kitten.

The little princess began to feel worried in the oven She knew that one day the wicked queen would come and stoke the oven and bake her and eat her. But the little princess was as wise as she was pretty and loving as she was wise. She curled herself up at the very bottom of the red bread oven and when the queen peered in she thought the little princess had died. The queen was alarmed and she opened the door of the red bread oven for a closer look. Quick as quicksilver the little princess slipped out of the oven and ran away into the forest. She lived in the dark forest with the wild beats; and she did not belong to anyone and she learned not to want to.

'You wait,' said the nurse, 'in a couple of hours you'll wake up and meet your lovely baby. Everything will be all right.'

But would it? Anna wondered.

But in the few moments she had looked so carefully the queen had seen how pretty and wise and loving the little princess was. The queen felt a new feeling and it was love, but she did not know how to feel it. Each day she went into the forest to look for the little princess. She was so busy looking and wondering and calling to the little princess that she did not have time to be wicked any more. But the little princess did not answer. She slipped away. She did not want to go back to the palace. She could not trust the queen never to be wicked again. She did not want to be baked and eaten. She preferred, on balance, to be eaten by the wild beasts who would eat her raw if they ate her at all.

Will they ever find each other?

THE TALE OF THE
VALIANT DEMOISELLE

I fingered the winterkilled grass, looping it round the tip of my finger like hair, ruffling its tips with my palms. Another year has twined away, unrolled and dropped across nowhere like a flung banner painted in gibberish. There is death in the pot for the living's food, fly-blown meat, muddy salt and plucked herbs bitter as squill. If you can get it. How many people have prayed for their daily bread and famished? In a winter famine, desperate Algonquian Indians ate broth made of smoke, snow and buckskin, and the rash of pellagra appeared like tattooed flowers on their emaciated bodies – the roses of starvation; and those who died, died covered in roses. Is this beauty, these gratuitous roses, or a mere display of force? Or is beauty itself an intricately fashioned lure, the cruellest hoax of all?

Annie Dillard, *Pilgrim at Tinker's Creek*

Mummy, Billy says I can't play soldiers with him because I'm a girl.'

'Well, don't play soldiers then; it's a silly game.'

'Mummy.' Exasperation, frustration, an answer not good enough.

'Well then, tell him not to be so silly, tell him you're Thérèse Figueur.'

'Who's she?'

'She was a soldier in the freedom army of the French Revolution. And later the great General Bonaparte himself gave her a medal.'

(But don't tell her, because eight is too young to know, don't tell her that on campaign in 1799 the Piedmontese peasants demanded that she should be given over to them, to be burned as a witch. And her comrades in arms consented.)

'Mummy, Billy says I can't be Robinson Crusoe 'cause he was a man; I have to be Man Friday all the time.'

'That doesn't make sense.'

Yes, it does, of course. Her own son. Oh, Christ.

'Tell him that there was a woman castaway over a century before Alexander Selkirk – he was the true man that Defoe made up Robinson Crusoe from. She was called Marguerite de la Rocque, and she was so brave that the Queen of Navarre put her into one of the first books of stories that was ever written in France.'

(But don't tell her, because eight is too young to know, that Marguerite of Navarre, sister of Francis the First, the most sophisticated, intelligent and virtuous woman in all Europe, had to lie, had to change the story, had to make it respectable, and had to present her whole courage as coming from her love of a man.)

'Mummy, tell me that story.'

Over four hundred years ago Columbus sailed across the Atlantic and discovered America. Then the Spanish and the

Portuguese went there and they brought back lots of exciting stories and lots of gold.

(And they killed and raped the Indians and destroyed their culture, and paid for their gold with measles and syphilis; but don't tell her that bit because she is too young to have to know.)

So then the people in England and France got a bit jealous and they thought they'd like to find some new countries too, and gold and spices and silk and adventures, so they built ships and set out. And one of the first to set out was a sailor from St Malo, in Brittany, and his name was Jacques Cartier. He made two voyages, wild and difficult journeys beyond the end of the world. You must understand how brave you had to be to go to the strange countries across the Atlantic which might not even exist: a few fishermen had gone before to fish on the Great Banks where the cod ran so fat and plentiful that they could be pulled up for the asking if you could make the crossing; but Cartier went beyond that, he sailed his little ship into a new sea, a new ocean, and he thought he had found the way across the top of the world and through to China. Actually, though, he'd found the Gulf of St Lawrence which leads into the Canadian interior. Some Indians he met told him that if he could travel up the great river he would come to a magic land called Saguenay, where there were gold and jewels and strange beautiful things, and people with one leg, and unicorns and spice trees. He spent one winter up the St Lawrence river, where Quebec is now, and no one from Europe had ever seen such cold, so much snow, such hard frosts; and they got scurvy and other diseases and the river was full of rapids; so he realised that if they were going to explore this new country and find Saguenay they would have to build a base, found a colony there on the river as a sort of launching pad for the interior. So he went home and asked the King of France to give him money and ships and people to go and found a city in New France. The King thought this was a very good idea, but he was a bit of a snob and he didn't think that Cartier, who was just a master mariner and captain, was the right person to be in charge of a new country. So he appointed another man, who was a nobleman called Jean François de la Rocque, Sieur de Roberval, to be Lieutenant-General and in charge of everything. But of course Cartier knew more about it all and was better at getting organised than Roberval, so he set out first with about half the people and equipment they needed, and he built the fort and spent another freezing, depressing winter in Canada; but at the end of the winter Roberval still hadn't turned up, and they thought he wasn't coming, and so many of the company had died and they were all fed up, so Cartier decided to go home.

In the meantime Roberval had finally got his act together, but I don't think he really had very much idea about what exploring was really like, because he took a very strange expedition, including lots of ladies and gentlemen who were friends of his, as well as sailors and soldiers and working people. And for the grand people it was all like an exciting adventure, a picnic almost; they didn't have the least idea about how dangerous and wild Canada really was. And one of the ladies who went was his own niece, a pretty young woman, about eighteen, called Marguerite, which means both a daisy and a pearl in French.

Imagine it: they sailed out of La Rochelle harbour in the spring winds of April, three ships with their square sails set and their high castles at the front and back. There were three hundred soldiers, sixty masons and carpenters, ten priests, three doctors, and all sorts of necessary stuff, like pre-fab carts to put together when they got there, and mills and ironware. And all the crowds of La Rochelle stood on the harbour and cheered and sang to see such a brave expedition going off under the King's Lieutenant-General to discover and conquer a New World. They had a safe and sunny crossing of the huge Atlantic and arrived in the harbour at Newfoundland; and they must all have felt very happy and confident.

But then, while they were resting in the harbour and in such high spirits, Cartier sailed in and told them that it would be impossible to defend themselves against the cold and the Indians, and that he for one was going home to France; his crew wouldn't face another Canadian winter and it was all Roberval's fault for not arriving when he had said he would. Roberval was really the commander officially, but Cartier was older and more experienced, and it was probably difficult for him to take orders from Roberval. Because, when Roberval ordered him to stay and return to the St Lawrence, Cartier took his three ships and stole away at night and sailed back to France.

I expect that everyone in Roberval's expedition was really upset by this, and probably a bit frightened as well. They had come all this way thinking that Canada would be a rich country littered with gold and jewels for them to pick up and have some good adventures on the way, but they

must all have known that Cartier was the most knowledge-
able sailor and explorer in all France and if he said it was
impossible then . . .

Then the excitement and the tension would have mounted.
The mutterings, fear and anger, and their dreadful, dreadful dependence on Roberval, now not the golden young
lord from Picardy who had friends at court and wit and
charm, but an iron man, a despotic, arrogant young man
who could not take advice from anyone. And wanting comfort, wanting fun, wanting reassurance . . . and he was so
pretty, so gallant and young and fine, and his wife was so
far away and perhaps they would never go home, perhaps
they would freeze to death and die here in the strange country. And it was high spring and the bright salty air filled
with sea birds in the May sunshine.

Perhaps they would never go home because they had
come to the New World beyond the dangerous ocean,
where the old harsh laws did not apply and they were
young and beautiful. Of course she had an affair with him,
sneaking down among the bales and goods in the lower
hold, sneaking away with him across the rocky beaches
where the sea birds were nesting too. His face so salty
under his beard and her legs so white under her petticoats.
To make love in the New World where even the stars were
different. And when the company sailed on again,
how could they stop? Roberval's gentlemen volunteers
were a young and brave band, unconventional, high-
spirited. Their lines of decorum shifting, what was and
what was not allowed. And, dear God, how she wanted
him; couldn't keep her hands to herself, in those cramped

close quarters and nowhere to get away. Just to see him toss his curls, his earrings dancing, made such shivers in her belly. She had to touch him. And when she touched him it was not enough, and there was no retreat. The sweetness of first love. She was crazy about him, greedy for him, lost her good sense, lost her good name, and three-quarters of the below-decks crew must know about it, the Governor's own niece, because there was so little space and it could not be kept secret.

So probably everyone was a little nervous and edgy when they sailed on. They went up the coast of Newfoundland and into the Gulf of St Lawrence through the Strait of Belle Isle. In the summertime it is stunningly beautiful — flocks of sea birds, great plunging gannets, little funny puffins, and seals disporting themselves under the cliffs of little rocky islands and to the north the low flat lands of Labrador and Quebec stretching away away endlessly into the unknown places. We don't exactly know what happened, but Marguerite did something that upset Roberval very badly and he refused to have her on his ship any longer. They were passing some little islands at the time — they're called the Harrington Islands now, they're quite little but luckily for her they have some fresh water — and he put her on one of them and sailed on.

Why could he not forgive her? Dear God, she had wept and sought forgiveness, crawled on her knees to him. She knew, she knew damn well, he was a Calvinist, a hard man wedded to his Bible, but . . . but he was willing to forgive her lover, and that hurt. It was she, she alone, who was damned; had gone outside his and his God's forgiveness. In the July sunshine the island looked pretty enough; it was not that. She could not read the meaning on her uncle's face. He could not forgive her, and he said it was God's judgement. He said they sailed with God and he would keep no blighting Jonah on his ship, no whores. He needed to show his power over them all. He could not stomach her beauty, her joy; she was radiant with her love, love flowered her flesh rosy and the sun and the sea flowered it golden. She was too beautiful for him to forgive her. He would, he said, have no befouling lust on his ship; but he was willing to keep her lover. It was woman flesh that stuck in his craw. She was the Gateway to Hell, and his gallant young men must not risk her corruption. A whore, a slut, a witch out of hell.

So he gave her few provisions and sailed on westwards towards central Canada.

He gave her a gun, he gave her a flintbox, he gave her a Bible.

Cartier had made a list, a list of the minimum supplies necessary to survive – 276 men, including apothecaries, tailors, carpenters, masons, blacksmiths, men-at-arms. He had written his list for the King saying they would need windmills, boats, anvils, food supplies, bales of woollen cloth, artillery, domestic animals and hens, geese, seeds, grain, cooking utensils and pig iron. They had all known the list and laughed at some of the meticulous details, and they had felt safe because Cartier knew his job.

He gave her a gun, a tinderbox and a Bible.

He wanted her dead.

He didn't want her blood on his hands.

He said if she was so damn free she could taste the freedom of the savages.

She had asked him for sugar and he had hit her in the face.

She did not know how to use the gun. He gave ammunition and powder, but he knew she did not know how to use the gun. One of the sailors putting her ashore gave her his own knife. It was a kindness, but when he slipped it to her he was careful not to let his hand touch hers. He set his mouth in silent embarrassment. The whole ship's company was embarrassed, but silent. No one raised a murmur for her. One of the priests had raised his hand to bless her and thought better of it. She was in mortal sin. She did not repent.

But just as the ship was sailing away her . . . her boyfriend leapt over the side and came swimming to the shore; he had decided to stay and help her.

The silly fool. The silly beautiful fool; his arms so long and white, cutting the smooth surface of the bay. His grin irrepressible, his body glorious. She went down into the water to welcome him as he swam towards her, standing almost to her waist in the soft sea, her arms stretched out. And there, in the sight of the ship's company, they fell into each other's arms giggling, laughing. For those few moments she had felt so bereft, she had felt the taste of loneliness and death and he had leapt into the sea to come to her. Holding hands they ran up the shingle, dripping wet, her dress clinging to her legs, his shirt clamped on his chest revealing his nipples. This was their paradise; they could fuck all day. Morality had abandoned them, they were free. Outrageous, bold, untrammelled, they waved handkerchiefs to the departing boat, laughing.

Then they lived very happily for a while. They built a hut out of the pine trees, out of logs, and they made furniture for it and got it all as cosy as they could, just like in *Robinson Crusoe* and *Swiss Family Robinson* – well, almost like; it couldn't have been so good, because they didn't have those handy wrecks the others had to get supplies off – they didn't have nails for instance, so the hut can't have been very secure. And an island in the Gulf of St Lawrence is rather a different thing from a warm sunny one in the Caribbean. But luckily Marguerite was very clever and creative, and she sewed and carved and made fishing lines by unravelling her petticoats; and her boyfriend shot and fished and they ate berries and fruit and stuff like that. It was hard work, but they did have a lot of fun.

At first. It was their paradise. Each morning she woke snuggled in the curve of his armpit. They played and teased and laughed and made love through a long golden summer, and at night the stars were heavy and golden; bigger brighter newer stars than they had ever seen, and they named new constellations in the honour of their loving. And she knew she was going to have his baby. It was their paradise and they giggled together and swore they would never eat the apple of civilisation again; and that when Roberval came back to rescue them they would laugh

in his face and tell him to sail away wherever he wanted for
they were content. The sun shone warmly and she grew
lean and fit and free in her limbs as she had never been since
childhood, and they wandered their kingdom naked and
unashamed as the savages were said to do.

But. Except. There was an undertow. A darkening
shadow. The sex was not as good as it had been on ship-
board: there was nothing else to do, nothing to hide, nothing to plot, no planning, no scheming, no exciting delays.
And he: he thought he had been so wonderful, so heroic
and generous and romantic, leaping off the ship for her. He
acted, just, at moments, hardly hinted, barely noticed in the
delight of sunshine, he acted as though she owed him
something.

But Roberval would have forgiven him, would have kept
him on the ship. Sometimes she thought that he, somehow,
somewhere, agreed with Roberval – and yet what had she
done that he had not? He thought that by forgiving her he
had earned her love. She would give it to him as a gift, but
not as a debt. But she did not like to say these things and
intrude on their happy laughter. And when the evenings
began to be cooler and longer she found that his conversation was not very interesting to her, and she started even to
read the Bible to amuse herself, and he resented it and she
felt guilty.

In Canada, you know, the autumns are extraordinary. They
had never seen anything like it, that wild extravagance of
colour; none of that soft mournful wet decline that we have
here in Europe but golds and yellows and crimsons and

scarlets after the first frost. There's a time they call the Indian Summer, St Martin's Summer, late in October, when the winds die down and the days are hot and hazy, and they must both have felt that all was well with them and that the rumours about the winter had been a mistake, a silly joke. Perhaps they played that they were a king and queen who had ordered one of the new Italian artists to come and decorate their palace for them, in the bright, brave, gaudy colours of that time.

And then the winter came.

Cold. She had not known what the word meant. They had been warned and like children they had not heard the warning, because they had no knowledge or experience to measure the warning against. Early one dawn the calm had been broken by a whirring noise, a low murmur with an inner beat, an unearthly sound. The heavy skeins of geese were passing, straight as arrows, running south and pulling the darkness of winter down on their strong pinion feathers from the north. She thought of the baby and she was frightened. And they went, innocent and ignorant as children, into the maelstrom of winter. Hell would not be hot, but cold and everlasting as that Canadian winter: and the weight of the snow drift, drift, drifting forever, or borne on the storm winds, battering out of the north; the bay rearing up against them, iced spume far flung; the great reefs of ice riming up along the shore, shifting and moaning like hellish harps at first, but as the cold locked down tighter there came an ominous and enormous silence in which there was no noise at all but the relentless wind. How could she help thinking about the baby and being frightened? The fear moved in, gnawing as fierce as the cold, and there was no escape from either. And the hut itself a feeble joke before the cold and the wind and the terror. Hunger. Thirst. Tedium and the smoky darkness of their frail shelter. The immense heartbreaking effort that the simplest task of survival used up. The weariness. And above and beneath and within all things, the numbing, bemusing, battering cold. And in the hut with nothing to do they tried to keep warm, clinging together not for delight, or for tenderness, or even for consolation, but for need – a need more gripping and impelling than the need of their lust in the faraway and almost forgotten springtime. And the bitterness of the need crept in between them and wedged itself there and there was nothing, nothing left at all of the golden loving but a bitter, cringing hatred and a bitterer and more cringing need.

And then, I'm sorry to say, that winter her boyfriend died.

She killed him. She was both whore and murderess. The bitterness had eaten them up and they snapped and snarled still locked together against the cold. Like bears in a den. Fire in them both, fires flaring for no reason, and violent savage sex afterwards that used energy and did not restore affection. And when he hit her, when he started hitting her, she grovelled before him, begging, pleading with him to stop, apologising for things she had never done and of which he had not even accused her, cradling her belly and her head, rolling on the ground, crawling before him on hands and knees, begging, beseeching, pleading. She hated him more for reducing her to that humility than she hated him for hitting her. She hated him and herself and they had come to a great black place from which neither could escape.

Finally she had turned, turned on him for no real reason beyond the cold and her sordid humiliation. She had half-broken the hut apart in the cataclysm of her fury, hurling abuse and objects and spit and spite: savage, animal, rodent, vicious. And where was the young and tender girl who had stood on the deck of the ship out of La Rochelle and longed to see the glories of the New World? She drove him in her mad anger out of the hut and into the wind. He was weak, confused by the cold and by her raving. He slipped. He gashed his leg. Hours later, frozen and blue-lipped, he crawled back into the hut. It had not seemed a bad wound at first, though quite deep, about two inches above his ankle. She resented him; resented shredding yet more of her inadequate clothing to bind the wound. She resented his clumsiness and the extra burden it laid on her. She resented her own guilt and the skill with which he had punished her. A few days later when she took off the bandage to re-dress the wound, she noticed that it was opening up, high and proud, and that the flesh above was puffy, greenish. He could put no weight on the foot. It was not getting better. A sweet, sticky smell pervaded the hut. Two nights later she heard the foxes howling outside and in the morning their marks were around the door. The skin above the bandage turned black. He had a fever, muttering through the night while the wild beasts howled. In his fever he said dreadful things, about her, about himself and about Hell. She knew that he was telling the truth. It took him three weeks to die.

She tried to dig him a grave, but the ground was too hard. She dragged his body into a snowdrift and it took all the strength she had. In the night she heard the foxes again, excited, with greedy snufflings and snarls. When she went out they were like white ghosts pawing and pulling at his corpse. She frightened them away and knew they would return. She dragged the body back into the hut and collapsed beside it. All night long she held him in her arms, rocking him and herself in a fever of passion. God how she loved him, how beautiful he was, how long and strong in the shadows, his skin so soft and sweet. She had loved him and sacrificed her life for him. He had betrayed her and deserted her. He had run away and left her, dishonoured and pregnant, cast out from society, alone in the wilderness, pregnant, alone and bitter. It was an old boring story, a woman's story, and she had thought herself to be above it. God how she hated him, and there was no love so sweet as this loathing, a hatred so strong that it warmed her at last. It enflamed her, she kissed his body all over, everywhere, long hard kisses, and she buried her lips in his gangrenous wound, tasting and probing the putrid flesh. He was dead. She was alone.

All that winter she guarded his body in the hut. She no longer minded the smell. The white foxes still came at night, waiting, waiting, waiting their chance. When she did not hear their shrill barking, she heard the deep and dreadful howling of the wind, tearing across the water, across the ice. Beating against the hut, seeking access, seeking her flesh with a wild lust that would not be tamed by her. And in the ghastly screaming of the wind, she heard a voice she could not hear, words she did not know. The hut was too small; she could not step away from him; his body bloated up, his lips pulled away from his blackened gums into a grin of malevolent triumph. He swelled larger and larger and she did too. But he was dead and she was alive. She ceased to care.

At last there came a day which felt different, though she could not tell what the difference was; an ending, a beginning, a changing. Outside it was as cold as ever, but along the rim of the horizon far away as she could see there was a separation: between slate-grey water and slate-grey sky there was a rim of pale pink. She gathered snow and melted it. She stripped off her clothes and washed herself. She covered his face with a rag: there were things that no man, alive or dead, should see.

She was in labour for thirty-three hours and there was no one to wipe the sweat from her face; it clogged her eyes, matted her hair and trickled salty into her mouth, and when night came she was wrapped in a shroud of ice. She screamed and heard in her own howls the echoes of the waiting foxes. She was animal. She crawled on the hut floor and chewed pieces of wood. She smashed at her own body. The pain threw her around the hut and shook her as a dog shakes a rat, and in the teeth of the pain she became a rat and snarled like a rat. And she screamed to him for help and he could not help her because she had killed him. She was far away from the places where there are other people. Then later she was weary, weary, weary with the pain and the loneliness, and there was no one to bring her vinegar on a sponge.

Just before the spring came she had her baby, all on her own in that little hut. It's very hard work for a woman to have a baby, and you really need to have people with you to help you and hold on to you. She must have been terribly brave to go through that all on her own.

Out beyond the place of courage, of choice, of free will, she came at last to the chasm, enormous and black, and she knew that it could not be endured any longer and she lay down on the floor almost quietly to await the end. She knew her body would be ripped apart by the devil flesh in it, and particles of her would be caught in the evil wind and hurled in flayed fragments across the island, out on to the icecap, and lost forever in the great white desert. And then, miraculously, she found a new strong rhythm, and she leaned on the rhythm and recognised in it some of the rhythm of her desire and it was the sweet rhythm of passion which had brought her to this last place. But it was a new place too, a new command, a new power, a new dignity. And she pushed down, bracing herself firmly against the wall of the hut. She was no longer herself, but a new strong woman, and not cold, nor hunger, nor death itself could stop her in the power of her striding. She would walk the great white plains beyond the ocean, beyond the sunset, and give birth to a child in the New World. And in the first shadow turning of the morning her daughter was born, tiny, white, bloody and screaming defiance and joy and life. And never, never, since the dawn of days, had anything been more beautiful and she was no longer alone and the spring would come with the child and they would blossom and flourish like the bay tree. She wrapped her tiny daughter as warmly as she could and they lay together watching the light creep into the hut, creep into the world, and she was filled with a fierce triumphant joy.

But sadly the baby died.

There wasn't any milk. The baby sucked and sucked and sucked. White and little and eager. At first it seemed to grow and strengthen, responding to the promise of spring and to her enormous, welcoming love. Soon, soon, the spring would come, the snow would melt and there would be growing things and she would stop bleeding and go out and hunt and put on weight and both the land and her breasts would flow with milk and wild honey, and the child would be the first daughter of freedom. But there was no milk. And she was too tired, too tired, too tired. So for six weeks she watched the baby die, its huge wise eyes uncomplaining, its tiny mouth still trusting, still hoping, still sucking. It shrank, shrivelled away just as the snow was doing, and suddenly in the middle of one night she knew that it was dead.

It could have hung on a little longer, just a little longer. Just a few days later from far away on the mainland she heard the gonging of the breaking ice and very soon she was able to bury them together, and with the burial it was springtime, and small white flowers blossomed among the rocks and the sea birds laid their eggs casually in the crevices of the cliffs. Then the great geese flocks pulled the warm weather with them as they flew northwards overhead to their nesting grounds. They passed so thickly that using the gun for the first time she was able to have roast goose for supper every night for weeks and the fat ran down her chin sweet and oily. She could not bear to think about her little white baby, so she did not. She had survived and the sun came out sweetly and warmed the cold marrow in the depths of her bones.

So that when the spring came she was all on her own and she must have felt that she would never get off the island. She could see other islands not too far away and on clear days probably the mainland too low in the distance, but she had no way of getting that far; probably she did not even know how to swim, because rich girls in those days weren't taught that sort of thing, but even if she could, why should she leave what little she had to go to another deserted island? That corner of eastern Quebec is, even today, one of the most godforsaken places in the world; there are still no towns, no roads, no nothing, just spruce trees and silver birches and scrub and rocky land for miles and miles and miles northwards until you get to the Arctic. Southwards was the great sea, reaching as far as she could see, and for all she knew it went to forever.

And perhaps this was really the time when her courage was most tested, when she was bravest of all. Because now she had no one depending on her, no one needing her like her baby did, no reason at all for keeping going. And she knew what it was really like; she knew there would be another winter, and another winter, and another winter, and she must often have wondered why she bothered at all. She must have been dreadfully lonely and desperate and miserable sometimes, but she kept struggling on.

She had to learn how to do all sorts of new things – things that no woman she had ever heard of had done. She must have learned to shoot and fish and hunt, and build fires and find eggs, and chop wood. She even shot a couple of bears.

And in a different way that second year was worse than the first had been, partly because she wasn't so strong and well as she had been the year before. She really wasn't getting enough to eat, and especially not enough vegetables and greens, and she had had the baby which must have worn her down. But also something very scary began to happen to her: she was attacked by demons. Well, I expect really they were just in her head, and perhaps she was going a little crazy or something from being on her own for so long and not knowing if she would ever see another human being in her whole life; and because of the sad sad things that had happened to her. But she believed in them all right, and all through her second winter on the island they tormented her, howling round her little hut and scaring her out of her mind. She even tried to shoot them with her gun, but that didn't work at all.

Busy. Busy. It was essential to keep busy. To wake up in the morning and make plans, and then to carry them out. Be organised. Be efficient. Today I will find grasses and mosses and stuff the cracks in the hut walls; today I will walk across the island and watch the seals playing; today I will check the lines and lay them for fish.

In the spring she shot a bear; a big, rough, brown bear. She never knew where it had come from; she walked through the spruce trees one day and there it was, its back to her, grazing. Almost without thinking she shot it dead, and realised with a deep joy that she would have a warm cover for the next winter. The bear meat made her sick, she did not eat it; but she had skinned the fur off, hacking bloodily, excitedly through a whole day, the warm fur, the warm blood and the distant memories of the pig-killings at the childhood farm in Picardy. And she stretched the skin and dried it and salted it and scraped it and it was a great victory. She danced for herself on the green grass and thought that she was the only French lady in the whole world who had killed a bear and stretched its fur for a blanket. There were so many little joys. She had to think about them and keep busy. She danced for hours before she felt silly and naked and self-conscious. Naked, bloody and dancing like a savage; if she were not careful she would forget how to be a decent Christian; she added reading the Bible to her daily tasks.

That summer she thought she was happy. She did not let herself think about the things that made her unhappy. She did not sleep much for when she was asleep dreams came to her and they did not make her happy. She stayed up through the nights and watched the heavy stars and thought about nothing and sang little snatches of old songs, and of new ones that she made up for herself. And as autumn came she noticed with amusement that like the animals her hair was turning white for the winter.

What changed? It changed the day she shot the second bear.

She saw them from her hut, the great swimming bears, white and strong, churning up the channel to her little cove. A huge white bear, creamy and immense, black nose and mighty forelegs. And with it two bear cubs; half-grown, snowier. She sat still by her hut and watched them, enchanted. The mother bear stretched out and the little ones curled against her great wet flank and they dozed a little on the pebbles. Then the cubs woke up and they played, such joyful play, and so like children, rolling and cuffing and delighting, nose to nose the two cubs and heaving up over their mother's body while she stirred in her sleep and pushed them off with those great fierce paws made gentle in mother-love; and they nuzzled her and rollicked in the autumn sunshine while the sea reflected a soft, playful approval. She wanted desperately to go and play with them, rolling and smothering in that density of white fur, that warm and vital softness. And she knew that if she moved, if she coughed or stirred, they would be gone, back on a sudden into the sea and she would be alone again.

Then she knew in all her being that her baby was dead and that she was alone and the realisation broke her heart. And in a great anger of jealousy for the bear mother, of jealousy and spite, she glided, crafty, graceful – oh, yes, premeditated; made – not wild and manic in her jealousy – but mean, mean. She got her gun and she stood at the door of her hateful hopeless little hut and she shot one of the bear cubs. At the explosion the mother bear leapt up on to her hind legs and roared; and she thought for one glorious moment that the bear would come, terrible as the Lord on Judgement Day, and kill her dead, and she could go where her daughter had gone and be silent as stone for always and for evermore. And even as she thought that she was reloading her gun, ready, determined.

The mother bear looked at her baby, poked it with her

nose, and then she and the other cub took to the sea, a great slither of white fur and hard muscle and they were gone. From the rocks beyond the cove she thought she could hear the wail of ursine grief, the great screams of a loving mother whose child has been stolen away by death. Slowly she went down the beach, slowly with her bare foot she touched the baby bear. It was not dead, it turned to her, its eyes pleading love. It was bigger than her baby, but white, white as an egg, and it had the same dark, puzzled, huge, wise eyes. Unthinking, she bunched her fist and put it on the cub's muzzle, and the bear sucked it firmly for a moment and then it died. She pulled it on to her lap. Sadly she stroked the thick white fur and she wept.

The soul of her daughter who had longed to live had travelled forth into the body of a bear cub because the thick soft fur would protect her from the cold. She had killed the mother bear's child and she had killed her own child. Everything that she touched she killed; his violence had not been in him, it had been in her. She had killed him. She had killed her daughter, and her daughter's soul had gone into the body of the bear, into the great rich womb of the mother bear and had come out safely again; her child's soul had found at last a real, a good, a mighty mother, but she had killed her child again.

So when the winter frosts came again she lay broken under the brown bear's fur, cuddling and caressing the fur of the small white bear, her daughter whom she had killed twice. And when the winds came the demons came too. She let them come. She gave them power. She let them come because with the white fur in her arms she could not refuse all the memories any more. For three weeks he had lain dying and she had hated him; she had killed him and she had hated him. For thirty-three hours she had laboured for her daughter, but it was not enough. The child had died and she had been there and had done nothing. She had not been able to save her. Slowly, cunningly she had crept into the hut, and taken the gun, and killed the snow-white bear, for no reason, no reason but spite and jealousy and greed for power.

The mother bear sent the demons.

The mother bear had come to the island to be her friend and guard, to let her burrow into that thick fur, to let her pass the winter curled up against the store of sweet fishy fat. And she had killed the mother's cub. The mother's child, her own child. So the mother bear had sent the demons.

No. The mother bear was a demon. She had come on the shoulder of the snowstorm to torture her with memories.

God had sent the demons to punish her, because she had killed another woman's child, for spite.

God did not exist. God had abandoned her. God could not endure the hellish cold. Here, in this land, she had gone beyond the power of God. She had come into the power of demons. God who had hung on the cross had given her, in his weakness, over to the strength of the demons.

The demons came in from the sea as the mother had come. They came riding the wind, triumphant and screeching. They came on the driving eddies of the snowstorm. They howled about her house, shaking the timbers and trying to get in.

Last winter she had known there were voices in the wind, but she had not heard their words. Now she could hear. Now she was open to them. Now she could not escape them.

Whore, they said, whore, slut, cunt, bitch. Adulterer, murderer, blasphemer. Whore, slut, cunt, witch.

They stripped her down to the bare bone.

The wages of sin are death. This is judgement. Yea, though you flee to the uttermost parts of the sea, we will find you. The wages of lust are death. There is no escape. The sweetness of your white skin in his arms; the sweet smell of putrefaction.

Whore, slut, cunt, bitch. Death is too easy for you. We bide our time. You hear our voices in the foxes singing for their carrion flesh. You stink of sin; they will not need to wait until you are dead.

You birthed us in the power you birthed your baby. You thought, you slut, that you were strong and free; in the maw of your stinking belly you gave birth to us. Your daughter is our mother. Her soul fled howling and angry to the north places and she bred us there. The daughter of sin, the child of adultery, bred demons and witches out of her tiny cunt. Monsters. We are your children.

Hairy, the Devil is hairy. Your gash is hairy. You let him put his foul, hairy member into yours. You encouraged him. You kissed the arse of the Devil and bound yourself to the demons. We are better lovers than he. You grovelled to him to tickle your slit. We will slit you, and you will grovel to us, beg, plead, whimper. Witch. Your uncle knew. A wise young man. Upright. Holy. Beloved of God. He was given the gift of discernment. He could smell your corruption and he rooted you out. He gave you to us because you deserved it. Whore.

They burn witches. The marketplaces of Picardy are sweet with the smell of cooked flesh. We are burning you, burning you to the bone with cold and grief.

Humble yourself, daughter of pride. Grovel. Beg. Beg us. You begged him and we are stronger. Much stronger. Grovel to us or we will break you. We will break your body. We will break your mind.

Calmer moments: the bright freezing nights, when the rocking and the pounding of the hut remitted. She would step outside to breathe, and the sky would be illuminated with the strange cold fireworks from the north, a spectacle making nonsense of the night and of the winter and of her puny littleness in the whole great void beyond the west of the world. And then they would come again, the demons, whispering, singing sweet and low, women's voices, kind and gentle, luring her to a more secret doom: you can escape, once and for all, you can get away, sweetly, easily. Walk away from the hut, walk out into the snow, out into the sea and all will be well. They promised her insanity and suicide and made it a gift. They whispered on the brittle air that there was a place without pain, without sense or meaning, a place where dark and light, good and bad, cold and warmth were all the same and all indifferent. And even the shapes and sounds of words collapsed inwards, imploding, shaken in their fabric, breaking down, down, down into a warm place inside which there was no effort, no end, no beginning.

Come down, they murmured across the shapelessness of the flat sea, come down, come in, come closer. Come, come, come. A small step, an infinite drop, down, away, and the cold as sweet as a blanket and sleep, sleep, sleeeep.

Dream a new time. A time before. Before there was anything; before the voice of God called the word of law across the void. When there was only the shapeless, wordless swirling. We can give you that, that formless, wordless rocking. We can give you that, if you submit. Let go. Submit. Bow down and worship us. Consent. You have only to consent. To let go.

And in the darkness she would cling to the frail hut, physically hold it, bite her own hands, hug the white fur until her ribs ached. She would remember, she would try to remember that the cold was a killer, that she must not leave the fireside. That spring came after winter, that order came out of chaos; and out of order came pattern and out of pattern history and life and herself. She did not consent. She did not submit. She was alive. She was still alive.

And then roaring again. Enormous. Fierce broken roaring. The noise so great it would break her ears open and her brains would strew the shore red on white. Slut. Whore. Cunt. SLUT. WHORE. CUNT. SSLLUUTT-WWHHOORREECCUUNNTT. Finished. You are finished, whore. We have the power here, cunt. We have the power and we will break you, slut. You are damned, whore; you are damned for all eternity. Damned, damned, Damned.

And on and on and on and on and on and on and on andon andon andon on on on on on on on on o n o n o n o n o n o nnnnnnnn oooooonnnnnnnn.

Until she cannot stand it any longer; and in a fury of destruction, anything, anything to silence their voices, she took the gun and shot at the wind through the roof, shoving in the shot, blasting wildly, great holes in the roof and powder burns on her arms and face. Bang, bang, bang. Enormous explosion – the wonderful great crashing of the gun at her behest silencing all other sounds, for a glorious and powerful time.

When the fury left her she saw she had used all her powder; there was none left. She had reached the end. She would die. And she lay on the floor of the hut, and their voices came again, no words now because she was as the animals are, just roaring and grunting and squealing and howling. How she had been in his arms. How she had been in her anger against him. How she had birthed her daughter. Pig grunts, and fox howls, and mewlings on her knees before his violence. And enormous growling, snarling, screeching and never never leaving her. And it was the end and all things were finished. And . . .

And no, she did not consent.

'I do not consent,' she said, and her own words echoed in the hut with a magnificent reality.

Words. Words at least were better. She seized the Bible. Grateful, even and suddenly, to Roberval who had given her nothing, but had not deprived her of human words, human contact.

> Out of the depths I have called unto you, O Lord; Lord hear my prayer. Oh let your ears consider well the voice of my complaint. If you, Lord, will be extreme to mark what is done amiss, Lord, who may endure it; but there is mercy with you and therefore shalt thou be feared.

And again louder. But their voices were louder still. WHORE. CUNT. SLUT. FOULNESS. ADULTERER.

Then he said to the woman taken in adultery, Go in peace and sin no more. He said, Do not be afraid, be of good cheer, for behold I am with you always.

WITCH. SLUT. ANIMAL. IN THE SILENCE WE WILL KILL YOU. YOU ARE DAMNED.

And the Word was made flesh and dwelt among us.

WHORE. SLUT. WHORE.

And he blessed her saying, Much will be forgiven her, because she loved much.

BELIEVE THAT, FOOL, AND YOU'LL BELIEVE ANYTHING.

And when they had mocked him they stripped him. And they led him out to crucify him.

Whore. Slut. Cunt. Starving bag of bones, careened in the desert, lost, lost, hopeless.

It is when you are weak that you are strong.
God chose what is foolish in the world to shame the wise.
God chose what is weak in the world to shame the strong.

Witch. Slut. Whore. Your uncle deserted you, drove you out from the camps of men, gave you over to us.

And the Spirit drove him out into the wilderness. And he

was in the wilderness forty days, fasting, tempted of
Satan. He was with the wild beasts and the angels ministered to him.

Cunt.　　Bitch.　　Whore.

He was with the wild beasts and the angels ministered to
him. Do not be afraid, be of good cheer.
The word was made flesh.

We have power.

He was in the wilderness, fasting, and tempted of Satan.

　　He was with the wild beasts and the angels ministered
to him.

　　Do not be afraid. Be of good cheer. For lo, I am with
you always, even to the ends of the world.

　　I tell you, her sins which were many are forgiven,
because she loved much.

　　I come that you may have life, and life more abun-
dantly.

　　He was with the wild beasts and the angels ministered
unto him.

silence.

The word was made flesh; and she wrapped him in swad-
dling bands and laid him in a manger because there was
no room for them at the inn.

silence.

The word was made flesh and dwelt among us.

silence.

There was silence. And in the silence there was a turning of the year and in herself.

My soul magnifies the Lord, and my spirit rejoices in God my saviour;
God who is mighty has magnified me, and holy is His name.
And all generations shall call me blessed.
He has put down the mighty from their seats and exalted the humble and meek. He has filled the hungry with good and sent the rich away empty.

It was an old song, a woman's song, a song of victory.

The winter was over. Naked, bloody, battered. Starving. She opened the door of the hut and fell forwards into the sunshine. The blood of battle stained her face. Emaciated, hanging on to life by a thin thread, the soft generosity of the white bear skin still in her arms. The roses of starvation flowering fresh on her back. She lay there, spread out. A deep and everlasting peace. To go so near to death that you have tasted its sweetness and decided against it. Decided for life. Hell had been harrowed, she had walked the unknown pathway and found the road home. Death had no more dominion.

Blessed are those who going through the valley of misery use it for a well, and the pools are filled with water. They will go from strength to strength and unto the God of Gods appeareth every one of them in Zion.

It actually wouldn't matter if she died now.

But I shall not die, I shall live and praise my God.

She had been in the wilderness, fasting and tempted of Satan. But there were words spoken, fur coverings chanced upon, and a sunrise, a victory, a triumph. The silence in her head was perfect and perfectly peaceful.

And by amazing luck, after that winter was over, some Portuguese fishermen, driven in from the Great Banks, saw her fire smoke and came and rescued her. They took her back to France and she went home. Later she told her story to Jean Alfonce, who had been Roberval's pilot, and he told it to his friend and patroness Marguerite of Navarre, and she put it in her story book called the *Heptameron* and that's how we know about her.

'Mummy, what happened next?'
    'She stayed in Picardy and taught school for the rest of her life.'
    'Oh. Mummy?'
    'Yes, darling.'
    'Can I have a chocolate biscuit now?'

THE SWALLOW AND
THE NIGHTINGALE

Revenge is said to be a dish best served cold, but they served it hot and spicy and were satisfied.

They work smoothly together in the empty kitchen. They have given the house slaves a holiday; they have sent them up to the mountain temple with two red cockerels and a picnic. The whole palace is peaceful, and the two women move about the space, synchronised and graceful. The meat is in a large pot, and before they hang it on the iron hook over the fire to boil, they sort through the pieces, their arms red almost to the elbows.

When Philomel scoops out the little penis, holds it up waggling it and making a dark sound which may possibly be laughter, Procne, for a moment, feels slightly nauseous, as she had in early pregnancy. But Philomel is smiling; she holds it up to her lips and flaps it like a tongue, and when she opens her mouth and there is nothing there, just the dark hole of silence, Procne's nausea passes.

She feels instead a fierce bright anger and expresses it in a slightly too high-pitched giggle.

Once upon a time there were two little princesses; they lived in a white palace under a blue sky and above a harbour in a blue sea. Their father was Pandion, King of Athens, a noble and warm-hearted man, skilled in the arts of both war and peace, blessed by the Gods and deservedly. Their mother was a serene and beautiful Queen, loved by her people and her household, the mother of two fine sons and these two little girls: beloved, delightful and bound together by the fine strong chains of a joyful childhood. Although there were fifteen months between them they reached adolescence so close, so alike, so inseparable, so happy together that their parents, their servants and even the poets who have since tried to tell their tragic story confused them – Procne and Philomel, Philomel and Procne, the nightingale and the swallow, the swallow and the nightingale – swooping, darting, singing about the palace. And chattering; they chattered all the time to each other, so that it seemed as though there were no gap between their thoughts and their words – fantastical, playful chatter, imaginative, voluble, springing and bubbling like a mountain stream. Their father thought they were good girls, because they would sit doing their charming needlework, like good princesses should; he was wrong as it happened, but that is how a father ought to think. And their sewing, like their eating and their dancing and their singing, was punctuated, enlivened, made interesting and engaging by their constant chatter and their happy giggles. They giggled together all the time. If they had not been so quick and light and lovely the incessant trilling giggles might have been annoying, but they were not.

Pandion was a good king and a devoted father. However it was not imaginable to him that his daughters would prefer giggling and chatting with each other to marriage with a royal hero, just like himself but younger. Tereus, King of Thrace, was, he persuaded himself, the very man for one of his two little chickens. Of course he was a Thracian not a real Greek and came from the cold northern forests, where the sea was black not blue and the hills were grey not gold – but he was a reliable ally and a well set-up young man. Put a little more bluntly he was a barbarian, but he was also, as barbarians often are for sweet and highly civilised princesses raised by gentle, noble parents in formal courts, extremely sexy. Procne was well up for it. Something in her responded deeply and joyfully to all that beard and muscle and stormy passion. He was her centaur, wild and wise with the wisdom of the beasts and the forests, which was so very different from and much more fun than the wisdom of the agora, and the long boring logical rhetoric of the philosophers, who seldom smiled and never chatted or giggled and admired self-restraint and young boys over women and laughter. Tereus paid her attention and she sensed his wild greed. Since she was fifteen months old she had never spent more than the occasional hour without Philomel, so it never occurred to her that she might miss her sister. For a bride gift Tereus gave her a little black horse, with delicate ankles and a moody wild character. She married him and they went north laughing. She rode the horse all day and Tereus rode her all night and marriage and Thrace seemed delightful to her.

But after Itylus was born Procne did not enjoy sex as much as she had before. She admired her sturdy little baby boy who looked ridiculously like his father, but she could not feel he was really hers. He was a Thracian baby. They took him away and pierced his ears with gold studs, and hung strange amulets around his neck and wrapped him in bearskin against the cold so that he smelled strangely rancid. The winter was long and dark. Procne felt heavy and inert. She was cold all the time and tired and tearful. She slipped into depression and she began to miss Philomel desperately.

Tereus took a mistress, but somehow he knew that was not quite the point. He wanted to make his exotic foreign wife happy. He liked her; he had enjoyed her laughter and her abandoned sexuality and her playful ways and her fierce courage on her fierce little horse. And somehow, he felt, it was not quite to his credit to have a sad wife. He did not like the idea that Thrace was unacceptable to a true Greek princess. And he wanted more sons. So when the snow melted and the first aspen leaves quivered gold in the morning sun, he told her he would go to Athens and bring Philomel to visit her. He was rewarded by a bright spark deep in her eyes and a burble of laughter, which augured well for a general improvement on the home front. So he leapt on his horse and accompanied only by his personal body slave headed south to fetch his wife's sister.

Procne was not stupid – frivolous perhaps, and brought up to be so, as all pretty little princesses are and should be, but not stupid. She knew all about the desire that Tereus' guttural Greek and huge energy had inflamed in her and she knew Philomel very well indeed. She knew that

Philomel would look exactly as she herself had looked when she and Tereus had ridden north together barely fifteen months before. She knew, too, that it was springtime and that they would ride north all day while the birds sang and the flowers bloomed and the damped-down blood of winter sprang fresh and hot in their veins. She knew these things and she was capable of drawing the fairly obvious conclusions from them – but she did not mind. And this was not simply because she was suffering from post-natal depression. She was a Greek princess, deeply civilised and sophisticated. In Athens it was considered vulgar as well as pointless to make much fuss about fidelity. Even the immortals did not, but disported themselves freely and gladly, Gods and Goddesses alike – where their desire alighted so too did their bodies, and why should mortals not follow that Olympian example? Love was in the meeting of minds, of thoughts and aspirations; love was in families and children and alliances and political will. She was the mother of the young prince of Thrace; Tereus was her husband and she had set up her loom at his hearth. It did not occur to her to insist on guards and maids and covered carriages. On the contrary, she was amused and tender towards them in her thoughts. In that beautiful golden land, in their beautiful white palaces, between the blue sky and the blue sea, princesses do not love deeply, but they do love joyfully.

She had no knowledge, no understanding, no pathway to knowledge or understanding of the silent dark hole of Tereus' passion. In the mountains where the sea is black and the land is grey and the winters are long, sexual desire does not come light as on a bird's wing, but huge and powerful as ice melt in springtime and dangerous and over-whelming. And because it is so real and so hard-edged and so demanding it is also set about with taboos and controls and restraints and rules and laws and deep, deep shame. Men hate their own lust and hate women because they arouse it; they try to protect women from other men and from themselves and fail and are ashamed.

And he did not know Philomel at all.

She was so pretty, so full of gaiety and life, so like Procne had been before the darkness came over her, and yet so cool and elegant and provocative. It simply never occurred to him that he had only to ask her and she would have lain with him laughing, and Procne would have laughed too when Philomel told her.

So he raped her.

Philomel saw it differently. She had been waiting to do this since Procne had described her own wedding night to her, over fifteen months ago. Procne had told her, part-awed and part-giggling, about the animal energy of sex with a barbarian, about the utter unadulterated maleness of it – boisterous, ebullient and fierce. What he thought was rape she thought was a game, a rather rough but highly amusing game; and she played it happily all through the spring night.

He hated her because she did not resist him, did not whimper or beg or scream, or not with any serious intent; he hated himself because he had raped his sister-in-law and was made ashamed. And in the morning as he woke he saw her sitting, with her little high breasts still uncovered, sitting cross-legged on the pile of skins where he had thrown her only a few hours before. He could hear his body slave in the next room; the man was his, by both ownership and love, but she could at least have sought his protection. He can see his own hunting knife not a yard from her hand, lying sharp and ready by the fireside, but it was still secure in its leather sheath. She did not call for aid, she did not cower in fear and she did not stab him in retaliation

She sat there and chattered.

Merrily she giggled and chattered. She was too well brought up to refer in any way to the wild passages of the night, but she chattered about breakfast and the day's journey ahead and how pretty the woods were and how much she was longing to see Procne and tell her everything. He could not bear it. He thought that she was a wanton slut, and then seeing her sweetness, her little round breasts and her innocent, somehow childish, gestures he hated himself for his own thoughts. She was a woman-child deserving his protection and he had raped her. Then, in terror, he thought that she was a subtle Athenian, and of course she would not say a word until she said it under the protection of his wife's hearth. There was a bloody hole in him, a pit filled with a howling darkness of guilt and fear and lust and shame.

She chattered on, babbling, giggling, and bubbling over. On and on, light, bright, glittering, frothy, sparkling, twinkling above his silent darkness. He could not bear it. He was baffled and appalled. He turned like a wild boar at bay. Something broke in him. He reached for her with his immensely strong arm, pulling her towards him irresistibly, and she did not try to resist. He pushed her down on to her back, and she was still giggling. With his other hand he reached for the hunting knife. He held the sheath between his teeth and pulled the blade free. He put one knee on her chest, shifted his weight and pinned her down; he jerked back her head by her hair and pinioned it with his foot. Now he had both hands free, kneeling over her, and she was still laughing, her mouth open, not twelve inches from his penis, which was hardening and swelling even now. He was so much stronger than she was that it took only one hand to force her mouth wider, pull her chin down, drag her tongue forward. Quite suddenly she stopped laughing, there was an instant when her eyes changed, when there was no longer delight but outrage and protest. It was too late. He cut her tongue out with his hunting knife and threw it across the room. The remaining stump still quivered in her throat, while the tongue itself lay pulsing and murmuring incoherently to the dark earth. It writhed convulsively, like a snake's tail when it has newly been cut off.

There was an appalled moment as their eyes met; and then there was blood, blood everywhere, and he leapt back and she struggled to turn her head not to choke on the blood, and it poured out on to the skins. He started to vomit. His eye caught the pink tongue still bleeding itself, and he picked it up on his knife point and threw it out the window. Then his uncivilised compassion for all living things obliterated everything else; he did everything he could do to alleviate her pain and distress, to keep her alive. She kept her eyes shut. She would not look at him.

She did not even try to speak.

By noon he had come to a decision. No one must ever learn what he had done. She could not speak. He would not tell. They would both be silent. In the nearby village he found an elderly couple; he committed her to their care; they were to be tender to her, feed her, amuse her, nurse, wash, and keep her. They were never to let her go. He did not even try to explain what had happened. He paid for their silence, and paid well. Then he and his body slave mounted their horses and road on northwards. They agreed that they would tell Procne that Philomel had taken a fever and died in the woods. He would be very gentle with his wife because he knew how sad she would be – but surely that was better, better for her, for everyone, to mourn sweetly than to know that your husband has raped your sister and then cut her tongue out to stop her chattering about it. He tried to tell himself he meant it for the best, but his dreams were filled with terror and his days with a hot wild anger and a dark silent shame.

His plan worked after a sort. Procne was very sad and very sweet to him in her sadness. He treated her with a new and gentle courtesy. This was made easier for him because he was impotent. She missed sex, but not as much as she missed Philomel. Like many marriages it was all right – not perhaps what either of them had hoped for, but dignified and even friendly.

She turned towards depression and mild hypochondria; she became obsessed by her needlework, fine delicate stitchery, creating patterns in sombre but lovely colours, stitching hour after hour. She spoke less now, having no one she wanted to speak to, so the court was calmer and more serene. He turned towards his son – seeing in Itylus all the promise that he once invested in himself. Surely, he thought, this novel combination of Thracian and Athenian, barbarian and Greek, would prove the breeding of the new hero. The broken father could heal himself in the new man, the perfect son, the one like a Centaur, wise with the logical wisdom of philosophers and the feral wisdom of the beasts, a joined nature, a wild glory. And in the meanwhile he was a charming child; fiercely courageous, he rode his pony with all the glee his mother had once shown and all the cunning skill that he learned from his father. He grew well and sturdy, he took no fever, his round head fitted into his father's hand and Tereus dropped his taciturnity to chatter with the lad, to boast of him to his friends and to caress him with the rough tenderness that was no longer expended on women.

Meanwhile in the cabin in the wood, tenderly nursed by her simple and well-meaning gaolers, Philomel survived. She survived and recovered, and so long as she kept her mouth shut she was nearly as pretty as before; but not as chatty, as giggly, or as merry as before.

Philomel knew with great simplicity and trust that if Procne knew where she were, if Procne knew what had happened, Procne would come and get her. Procne was her big sister, fifteen months older than she was, and it was among the tasks of the big sister to come and find the little one, just as it is the duty of the little sister to assuage any parental wrath. Sisters who love each other know these things almost before they know anything else. If Procne did not come, and Procne did not come, then it was because she did not know. The only problem was how to tell her, because, although she had recovered her health and her looks of course Philomel had not recovered her voice. At most she could make an ugly gurgling sound, but she could not speak, could not tell, could not relate. She was silenced and so silent.

Philomel was not stupid – insensitive perhaps, and brought up to be so, as all pretty little princesses are and should be, but not stupid. From a very early age she had associated sewing with chatting; they had sewed and chatted together, punctuated always with giggles. Even if she could not speak, she could still sew. She sewed the whole sorry story into a tapestry; stitching away hour after hour, fine delicate work, creating pictures in sombre but lovely colours. Her devoted attendants were impressed by the delicacy of the work and went out of their way to bring her coloured threads and new sharp bone needles – it seemed a minor kindness as well as a reward for her quiet diligence which made their job all the easier. It was a large work and she stretched it on a frame, both for convenience and for secrecy, so they never saw or dreamed of what she was up to. It was not only beautiful but also witty, subtle, allusive, full of puns and references and metaphors; it was a work of art. Silence drove her to meaning as speech had never done and she knew that Procne would, if she ever saw it, read it as easily as she could hear chatter. Though she probably would not giggle.

When it was finished she gave it to a passing chapman, having ascertained that he was heading north. She knew what she had made, she knew that he would take it to the next court on his road and sell it to the Queen there. The next court, travelling northwards, was Thrace. It was perhaps chancy, but it was the best chance she had.

So a few weeks later, via various middlemen and court-iers, Procne had the joy of learning that her sister was alive and calling out to her. For the first few hours that was all that mattered, that rising froth of hope and relief and delight; she was almost giggling as she perused the fine detail of the tapestry. It was Philomel, Philomel alive and giggling. It took longer for her to absorb the story, the story in all its vile detail, nothing held back, nothing glossed over. She was dumbstruck, as silenced as Philomel for a while and then she moved into action. She did not say a word to Tereus. She decided to bide her time on that confrontation. First of all, and swiftly, she went down into the woods and found her sister.

There was neither chatting nor giggling in that meeting, but there was a dark joy.

Procne brought Philomel home with her and hid her in a small room high in a tower of the palace. There was only silence where there had been chatter; there was only ugly gurgling where there had been trilling giggles. The love that had always been between them had no way of expressing itself – they were frivolous and insensitive, but they were not stupid. They planned their revenge.

At first Philomel wanted to castrate him. She mimed the fine slash of a hunting knife and the casual tossing of his treasure across the room. She mimed the remaining stump still quivering between his legs, while his penis itself lay pulsing on the dark earth. She mimed it writhing convulsively, like a snake's tail when it has newly been cut off. Procne started to giggle and then stopped abruptly. She told Philomel that the two of them had already done that, they had made him impotent, they had castrated him once already, a deep castration inside his head. There was no point to a physical one. It was not about sex any more. He had cut out their words, they would make him eat his word – his dearest word, his statement to the future, his glory, his son. Philomel, for a moment, feels slightly nauseous, but Procne is smiling.

So they kill Itylus and dismember him and put all the pieces in a large pot. Then they give the house slaves a holiday; they send them up to the mountain temple with two red cockerels and a picnic. They work smoothly together in the empty kitchen. The whole palace is peaceful, and the two women move about the space, synchronised and graceful. They stew the little boy with onions and paprika, the pungent earthy flavours of the north, spicy, rich and hot.

Procne serves the stew and watches from inside the dark hole of her mind while his pink tongue licks the juices from his full smooth lips and from his rough beard that surrounds them. Pushing back his chair contentedly he calls for his son and Procne, as serenely as her mother had told her father of his little girls' playful days, tells him what they have done.

In the brief pause of his disbelief he is silent.

Philomel enters. She carries Itylus' skull, inverted and filled with red wine. She offers it to him with her mouth open – she has become a poet without words, neither frivolous nor insensitive.

Tereus leaps up in horror. He will kill them both and then himself. There was no cause. There was cause. There is only horror. He draws his sword . . .

This is a terrible story.
And it makes so little sense. Is it a story about sexual perversion? A story about men's violence and women's

malice? A story about men's shame and women's shame-lessness? A rare dangerous story about a woman who loves something more than her own child? Is it a story about cultural difference, about Greek and barbarian, about male and female, about speech and silence, about tongues and penises?

Even the poets cannot bear this story. They end it so awkwardly, those golden-tongued bards. Tereus draws his sword but before he can cut off anything more, even life itself, the Gods intervene. All three of them are turned into birds.

Tereus is a hoopoe, which is one of the most striking and distinctive birds of the whole region with a feathered crest that fans into loveliness as it alights, but with a flapping and uncertain flight.

Philomel is a nightingale, which sings its mournful lovely song deep in the woods, but is rather plain and dull when seen close to.

Procne is a swallow, which has no song, but is free in the air. It can never rest on the ground and nests in a dark hole that it makes for itself.

SEAL-SELF

In Cleveland it was well known that any wild goose which flew over Whitby would instantly drop dead; and that to catch a seal it was first necessary to dress as a woman.

Keith Thomas, *Man and the Natural World*

It is cold when he wakes, stirred from forgotten dreams by the deep whirring in the air. The goose flocks are driving north again. It is cold and still dark, too dark to see the great wide arrowheads, spread wide, not yet re-gathered since they had split up to avoid Whitby, but he can hear them and he shivers. They stir his blood each equinox with their coming and going, up there, out there, beyond. He does not know where and he could not imagine. Last week he had seen the falling stars, the serene and magic performance of the heavens to celebrate the turning of the year. And after the falling stars the wild geese, uncountable also, will pass over along the pale coastline. For the next week they will appear, from the south, at dawn and at dusk, through the night watches and in the morning, as swift as falling stars flighting northwards towards the cold wind.

And after the wild geese have passed, the seal mothers will surge up from the icy water and lay their pups on the great flat sands below. And he . . . but he does not want to think about it.

He twisted into himself seeking what warmth there still might be in the bed, wrapping his arms around himself, deliberately seeking the safety of sleep, but the deep whirring noise over the cottage roof continued unabated until it was fully dawn.

His world is shaped by the stripes. Green stripe. Yellow-gold stripe. Lead-coloured stripe. Blue stripe. Across the stripes, at right angles to them, ran another stripe, invisible but every bit as tangible; the fierce east wind that rushed in from far away across the ocean, coming at him, vicious and greedy, coming in a straight and evil line, down the sky, the sea, the sand, the fields. May God have mercy on his soul. He crosses himself, half-scared, half-scornful, for this is old women's thinking, and he is ashamed; and men now do not cross themselves, for times have changed, and his mouth curls in scorn of his mother and her fussing ways, for he is a man, and when the goose flocks are passed over and the seals come to play on the beaches, he will prove he is a man.

For the next ten days the wild geese pass over. He knows they are watching him, his friends, the geese, even the rising sun. His mother. In the village when he passes across the square the young women look at him, curious and questioning. The tawny maiden from the high farm-stead eyes him, direct and challenging. She is taller than he is, and her legs run up under her skirt, legs so slender and long that they must lead somewhere good. She tosses her head in the pale April sunshine and diamonds scatter from her hair. He is bewitched by her long cool stare. As he carries the milk pail she passes by, almost brushing against him, and her clear voice bells sweetly to her friend. 'They say the first of the seal mothers are come to the sand dunes. I would love a sealskin cloak this year.' He hates her suddenly and brilliantly, bright as the April sunshine, but his penis stirs and he watches her breasts. She smiles at him, promising him. And if not her then another. They all promise him together.

Last year he could not bring himself to do it. It is not the killing; he has cut pigs' throats, catapulted birds out of the sky, snared hares, wrung chicken necks, drowned kittens, baited bears, put his evil-snouted ferret to the rabbits' warrens. It is the other. They do not understand. His mother had smiled last year when he had tried to tell her. She had laid out the apparel for him even. His stomach feels sick to think about it. His dreams fill with it. And it must be this spring, for by next year his beard will be upon him. Now is the time. He knows it. He is frightened. For it is well known that to catch a seal it is first necessary to dress as a woman.

He wakes again in the darkness as before, and there is silence; the whirring of the goose flocks has vanished northwards, and though it is still cold there is a new softness in the air. His fear is very present to him. He strips off his clothes and stands naked. He pulls on his mother's skirt and arranges it at his waist, it falls lumpenly, ugly, and his hairy feet appearing at the bottom strike him as ungainly and ludicrous. He knows, blindingly as dawn, what his fear is. It is pleasure. It is pleasure and desire. He tiptoes to his mother's kist, and takes for himself her boned corsets, her linen hose, her full Sunday petticoats, her best bonnet.

Before he is half-dressed his hands are wet with his own juices: his fingers tangled with bodice ribbons and semen, his mind with delight and shame. But after that he knows that it must be done well and fully. He takes great care, padding his hips with fleece, tightening the corset with gentle concern. The skirt hangs better so. He chooses for himself breasts not too large, too heavy, but high and delicate like the tawny maiden from the high farm. He smiles for himself that smile of veiled promise that she gave him in the village square. Then when everything is ready he realises that it will not do. He takes off the petticoats and skirt again; he takes a hair-ribbon, soft satin smooth, the same rich rose colour as the chaffinch's breast, that his mother brought home from the Whitby Fairings; she never wore it, it was too fine for her, she said, she wanted it only because it was a pretty thing and no one bought her pretty things any more. He ties it now gently round his penis, which is soft and pleased and sleepy, and draws it back between his legs, folding his testicles carefully. He feels the flat firm skin behind them and knows that there should be a hole, a place of darkness and wet that he will never know. It cannot be helped. He attaches the other end of the ribbon firmly to the bottom hole in the back of the corset. Now when he pulls on yet again the skirt and petticoat he knows that it is almost right. Shoes he must do without, for he will not mar his own loveliness with cloggy boots but none of his mother's will fit him. But stockinged feet are charming for a maid out in the fields at daydawn.

As he passes the parlour he sees in the half-light himself in the mirror-glass, gold curls fluffing out under the sweet bonnet with its delicately ruched and pleated inner brim. How pretty she is, he thinks, so much prettier than the tawny maid from the high farmstead. He smiles. How pretty I am, she thinks, and she raises the latch craftily and skips out, silent and dainty, into the waiting springtime.

The preparation has taken longer than was planned. Now it is dawn already; the great stripes of the countryside have already divided themselves, though not yet into colours, only into different greys. But there is a ribbon, laid tidily between the grey stripe of sea and the paler grey stripe of sky, a rose-pink ribbon holding the world in shape, the day-spring whence the sun will be born.

She shivers in the cold dawn and wishes that she had a sealskin cloak to snuggle in, a cloak made from the softness of baby seal, white and thick and dappled. A sealskin cloak trimmed and fastened with rose-pink ribbons, she thinks, and then she laughs at herself for her vanity. Nor would she wear one if he gave it to her, for seals are friends to honest women, and she is going now to meet her friend Seal Woman and greet the new Seal Child who will have been carried in the deep waters all through the winter, wrapped in thick sweet blubber and rocked in a secret bay between the promontories of her mother's pubic bones, safe within the greater ocean. And who would now be pupped in the soft golden sand, clumsy and enchanting, pug-faced, soft-furred, playful and unafraid. No woman of sense or worth would accept a sealskin cloak, not from the King himself were he to come to the cold coastland north of Whitby and hear the wind rush in from far across the ocean; nor would she wear one and mock the mourning of Seal Woman for her child.

So she laughs, though kindly, at herself and her vanity and walks across the grey meadows towards the seaside; and as she walks the light seeps gently into the air and grass turns towards green and the birds begin to sing and the sea sedge and saxifrage are pale pinky-mauve and the celandines are yellow. The pink ribbon beyond the sea widens and pales and the broad sweep of the sky overhead is almost as white and pure as the frothed edges of her petticoats, bleached out with love and joy.

Closer to, the line, which from the cottage seems so precisely drawn between grass and sea, is blurred, indefinite, hesitant. First there is grass and woolly sheep still huddled against the night, then there are scrubby plants mixed in with bare patches of earth, of sand, then there is mostly sand with the occasional bold push or outcrop of reedy grass, and then almost unnoticeably there is only sand, great reaches of it in rolling hills, swirled into fantastic shapes by the long-drawn wind from the sunrise side of the ocean. And finally the hillocks settle, flattened out by the waves, and there is a wide wet beach changing constantly with the long pushes and tugs of the tide.

And when she comes at last to the very end of the dunes, to the edge of the tide beach, she heaves a great sigh of relief, coming home, united in her belly with the pushes and pulls of the tide, of the moon, of the great spaces of the sea. Quietly and easily she folds her legs, her skirt ballooning softly around her and sits in silence watching the long waves roll in, smooth and strong from out there, out beyond her eye view, and each wave is different and each wave is exactly the same forever and ever and she feels calmed, rocked, soothed, contented.

And as she sits there, waiting for the sun to rise, the seals begin to emerge. Some from the sea where they had gone at her approaching, and some from the dunes where they had slept. Now they flop, heavy and clumsy, on the shining golden sand by the waterline. Some are still gravid, ponderous and careful, and some have already pupped and their tiny young lurch around them or frolic idiotically in the wave edges. Not thirty yards from the shore a mother seal floats on her back, her tail flapping balance against the wave tossings, her little white pup held, flipper-fast, against her breast to suckle. So water-graceful, land-clumsy; so strong, so tender; so like and so unlike herself. She forgot the reason and the manner of her coming and waited only on the movement of the tide and the rising of the sun.

'Good morning, my dear,' says Seal Woman, 'and welcome.'

She springs to her feet to curtsy.

'Hello,' says Seal Child. 'I'm new.'

And new she certainly is, but already with bright black eyes that look and see, and with flourished whiskers, moustaching out from her black nose, and dappled white-grey fur fluffed in the sun. Barely two feet long, neatly constructed for an environment that cannot sustain her, at home in no element, timeless, lovable, perfect and preposterous. She smiles and reaches out a hand to touch Seal Child's nose.

And now, now he is meant to take a stone now and smash it down on Seal Child's head, blanking out the

shiny eyes forever and carrying off the soft skin to the
tawny maiden from the high homestead to wear as her
victor's spoils, and to prove to the village that he has
become a man, but she has forgotten this, lost in the wide
free space of air and ocean, lost in the wide loving gaze of
Seal Woman.

There is no need to talk much, or to talk of anything in
particular. She sits, Seal Woman sprawls, and Seal Child
suckles unhindered, occasionally wriggling or squeaking in
delight. And all across the wet beach there are a hundred
other seal mothers suckling, snoozing, sprawling, and now
the gulls come swooping, wailing, to join them, and out on
the breakers the older pups play and beyond that the sea
pours in, in, in, a long solemn, musical procession, ancient
and careful. And, quite suddenly, the sun rises.

Seal Child waggles her flippers in delight, tosses her tail,
gambols a little. Seal Child says, 'Will you play with me?'

'Yes,' she says, 'yes, please.'

'Mother, come too,' begs Seal Child.

'Of course,' says Seal Woman.

So together the three of them go down to the seashore
and plunge in. And suddenly she is not woman to woman
with Seal Woman, but child to child with Seal Child. In the
water it is a new Seal Child, graceful, strong, rhythmic;
suddenly no longer little and sweet but powerful, fast, the
fur no longer soft and fluffy but streamlined, completed.
Together she and Seal Child splash and paddle in the
breaking water, dance in and out of the foam, going
deeper, deeper, deeper in. The waves mount around her,
lifting her skirts gently up and down, until they are soaked
through and dragging at her legs; her balance fails and she

falls into the next wave, is lifted by it, raised up, brought down, and left as it runs on in towards the sparkling sands. When she realises that her feet will not touch the bottom again she is, for a moment, scared and then it does not matter because she too can swim like a seal, strong and shapely, powerful in the water as never on the land. And deep new places opening in her lungs so that she can go down and under and be there unafraid.

And now they swim and swim; the dark cold waters are the breeding grounds of fishes who move in vast shoals hard to see. But flipping over and rising upwards the surface is a great starry sky, brighter and fiercer than the terrestrial constellations; where the water meets the air there is a barrier, a great spangled ceiling, chandeliered with light, with air, water, sun-fire sparkled. And turning downwards, down, down into the dark there is the everlasting silence, the great underwater drifts and waves and forces of currents unlit by the sunshine, and great still mountains, cliffs, ranges, beflowered in dark growths whose shadows deepen the green darkness and whose rhythms are from before the beginning of air breathing, and Seal Woman flows between her two children, guarding them, hovering over them, around them, protecting them, remembering them in the forgotten places. And there is no weight, no gravity, no memory, and deep, deep below there is the ocean floor whence they all came and whither they do not choose to go and they are carried above it joyfully, on the strength of their own limbs, wings, fins. And Seal Child, using flippers and nose, pulls away the ties on the sweet little bonnet and it floats a moment in the water, like a dark jellyfish, and is gone.

Then, on another shared thought, they all turn and shoot upwards, breaking the surface into sprinkled jewels, whooshing into sunlight, their lungs pulling in new fresh air, bobbing upon the surface and laughing together. And Seal Child, using tail and teeth, strips off the knitted hose and chases them playfully across the wave tops till they drift away.

They swim far north to the gathering and gossiping grounds of the salmon, under the shelter of the great ice pack, where the waters teem with microscopic life, and are greener than the grass. They swim among the mating places of the wild geese and see the cold slopes where the white swans winter. They watch the dignified icebergs sail regally out towards their death, glittering bravely in the bright sunlight, and they dine without effort on the herring shoals that drift on unseen currents across the sub-polar waters. And Seal Child, using nose and mouth, nuzzles off the skirt and petticoats, the bodice and sleeves, and lazily they float away to provide refuge for some weary tern in some other distant sea.

And then they turn and drift slowly southwards, following the cold current that finds its way along the eastern coast of Scotland, leisurely riding the water and watching the ships in the distance break the tidy line of the horizon. And the sun comforts those bits of them that break the surface of the cold sea, so they turn on their backs and let their tummies feel the gentle spring warmth in the morning light. And they play in the rocky pools off Lindisfarne, the Holy Island; and watch the great gannets drop sixty vertical feet through the air, white streaks of power; and they tease the gaudy puffins who bob and wimble under those serene cliffs. And Seal Child, using tail and flippers and mouth and nose, unties the corset cords and pulls the garment off and with a weary sigh it sinks down and down to amuse poor drowned sailors from years and years ago.

And as they come back to their own golden beach to the north of Whitby, the end of the rose-pink ribbon, which she had tied to the corset and which had worked its way in between her buttocks, floats loose and drifts like the colourful seaweed in a coral lagoon two thousand miles away to the south and west. Seal Child plays with it as it dangles and they all laugh, riding in on the breakers and coming to rest at last on the sunny wet sand in the first early hours of the day. And Seal Woman and she lounge on the beach and talk of those things that women talk of when they have had good physical exercise and are met in magic places, while Seal Child frolics around them playing with the ends of the pink ribbon and with her penis.

Seal Child says, 'I love you.'

She says, 'I love you too.' All three of them grin peacefully. And it is simply true.

Seal Child is still very young. Love means warmth and cuddling and feeding. Seal Child scrambles up on to her body and tries to suckle from her, not finding flat breasts, small nipples or a soft furred chest anything out of the usual. She holds Seal Child under the front flippers to steady her, feeling with great pleasure the softness of wet fur against her own belly. Seal Child's whiskers and soft mouth tickle, she giggles and rolls over with her; mother child; child puppy; child child; happy. Seal Child tries again to suckle, her mouth is round and pink, her lips firm and sweet against the nipple. And suddenly the soft and floppy penis, still bedecked with rose-pink ribbon, springs up, awakened. She rolls over on to Seal Child who wriggles in the sand. Suddenly he looks up. Seal Woman is looking at him, not just with anger, but with great sadness and greater amazement. He springs to his feet, the ribbon still dangling.

'I'm sorry,' he says to Seal Woman.

'Come and play some more,' says Seal Child.

'No,' says Seal Mother.

Seal Child looks puzzled. She is about to start whining. She flops to her mother and finds there the milky sweetness she had been seeking; with enthusiasm she begins to feed.

'I'm sorry,' he says again.

'I have never been fooled before,' says Seal Woman. 'Why is it?'

'I was naked,' he says, beginning to be annoyed. 'You could have seen. You must have known.'

'That's not what counts,' says Seal Woman.

They are still. They both look out at the sea, where the waves break still. They both look at Seal Child sucking. For a last moment they both share equally the desire to protect the baby at all costs.

Feeling their attention on her, Seal Child breaks her sucking and grins. She flops affectionately over to him and for a moment Seal Woman just watches them. Seal Child tugs at the wet pink ribbon. His penis swells again.

'You must go now,' says Seal Woman sadly.

Seal Child, silky wet, rubs her flat face across his belly.

'I could cut it off,' he offers; and for a sweet moment of fear, excitement, desire, loss, he means it. Seal Child's snout snuffles downwards, nibble-mumbling his soft hair;

her whiskers tickle him. His penis stirs, Seal Child and he giggle.

'No, that's not what counts,' says Seal Woman.

'No,' says Seal Child.

'No,' he agrees.

'Please,' he says.

Now, he thinks, now I should take up this heavy stone, that is here, by good fortune, here just beside me, here at hand, and bash in her head and strip out her blubber guts and carry home her soft sweet fur and have her forever and be a man. This is what I came for, he thinks, and his penis stirs again.

'Please,' he says, 'please let me stay.'

And if they will just do what he says, wants, needs, he thinks he will not have to hurt them.

'No,' says Seal Woman. She knows his thoughts but she is not afraid. She is angry-sad, sad-angry. 'No.'

They vanish.

They have taken from him even a moment of choice. The stone is there, round, heavy, fitted to his hand, but he had not decided. Round the very base of his penis, tangled in his golden pubic hair, is one long whisker caught underneath the rose pink ribbon, but he had not decided. He will never know what he would have decided.

It is full morning, suddenly, bright beyond bearing. On the golden stripe of the beach there is nothing but his golden body. Out in the leaden-coloured stripe he sees their leaden-coloured heads bob, spaniel-eyed, sad and smiling.

He goes home. He crosses out of the golden stripe and into the green one. No one sees his solemn, naked procession.

Later he says, 'It is well known that any wild goose which flies over Whitby will instantly drop dead; and that to catch a seal it is first necessary to dress as a woman.'

Later he says, 'I caught a seal, but then I let her go.' He does not know if they believe him; he does not know if he is a man.

The Diviner

Joe Cassidy lives with his wife and family in Co. Kildare. His daughter is the author Laura Jane Cassidy. He has been practising as a diviner in Ireland for over a decade.

The Diviner

The inspiring true story of a man with uncanny insight and the ability to heal

JOE CASSIDY

PENGUIN
IRELAND

PENGUIN IRELAND

Published by the Penguin Group
Penguin Ireland, 25 St Stephen's Green, Dublin 2, Ireland (a division of Penguin Books Ltd)
Penguin Books Ltd, 80 Strand, London WC2R ORL, England
Penguin Group (USA) Inc., 375 Hudson Street, New York, New York 10014, USA
Penguin Group (Australia), 250 Camberwell Road, Camberwell, Victoria 3124, Australia
(a division of Pearson Australia Group Pty Ltd)
Penguin Group (Canada), 90 Eglinton Avenue East, Suite 700, Toronto, Ontario, Canada M4P 2Y3
(a division of Pearson Penguin Canada Inc.)
Penguin Books India Pvt Ltd, 11 Community Centre, Panchsheel Park, New Delhi – 110 017, India
Penguin Group (NZ), 67 Apollo Drive, Rosedale, Auckland 0632, New Zealand
(a division of Pearson New Zealand Ltd)
Penguin Books (South Africa) (Pty) Ltd, Block D, Rosebank Office Park,
181 Jan Smuts Avenue, Parktown North, Gauteng 2193, South Africa

Penguin Books Ltd, Registered Offices: 80 Strand, London WC2R ORL, England

www.penguin.com

First published 2012
001

Copyright © Joe Cassidy, 2012

The moral right of the author has been asserted

Set in Garamond MT Std 13.5/16 pt
Typeset by Jouve (UK), Milton Keynes
Printed in Great Britain by Clays Ltd, St Ives plc

A CIP catalogue record for this book is available from the British Library

ISBN: 978-1-844-88287-8

www.greenpenguin.co.uk

ALWAYS LEARNING   **PEARSON**

For my mother, Mary – the source of my strength

To AINE

hope you enjoy
the Book

Joe

Contents

CONTENTS

PART III

Prologue

Last year I attended a class reunion in Naas. I can get nervous when I'm going to a thing like that, because people always ask, 'What are you doing with yourself?' I didn't mind when I was a builder and stonemason, but when I tell them that I'm a diviner and a healer, many people haven't a clue what that means. Because it's different. Because *I'm* different. And occasionally I'll get a bad reaction.

I remember going that evening, and thinking that it could be awkward. And halfway through the night, when I was standing at the bar waiting to be served, somebody asked me what I was doing these days. And I told him, 'I'm a healer.'

There was another guy at the bar, and he nodded. 'Yeah, I heard that,' he said. He seemed fine about it.

But the first fellow turned round and said, 'Joe, I didn't know that.'

Here we go! I thought.

Then he said, 'I'm not surprised.'

'You're not?'

'Not at all.' He beckoned me to a quiet corner of the bar.

'Now I don't know if you remember,' he said, 'but one day, when we were very young, we were walking along the road. We were going swimming, I think.' He paused and took a sip of his beer. 'I remember we had our togs rolled up in our towels. We were walking along without a care, when suddenly you started to scream at me and at another boy. You were shouting, "Get off the road!"'

'Why would I do that?'

He shrugged.

'We were wondering, *What's wrong with this fellow now?* We didn't really take any notice. So you ran up and started pushing us towards the ditch. We all fell over and started to shout back at you, but then this lorry came round the corner with a punctured wheel. It was out of control, swerving all over the place. And if you hadn't done that, if we had kept going, it would have swept the two of us right off the road.'

I don't remember that one. I honestly don't. It's a difficult thing. When you realize that you're different, that not everybody can do what you do, you suppress it. It hasn't been easy to find myself. To find out who I am.

That night at the class reunion was a good one for me. It was as if life had come full circle. For a number of years there were things I had to say to the doubters and the sceptics. I had to prove myself. Now I am happier to tell people that I work as a water diviner and a healer, because I have fully accepted who I am.

PART I

1. Early Childhood

There was something different about me, right from the beginning. I was born on 25 March 1961, the fourth child of Paddy and Mary Cassidy, in Naas, County Kildare. But I wasn't expected to live.

When my mother was in labour with me, the doctor was called for. He didn't like the look of the way things were going, so he called an ambulance. My mother, who must have been in a great deal of pain, was afraid for her life when she overheard the doctor saying to the ambulance driver, 'How long does it take you to get from here to Holles Street in Dublin? I mean, how fast *could* you do it in?'

The ambulance man said, 'Twenty-nine minutes – at this hour of the night.'

The doctor replied, 'Well, if you do it in that time tonight, you'll save this mother. If you're much longer than that, then you'll lose both her and the baby.'

Luckily, the ambulance *did* get there in time. My mother was saved and in due course I was born. But it seems that I wasn't at all well. In fact the doctor said to my mother, 'Pray that God will take him. He'll never be anything, only a vegetable.'

Now my mother is a strong woman. She will never just take what she is told. So she went straight to the church and prayed that God would save me. I ended up in an incubator for the first months of my life. My mother had to leave me in the hospital when she went home, but she came up to see me as often as she could. And, against the odds, I came out of the incubator and was brought home. However, that wasn't the end of it.

Although my mother was a young woman, she was used to rearing children, having already had three before me. But I didn't react the way my brothers and sister had done. The others had cried when they were dirty, hungry or wet, but I never cried, and that worried her. I never slept either. My father would often get out of the bed and check me in my cot. One night my mother remembers him getting back into the bed and saying, 'He *is* a vegetable.'

It was years before I heard this story. I thought my birth and babyhood had been uneventful. It wasn't until I was grown and had children of my own that it was told to me. And I might never have heard. But when I began to work as a water diviner and healer, some of my brothers and sisters were sceptical. Their attitude was, 'You're a grand fellow, Joe, but what is this?' The only one who took my news well and didn't seem too surprised was my mother.

'Joe, I've something to tell you,' she said, when I visited her one day. And that's when I first heard the story.

I was intrigued. It didn't make any kind of sense to me. I remembered running around as a small boy, and there was never a mention of me being backward.

'So what happened?' I asked, as my mother took the kettle off the range and made the tea.

'I was going down the town of Naas one day when I saw Father Swayne. He came over and said, "Mary, I'm sorry to hear of your trouble." And I said, "Ah, sure, Father, God is good." '

'But what did he mean?'

She looked at me strangely. 'That I had a handicapped child.'

'Handicapped? Is that what people were saying?'

'It was. And he said, "You already have three children. You'll never be able to look after this one, because he'll never be able to do anything for himself." Then he said, "I must bless him for you." I asked him when he could do it, and he said, "Sure, I can do it today." So I went home, and he went off to collect his oils.'

'Oils? What for?'

'To bless you with.'

She poured the tea and cut me a piece of chocolate cake.

'So I went home. And Father Swayne arrived and had a cup of tea with me. And eventually he went in to where you were – you were in a Moses basket. And he blessed you.'

I took a bite of the chocolate cake, which was delicious, as all my mother's cooking was and still is.

'That was normal back then, wasn't it?' I remembered that you'd often see the priest walking down the street talking to everyone. He'd call over any child he saw, put the sign of the cross on their forehead and say, 'Bless you, child.' We never thought anything of it.

'That's right. Priests could *be* priests in those days. Anyway, this day, after he went, I stood by the front door, near the green area you loved so much growing up. He got to the corner, turned around and waved. I waved back and then closed the door. Now.'

She reached for the teapot and topped up our cups again.

'You may not believe what I'm about to tell you, but it's true.'

'What is?'

7

'When I closed the door it was like flicking a switch.'

'Yes?'

'You were crying for the first time. And all I can tell you is that it happened after the priest blessed you.'

My mother went on to have four more children. She had eight altogether, and she told me that when the last one, Stephen, was born, the doctor in the hospital had asked her at what age I'd died. 'Joe?' she'd said. 'He's not dead.'

'I mean that fellow you had,' the doctor had said. 'The one we cared for in the incubator.'

'There's not a bother on him. He's flying.'

The doctor had looked totally bemused. 'What do you mean?'

'He's fine. Really he is. He's at school now.'

'Will he be up here to see his brother?'

At that time we had a van, and we'd all be thrown into the back of it.

'He will, yeah.'

As my mother was telling me all this, a flash came into my mind of being in a room with doctors. Doctors who were pulling at my legs, my ears, my nose and the whole lot. So I asked her, 'Did they bring me into a room by myself that day to check me over?'

'They did.'

'Well, what did they say?'

'They walked you back into the room and said, "It's a miracle. We can't believe this is the same child."'

'And you believe it was the priest's blessing that saved me?'

'I'm only telling you what happened. But Father Swayne was a really good man. I don't think it was a coincidence that I met him that day.'

*

I was happy as a child; very happy. I was born and reared on a council estate in Naas, and although we didn't have a lot of money, neither did a lot of people back then. I remember a neighbour would often knock on the door and ask, 'Have you sugar to spare?' And you might go to that neighbour a couple of days later and ask, 'Could you lend us a drop of milk?' That was the way it was. You didn't know any different. There was a good community feeling. People cared about each other. There was no shame in going to a neighbour looking for that half a jug of milk. You didn't feel in any way less well off. You just felt that was life.

Looking back, though, it wasn't easy for my parents at times. My father worked as a builder, and often when I was growing up I knew money was tight; I'd be aware of that. I remember in later years seeing my father under pressure from a lack of money. I could see the strain on him. But it was never desperate for us. There was always food on the table, even if, as one of a family of eight, there wasn't enough money for new runners.

We had a lot of freedom. As a young boy, I remember playing out in the garden or running around the green with my friends. My mother would be in the house doing the cleaning, the washing or cooking. She was a skilled cook. Watching her make bread was like watching a master craftsman at work. She'd be holding a conversation with you, and pounding and rolling the dough at the same time. It was as if the art just came to her; it looked so natural. My mother took a lot of trouble over our dinners. We'd have stews, and bacon and cabbage. But my favourite was always shepherd's pie.

For a number of years I shared a bed with my brother. And later on, when a fourth lad was born, we had bunk beds. There was a boys' room and a girls' room, with four of us in each. These days eight children in one family is almost unheard of, but back then it was normal. I suppose that was because of the Catholic ethos: you had the priest on the pulpit saying that contraception was a sin. And anyway, back then you couldn't have got contraceptives for love nor money.

Even before my younger brother and sisters were born the house was crowded. When there were eight of us it must have been even more difficult, but I don't remember thinking that. You don't think about it when you don't know any different. We had to be quite organized though. I remember there was a chart on the kitchen wall that told you who was having a bath that night.

I will never forget my first day at school. I was almost five when I was sent to a convent in Naas. I remember being brought down by my mother. I don't think I made a big fuss about going to school on my first day; I think I was just going with the flow.

I remember the rows and rows of small desks, and having to share one. It was a big class. There was more than thirty in it, and all were junior infants. That first day some people were crying, but not me. I was happy enough to be there. When my mother left the classroom, there were no tears either. I sat there for about ten minutes, taking everything in. I was fine. But then the teacher handed me a black slate and told me to write on it. That's when I realized I was expected to sit there and not move. And I knew then that I didn't want to be there. My brain just kicked in. But still I didn't cry. And I didn't say anything to the teacher. I just got up and left. I got as far as the door when the teacher noticed and roared out my name. But no way was I going back in. I started to run. I ran down the corridor, out through the playground and up the main street in Naas. I was running as fast as I could, but when I turned my head, I noticed the nun still chasing me. She was running, holding up the skirt of her habit. I remember dodging people on the street and a woman laughing. Eventually the nun caught me and brought me back to the classroom.

The next day I did the very same thing. I went to school. I didn't cry, but at the first opportunity, I took my chance and ran. And the nun chased me and brought me back. It happened every day. I'd get up and leave, and they'd catch me and bring me back. It wasn't that I was unhappy exactly; just that I didn't see the sense in school. I didn't understand why I had to be restricted. And I wanted to be back home.

My elder sister Esther was in the same school. The nuns brought her over to sit with me for a while, and she was made to look out for me in the playground too.

After a week or so, I stopped trying to run away. Part of that was because of the buns. We were given them every day with a glass of milk. They were like hot cross buns and they were delicious. I can almost smell them now, and to this day I love a hot cross bun. I suppose I thought, *If I stay here I'll get a bun every day. So maybe this is not the worst place to be.*

I don't remember much about what we learned at that school, although I do remember that for Irish we had these felt figures that stuck onto special cardboard.

After the junior infants you moved into the senior infants, and after that, you went to the boys' primary school. But when it came to the end of my time in the convent, the head nun asked to see my mother. 'We're going to hold on to Joe for another year,' she said. 'He seemed a bit young at the start. And it took him all that time to settle down.' That was fine by me. I didn't mind at all.

In the days before I finally left that school, after I'd stayed for that extra year, the nuns gave me some pictures. I don't know if work was going on in the convent, whether they were changing the decor, but they kept giving me these pictures. I can still see them in my mind. One was of O'Connell Street with Nelson's Pillar before it was blown up. There was a green bus in it too. I remember those pictures being consigned to the attic later on. I often think to this day, *Why did the nuns give me those pictures?* I also remember that the nuns started dropping me home. And I've no idea why.

2. Growing Up

My mother is a very religious person. She's eighty-two now. And she's a very healthy woman, thank God. She lives life to the full.

There was a lot of respect for priests and teachers back when I was a child. But my parents were never the type to bow to any pressure. If there was a problem in the school my parents would back us. They did that for us on several occasions. If they felt they had to go up to a teacher, they would.

My mother encouraged me and my two older brothers to serve at Mass. My brothers enjoyed it. If you were serving at a wedding or a funeral, people gave the priests money, and they'd give it to the servers. I don't know why, but I hated serving at Mass. It was probably because I was very shy and reserved as a small child. And I just didn't see any great benefit in it. I only agreed to do it because my parents wanted me to. I wasn't too long at it when I said, 'I don't want to go any more.' And that was it. I don't think they put any great pressure on me to stay. It was nothing to do with the priests. I never encountered abuse or anything like it – not when I was serving, and not at school, either.

My second primary school was run by the Christian Brothers. It was in Naas, and I was able to walk there. I was happy in that school, and I made some good friends. I was good at Gaelic football and we did very well in competitions.

My father would come and cheer me on at the football matches. I loved that. It was really important to me.

I loved Christmas too. I loved everything about it: the lights in the streets, the carol singers; I loved the magic of it. I loved it then and I still love it today.

It started early in our house because my mother liked to be organized and to do things ahead of time. I remember her making the Christmas puddings. She'd do that in October. I'd help her to stir the mixture, which I particularly enjoyed because it meant I could make a wish. She'd use a large mustard-coloured china bowl to mix the puddings, then she'd put the mixture into china basins. I'll never forget the smell of all the spices, or of the steam in the kitchen when she was cooking the puddings. Sometimes she wouldn't bother to open the window.

There's one Christmas I remember very well. It was the year of my confirmation, and my mother had bought herself a new coat for the day, which was a big thing for her. That same Christmas she bought my father a long leather coat. It wasn't new. She got it second hand because we hadn't much money – money was tight that year because it had snowed, and when the weather was bad there was no work in the building trade – but I remember him wearing it while we opened our presents and he looked so proud. Proud of his coat and of his family. He stood there, beaming at us all. Even when money was tight, we'd always get good presents from Santa. I remember getting cowboy hats and guns. I felt like John Wayne. And we always had a big tree.

We ate like kings, too. We always had turkey and ham at Christmas, and along with the Christmas pudding there would be trifle. My mother was such a great cook. In later years she would make a beautiful curry stew with the leftover turkey. Before Christmas week was out, we would have finished the turkey and ham.

The week after Christmas we would take a trailer and go out to the bog near Coill Dubh to collect loose turf for the fire. That year, the year of my confirmation, it was snowing when we set out. I remember my father said he'd bring the gun, and he put it in the boot of the car. We drove along the road, which was packed with snow. We drove round a corner, and on the bend, with the snow falling, we saw two beautiful pheasant standing in the middle of the road. I can still see it, as if it were today. My father stopped the car and got out, walking lightly, and he went to the boot to fetch the gun. Before he left the car, he tapped me on the shoulder, and said, 'When you hear the shot, run and pick the pheasant up.'

I remember thinking, *Run? On the slippery snow?*

Now my father was a great shot. He got both pheasant, and I ran along the snow and picked them up. I remember the thrill of it, knowing we were doing something that perhaps we shouldn't. Of course a real sportsman shoots legally with a dog, but my father was thinking of the bigger picture. I got into the car with the two pheasant and threw them onto the back seat. He rubbed his hands together and said, 'We have the dinner anyway.'

I will never forget that day. Never.

I remember one day I was playing soccer in the green area outside our house. I was about twelve and still at primary school. It had been a good game; I'd been scoring a few goals. I stopped playing because I needed to go to the loo. My intention was to go into the house, go to the loo and get out again as quickly as I could, so that I could score another goal. I didn't want to miss out.

I ran down the stairs so fast on my way out that I slipped at the landing window. As I picked myself up, I looked out and saw the neighbours who lived across the road. The man and his wife were walking slowly up the pathway together, their arms linked. As I glanced at them, my sixth sense kicked in. I saw a distinct picture of what had happened to them. It was like a newsreel in my head.

I could see that the couple had been in a crash. And the man who had hit them was drunk. I recognized the village where the crash was. It was Sallins. I called out to my mother as I rushed to the front door, and said, 'Mam! Mr and Mrs May.'

'What's wrong?'

'They're after being in a crash.'

'What? Are they hurt?'

'I don't think so.'

'Where was it?'

'Down in Sallins. And the man that hit them was drunk and their car is a write-off.'

'Who told you?'

'I don't know. I just know.' I went out then, and continued playing soccer.

A while later I was called in for my dinner. It was a beef stew with potatoes and carrots. When we were having the dinner, sitting around the kitchen table, another neighbour from across the road came in. She said to my mother, 'Did you hear about the crash?'

My mother said, 'Where? What happened?'

The neighbour, who'd just heard from one of their children, told her. The couple weren't hurt, but they'd been really shaken and hadn't left the house since they'd been dropped home.

My mother looked over at me and said to the neighbour, 'Oh, Joe – that fellow. I don't know what to do with him.'

'What do you mean?' the neighbour asked.

'He told me that earlier on. And he hasn't been talking to anybody.'

My father wasn't there just then: he must have been working still. It wasn't a strict thing that we all sat down together for dinner. Those of us who were there would sit round the tables, on the benches or a chair, but if someone was out playing sport, their dinner would be kept warm over a pot on the range.

I don't know if my mother told my father that I knew about the crash. But I *do* remember my mother's reaction. I felt it bothered her.

I don't think that was the first occasion that kind of thing had happened. I remember as a younger child I'd sometimes see visions. We would visit relations in these different houses, and for a split second I would see someone who didn't live there at that time.

There was one house in particular that we used to go to down the country. It was in a town called Killashandra in County Cavan. A relation of my mother lived there; we called her auntie, and we would go about twice a year. I used to love going to that house, because the woman kept a few hens. I would look out from the back of the house, see the hens in their run and tell myself that one day I could have hens of my own.

I remember it was a rather gloomy house. It had a dark kitchen with an old range, and the living room was off it. One day, in the kitchen, while my auntie was making the tea, warming the pot with her back turned, this older person walked out from behind her. She just appeared, and walked across the room. I remember she glanced back. She was dressed all in black. And, I remember, she was wearing a dirty white apron. All this was really distinct. I was waiting for someone to introduce me to the lady, but nobody did. They acted as if she wasn't there. I don't think I said anything.

On another visit, a year or two later, I was looking through a photo album. There were all these faded black-and-white prints stuck in with photo corners. A few photos had fallen out. I picked up one of those and saw a photo of the old woman I'd seen. I asked my auntie who she was. And she told me she'd lived in the house years before.

'Does she visit sometimes?'

'Goodness, no! She's long dead,' she said. 'She died years ago – long before you were even born.'

I realized then that she had been a spirit. I don't remember finding that especially strange. To me, that must have been normal.

And because it was normal, I thought everyone saw the things that I saw. It wasn't until that time the neighbours had the accident that I became aware that I must be different. I knew because of my mother's confusion, as she tried to work out how I could possibly know about the crash.

I didn't much like it, the thought of being different. I certainly didn't see the visions as a gift. So I started to suppress it. I was trying to understand it, and I didn't want to talk to other people about it for fear of being different. I was just wondering, *What's going on?*

3. Teenage Years

I went to my final school when I was thirteen. It was called St Patrick's Vocational School, and it was in Naas. School-work was a bit of a struggle for me. I suffer fairly severely with dyslexia, and it was a real problem when I was a teen-ager. I remember teachers saying to me that I had brains to burn but I wasn't using them. I remember my mother and father going to a parents' evening and being told that here is a boy who seems to be very bright, but just doesn't perform.

The teachers didn't understand. They weren't qualified to understand and so I was a puzzle to them. I was a really good talker – so much so that I was head of the debating team. Even if the subject of the debate was something I wasn't familiar with, I was never daunted, and this confused the teachers. If I had all this information in my head, why couldn't I get it onto a piece of paper? I think it frustrated them.

Now, of course, there's a lot more understanding about problems like dyslexia. People are given help. But not then. Back then it was, 'You are a lazy devil. We'll bring your par-ents in.' So school was tough.

But at least I had my sport. Life as a teenager could have been very difficult, but being good at sport made me feel appreciated and respected. Without it, I don't know how I would have fitted in.

There were occasions, though, when I was younger, that I behaved strangely even around sport. I was on the Gaelic football team, and sometimes we would play a match maybe ten or twelve miles away. I knew I was good at football and I knew I would play a good game, but for some stupid reason I'd find myself saying, 'I can't go.'

There wouldn't be a real reason. I'd just make up a story. I'd say, 'I have a pain in my tummy,' when I didn't have a pain. I've no idea why I did that. I remember on one occasion two teachers coming up the road saying to my mother, 'Where is he? Where's Joe?'

I'd be hiding somewhere. Maybe behind a bush along the canal. And eventually I'd come out and I'd go and play the match. And once I was there I'd enjoy it. I've often thought about why I behaved like that. I wonder, now, if it has anything to do with my being a healer, with my being different.

It wasn't just Gaelic football that I was good at. I was also good at soccer, long jump and, later on, at tennis. We were lucky in the council estate. When I was thirteen there were two men in the community who worked to create a tennis area. They built two tennis courts and a basketball court too. I really loved tennis. I never had lessons, but I picked it up fine. My sister played it first. She'd been given a racket for her birthday, and I used to borrow it from her. I played it a lot.

Back then I loved watching Wimbledon. This was when Bjorn Borg was the top seed, and he was my hero. I made sure to watch all his games. I identified with him a bit, because he seemed to be different from the other players. He was ice cool, and when he was playing he seemed to be living in the moment. I thought he was perfect with his long blond hair. I used to have a long head of hair back then too. He was brilliant!

When it came to girls, we were all very innocent back then. We were starting to get an eye for them, and our hormones were raging. And we did go out with girls. But all it meant to go out with a girl was walking her down the canal at lunchtime holding her hand. I did a bit of that, mostly to fit in.

Like all teenagers I loved music. It was a big thing in our family. There was a back room downstairs, and we had the stereo in there. Originally it was a dining room, and we used it every year for Christmas once the family grew bigger. We all loved music. My oldest brother Pat was into Bob Dylan, John Denver and Neil Young, and I followed suit. I loved Rory Gallagher too; he was very big in our house.

Even though I wasn't good academically, I was happy at school on the whole. We had some good teachers. But there was one day when I was treated unfairly.

A boy in the school had died. He was a good friend of the family, and his was a large family too. We would have all been in and out of each other's houses. The whole school went to the Funeral Mass, and we were all marched down the road to the church. We stayed for the service, but we were told categorically that we couldn't go down to the cemetery for the burial. I thought that was totally unjust. He was one of my best friends. I felt I *had* to be there. When we came out of the church gates, I couldn't face going back to school. I remember thinking, *This isn't fair. I'm going to the cemetery.* And I slipped away.

When it was all over, I walked back to the school. To get to the classroom, I had to go through the car park and then through some double gates. I was walking along in a daze, thinking about my friend and how much I was going to miss him. It was terrible to think that he was dead.

Just as I was passing the gate, a teacher appeared from nowhere and grabbed my collar. I jumped in fright. We were all terrified of this particular man. He asked me where I'd been, and I told him I'd been at my friend's funeral. He started roaring and shouting.

'You were told you couldn't go to the cemetery!'

'I know, sir, but he was one of my best friends. I felt I should be there. So I went.'

He still had hold of my collar. He practically lifted me off the ground in rage and he laid into me. Though he was well known for his bad temper, the force of his anger on this day really shocked me. I fell back against the wall and I could barely stand.

I didn't tell my parents what had happened. I suppose it didn't seem important on the day that my friend had been buried, because the funeral took over everything. But if I had told them, I know they would have been on my side. Of course, it was a different era. Children were often shielded from death back then, and maybe the school was trying to protect us in a way. But I do feel someone should have checked to find out who the boy's friends were. I was being lumped in with people who wouldn't even have known what he looked like.

When I was sixteen, I had to do the inter cert: our first state exams. I remember going in to each one, sitting there in the exam room and knowing that I would fail the exams. I just knew it in my heart and my soul. And I dreaded the day in September when we would get the results. Finally, after the summer holidays, that day came. We stood in line, ready to be called in, one by one. And it was the teacher who had laid into me the day of my friend's funeral giving out the results. I'd never had much respect for the man, but since that day I considered him completely lacking in compassion. When it was my turn to get my results, I went in slowly. He looked up at me and sighed.

'Ah. It's Joe Cassidy. Tell me, Cassidy. What are you going to do with your life?'

I said nothing. I remember standing in front of him shaking.

He said more loudly, 'What are you going to do with your life?'

I looked up at him. 'I'm not really sure, sir.' No matter what idea I had I wasn't going to tell him.

He said to me, 'Sure, you're going to have to do something.'

'I'll probably end up working with my father or my brother. On the buildings.'

He said, 'Oh, fine.' And he threw the piece of paper at me.

I picked it up and looked at it. I remember my hands were shaking so much I could barely read it. The grades were not great – with my dyslexia I was never going to perform well in exams.

'These results are disgraceful,' he said, and he gave me a look of pure venom. 'Have you anything to say for yourself?'

'No, sir.' There was a silence then. I could see a vein throbbing in his neck.

He took a deep breath. 'Well, I have something to say to you.' He pointed at me. 'You were never anything in here. And you'll never be anything out there.'

I wasn't going to take that from him. He was just a bully. I looked over my shoulder and saw that the door was open. And, gathering my courage, I said, 'Sir, I have something to say.'

'And what would that be, Cassidy?'

'I'll be the happiest fellow in Ireland that I'm leaving this school today.' I paused for dramatic effect. 'And I'll never be back. But,' I said, 'you should ask yourself, are you happy?'

Then I ran across the playground to a fence with timbers between brick pillars. Beyond it was a busy road. He was running after me, as I'd guessed he would. But I'd had a head start because he'd been sitting at his desk and he needed to get up from behind it. He was several yards behind me when I jumped the fence and crossed the road. I looked back and he was just standing there, staring at me.

I never forgot his words. I'd dream about that moment time and time again. That dream only stopped when I was acknowledged for my philosophy essays as a mature student in Maynooth College.

Years later, I visited the school again for a reunion. They were moving everyone to a brand-new school, and we were asked if we would like to visit and meet the teachers again. I was happy to be back because I had good memories from that school too; there were some very good teachers there.

As I walked around, going to the metalwork room and the woodwork room, it all looked very much as I remembered it. I enjoyed reminiscing with the teachers, and I was glad I'd been back. In some ways, it got rid of all those negative memories.

4. Love of Animals

I've always had an affinity with animals. The first dog I remember in the family was a mixture of all sorts, called Trixie. But it's the next one, Pandy, a Jack Russell, that I have the most memories of, because she was bought for me. I was eleven years old. We went to see the puppies when they were too young to leave their mother, so we had to wait a few weeks. I was so excited that I went up every day to see the pup until it was old enough for us to bring home. I didn't go right in, but I'd walk up to this car park that overlooked the garden where the man with the pups lived. Every afternoon after school I'd go there, look down at the garden and think, *Soon I'm going to have a dog.* And when eventually we got the dog, I had a few friends around to play with it.

I loved having Pandy. We all did. Everyone in the family helped to look after her, but I loved that she was mine. I loved looking after her, taking her for walks and getting her to run after a ball in the garden. Often she slept in the bed with me; nobody minded.

It was around that time that we had a mobile home in Wexford. It was in Blackwater, not far from Kilmuckridge. We went there for holidays for a number of years, and we would go down there for some weekends too. We loved it, and Pandy loved it most of all. We would throw sticks into the sea for her, and she would swim out to get them. Those are great memories.

Owning Pandy gave me a taste for owning animals. When,

sometime later, my dad mentioned that he knew of some hens looking for a home, I begged him to get them for me. It was great driving out to get the hens together, just him and me.

'God, your mother will kill me, bringing home hens,' he said with a chuckle.

And I said, 'No she won't.'

He looked at me then, thoughtfully. 'You know what, Joe?'

'What?'

'You remind me so much of myself when I was growing up. I always wanted animals. But you know, we couldn't always have animals. Times were tight.'

'Yeah?'

'I'll tell you a story. One time I had a goat. I had her at home. My mother said to me one day, "There is no way we can afford to keep this goat." So I was to get rid of it.'

'How did you do that?'

'Ah! Well, you see. I brought it down to the canal in Naas and tied it to a tree. And I went down every day to feed it, and look after it there.'

'And she didn't know?'

'Not at first. But eventually she found out. A neighbour warned me she knew. And I knew she would be furious. I knew there would be a chance she would take a swipe at me with the sweeping brush.'

'What did you do?'

'I went home. And I cut through the handle of the sweeping brush.'

'Why?'

'Because when she came in, sure enough, she picked it up and took a swipe at me. And because I'd cut through it, it broke.'

'Did she realize?'

'No. I pretended I'd been really badly hurt. I fell on the floor going, "Owwwww." And she felt guilty, as I knew she would. Because she was very soft really. She said, "Oh you poor young devil, come here." She gave me a hug, and I was allowed to keep the goat.'

I loved hearing that story. It made me feel even closer to my dad. And as time went on I got more dogs, along with some pigeons and rabbits. And we had the hens. I loved looking after them all. But that wasn't all. I liked rescuing animals too.

I remember one time finding a bird, a heron, beside the river, and I brought it home. I was only young, and I can't have been taught how to handle injured birds, but I found myself going out into the road and picking up ice-pop sticks and different twigs. I brought them in and made a splint for the broken wing. Then I taped the splint to the wing. It just seemed like the right thing to do.

I kept the injured heron in the pigeon loft; well, in the shed my father had built where I kept the pigeons. The pigeons went up on the perch and the heron was on the floor. I kept him for a while, until I felt his wing was mended. Then I took the splint off his wing and carried him down to the side of the canal. It was only about 150 yards from our front door. I gently put him down, and he took off. He was fine.

People must have heard about it, because I got something of a reputation. After that people would often call round, saying, 'Hey, Joe, I found this bird' or 'I found this cat', and they would give the injured animal to me. At that time people hadn't the money to run to the vet with everything they found. I often wonder, looking back, how I came to do that when I never learned how to. But I did it. I helped animals from about the age of eleven.

I don't know if my parents thought anything of it. With my mother having eight children, and there being three before me, maybe there was no time to think about it. She was so busy rearing us, and Joe was just Joe.

But I do remember a neighbour saying one day to my father, 'That fellow! He has a way with animals.'

5. Death of My Father

When I was very young, I don't really remember money being an issue in our family, but when I was in my teens, I noticed sometimes that my father was under pressure because of it. My father never saw the bad in anybody. He would give someone an estimate for a job, and if the job was more involved than he'd expected, he felt sure that the man would pay him for the extra work. But often, when it came to it, they didn't, and people ended up owing him money. They didn't compensate him for the extra work that he had done.

I met people in later years who said, 'You are the spit of your father' or 'You have the personality of your father', and it's true. I'm good with people, like he was. And, like him, I'm not always business-like. But I can sense that my father was too trusting in his work. He was too helpful. And he didn't like asking for money. He wouldn't always confront people.

On one occasion, I could see it had really got him down. He was under a huge strain. As a young boy I would work alongside him on site, and I feel I knew my father really well. And maybe, with my sixth sense, I could see things in him that perhaps others couldn't. But what could I do? What does a fifteen- or sixteen-year-old boy say to their father? I noticed these things, but I never said a word.

I remember my father being very low for a while. I even worried he was near to having a nervous breakdown. He was in this state for a week, and it can't have done his health any good. I remember he was lying in bed one day when I got

29

home from school, and I went up to see him. He said, 'How're the pigeons?' I had some show pigeons at the time. They were beautiful black-and-white birds called Fantails. And I brought one up onto the bed. He stroked it on the back and said, 'God, it's lovely. Let it out the window now, and it will go out round to the loft.' He didn't tell me he felt bad. But being a child, I knew from just looking at my father that he was a broken man.

I never heard anyone say he was depressed. Certainly, he wasn't treated for depression, although something wasn't right. But he got over it. And after that low period he got on with his life again.

I remember one time I was working with my father on a house where he was doing the sewerage. He was putting in the manholes and the pipes leading to a septic tank. I was still at school then, and would sometimes go to the site with him on a Saturday.

One day we arrived there as usual, and there was a container in the garden that hadn't been there before. For some reason it made me feel horrible just to look at it. Dad said he was storing bags of cement in there, and he asked me to go and get a bag. I don't know why, but that was the last thing I wanted to do. It made me feel almost ill, but I'd no idea why. Anyway I ran and got the bag as fast as I could.

There was a load of furniture in there too. Dad told me that the people he was working for had lived in Africa, and all their stuff had been shipped over. The next time I was up there, helping my dad, the container was almost empty. The people had taken everything they wanted out of it, but the foreman told Dad he could have a knick-knack if he wanted as they weren't wanted by the family.

My heart sank when I heard that. I thought, *Jesus, no!* I wanted nothing to do with anything that had been in that container. And my father, being my father, would, I knew, pick some things out. He was well known for collecting clutter. I remember going to a dump with him one time. We'd taken a trailer load of junk to the dump, and we ended up taking a trailer load of stuff home again.

I wanted to tell my father not to take anything, but he was already rooting through it and so I didn't say anything. He picked out a couple of flower vases. One was black and white with handles at each side. When I looked at it, I wanted to break it. I didn't, though. I couldn't, because how would I explain why?

I always hated that vase. Dad put it in the sitting room, and it always gave me a strange feeling when I looked at it. The odd thing is, that when I was talking to one of my sisters in later years, it turned out she had hated that vase just as much as I had. It had frightened her too.

One of the first things I did when my father died, before he was even buried, was to go down and look at that vase in the room. It was as if I was being drawn to it. And even though he wasn't long dead, I carried it away and I broke it into bits. And I threw the bits into the river.

I would go shooting rabbits with my father too, and I really enjoyed it. I know that seems strange coming from an animal lover, but rabbits were food. My father was good to me. He'd arrive home from work, and there must have been times he wanted to put his feet up; but if he knew I wanted to go shooting on a summer's evening, he'd drop everything and take me. I'm sure he enjoyed it, but being the father he was, he put himself out a lot for me.

After we had shot the rabbits we usually gutted them in a little stream and put them and the gun in the car. One day, after we'd done this, he said, 'I want to talk to you.'

'What's this about?' I asked.

We sat down, and he said, 'I want to tell you stuff about my childhood. About my upbringing.'

So we sat there as the sun went down, and he talked and talked, and I just listened.

My granny had died when my father was very young. He was one of five. It was hard for my grandfather. He had dealt with his grief through alcohol, and that had made him tough on all the children. I think it was worst of all for my father, because he took responsibility and found himself running the show.

Much later, when all the children had left home, my grandfather had married again and he had a child from that marriage. She's very close to our family. I thought of her as a cousin when I was growing up, because she was just a year older than me, but I suppose really she is my aunt.

My father loved his father, but he wanted me to know how bad things had been. I had never known that before. I had a good relationship with my grandfather; he could be a little dictatorial, but I'd never had a problem with him. It was a bit awkward hearing all these things I never knew, and learning that the man had these issues.

'Why are you telling me all this?' I asked.

'Because I want you to make me a promise. You're going to be out working soon. But I want you to promise that you'll make time to visit him for me.'

'Grandad? But I do visit him.' I was finding this conversation really strange. 'Why are you talking like this?'

'I don't think I'm going to be here much longer.'

'What do you mean?'

'I don't think I'll be around much longer.'

I stopped asking questions then, because I was so worried. Worried and very confused. As far as I knew, my father wasn't ill. And if he wasn't ill, why was he talking about dying? It didn't make any sense. Yet I didn't go home and tell my mother.

There was another thing about that day that was curious. Why did he pick me, the fourth child, to tell? Why not the oldest? Or the second oldest or the third? He didn't tell any of them anything, as far as I know.

I'm pretty sure that at the time of our conversation all was well with my father. But soon afterwards he began to have a bit of heart trouble. I wondered if it was something to do with the strain from that job that had brought him down. Anyway, he went to the doctor, who tested his blood pressure and gave him some tablets, along with a spray to put under his tongue when he had an attack of angina.

I had always got on with my oldest brother, Pat. He was five years older than me, and perhaps he was the most like me. I don't mean that he had healing powers. When, later on in life, I told him about my healing, I think he was concerned for me, as he said, 'Joe, what is this?' But he was very easy-going like me. He was a stonemason. And I had always loved stone. I loved the feel of stone, and I loved working with earthy things. I still love working with soil in the garden, and with clay. I get a connection from touching stones and from touching timber. We're walking this earth, and to me we are part of it. That, to me, is what life is all about.

So after I had left school, at sixteen, I decided to go and serve an apprenticeship with Pat. And I took to it like a duck to water. I loved it, and I was very good at it too. We worked well together. Pat was the brains. I really enjoyed working with him and I loved having that bit of money. I started to buy clothes and to live the high life. Things were good.

At that time, if you were doing an apprenticeship, you went to college for one day a week. I was going to Bolton Street College in Dublin. One morning, when I'd been working for a few months, I was getting ready to go in. I was getting a lift with Pat, because he was tutoring at the college on a part-time basis. It was great being able to go up with him. He was driving a blue Fiat with a red interior at the time; I think it was a 124. It was cold that morning, and it was actually icy. My father was around. He'd had some scares with his heart, but he was still working away. I remember he got up from his breakfast and was boiling the kettle and helping us clear the windscreen.

As I was opening the car door to get in, he said, 'Oh Joe, just before you get into Blackchurch ...'

'Yeah?'

'... I was going up there a few days ago, and I saw the first lambs of the season on the left.'

We drove off. And right enough, just where my father had said, I looked to the left and I saw them. These tiny lambs. It made me smile to myself. The day at college went well, and afterwards I got the bus home. Pat wasn't coming home that evening; I think he was probably meeting his girlfriend. So I got off the bus, and I was walking along whistling – I'm always singing or whistling. I was then, and I still am today. My mother says, 'You'll always hear Joe before you'll see him.' I remember coming up the road alongside the canal and meeting a neighbour of mine, who was younger than me. He was looking at me. I remember that, because he seemed to be uneasy. I got a sense that he was looking at me strangely. I said hello to him and he just said 'Hi' and walked on. I wondered why he seemed so awkward, but I continued on.

I was nearly home, just a few hundred yards away from my front door, when I noticed there were more cars on the road than usual. They were parked awkwardly, and some of them were blocked in. I got to the front door, and before I could open it one of my sisters did. And she said to me, 'Daddy is dead. Daddy is dead.'

'What?'

'He's dead.'

I went into shock. It was a horrible way to find out, but obviously she was in shock too and could not have been expected to manage things with me when she was shattered herself. I think I'd have preferred it if there had been somebody to meet me at the bottom of the road, rather than get home and be told – or even if that young fellow had told me. But that's how I found out. And I suppose there is no good way to hear news like that. My father wasn't old. He was forty-eight.

It's terrible when something like that happens, suddenly. You go into this haze. You can't take it in. You're just not prepared. It's not as if he'd been in hospital, and I'd been going in to see him; seeing him sick, and knowing he was going to die. I kept thinking of the last thing he said to me: 'Look out for the new lambs.'

I don't think I ran off crying. The first thing I did was to go and see how my mother was. I found her in the kitchen having tea with the neighbours. They didn't know what to say to me. Of course, they'd had a few hours to deal with my father's death, before I came home.

I feel cheated, in a way, that my father died so young. I wish I'd known his philosophy about life. I think he was a little like myself – a bit different – although he never showed it much. He certainly had a way with people, and I'm told that I do too. I have to. Part of my healing is talking to people and connecting with them. Most of my father's life was caught up in work. It must have been tough with ten mouths to feed.

I didn't know how my father had died; not at first. There were so many people in the house, and there was so much going on. But I heard, later, that he was working in a house not far from where we lived. He was making some kitchen presses for a woman. But he didn't feel well, so he went home again around lunchtime.

He went upstairs to rest, and asked my mother to call the doctor. First, he wanted to wash the grime off his feet. He headed for the bathroom, but my mother told him to rest and said she'd bring up a basin of water and wash them for him. She left him, and went to fetch the water. She didn't take long, but when she walked back into the bedroom, he was dead.

I've never really discussed my father's death with my mother. I don't know if he'd told her what he'd told me – about not being around for much longer. He had had a few scares with his heart, but you don't expect someone to die in their forties.

By the time I got home, the body had gone to the hospital. The ambulance had been called after he'd died, and he'd been taken to the morgue. It must have been terrible for my mother.

That evening, as was customary, the neighbours gathered for the rosary. I remember one neighbour, who lived across the road, came in a fur coat. That caused a few comments. Just before the rosary started, somebody blew off air in the sitting room and people were giggling. I remember thinking, *Who do they think they are? My father is dead, and they're laughing.* I took it so personally, but that's stupid. Life has to go on, and death makes people feel uncomfortable. People deal with something like that in their own, different ways.

There was a good atmosphere in that room. I got the feeling from people in the housing estate that he'd done a lot for the couples in the area. If they were going through troubles, he would be there for them. He would call over and just chat to them about it. So I did feel a huge sense of loss in the room, and not just from the family; it came from some of the neighbours too. It made me realize that, in a discreet way, he probably had friendships that were a bit more than friendships. A lot of people would have laid bare their soul, and told him their worries and concerns.

My father's body never came back to the house. I imagine that was my mother's decision. She probably wanted to protect the sensitivities of my younger sisters and brother. The youngest, Stephen, had just had his holy communion the previous year, and I think she felt it wasn't appropriate to have my father laid out in the house. She wanted Stephen to remember his father the way he was.

Us older ones went down to the morgue. The coffin was being taken from there down to the church. Prayers were said at the morgue, before the lid was put on the coffin. I distinctly remember standing there, looking down at my father in the coffin. My main concern was that I hated the colour of the lining. It was a marmalade colour, and I felt it didn't suit him. So at that momentous moment, when I should have been saying goodbye to my father, telling him I loved him and saying prayers for him, I wanted to take my daddy out of the coffin.

After that we went down to the church and said more prayers. Then we went home for the night, and his body stayed in the church. The next day we had the full-blown Funeral Mass.

It was a big funeral. I remember everyone coming up and paying their respects, but I don't remember very many details about that day. I was just trying to live in the moment. It was a case of getting through it.

I don't think I cried; I was much more concerned with my mother. She was only forty-seven, and she had so much to cope with. She couldn't just give in to grief. I watched her carefully in the weeks and the months after my father's death.

She had buried her husband. But still, she was a mother of eight, and all of them were living at home. Two or three were working, and I had just started work. The main income had now gone out of the house. It's not easy to grieve when the food has to be put on the table every day.

She did grieve. Of course she did. I remember coming into the house one day when my mother was busy peeling the potatoes before putting them on to boil. She hadn't the tap running, but it wasn't necessary. The tears from her eyes were splashing onto the potatoes.

I saw that. And I knew I should have gone over and put my arms around her. But I didn't. I was a boy of sixteen, and I felt helpless. I felt sorry for her, but I didn't discuss her emotions. I couldn't. I suppose that's a male thing.

One day, though, I was really able to help my mother. If I hadn't been around, we might have lost her too. I was working, and I was big into buying clothes. I remember I was going off to Dublin to buy some shoes, because back then I couldn't get anything I wanted in Naas – not like now. Back then, Dublin was it.

My mother was doing the washing. She had one of those old-fashioned twin-tub machines. I was going to catch the bus, and I was late. I turned round to say goodbye to my mother, and she was literally stuck to the machine. She wasn't saying anything, but I realized, to my horror, she was being electrocuted.

I hadn't time to think. I just grabbed hold of the sweeping brush, which was propped against the kitchen wall, and pushed her hard, away from the machine, with the wooden handle. She fell to the floor. She lay there for a while, shaking. It was terrifying.

'Mam, are you OK?'

She shook herself and pulled herself to her feet.

'Ah. I'll live for a few more years now.' She flicked the electric cable with the brush handle to disconnect it, took the clothes out of the machine and hung them to dry with not a bother on her.

'That's good for you, then,' I said, and ran off to catch my bus to town. Neither of us ever referred to that incident again.

Even at that time, I didn't discuss my father with anyone. Yet I missed him more than I would admit. I'd lost the person who understood me best. I feel in later years he might have acknowledged what I do now. I think he would have been quick to support me.

6. Meeting Jean

My father had died on February the 15th. Two nights before he died, on the 13th, my sisters Esther and Martina were busy writing cards for Valentine's Day. They were slagging each other, trying to find out who each was sending a card to. I ignored them as I watched TV. I remember my father peering over the *Evening Herald*, chuckling at them. Then he glanced at me.

'What about you, Joe? Are you not sending a card?'

'Oh – I dunno.' I didn't look at him, I just concentrated on the screen. But I probably blushed.

'Is there someone that you'd like to?'

'Yeah. Sort of. But I don't even have a card.'

He pulled himself out of his chair, came over and hit me playfully with his folded newspaper.

'Then get a card.'

He didn't ask me who I was thinking of. But I went to the shop on the estate and picked out a card. It was a huge, extravagant card, with flowers and hearts all over it. I ran across the road and pushed it through a neighbour's letter box. I didn't, of course, write my name.

So my father never knew that I liked Jean. It had taken me long enough to realize that I liked her. It was her smile that did it. Her smile and her lovely green eyes. She looked like someone I could connect with. I'd known her all my life. She'd always been a neighbour, and she was a friend of my younger sister, Martina. She'd always been in and out of our house, but I'd never thought of Jean as a possible girlfriend. Never until then.

It was only two weeks after my father had died when I decided to risk asking Jean out. I was nervous about it because she was a year older than me, and I knew she had other fellows running after her. But there was something about her. It was an aura; her glow would light up a room.

I saw her leave her house one day, and I purposely followed her. I caught up with her just outside the shop.

'Hi, Jean.'

She stopped, turned round and gave me the benefit of that glorious smile.

'Hi, Joe.'

'My sister Martina told me it was your birthday next week. Would you like to go to the pictures?' I blurted out.

She looked at me for a while, as if she was considering it. *At least*, I thought, *she's not laughing in my face.*

'OK.'

'Yes?' I couldn't believe it. I felt like throwing my arms round her and hugging her, but I managed not to. I managed, somehow, to keep looking calm and collected.

'Yeah. Why not?'

I thought I was so cool back then. I had a head of long hair, and I was big into clothes. I had to have the latest denims; I loved Wranglers, and I'd wear those Clarks boots with the buckle on the side – the ones that were German-looking. I had a Puffa waistcoat, too, which I'd walk around in all summer. I probably looked like a gobshite, but I felt *I had* to wear it. It was all about the latest fashion.

I don't remember which movie we saw on that first date. I don't think Jean remembers either. I'd love to think that's because she was too excited about being out with me, but I doubt that. The date went well, and we started going out twice, maybe three times a week. It was all pretty innocent. We'd hold hands and kiss. But, of course, I'd be looking for more.

We dated for a few months, but then we drifted apart. I think that was my fault. I was maybe in a bad way still, because of my father's death. And, with the money I was earning, I was going out and having the good life. I'd be out drinking pints, and Jean doesn't drink. We probably stopped going out together because of that.

We'd spend a few months apart. I'd think I didn't mind. Then I'd see other fellows dropping her home and I didn't like that one bit, so I'd come to the decision that I had to act and I'd make a move again. I'd promise her the sun, the moon and the stars. I'd try to convince her that yes, I was going to change. And to cop on. But I was all over the place with my emotions. She was probably getting the brunt of my pain from my father's death, and that, I knew, wasn't fair.

Everything was very innocent in those days. We were young, we were neighbours, and we were going out together, but you'd be careful not to go too far. Any mother's biggest fear at the time was that their daughter would get pregnant. And we weren't taught at school about contraception. It was all a bit of a minefield.

If she had become pregnant, I'd say they would have killed me. Certainly things would have been difficult.

About a year later, we were at a disco, dancing close. Eric Clapton was playing 'Wonderful Tonight'. I looked at Jean, thinking how true those words were. I remember she was wearing jeans and a cheesecloth tunic, and she was glowing. I hadn't planned it, but I found myself whispering in her ear, 'Will you marry me?'

She looked up at me, smiled and murmured, 'Yes.'

I hugged her tight. I think I'd been expecting her to say, 'Cop on to yourself!'

The next day I was worried whether she had meant it, and I asked her again. I said, 'I'm not the biggest romantic, Jean, but are we going to get married? Will you really marry me?'

She laughed and said, 'I said so, didn't I? And it's still yes.'

So we agreed. We were definitely going to carry on and get married. But we were not ready to tell the world just yet. Jean wanted to wait until at least her twenty-first birthday. I knew I was going to marry Jean from the start – I just knew it, maybe because of my sixth sense. But I was at an age when in other regards I didn't know my arse from my elbow. I was earning good money working for my brother as a bricklayer and stone-mason. I was doing as much work as he was, and I enjoyed my job, mostly. I was good at it. And I had money to spend on clothes. I had a car too. It was a good car, an Escort 1.3. For all that, I'd say people were looking at us, saying, 'She's mad.'

My brother and I were always extremely busy, and we were very well paid for the work we did. We worked on housing estates and on one-off houses, on a lot of schools and on churches. I was happy – mostly. But sometimes, over the cup of tea at ten o'clock, the conversation with the lads could get me down. Page three would often be the topic of the day. I'd be looking at these grown men and wondering why their conversation was so limited. So, though I loved what I was doing and loved the environment, I would sometimes feel, *Jesus! Is this it?*

I wasn't displaying anything of who I was – of Joe the diviner. And maybe I was running away from that. Maybe that was why I was spending money on drink. I was at home still, and I was living in the moment. I was spending the money I earned, and not thinking about the future. I was saying to Jean, 'We'll get our own place,' but there wasn't much money in the bank, and not much chance of it either.

I'd go to the bar a lot, and when I was there I'd have no problem downing six or seven pints. It was the culture. I wouldn't go out to get drunk. But the drinking was a big problem between me and Jean. I wanted to marry this girl, but when she said it was time to go home, I'd want to stay for another pint. I'd be the first in the bar and the last one out. I'd never think of going home before closing time.

Jean must have been exasperated. I haven't an excuse, but I was probably playing the pity card, saying, 'I'm drinking because my father's dead and my mother is up there in an awful way.' There was probably too much of that. I must have been one of the hardest fellows to go out with under the sun – and not only because of the drinking.

I remember one night, when the relationship was off, I got into my car, thinking to myself that I had to find Jean. I had to see her. I hadn't a clue where she was, and I didn't call to her house to see if she was there. I just took off in the car and ended up in Newbridge, a town about seven or eight miles away. I parked my car and walked straight into a pub. And there she was, sitting with her friends. She was drinking Club Orange. She looked astonished to see me.

'Joe? I wasn't expecting to see you. What are you doing here?'

'Just passing.'

'But who told you I was here?'

'No one. I was in Newbridge and I fancied a pint.'

She knew I never normally drank in Newbridge, and must have guessed that I was only there to be with her. But she let the subject go. I stayed to speak to her for a few minutes, then I drove home again. That wasn't the only time it happened.

I'd pop up in all kinds of places, and I remember Jean getting a bit irritated. She'd say, 'You just appear out of nowhere.'

Maybe she suspected that I had sixth sense. Maybe, deep down, she knew.

Jean has told me since that she always knew she would marry me, even when I was messing her around. There would be times when I felt out of my depth. Things would seem complicated. Jean would say that I never talked my problems through. She hated that I'd just go off to the bar and have a good time instead of talking. They were the only times we ever really fought.

At the time, Jean was working in an office in Naas. She was still there when we decided to go away together for a weekend. We went off to Dublin. It was a very special time. We hadn't been alone together for as long before, and we found that we enjoyed each other's company so much.

And because I was with her, I had no desire to go to the bar for a pint. I didn't drink alcohol at all that weekend. We both drank water or a mineral with our meals, and we just enjoyed being together. When I'm alone out with Jean, I still don't drink. Later on, the year before we were married, we had another weekend away. That time we went to Scotland.

A few years before we married, Jean decided to train as a nurse. She worked specifically with people who had intellectual disabilities. She was twenty-one by then, and she began to live away from home. She shared a house with other nurses, but she had her own room, so I was able to stay over with her.

That's when the relationship became more serious. I could never have moved in with her officially, not without being married. At that time, that sort of thing was frowned on. And anyway, her hours were very difficult when she was training. She had lots of weekend work and she often worked nights.

It was around that time that we decided we would make

our engagement official. We drove up to the docks in Dublin and I proposed once again. That area in Dublin is lovely now and we often go back there just to reminisce. A friend of mine helped me buy the ring. When I told him I was getting engaged, he said he could get me a good deal in O'Connor's, the wholesale jewellers in Harold's Cross, as he had a contact there. It was the jewellers made famous by 'The General' – Martin Cahill – when he stole a load of jewels from there.

We picked out a petite diamond ring, which Jean loved, and set a date for the wedding. It would be a few years down the road, when she was twenty-five and I was twenty-four. And from that time, we went out continuously. There was no more breaking up and coming together again. I think the break-ups happened because of frustration. You want to be with this person and you can't find a way to be. Once you can be together more, you get used to each other and you feel, *This is it. This is the person I want to spend my life with.*

We got married in 1985 – the year of Live Aid. We had 120 guests, half from Jean's side, half from mine, and it was a great day. We had a church wedding in Cill Mhuire, Newbridge. It was what you did back then. I had built that church with my brother; we did all the block work on it, so that made it feel even more special.

Jean's dress was lovely. It had a dainty headpiece. When I saw Kate Middleton's dress, it reminded me of Jean's. And when I said that to her, she said yes, it was a similar style. She was chuffed that I remembered that, twenty-six years later.

The singing in the church was gorgeous. Jenny, Jean's cousin, sang 'Ave Maria', and 'In a Country Churchyard' by Chris de Burgh. Afterwards we went to Lumville House, a small hotel on the Curragh. We went to the Derby at the Curragh Races the next day. Then we set off for our honeymoon to Jersey.

7. Early Marriage

We were building a house in Ballymore Eustace to live in after our wedding, but it wasn't completed in time. So, meanwhile, we rented a flat in the village. It was pretty small and basic, but we were happy. It was just me, Jean and the mice.

I wanted children right away. I don't think Jean was as keen as me, though we never sat down and discussed it. We were just going with the flow. We'd only been married a few months when our first child was conceived. A few months later, the house was finished so we moved in. I was still working with Pat as a bricklayer, and Jean was working in Celbridge. She travelled up and down every day and was still doing shift work, which could be tough.

We were settled there by the time Laura was born. I remember taking her there from Holles Street, wrapped in a blanket against the cold. That year there was a really hard winter. The snow was unbelievable. It was difficult when we first got her home. It was like a wake-up call. There was a feeling that now, suddenly, we were on our own.

Laura was a colicky baby. Now people come to me with babies who have colic, and I put my hand on them and make them better. But back then I hadn't clicked that I was a healer, and I went through months of torture with my own daughter. It was particularly bad when she was teething.

I had a head of curly hair at the time. I used to lean over the cot, and she'd get a finger in the curls and twirl it. I'd be singing to her. And she'd go to sleep and I'd back gently away from the cot, and the next thing she'd be screaming again. So I'd start singing again. She used to love that. She loved to hear me sing.

I didn't sing nursery rhymes or lullabies. Well, I couldn't. I didn't know any. I'd sing her some Garth Brooks or Eagles, and she used to love the song 'Woodcarver'. Her bedroom in that house had pink walls, with these big murals of cartoon characters on them, which a friend of Jean's had painted for us.

We didn't know many people because we were new to the area, and for a while we were snowed in. We weren't well organized, and money was tight after we'd done up the house. We were living from week to week.

I remember fuel was a problem. I'd walk down to the village for a bale of briquettes, and on the way back up the hill I'd be slipping and sliding and falling all the way down again. It was mad.

Jean went back to work once her maternity leave was up, and her mam looked after Laura for us. She lived in Naas. I'd drop her in on my way to work.

Round about that time, though, building became a bit of a challenge. I'd get this desperate fatigue and have muscular problems, along with other strange symptoms that made me feel very unwell. There were times I was too sick to work. I went to the doctor with one thing after another. They would send me to the hospital for scans and tests. They thought it was this, then that, then the other. They mentioned ME at one time, but they never settled on any kind of diagnosis.

Soon a pattern developed. I'd be really unwell, so I'd be off work. Then I'd get fitter, and would go back to work again. I might be fine for a while, but then I'd suddenly find I was going downhill again. In the end I gave up working for my brother. I just couldn't cope with it any more. After that I did a bit of security work, which was easier.

In 1989, by which time we'd been in Ballymore Eustace for four years, we sold the house and moved back to Naas. We moved partly because it was easier to have Laura minded, and partly because we missed living in the town. I don't know if we said those were the reasons. You might think you are moving for one reason, when really it's for another.

At first it was lovely to be living back in Naas. But even though I'd been born there and had lived there most of my life, now that we'd been in the country for a while, I soon found myself feeling cooped up there, and I wanted to move again.

Over the next few years another pattern emerged. I'd buy a house that needed renovation. I'd do it up on a part-time basis, and Jean's father would help me. He'd retired at that stage and I think he enjoyed helping out; I'd certainly never have been able to do it without him. And when I'd finished we'd move on. I was minding Laura a lot at the time too, and Jean was still working full time.

One day my father-in-law was putting in a kitchen counter-top for us, and we needed some offcuts of timber to support it. I drove up to a building site where I knew the builder. He wasn't there, but a carpenter was working on the house. I'd never met him before, but he knew who I was.

I explained to the carpenter that I was looking for some bits of timber, and he said, 'Oh, there's loads out there waiting for the skip.'

As I was talking to him, I got a very strange sensation in my body, which made me feel extremely unwell. This resulted in yet another trip to the doctor. To say that I felt sick after being in that man's company was to put it mildly.

A while later, I got a phone call to say that this carpenter had been arrested for the abduction and rape of a young girl in the Dublin mountains. When I heard it, I thought immediately of how sick I'd felt, standing in his presence. The man was subsequently convicted of the crime and served a jail sentence. When I met him, I hadn't understood the strange feeling I got, but now I know that it was to do with energy.

Liam was born when we were living in one of the houses we were renovating. I don't remember as much about his babyhood as Laura's, but I do know that he didn't cry anything like as much as Laura did. Maybe he didn't have colic, or perhaps it was because we now knew what we were doing. There is one incident from back then, though, that I remember really clearly.

When Liam was a small baby, maybe just one or two months old, Jean said, 'Let's go into the town and do a bit of shopping.' So we all went in. Laura and she went off to do their bit of business, and they left me in the car to look after the baby. I had been sitting there for ten or fifteen minutes when time really began to drag. So I thought, *What am I doing, sitting here on my own in the car? I'll go up the town and meet them.*

I was walking up the town and after a while I spotted Jean and Laura coming down the street holding hands. I smiled at them and waved. Jean looked at me and stopped dead. And then I noticed horror in her face.

'Where's Liam?' she said.

'What?'

'Where's the baby?'

'What baby?'

I know it seems strange, but for that short period, I completely forgot that we had a new baby. When I realized what I'd done, I turned and raced back to the car. And there was the baby, lying there without a bother on him. He was fast asleep.

8. Sickness and Animals

One night, when we were settled in our third house, the one in Eadestown, we were sitting watching TV when Barbara Woodhouse came on. She had a programme where she taught obedience to dogs. Everyone was talking about her at the time. She seemed able to do anything she wanted with the dogs, and it rang a bell with me. I remembered the animals I'd had as a child, and I thought if she could do it, then so could I.

This was back when my health wasn't great. I spent so little time working with Pat, and I needed an income. I thought that initially I'd board a few dogs. The first thing I did was to convert the garage into three or four kennels, and I started to take dogs in. I liked it. It came naturally to me. I found that I still had a way with animals.

So I decided to expand. I applied for planning permission for a purpose-built kennels on the site. It came through, and I ended up with about six or seven kennels with a large exercise area. I remember I had to put in a whole new sewage system.

We had our own dogs, too, at that time: two King Charles spaniels, Pal and Holly – one brown and one black – and a golden Labrador called Princess. I remember one night, before we opened the kennels, Jean and I were at my brother-in-law's wedding. We knew we were going to be late, so we'd arranged to stay over at Jean's mother and father's house.

We were tired, and I went to sleep as soon as my head hit

the pillow. But a few hours later I woke with a jolt. I'd had a nightmare and was in a real cold sweat. I sat up in bed. Jean grabbed the bedclothes, mumbling that I'd let all the cold in.

'What's wrong? Why aren't you asleep?'

'I have to go.'

'What? Where? What time is it?'

'It's five.'

'That's the middle of the night.'

'I have to go home. There's something wrong with Holly.'

'What do you mean?' She sat up, gathering the bedclothes around her.

'I've this feeling.'

I was up by then, pulling on my now-crumpled suit.

Jean went a bit quiet. I think she was beginning to realize that this man she had married was a little bit different. But I could see that she took it on board. She sighed, rolled over and fell straight back to sleep.

I drove out to where we lived, about three miles outside the town, and went into the kennel. Princess was sitting there covered in blood. Holly was lying down underneath the bench; it looked as if her throat had been slit. It was horrifying.

I pulled Holly out, wondering whether she was alive. She was listless and in a very bad way. She'd been bleeding heavily. I checked the bleeding, which seemed to have stopped, wrapped her tightly in a jacket and laid her gently in the car. Then I rang the vet and drove in. The vet on emergency duty stitched her up, and she pulled through. But he did say to me that if I'd left it much longer, she could have bled to death.

It was clear that the dogs had been in a vicious fight and that the Labrador was involved, but that didn't make any sense to me. All the dogs were placid. Princess had *never* shown any aggression before. She was wonderful with children.

She'd let them tug her around the place, and even ride on her back. And if other dogs growled at her, she'd generally back away.

When I got home, I noticed some marrowbones in the kennel, and I realized what must have happened. I never gave bones to the dogs when they were in a confined space, because Holly became fiercely protective of them. But on this occasion I'd asked a friend to feed the dogs while we were at the wedding. I had warned him not to give them the bones, but he was a bit deaf. I expect he thought he was doing me a favour. Holly must have started a row over them. I knew that even if there were ten bones to share, Holly would try to stop the Labrador from having even one. I imagine that Princess went for a bone, Holly tried to snatch it and Princess defended it a bit.

That incident made me think again about my sixth sense and how I wanted to pay more attention to that side of me. I remembered that if I was sitting in the house as a young child and I wanted to check on the dog, I could do that by just tuning into him. Whereas most people would automatically go and find the dog, or call him, I'd think about him. I'd think hard, I'd visualize him; and the next minute the dog would be standing beside me. I suppose it was telepathy.

That might sound odd to other people, but I grew up with it. It was natural to me. It didn't occur to me when I was younger that other people might not be able to do the same thing.

Soon after the kennels opened, a man brought his dog to me. It was a German shepherd. It was a lovely gentle dog, but the man had a problem with it. He'd had a stroke, and was paralysed down one side. It was the side that the dog had been trained to walk, and the dog just wouldn't walk on the other side. He didn't seem to want to, and the man hadn't got the strength to hold him any more.

It had got to the stage where the man wondered if he could keep the dog, but the thought of giving him to someone else broke his heart. He was so worried. So I said, 'If you like, I'll work with him while he's here, and try to get him to walk on the other side.'

It took the dog a while to respond to me, but by the time the man came to collect the dog, he'd got the idea. So I taught the man how to do it for himself. He was really pleased, and the word spread. I decided to move more into obedience training, and the business began to grow. I really enjoyed that.

Soon after that incident, a springer spaniel came to board with me for two weeks. She was a beautiful dog and settled down with not a bother. But the day the owners were due to pick the dog up, I went out to the kennel and found the dog barking hysterically. She was chasing her tail and going mad, desperate to get out. She hadn't displayed any of these tendencies before, and she didn't seem to be angry or upset. She was wagging her tail. She was just totally excited. I put her on the lead and brought her out. She looked at me and barked gently, as if she was trying to talk to me.

A few minutes later, lo and behold, the owners drove in. She went mad with excitement, and they were delighted to see her looking well. As they all drove off, I said to myself, 'That's very weird. The dog goes mad, and two minutes later the owners drive in.'

After that, I began to notice the same kind of thing. It was like the dogs were sensing that their owners were near. It didn't happen to all of them, but it did happen with a good few. And the routine in the kennels was no different on the day the owners came, so that can't have been the reason.

55

It's easy to turn a blind eye and say everything is a coincidence, but I had the same springer for a few days a few months later. The dog behaved perfectly the whole time; there wasn't a bother on her. Then a few minutes before the owners came to collect her, the very same thing happened.

So then I started practising with my own dogs. If the dog was outside and I wanted him to come in, I'd visualize the dog. I didn't move from the table. I just sat there with the back door open, and the next moment the dog waggled in. She'd look at me questioningly, as if to say, 'What's wrong with you? Are you looking for me?'

I taught obedience training much as I had seen Barbara Woodhouse practise it on television. But I added an extra element: I helped people to communicate with their dog without actually talking to him; to zone in to his way of thinking. I taught them to connect. It's similar to the way a horse whisperer connects to the horses; a lot of it is to do with self-belief.

I think the dogs were good for me. I was helping them with their training, but that help was going two ways. By working with the dogs, I was rediscovering that connection to animals.

A lot of people believe you can't teach an old dog new tricks. I don't believe that. The German shepherd wasn't young, but I got him to change the side he walked on. It took time, because dogs are creatures of habit, but it worked. Many owners are happy to let the dog rule the roost. You can train a dog, but you have to put the effort in.

I trained dogs and their owners individually, and I put classes together for an evening a week. It worked out well. For the group sessions I mainly taught puppies – getting them to sit and stay. A dog should learn basic manners. It should be part of the household and should never control it. But there is a balance. A dog is not a computer. Dogs need the freedom to express themselves.

Having the kennels suited me, because it meant I was also there for the children.

I enjoyed being there for them. And I realized that children, like dogs, need their freedom. I worry that today so many parents just sit their children in front of the computer or the TV. Children sit when they're in school, and then they come home and sit – sometimes for hours on end until it's time for dinner. It was so different when I was young. When I was a child we had lots of freedom. We might head out to play in the woods, and we were always out playing on the streets and riding our bikes. Our parents weren't constantly thinking, *Will they be OK? Are they going to be abducted? Is there a paedophile about?*

But now, how do you get the balance? Of course you have to tell them not to talk to strangers, and let them know that there are dangers out there, but if we don't let them out of our sight we're taking them away from the elements and away from nature. And that can't be good for anyone.

I gave Laura and Liam lots of freedom. I'd let them cycle off to a friend's house and I would not be standing at the gate worrying. I'd know, somehow, that they'd be OK. I suppose I was subconsciously using my developing sixth sense.

We were happy in that house for quite a while, but one day, in 1996, I'd had enough. I remember deciding, *I don't want to live here any more.* I remember the day it happened. Jean came home, tired, from work. By then she was working in Newbridge.

'Any news?'

'I rang the auctioneer.'

'What?' She turned from hanging up her coat, and stared at me.

'To value this place.'

'Why would we want to do that?'

It was a rhetorical question. Because she knew. She could see in my eyes that I needed to move. We'd lived there for five years, and we'd been very happy. But I suppose I missed the town. And the house was now renovated and ready to sell on, so it did make sense.

In later years she said to me, 'I remember coming home one night, and you mentioned an auctioneer. And before I knew it, the house was for sale.' And from the way she said it, I knew that, at the time, she hadn't felt that a move was entirely necessary. But I wasn't looking at it in the same way. I was finding my sixth sense, and it was like it was meant to be.

9. Confronting My Gift

I was keen to move back into Naas again. I persuaded Jean, and we found a house and made the move. And if she minded the hassle of it all, well, she didn't complain. I've come to learn that she likes moving. It's like a new house gives her a new lease of life.

It was good to be back in the town — at first, anyway. The country had felt too quiet at times — too isolated. But after a while I didn't like it much back there either. On a Saturday morning, you'd wake up and everyone was mowing the lawn. We listened to lawnmower after lawnmower. It did my head in after a while. I got to feel that if I wasn't out in the morning mowing the grass or using the hose, I wasn't part of the neighbourhood. I felt I should be out washing the car. It got so that I felt guilty if I had a lie-in. That kind of thing, it's not for me. I didn't want to be part of the Residents' Association; I felt I didn't fit into the neighbourhood, and it got to me in the end. I lasted there for only twelve months, and in 1997 we put the house up for sale.

This time, Jean was as keen as me to move. She'd quite liked living in the town, but she realized I felt I *had* to get out. Because of that, she found it difficult living with me there. She was concerned for Laura though, because it might mean she'd have to move schools, and she was already in her second primary school.

Our house sold fast, but we still had to find a new one. We were driving around the place any spare time we had, but we couldn't seem to find one. It was just at the start of the boom, and the moment you saw a house, it was sold.

One day, we'd been down to Aughrim. That was much further out than we had planned to live, and we were losing heart. And, truth to tell, I was feeling a bit guilty. We went into my sister's house one day. She took one look at us, and said, 'Is everything all right?'

Jean sighed, and just looked at me.

'The house is sold,' I said. 'We have to be out of it. We can't get a house. Not anywhere.'

My sister looked thoughtful as she made some tea and put out some biscuits. 'So you're getting desperate then?'

'A bit.'

'Well, there's a house down the road here. In Two Mile House. It's not ideal. It's been on the market for quite a while and a lot needs to be done to it.'

My ears pricked up.

'But with your background ... there isn't a sign on it, but it is for sale.'

'Where exactly is it?'

'Oh, it's in a good location all right. It's outside the village and has a lovely view across fields.'

'It's worth a try, I suppose,' said Jean. '*Anything* is worth a try. Why don't you go and have a look, Joe? I'll stay here with the kids, and if it's any good I can come and look later.'

So off I went. The house looked more than a little run-down. The paintwork was flaking, there was ivy snaking up the walls, and the path was overgrown with weeds. But there was smoke coming out of the chimney, and a car in the drive-way, so clearly someone lived there. I knocked on the door and a man in a flat cap answered.

'Yes?'

'Is this house for sale?'

He took his pipe out of his mouth, and looked me up and down. 'Well, it is.' He paused. 'And it isn't.'

'Oh?'

'It has to be cash.'

My heart sank. I thought, *If it has to be cash, there's a story here*, but I asked if I could look around. There was something about the place that appealed to me.

In truth it was a bit of a wreck. The kitchen needed gutting and the whole place needed an overhaul. But I knew I'd be able to fix it.

'Look, I might be interested. Can you give me your number?'

I took Jean to see it the following week. And though her heart fell a little when she saw the condition of the place, she was prepared to give it some thought. I told her the changes I thought we could make, and we discussed them. Jean is good at imagining what a place *could* look like. Once she'd given it the go-ahead, I did a deal with the man.

But there was a problem. Some years earlier, he'd extended the house and he had encroached onto the neighbouring land. I don't know why. There'd been no need to do it. But the farmer, it seemed, had let him get away with it. The problem was that although the farmer was happy enough, it had never been made official. The maps hadn't been redrawn, and that made the legal side problematic.

When I went into the local building society to explain I was interested in the place, the manager said, 'You'll be lucky.'

'What do you mean?'

'You're the third or fourth person who's been in here trying to buy that house. You won't get a mortgage on it.'

That was worrying. If I couldn't get a mortgage, I'd have

to spend all my cash on the house. Then I'd have no money left to do it up. I couldn't expect Jean to live there the way it was – or the kids come to that. But I was still interested in the house, so I approached the farmer who owned the sod; I explained the problem and asked whether he would help me out and sell me a piece of land. He said he would.

I went to the Land Registry Office in the Irish Life Building in Dublin. A man I knew from my local pub spotted me in reception and asked if he could help me. I told him I was up trying to sort land, and he brought me into his office. I had Laura there with me, and they gave her a biscuit while we sorted the whole thing out.

So, eventually we got the place. It's an interesting house and it has a history to it. It had a number on it when we bought it, and I think it might have started life as a council house. I imagine it was built for the people who worked on the canal at Corbally Harbour. I enjoyed renovating that place. I did a lot of stonework on the outside of the house, which gave me great satisfaction, and my father-in-law helped me a lot.

My health at that time was still bad. One of the doctors was convinced that I had ME, and he put me on tablets that were supposed to help. I found out later that they were actually antidepressants. Shortly after I'd started the course of pills, I was out in the car with Jean when I realized I didn't feel at all well. We were on the way to my mother's house, and when we arrived there I felt even worse.

I remember sitting there not able to move. I literally could not get off the couch. Jean was worried, so she rang the doctor on call. He asked which tablets I was on, and Jean told him. When he heard they were antidepressants he wasn't too concerned. I suppose he thought I was immobile because of depression. But when things didn't improve, Jean rang him again an hour later and said, 'My husband really isn't well. *Please* could you come out? There's no way I can get him into a car to come and see you.'

The doctor arrived in, looked at me and then took my blood pressure. It was dangerously low, so he called an ambulance at once.

I remember being brought into the Accident and Emergency. There was panic and mayhem everywhere that night, but a lot of the panic centred on me. I had drips put into me and I was wrapped in tinfoil. I'd no idea why. Jean has said since that it was the only time she felt I was going to die. She left Naas Hospital, went home and cried her heart out. To all intents and purposes, I was in a coma by then – or that's what the doctors thought, anyway.

I remember looking out through the door to the entrance hall, and this lady was walking out carrying a briefcase. A voice in my head was saying, 'You have to get her back.' I didn't know why, because she wasn't wearing a doctor's uniform. She could have been anybody. She was just getting to the exit door of Naas Hospital, and the doctors were starting to wheel me in. The voice kept saying, 'You have to get her.' I was zoning in on her; I wanted to get this woman to turn round. It was like I had to. She had her hand on the door, and as I focused on her, she turned round. She saw the mayhem going on, and to my surprise and relief she came back in.

She thought I was in a coma – everybody did – but I can remember everything that happened, even down to the tinfoil. It was very strange, because at one stage I felt as if I had left my body. I was up in the corner of the room, and I was looking down at the doctors working on my body. It's hard to explain. And the odd thing was that I didn't feel any sense of panic. I just thought, *Oh, there is my body. They're working on my body.* But I'd no fear; I wasn't thinking, *Oh God, I'm going to die.* At the same time, I didn't have any fierce will to go back to my body. Where I was seemed to be paradise. I had no pain; just an unbelievable sense of peace.

Eventually I returned to my body, and this woman was working on me. Then they wheeled me through to the ward. But I sensed after a while that these doctors didn't know I was conscious. They were talking over me as if I wasn't there. And I remember lying in the bed, but I couldn't talk to them. It was frightening. I was thinking, *They haven't a clue that I am aware of everything that is going on.*

I remember watching this clock going tick, tick, and the doctor was sitting beside my bed and she was nodding off to sleep. I was trying to tell her, 'I'll be fine. Will you ever go off and have a rest?' Then a nurse tried to persuade her to go off for a coffee break, and she looked at me, considering.

'Oh, I don't know.'

'Go!'

She sighed. 'All right. But if anything happens to this man, anything at all, be sure to bleep me right away.'

She left the ward, but was back minutes later to adjust my drip. Then she went off again, turning round at the door for one last look.

A few minutes later the nurse came to check my pulse. As she was writing in my chart I sat up and said, 'Could I have a cup of tea, please.'

She jumped and dropped the chart with a clang. Then she ran off to get the doctor, my tea forgotten. The doctor ran in, her stethoscope flying over her shoulder. The first thing she said was, 'My God, Mr Cassidy, you are one lucky man. We were very concerned about you.'

I said, 'God, yeah, I remember.'

'Sorry?'

'I remember all that. And I remember earlier on you said you were going for your coffee, and if anything happened, the nurses were to bleep you.'

She turned to the nurses. 'Have any of you been talking to this man?'

'No,' one of them replied. 'He just asked for a cup of tea, and I went for you straight away.'

She sat down with me then. 'Do you remember everything about last night?' she said.

'Yeah,' I replied. And I went over it all for her, from the way I'd focused on her to get her to stay, to seeing the team working on me. Her face was a picture. She looked dumbfounded.

'And you know what the problem was?'

'I'm allergic to those pills I was given. For the ME.' I'd heard them saying that too.

'Can you explain what it felt like, when you were trying to get me to come back?' she asked.

'It was like a slow-motion film. I knew I *had* to get you back. I didn't know why.'

'That's extraordinary.'

We sat in silence for a while.

'I was trying to leave the building.' She looked totally bemused. 'I'd been working a long shift. I was tired, and I was thinking about the hot bath I was going to have the minute I got home. And the glass of wine, and the early night, and the lie-in the following morning. I was thinking about how I'd spend my time off. My whole weekend.'

She laughed. 'I can't explain why I turned round. Crises happen in Accident and Emergency every day of the week, but for some reason I was drawn back.'

That incident changed my life – though at the time I didn't realize it would. And soon after we moved into the house in the Kildare village of Two Mile House, I met another lady doctor who made me think more seriously about my gift.

When I'd been going through all that sickness, I was in and out of hospital having tests for all kinds of things. At one time they were convinced I had multiple sclerosis, then they thought I had ankylosing spondylitis. I had a lumbar puncture one time, and tests on my heart. But however bad I was – and at my worst I could barely walk – they couldn't find out what was wrong with me.

It so happened that one of my doctors was attending a medical conference in London. He was talking things over with his colleagues when one of them asked him if he had any interesting cases on the go. 'We do have this one guy,' he replied. 'We don't know what to make of him.' And he explained my case.

His colleague was a neurologist, and she said, 'I'd be interested in seeing him.' She was doing some work in the National Rehabilitation Centre in Dun Laoghaire.

When I heard they wanted me to go there, I was bemused. I didn't need rehabilitation; I needed a diagnosis. But it so happened that a psychologist who worked with Jean knew of this lady and had heard that she was extremely well thought of, so I agreed to go.

They do great work at the Rehabilitation Hospital; it's well known as a centre of excellence. But it's an old, forbidding building, and when I went to the day-care centre, where I was meeting this lady, I had to walk through a long, old-fashioned ward. As I did so, I got this eerie feeling. I picked up on the people's energy of sadness. And that made me feel even worse.

The doctor seemed nice enough though. She was younger than I had expected – in her thirties – and she asked me how I was.

'Well, I got here,' I said. 'At the moment I can walk. That's something. I'm bad on the legs at times. But I do wonder what I'm doing here.'

'What do you mean?'

'Well, I have no idea why I would be sent to Dun Laoghaire. No one has really explained to me why I am here.' I didn't understand what I was doing there. I hadn't had an accident or a stroke. I knew I wasn't there to have a scan or an X-ray. All I *did* know was that this doctor was considered an expert in her field.

What they had actually planned for me was a series of memory tests. It mostly involved me looking at pictures of buildings, people and objects. I would then have to recall whether the ones they showed me next matched what I had been looking at. I didn't understand what all that was about. It felt like being in Guantanamo Bay, and afterwards my brain felt fried. I'd be so very fatigued.

After a few days of this, I was taken back to see the doctor. She read all my notes carefully; then, closing my file, she looked up. She was thoughtful.

'What is it about yourself?'

I raised my eyebrows.

'Are you suppressing anything?' she asked.

That did it! I went, 'Oh Jesus! Not that again! Are you suggesting I've been abused?'

'No, Mr Cassidy.' She looked shocked at the thought. 'No! Nothing like that.'

'That's fine then.' I relaxed a bit. 'Because I've been down that route. And no, there was never anything like that.'

'I know that.' She pointed at my notes. 'But is there anything. Anything else …'

That was when I let rip. I don't mean I shouted at her, just that I couldn't somehow control what I said.

'I'm psychic.'

It was the first time I had ever used that word about myself. In fact it was the first time I'd even admitted it to myself, let alone to anyone else.

'You're psychic?'

'That's what I said.' If she'd been shocked at my words, she wasn't half as shocked as I was. 'It's the only word I can think of to describe it.'

'Can you prove it to me?'

'Well, I can. But before I do that, let's get one thing clear. You know everything about me, because you've got files this thick. I know nothing about you, only that you were highly recommended.'

'That's true enough.'

Now, I didn't know what I was going to say to this lady. And I hadn't realized this was the way the morning was going to go. So I just plunged in.

'Your father was a diplomat.'

'Yes,' she said. 'He was.'

I paused after that. I sensed that some of the questions I was going to ask her might upset her, as they were very personal. So I said, 'If I ask you a question, please will you tell me the truth? Because if you don't, if you try to divert me, this will get complicated and the conversation will get us nowhere.'

'OK.' She fiddled with her pencil. 'That's fine.'

'Your grandfather was a diplomat.'

'That's right.'

'And forgive me for saying this, but there was wealth within your family.' She reddened. 'Much more than a diplomat would earn, I mean. Had your father inherited a vast amount of money?'

'Yes. Yes, he had.'

'But would I be right in saying that he wasn't exactly mean but he didn't throw money at you. He wanted you to find your own way.'

'That's right.'

'I'm getting that you were in boarding school.'

'I was, yes. From the age of eleven.'

'While you were home one weekend, you said you needed some money because you were going on a school trip.'

'That would happen sometimes – yes.'

'And I see that your granny was living with you at the time. She wasn't well, she was living in an annexe.'

'Yes. I was still at school when she moved in. That's right.'

'Going back to the money, you knew you'd get a few pounds from your parents. But you wouldn't get as much as your girlfriends in school would get.'

She nodded.

'You stole money from your granny's purse, and that gave you more than the other girls in school.'

She looked at me in silence. The seconds passed. I was afraid I really *had* offended her. Then she said, in her English accent, 'Mr Cassidy. You have to use this gift.'

'I'm sorry?'

'You have to use it. For the sake of your health.'

'What?'

'We deal with medical science here. Obviously I have you here because we're trying to understand people like you. You are different. I've met people with powers before, but I've never met anyone with powers as strong as yours seem to be.'

'You mean, nobody else has accused you of stealing a fiver from your granny's purse?'

She laughed. 'Well, that's true enough! But the important point is that you need to use your gift if you want to get better.'

'Is that so?'

'It is. Because the last patient I had with healing powers got so sick from suppressing her gift that she ended up in a wheelchair. You're having trouble with your health now, but if you accept and work with the gift you have, I think you'll find your health will improve. It's suppressing it that's causing the problems.'

She wrote down some telephone numbers.

'Mr Cassidy, here are some numbers of people who practise various forms of healing. If you ring them they might be able to help you.' And then she tore up the piece of paper with the numbers on it. 'On second thoughts, don't bother. Just go away and do it. You have to.'

I remember going home from that appointment in a daze. Later that night, I went outside and looked up at the sky. The stars were magnificent. I stared into the universe and said to God, or to the higher power, 'I'll go with this. But if you let me down, I'll f***ing kill you.'

10. Setting Up

It took me a while to come to terms with the idea of using my powers. I was reluctant. I knew that I would be putting myself up for ridicule, and that's not easy. It's fine if you're on your own, you can do things yourself and be judged for it; but I was a married man with two children. In a marriage you're committed to protecting your wife, and as a father your instinct is to protect your children. And here I was, going into an area of practice which could bring, at the least, funny looks – not just for me but also for my family.

I thought back to another incident. I had been in hospital a few years previously when they'd been investigating my illnesses, and a nun used to work in the hospital. She sat down beside me one evening and started to talk to me.

'You know, Mr Cassidy, the way nobody can put a finger on what's wrong with you?'

'I know.' I was wary of conversations like this.

'Well, I was reading a book the other night about a water diviner. He lives in Wales. Before he realized that he had the gift of divining, his health was bad too. His story, back then, was very similar to yours, right now.'

I hadn't taken much notice of her at the time: I was too taken up with what the doctors were saying about the various illnesses they would test me for next. But when, two years later, I met that female doctor, I said to myself that maybe I should read up on what the nun had said. I found the book and read it, and she had been right. It was almost a carbon copy of my own life.

I thought, *Maybe I do have divining powers.* So I took a rod into the garden, and I practised and found that I could do it. It's like everything. It just seemed to be very natural to me. When I started doing it I could feel the water, and I could visualize it under the ground as well.

Jean had a bad back around that time. She was taking pain-killers for it and she tried using heat pads to stop the pain, but she was still uncomfortable. She was wriggling on the sofa one night, trying to ease it, when I asked her if she would like me to give her back a rub.

She pulled up her jersey and showed me where her back hurt. But then, something strange happened. I found myself first putting my left hand on her forehead. I expected her to stop me, but she shut her eyes and relaxed. Next I put my hand on her chest, and then to the area where her back had hurt. Jean was smiling.

'That's amazing, Joe,' she said.

'What do you feel?'

'I feel heat. But most of all just relief. Relief from the pain. How did you do that?'

'I think it's energy,' I said. 'I think it's energy from the universe, and I'm a conduit for it.'

'It's strange.' She was still smiling. 'It doesn't feel like you touching me. This touch is different.'

Jean said that I really must use my gift. I decided, then, to set up as a water diviner and healer. The problem was that I hadn't a clue how to start. Around that time, Jean went to Dublin and enrolled on a feng shui course. A guest speaker gave a session about the Diviners' Association. I looked them up and found a diviner who lived not too far away from me. I decided to go and see him.

I told him about all the coincidences in my life and about my childhood experiences too. He asked me a few questions. We met a couple of times, and he told me he felt my powers were strong.

'Obviously you're very in tune,' he said. 'You're very strong in your abilities.'

The best thing about meeting that man was that I didn't have to explain myself to him. He knew what I was saying and he believed it all. Later on, he introduced me to a few more people who were in the healing field.

I had a call from him one day, asking for my help.

'I've been working on some animals round here,' he said. 'I think it must be a problem with the land. Some cows have died, and others are ill.'

'You think I can help?'

'I don't know, Joe. But I'd love to see you try. I don't seem to be getting anywhere with them, and the farmer is becoming distraught. Would you mind taking a look?'

I went, and worked on the land, and I asked the farmer not to say too much. I always do the same in cases like those. And when I'd finished my work, the animals stopped being sick. The diviner rang me again. He sounded really impressed.

'That's amazing, Joe, what you did. I think that's the area you should be working in. With land, and with animals.'

I felt excited. If I could do things that this man – who himself was a diviner – could not do, then I surely should be working as a diviner. I told my mother, and other members of my family heard too. I was expecting everyone to share in my joy, but I didn't get the reaction I was hoping for.

My mother understood. It was soon after I told her that she told me about my birth, and how I'd always been different. She understood, but I think she was worried for me. And others in my family thought I was going off my head. The thing is, my brothers and sisters were all in regular jobs. Some of them were thinking I was crazy to give up on construction now that my health was back. The attitude from some was, 'Joe, you're a grand man, but people are going to ridicule you for this.'

I was trying to tell them, 'Look, I have to be who I am.' But I got the feeling that they just didn't want to hear about it. So I stopped talking about it to them. In a way I distanced myself from them, and that was a shame.

I do, of course, discuss my healing with Jean, and with Liam and Laura. Jean, I think, was just happy that I'd found something I could do. We'd been close to desperation. Every time I'd gone back to building work, I'd become very ill again. And here, perhaps, was something I could do that would not compromise my health, that would most likely make me better.

I didn't make a miracle recovery. My legs, particularly my left leg, are not as strong as they might be. If I have to walk a long distance, I still use a walking stick. But as soon as I used my gift, my symptoms began to disappear.

The family's doubt did impact on me, though. I remember feeling I had to prove my gift to myself. One day, I was pulling out of Naas when this car overtook me. I caught a glance at the people in the car. I was heading to Dublin at the time, and I remember saying to myself, 'Those poor devils. That child is sick, and they're on their way to Our Lady's Hospital for Sick Children in Crumlin.' I just knew it. But to check my gift, I tucked in behind that car and stayed behind it until it turned into Crumlin Hospital. I did that for my own peace of mind.

People often ask Jean whether she believes in my sixth sense and my healing, and she says that she didn't set out to believe it. She simply lived it. It was there. A fact. And it's what her life is.

Liam was only five when I started out as a diviner, and he loved the idea. It was harder on Laura. She grew up with me being in and out of hospital a lot, and she worried about that. She told me recently that my illnesses had really hit home when she was eight. In her primary school there was another girl whose father was ill and, like me, was in and out of hospital a lot. The two of them would paint cards in art class for the two of us. Then her friend's father died. Laura realized that sometimes people didn't come home from hospital, and this scared her and made her very protective of me too. When I started doing the divining and healing, I don't think she knew what to make of it, and I probably tried to shield her from it.

When we moved to Two Mile House, I believe there was a reason that we moved into that particular house. It was meant to be. I'd always felt that, but it was a couple of years before I realized why. When I was established as a healer, a man brought his wife along to see me. He asked if he could sit in on the session, and I said that was fine with me. Sometimes people are nervous, and as long as the person being treated is genuinely happy to have someone there, it doesn't worry me one bit. There are occasions, though, when a husband urges me to let him sit in and it later transpires that he didn't want his wife to have a healing. This usually happens if there are problems in the relationship anyway, but this was not the case with this gentleman. When the healing was over and we were chatting, he said, 'You know, it's amazing. I was at this house before.'

'You were? When was this?'

'Ah,' he said, 'it was many years back. I was here with my mother and she's been dead a while. The woman who lived here back then had the cure for the shingles.'

I was really taken aback. 'You're sure it's the same house?'

'Oh, yeah. You've done a lot of work to it, I can see that. The stonework wasn't there before, but it's the same house right enough. I remember the driveway, and that view across the fields. I couldn't believe it when I arrived.' He turned to his wife. 'I said it to you, didn't I?'

That really interested me. I did some research around the area, and right enough, the woman who'd lived there *had* cured shingles. She was now long gone. I'd bought the house from her son. But it was interesting to me. The energy of healing had lingered on. And now, here was I, working as a healer.

PART II

11. The Ancient Art of Divining

Water divining goes back several thousand years; it's been in evidence since ancient times. It was practised by the Greeks, the Romans, the Egyptians and the American Indians, to name just a few, and it is referred to in the Bible when Moses was in the desert. Diviners have also been used during times of war to detect landmines.

In Ireland years ago, nearly everyone knew of a diviner. If you were building a house in a rural area, it was common practice to call the diviner so that he could identify the best location for the house. An elderly woman once told me that when she was a child, the saying went that if you didn't get in the diviner before you built, you would never be without headaches.

In my grandmother's time, dowsing, a form of divining with the use of a pendulum, was commonly used by anyone who kept hens. They did this to determine the sex of a chick in the egg. And before we became reliant on technology, the water diviner could regularly be seen checking for leaking pipes, locating a well, finding buried objects and even searching for gold. There was a time when the diviner was appreciated for all his gifts, particularly by people of the land.

Today, divining is often taught at workshops. I am of the belief that some people can be taught how to divine for water, but the intuitive element that many diviners have cannot be taught. The gift to heal is not common to all diviners.

The art of divining and healing often runs in families. When I first set up, I asked my mother if there had been any healers in the family, going back. She thought hard for a minute.

'Well, there was my uncle of course. This would be your great-uncle.'

'He was a healer?'

'He was. He moved away from Kildare when he was a young man. He settled in Cork. I'm not sure that he healed people, but he had a wonderful way with animals. The local vets would call him if there was a beast down; a cow or a horse. Word got around. People would call on him, and their animals would get better.'

'Was he a water diviner too?'

'I think I heard that he was. But it was the animals he was known for.'

'Were there any other healers – on either side of the family?'

'Not that I heard of.'

I've always had a strong connection with animals, but it's my son, Liam, who now has an interest in healing them.

I use my divining skills to treat houses and buildings that are affected by geopathic stress. The word 'geopathic' comes from two Greek words: *geo* meaning 'of the earth' and *pathos* meaning 'disease'. In my experience, most cases of geopathic stress are caused by the effects of underground water lines, excavation disturbances, or energy ley lines interacting with the electromagnetic fields in houses or buildings. If you build your house over these natural underground water lines, a negative energy may well build up in your house, which can lead to all kinds of problems for the people who live there.

When I'm called out to a house, I bring along my divining

rod and I determine the location and width of the water lines. Then I neutralize them. I do this by earthing the water lines, which is similar to the principle used in acupuncture. I acupuncture the earth by puncturing it with steel bars. I put a bar into the ground, in the middle of a water line I have identified. The bar doesn't divert the water, but it breaks the water at the point of insertion. This diverts the energy of the water downwards away from the house.

When I am divining for geopathic stress, I use a Y-shaped branch, usually from a hazel tree. I hold the two parts of the Y in the palms of my hands and I walk around the perimeter of the house. As I approach the water line, the straight part of the branch will turn upwards towards my chest. The force of the pull on the branch indicates to me the strength of the water line.

These days, obviously, technology is more commonly used than the ancient art of divining. However, as a diviner, I am not convinced that the results are always as accurate. Take one instance, where the most up-to-date technology was used on a plot of farmland to determine if it was suitable for use as a quarry. Someone who worked for the quarry company made me aware that the land was being tested, and I, naturally, took an interest in it. The company had been assured that the land was of the highest quality, and that a good supply of materials could be excavated quite easily.

I purposely went walking across that land one evening with my dogs. I took my divining rod with me and divined the land. And I was not convinced that this land was of the highest quality for excavation. The materials were a lot deeper underground than I had been led to believe. I took a keen interest in the progress of the excavation. It took months for them to reach materials of sufficient quantity and quality. I believe, if they had used a combination of technology and divining, it would have saved them both time and money.

I believe that divining and healing go hand in hand, but a lot of diviners choose not to practise healing. Ireland has a long history of healing, and some people have what is known as 'the cure'. It is well known, for example, that when someone has shingles, warts or perhaps ringworm, they might go to a local person who has the cure. I am often referred to as having the cure, but my gift of healing is far more extensive. I work in all kinds of different areas, and I have worked with people from all walks of life since I started using my gift.

I don't advertise. All my work comes from word of mouth. I would never suggest to someone that they should come to me. I strongly believe that if someone is meant to come to me, they will find me.

My hands-on healing works on energy that is blocked in the body. When I give someone a healing, the general procedure is always the same. I ask them to remove their shoes and their jacket, and to lie back on a plinth. I always play music to relax them. At the moment I tend to play music by the blind singer Geoffrey Gurrumul Yunupingu. Sometimes people become so relaxed that they actually fall asleep. That happens in about 30 per cent of cases.

I always start the healing by placing my hand on the person's forehead. I then go to the top of their chest, to each side of their stomach and then to their feet. After that I'll go back to their head again.

I instinctively know which part of a person needs healing and I am drawn to that area. I always heal with my left hand. My right hand doesn't have the same power. I use my left hand to get a person's energy flowing again, and people tell me that they feel a sensation of heat or tingling.

When I started out I used this procedure instinctively, and it's the same procedure that I use today. I use this procedure for everyone, regardless of what they present with. Healings work with all kinds of conditions, from the physical to the emotional.

12. My First Few Cases

My first official case came to me quite by chance. I was in the bar one night having a pint or two when a friend of mine came in. He asked how I was, and I told him that I was setting up as a water diviner and healer. We carried on talking. I bought a round, and then he mentioned a friend of his who was very ill.

'He's a neighbour of mine,' he said.

'Yeah? What seems to be wrong?' I asked.

'He's not sure. He's been with a local alternative practitioner here in the town, and she has told him his symptoms could be the result of geopathic stress.'

'That's interesting.'

'Do you work with that, Joe?'

I said I did, and that I knew there were a lot of water lines where the man lived.

'Then I'm sure he'd be interested to hear about you. I'll suggest he gives you a call.'

And he *did* call. I checked the house out with my divining rods, and sure enough, there were a lot of water lines underneath the bedroom where the man slept. So I treated the water lines and his health improved enormously. After that, I gave him some hands-on healing to improve his energy. That was a success too. He was happy, and I'd gained some confidence.

The next case I treated was a horse. He had a lump on his neck. The vet wanted to remove the lump, but it was going to cost more to operate on the horse than he was worth. So the owner called me in. I went to the stable yard and met the man. He took me over, opened the stable and we both walked in. He put a head collar on the horse and talked to him with great affection.

'He's a lovely horse, and I worry about him. Every day when I go into the stable to give him his water, his feed and his hay, I like to pat him on the neck. And he has this great big lump. Do you see?'

I did see it. Well, you couldn't miss it.

'That's big all right.'

'It is. And it's growing fast. I feel sorry for the fellow.'

He was a lovely, big, grey, heavy-boned animal. I went down and treated him every morning for a few days. And afterwards, when I'd finished, the man patted the horse as usual when he went in to feed him. And he couldn't believe it. He put his hand on his neck, and the lump was gone.

After that, word spread. It started with one or two people ringing, looking for me, but soon I was working all hours. I didn't advertise. I never have, but people always come. They hear about me from friends or sometimes from professionals. At one stage it got so that I had no time for myself. I was at the healing all day, and that takes a lot of energy. I had to give the same amount of energy to someone I saw in the evening that I'd given to someone in the morning, and that took it out of me. It was extremely tiring.

I designed a clinic area within the walls of the house. It was under the roof at the gable end. It had a treatment area, a waiting room and a bathroom. There was a separate door from the outside, and you couldn't gain access from the house. So that's where I started off. Later, I built a clinic in the grounds, and that's where I practise today.

Now, I'm the first to admit that I'm not a businessman. I'm good with people. I've always had a way with them, but people tell me I'm too easy-going. And when I first started divining and healing, I was doing it for very little money.

One day, I remember, a nun came along for some healing. She was lovely; old and very gentle. She was a traditional nun and wore a habit. The minute I saw her I thought that I wouldn't be looking for any financial gain from this one. It didn't seem right. And when we were finished, she said, 'How much do I owe you?'

'No. You're fine.'

She was still scrabbling in her purse.

'Say a prayer for me,' I said. 'Will you do that?'

'Well, of course I will.' She looked embarrassed. 'But I *have* to give you some money too.'

I looked at her and decided to test her out. The question of money had been worrying me ever since I set up.

'Sister, if you don't mind me asking you, this has been on my mind for a while. What way would you look at a man who claims to be a healer taking money off you?'

She smiled. 'I have no problem with it.'

'Really?'

'The ring on my finger says that I'm married to God. If you think back, God didn't work for nothing.'

'He didn't?' This was news to me.

She shook her head.

'Through Jesus, he walked around and preached. He had food. He had a bed. He had somewhere to sleep. So, maybe he wasn't given money – it was more bartering at that time. But as far as I'm concerned, God got something for what he did.'

Now, I can see that might sound like a contradiction.

86

Because if we go with the Bible, he didn't need anyone to give him bread. With miracles he was able to pull bread down from the sky, so did God ever need anyone to give him anything? But she paid me, and after that, I felt better about taking money.

I'm still not a good businessman. When I worked in the construction business with Pat, he took care of all that side of things. I'd never had to deal with it. And I've never really got the knack of it since. Jean says I've no respect for money, and maybe she has a point. I've got three wallets, but my money is always scrunched up in my pockets.

I charge people, of course, and they pay the rate I ask. But if someone genuinely hasn't access to enough money, I'll charge them what they can afford. When you're in the healing game, not everything is for financial gain. That's the way I see it.

13. Working with Cows

I regularly get phone calls from farmers, and it's not always someone I know. I often hear from farmers I haven't met before, and might never meet. They ring me from all over Ireland: from Cork, from Mayo, from anywhere at all. And it's usually for the one thing. They'll say, 'Listen, Joe. I've a cow down.' This is almost always a cow who has had a calf and hasn't got up again afterwards. My understanding is that if a cow does not get up again within a certain period of time after giving birth, it can lead to her being paralysed. If that happens, the cow has to be destroyed.

I ask the farmer a few questions: What colour is the cow? What breed is it? Where do you live?

I then visualize the cow, and send it healing. And more often than not, the farmer will ring back to say the cow is fine. If he doesn't ring, I don't check. But I hear from the same farmers time and time again. They keep my number. Only last night I had a farmer on the phone. He was saying his cow had got up, and it was the fourth cow I'd got up for him.

I don't ask for payment, though the other month a farmer sent me two fifty-euro notes with a letter saying, 'This is to thank you, Joe, for all the cows that you have got up for me.'

It all started with a cow on a local farm about ten years ago. I kept two horses there, and the farmer, whose name is Jimmy, was telling me about this cow who had calved. The cow was down, and it wasn't looking good.

I went over to the cow and started giving it a healing. It was instinctual. I started with the forehead and then I moved to the cow's hips. When I had finished I put the sign of the cross on each hip. I don't know why. It just came to me. Then I went back to the head again. Jimmy was just standing there, watching.

'What are you doing there, Joe?' He laughed. He knew I was a healer, but he hadn't a clue that I worked with animals. Anyway, he soon stopped laughing. Because no sooner had I finished with the cow than, lo and behold, she slowly but surely got herself up.

'Jesus!' He couldn't believe his eyes. And to be honest, neither could I. I'd no idea I would get a reaction like that.

A week or so later, Jimmy was driving along the road when he came across a neighbour of his, another farmer, who was out for a stroll with his sheepdog.

'How're things?' Jimmy asked.

'Ah.' He shook his head. 'To be honest now, Jimmy, they could be better.'

'What's the problem?'

'I've got a cow down.'

Hearing that, Jimmy said, 'Well, give a call to Joe Cassidy.'

'Who?'

'Joe Cassidy. He got one up for me.'

'What do you mean, he got a cow up for you? Joe's a builder, isn't he? Not a vet.' Jimmy explained to him that I was now a healer, and he said, 'Well sure, it can't do any harm.'

I remember going up there that day. He told me the cow had had a very large bull calf, and that was what had caused the problems. The cow had been down for a few days. That worried me, because the longer a cow is down, the worse the problem can be.

The cow was in a shed. It was a very confined space. We both went in, and before I worked on the cow I started chatting to the farmer. There's nothing I like better than chatting to these farmers. They share my love of animals and of the land. But I was worried by the lack of space.

'Now you watch yourself,' I said. 'I don't want the cow knocking you over.'

'I will.' He chuckled. I think he was a sceptic and I can see where he was coming from. The cow had been down for a few days. He'd been worrying about her, and he must have been thinking, *She's hardly going to be standing in front of me in two minutes.*

Now sometimes it takes a while for a cow to get up. Other times she doesn't get up at all. But this time, the results were dramatic. I'd no sooner put the sign of the cross on her hips when the cow jumped up.

'Look out!'

I hadn't even gone back to her head. I jumped to one side, but the farmer was pushed back a bit as the cow rushed out of this narrow doorway. I'd never seen a cow move like it. It was more like a horse.

The cow ran down the field, and the farmer and I were just standing there, looking at it. The farmer's mouth was open. After a while he started saying, 'Oh Jesus, oh Jesus, oh Jesus.'

'What's wrong with you?' I asked, thinking to myself, *Isn't he pleased the cow is running?*

'If she doesn't stop there'll be trouble.'

'What do you mean?'

'If she doesn't stop she's going to go over. There's no fence down there at the moment.'

'Ah!'

'And the other side there's this great drop into a pit.'

The cow was running hell for leather, and the farmer was trembling with worry.

But then, just like in a children's cartoon, the cow suddenly realized she was coming to the end, and she put the brakes on. She was sliding with her front legs splayed in front of her until she came to a stop. No harm done.

'Well, thank Jesus!'

Then she turned and ran the whole length of the field up to us again, before she stopped and just started to graze. The farmer was speechless. He looked at me, and he looked at the cow. I don't think he could believe what he had witnessed. I will remember that day for evermore.

After that, word spread further and more farmers would ring me. I would go out and see them and I'd treat the cow; more often than not she would get up, though sometimes it took a few days. The problem was that not all the cases were local ones. And after a time of this, I thought, *Hang on a minute, if a man's ringing me from Offaly or from Tipperary, I'm not getting into the car to do a healing on a cow*. Instead, I would ask the colour of the cow and the breed and where the cow was. And I'd say, 'I'll see what I can do.'

It happens still. I will visualize the cow and send healing. And almost always, when a cow is down because it has given birth, the cow will get up again. Sometimes people ring about a cow that is down for other reasons, and in those cases, the healing is not always successful. The healing seems to work better when the cow has given birth.

14. Animal Stories

Early on in my career, I rang *The Gerry Ryan Show* on RTÉ Radio Two. There was a woman on that morning who was worried about her teenage son. He could barely put his feet on the ground because he had very bad verrucas. He had tried everything to get rid of them, from ancient remedies to ointments, and his mother was in despair. She wondered if any of Gerry's listeners would be able to help.

I rang to pass on my number to this woman. I felt healing might help. I spoke to the researcher, and they put Gerry on during an ad break. I emphasized to Gerry that I hadn't rung for financial gain. I said I felt that maybe healing was needed.

'I will drive to the boy at my own expense. I really think I can help.'

'Will you go on air?'

'Oh, I don't know.'

I wasn't keen. But before I knew it, I was on and the interview went well. Gerry wasn't judgemental. Afterwards I worked with the boy. I gave him some healings and they brought him a lot of relief. His mother rang to say he was walking better. Certainly, his life was better.

Another day I was on the radio show *Liveline*, with Joe Duffy. Again it was in response to a caller. She was having problems, and I felt her house needed cleansing. I rang in and said I felt that I could help in the scenario, and once again I found myself on air.

I spoke from the heart that day. I was talking about my

work on houses and how often houses needed cleansing. Joe was challenging. I felt he was trying to test me, to make sure I could back up what I was saying. But the interview went well. I explained the divining and healing work that I did and I was on the line for a long time – ten or maybe twelve minutes. I was conscious of the time because I was due to collect Liam from primary school. I always managed my work around that. Back then, I was one of the few men at the school gates.

It was Daffodil Day. Every year, without fail, I'd give my twenty euro to help with cancer research, and that day I rushed down, leaving a few minutes early so I'd have time to hand in the money at the hall beside the school. When I went in, all these women, who were drinking coffee in there, started clapping and cheering. I couldn't think why.

'We were after listening to you on the radio,' said one. 'You were fabulous!'

It was funny. Of course I'd known I was on air. But it didn't enter my head that the nation was listening. I just spoke without thinking about it.

The next day I was in Baltinglass doing a job, when my phone rang.

'Mr Cassidy?'

'That's me.'

'I'm the researcher on the Joe Duffy show.'

'Oh yeah?'

'Your call yesterday caused quite a stir.'

'Did it now.'

'The phones have been hopping here. Do we have your permission to give callers your phone number?'

I said that was fine, and then it was *my* phone that was hopping. Some days it never stopped ringing. Some people rang about their houses and I met a few of them. I gave distance healing to others. I asked them to send a photo of themselves or of the person who needed the healing. They'd send it with a note, and I'd work on the healing. Most of them enclosed a note asking what the donation was. I never got back to them. I just worked with the photo.

There were others who got a healing just by talking to me about their ailments over the phone. And other listeners of the show, who didn't get in touch, most probably got some comfort simply from hearing the show. They might have felt they now had answers. Because often, healing comes from inside a person. I'd say that radio interview led to quite a number of new clients. Publicity like that certainly spreads the word.

One day I had a call from the late Dr Michael Corry. He was a psychiatrist and psychotherapist who founded the Wellbeing Foundation. He was known to have a holistic approach to mental illness, and he'd written several books. He'd heard me on *The Gerry Ryan Show*. He was interested in what I had to say, and he asked if we could meet up. We met the first time for a cup of coffee, and seemed to hit it off. I remember he gave me his latest book to read. And after that we'd meet on a regular basis. He'd discuss his philosophy on life, and I'd discuss mine. He became a good friend.

One time he asked me to his house near Laragh in County Wicklow. He wanted me to pick up on the energies there. I drove out to the house. To get there you drove along this lovely quiet country road and over a bridge. As I was driving along, a big stag jumped out and narrowly missed the bonnet of my car.

The house, which was an old one, but renovated, was in a beautiful setting. There was a wooded area near the back. It was right in the middle of nowhere. What I really remember is the quiet. All you could hear was the song of birds. I walked round the garden and picked up that years ago, Mass had been held there. It turned out that the house had been built where a Mass rock was.

Michael loved horses. He spent most of his spare time riding them. He owned a couple, and kept them at a yard near his house. He was also involved with fundraising for an animal sanctuary in the area. There was a horse up there who wasn't responding to treatment. It had been abused and wasn't getting any better.

The lady in charge of the sanctuary, Sharon, used a vet who was very open-minded. He used conventional treatments, but he used homeopathy as well. This horse wasn't responding to either, however. It had been wormed, and this had made no difference. They were trying to feed it up, but it was skin and bone and it stayed the same weight no matter what extra nourishment they tried. Sharon was talking about the horse one day, and Michael mentioned me.

'I know a healer who's had some success with animals. Maybe we should give him a shot?'

So he passed on my number and Sharon rang me. I went to see the horse. I'll never forget my first sight of him. He was standing in the middle of the field with his head hanging down. He'd no interest in life. He hadn't a pick on him, and his coat was dull.

'What we have here is a depressed horse,' I said.

'But can you help him?'

'I'd say so.'

Now it so happened that a man from TV 3 was there that day. He was going to be filming at the sanctuary, and Michael and Sharon thought it might be interesting if they filmed a segment of me working with the horse. They brought the guy over to meet me.

'What do you think, Joe?'

'Well, I've no objection,' I said. 'But I don't want to be filmed as a one-off. There's no point in my going in front of the camera with this sick horse and then never going in front of it again. If that happened people would be left hanging. They'd be left wondering how the healer had got on with the horse.'

'Fair enough. So how do you suggest we do it?'

'You can film me working with the horse today. And you can come back in, say, six weeks and film me again. Then you should see some difference.'

I didn't ask them to tell me the history of the horse. All I knew was that it had not been well. So we were standing in the middle of the field, and Sharon was there with me, along with the fellow with the camera. They interviewed the vet first, then they started talking to me.

I put my hand on the horse's head. I picked up that he'd been neglected and that the person who had owned him had fallen on hard times. When this horse was a young foal, it had been left in a bare field with no grazing. Whether this was because the owner had bad health or because he hadn't money, I'm not sure. The foal's mother died of starvation, right there in the field. And that poor foal was left standing over its dead mother for several days before someone noticed and rescued it. I picked all this up by connecting with that horse. I got a feel, from him, of what he went through. No wonder he was depressed. He wasn't the first depressed horse I'd come across.

I went up to the sanctuary once a week for the following six weeks to work on the horse. I was doing hands-on healing. And each week his condition improved. After six weeks, true to his word, the fellow from TV 3 came back, and he filmed the horse again.

When they broadcast the clip, they split the TV screen in two. On one side they showed the horse at the start of the six weeks, and on the other half they showed him at the end of it. It was like looking at two completely different horses. For a start the horse was now in much better condition: it had gained weight and its coat had gained some gloss. But the main change was in the look of the horse. This once depressed horse with its head hanging down was now standing upright. It was looking at the world with pricked-up ears and a bright eye. You could see that this horse wanted to live again.

I did more work up there for a while. I remember one time, when I went into the yard, the farrier was there. I was chatting to him and he said he was crippled with back pain. He asked me if I could do anything for him.

'I'm sure I can, if you want me to,' I replied.

'Well, I don't suppose you'll do me any harm.'

I waited until he'd finished with the horse, then treated him in the tack room. He told me later it had brought him marvellous relief. A few years later I saw that man again when he came to me for another session or two.

I stayed in touch with Michael Corry over the years, and at times he'd recommend that one of his patients get in contact with me. He'd say, 'I think you should ask this healer I know to come to your house. Maybe, if he clears the energy, it could help you.' Generally these would be people who had been labelled as depressed on a long-term basis. And some of the patients did benefit a huge amount from having their house looked at.

There is one woman I remember in particular. I'll call her Paula. She had been a patient of Michael's for a long while, and she was in a bad way. She was so low that she hadn't drawn the curtains back in the house for something like ten years. It was as if she was shutting out the world. She was doing no real socializing.

The day I first went round, I could see Paula had little interest in life. She was an attractive woman, but she had given up on keeping herself looking well. Paula's husband was there that first day. He was a real gentleman. My first reaction was to pity him. I thought, *God love him!* He clearly loved his wife. He seemed very sensitive to her distress, but the sadness in that house was just dreadful.

The story was this: when Paula was younger she had become pregnant and she was put in one of those institutions. She had to give up the baby. At the time she seemed to take that all right. Of course, it would have been kept an absolute secret. She got on with her life. She worked with people with mental-health problems in a large institution. She loved her work and was confident at her job. But perhaps her job was where the problem started.

Paula was going in to work every day, dealing with people who had a low energy. It's possible that because she was walking into this low-energy field, she started to pick up that low energy herself. This does sometimes happen. And as Paula's energy got lower and lower, her sadness from the past started to resurface. Had Paula been in a different career, her trauma might not have resurfaced. Once it *had*, however, she could no longer cope with her job, so she left. But this didn't solve her problem; instead she found she couldn't deal with the knock-on trauma.

The sadness in the house was lingering. I worked on the

energy, but it was a difficult case. Whatever tablets Paula was on – and I think she'd tried many – she was keeping the bad energy in because the curtains were drawn. She had implanted all this bad energy and it wasn't able to escape, so how would she ever get better?

I continued to work on the energy. It was an ongoing process. And one day I gave Paula a hands-on healing in the house. It was such a sad case. I could see through Paula's depression to the wonderful person she had been before she shut down. She was tall, and I could tell she had a beautiful spirit. But you couldn't reach her. I felt so badly for her, and for her husband too.

He kept telling me, 'This person you see is not the person I married. She is the most amazing, glowing woman, but she's broken.'

'I can see that. I'm picking it up from her. Really. You don't have to tell me what a beautiful person she was.'

You could see the love that had been between them. And he, God love him, was heartbroken because his wife had become the person she now was. He was a very positive person, but it wasn't easy for him. He tried endlessly to get Paula to engage with the world. He tried so hard to get her to draw back those curtains, for example, but she never would. She was intent on cutting out the light.

Just imagine what his life was like. He went out to work, but while he was there he was concerned about his wife. He was worried that one day she might take an extra pill. Or a lot of extra pills. When he got home from work, there was his wife with the curtains drawn. He had to make the dinner for them both and for their teenage son. He was doing all the driving, all the shopping; he was doing everything. And to make matters worse, she wasn't connecting with him. So it was a terrible situation for Paula, and it was terrible for him too.

It really didn't help the house's energy that the curtains were all closed. Bad energy lingers on when the world is shut out. In the past, when houses were spring-cleaned, the furniture moved and the whitewash put on, houses were cleared of bad energy. In that house, the energy was stagnant. Natural light makes flowers grow and nourishes us. But if a woman is in a shut-down room, dreaming about the horror of losing her baby, the bad energy has nowhere to go.

One day, after I'd been treating the house, Paula offered me a cup of tea. I accepted and we sat at the kitchen table. I was worried about her, and concerned that I hadn't got to the bottom of her problem. I remember saying this to her. And she said, 'For what it's worth, Mr Cassidy, I'll give you one thing. You have something.'

'And what might that be?'

'I wouldn't sit with any other male — not with anyone except my husband or my son. Yet I'll sit here talking to you.'

'Well, that's true enough!'

'So in that you've achieved something.'

I got up then and walked to the window, deep in thought. There were venetian blinds at the window and I could see out to the back garden. And that's when I saw the dog. It was a white husky-like dog. I'd say it was a cross breed. But it was the nearest thing to a wolf that you could get.

'Is that dog yours?'

'Yes. At least, it really belongs to my son.'

'I haven't seen him before.'

'Well, we keep him out of the way. He can't really be trusted with strangers.'

'You mean he's vicious?'

'Not that. Nervous more like. But he might snap.'

I felt drawn to the dog. 'Do you mind if I go out there and take a look at him?'

She looked hesitant.

'It's OK. I have a way with animals.'

I went out and tried to talk to the dog. He stalked round the edge of the garden, looking at me out of the corner of his eye. I was picking up that this dog, like Paula, had shut down. He was locked in on himself. I reckoned that he was picking up on Paula's energy and on all that sadness in the house.

There was a wildness in that dog. Confinement didn't suit him. While he was being kept in he couldn't properly express himself. But the main problem, I thought, was that he'd taken on Paula's personality. She was in the house, and she'd shut down. And the dog was out the back, and he'd shut down too.

Gradually I won the dog's trust. I connected with his energy, and eventually he let me go over and pet him. But he wouldn't make eye contact. Not at first. It was important, I felt, to persevere though, because it struck me that if I wanted to help Paula get better, I could perhaps help her through the dog.

Finally he made eye contact. I looked at him, and said, 'I know it's not right for you to be confined here. You should be out more, and you should be walked more. You should be allowed to be yourself. But with the energy in this house, nobody can be themselves. Paula can't be; her husband can't be; and you can't be. Your water is being put out for you, you're being fed, but you're not being properly looked after because of the depression. And you're picking up on it.'

I was telling him that I believe in the power of animals.

I was telling him through telepathy. I was saying, 'I have respect for you.' And then I asked him if he would work with Paula.

'The next time you come into her company, don't shy away from her. Instead of that, make some connection. Will you brush against her? Will you lick her ankle? Will you make every effort you can to connect with her?'

The dog began to take some interest in life and he started to make overtures to her. And eventually she started to interact with the dog. It was the first real interaction she'd had for years. The dog became a real part of the family, and gradually Paula began to get better. Then one day, finally, the curtains were drawn back again. And she seemed to come out of her depressive state.

Michael Corry found that case fascinating. And it was. It was the first time ever that I had worked through a dog to help someone heal.

15. Freeing Spirits

When someone asks me to clear the energy from their house, or when they say there is a spirit there, or strange things are happening, I don't ask for details. And if they start to tell me the story around the happenings, I stop them. I don't want to know too much. I prefer to pick up on things for myself.

Thirteen years ago, a woman called Mrs McKenna rang me and said her son wasn't sleeping well. 'He's being disturbed by a spirit,' she said. 'And his room is always cold. It's really strange.'

I tried to say, 'Don't tell me any more,' but it was hard. This woman sounded really distressed. She told me much more than I wanted to know. It was as if she had a need to talk to me. I got a vision of the house, which was in County Carlow. I asked for directions and a brief description of the house, and arranged to visit the following day.

She had told me it had originally been a cottage, but had been converted and was now a good-sized family house. Before I arrived, I had a vision of exactly what the house looked like. It was a sunny spring day, and the house was welcoming. There were tubs of geraniums on a windowsill, and potted trees either side of the door.

I rang the bell. 'Mrs McKenna?'

'Call me Jane.' She was an attractive woman, but her smile was tight. She seemed agitated as she led me through the narrow hall to the kitchen, where her husband sat reading the *Irish Independent*.

'Mr Cassidy.' He extended his hand. 'I'm James. I hope you can help us. It's our son's room. It's always cold in there.'

'But there's more to it than that,' Jane said. She looked really worried. 'He swears he sees someone at night-time. He says someone tries to take his duvet off the bed. He says it's a little girl.'

'I really don't believe in ghosts,' said James. 'I never have. But this has been going on a while. I'm starting to think there may be something in it.'

'There has to be,' Jane said. 'The whole house has an atmosphere. But Jake's room is the worst.'

She would have talked on, but I decided to check round the house and see what I could find. The young boy wasn't there that day. He was at school. I asked the couple to show me round and then, I told them, I'd wander around on my own.

First I walked around outside, checking for water lines. As I walked to the side of the house, I saw these old sheds. I remember thinking they looked out of character. And then I looked again, and the sheds weren't there any more. In their place was a spanking new extension. I was startled. I wondered what was going on here. I was puzzling over this as I walked back into the house.

I will never forget walking into the boy's bedroom. It was a typical boy's room. There were posters of Manchester United footballers, and football boots left abandoned on the floor. But there, in the left-hand corner, I saw a young girl with long fair hair. It was the clearest spirit I have ever seen. I would have taken her for a living girl, except that she was floating. Her feet weren't touching the floor, nor her head the ceiling. It was so clear that it took my breath away.

Now, spirits don't talk to me the way a living person would.

But they do communicate. It's done through telepathy. And this girl was keen to tell me her story.

Her parents had got married late; her mother was in her late thirties and her father older still. She had been their only child. They were simple people, but they were happy. And they adored their small daughter.

She had died when she was still a small child, and her parents were heartbroken. She said they'd never got over their loss, and the experience had changed them. She said the energy from their loss lingered on.

Then she told me something that sent a tingle down my spine. Her father kept goats in a shed. She loved those goats, and one of her happiest memories was going out with her father to mix their feed and check their water. All the goats had names.

One day, though, she saw her father killing one of the goats. She couldn't believe that her good, kind father could do such a thing. It seemed so out of character. Now, the girl wouldn't have known it, but keeping goats to use as food was a common farming practice years ago. Goats were reared to be eaten. I don't know if her father tried to explain this, but the whole episode had made her think less of him. *Why*, she thought, *would someone who was so good with animals, who cared for them so well, then turn round and kill them?* This memory had lingered with her, and gone with her to the grave.

When she described the old sheds I realized I'd had a glimpse of the girl's world. The sheds weren't there now, but they had been there when she was a child.

When the McKennas had bought the house, it was in quite a dilapidated state. They had renovated it, and had also built an extension. It looked wonderful. But the extension had been built on the site of the goat sheds. That was why the atmosphere in the house was still bad.

The girl had died eighty-four years earlier. The renovation had disturbed her spirit, and she was no longer at peace. She felt unable to move on. That's why she had appeared to the young boy. She wanted the energy in the house worked on. Then she would be at peace.

I looked round the rest of the house and, although the atmosphere was a little stagnant, especially in the rooms that had not been renovated, I didn't find anything else of significance.

I joined James and Jane back in the kitchen, and I told them what I had seen.

'Tell me this though,' said Jane. 'We've lived in this house for five years now. It was peaceful for the first four. Why would a spirit not make her presence felt until now?'

I explained that it's not until walls start to come down that spirits appear.

'Before that the energy is stagnant,' I explained.

'OK. And another question: why can Jake see her spirit, when we can't?'

I explained that children are better at picking up on these things, that they're more open. 'And he's about the same age as that little girl was when she died. That would give him a closer connection.'

I worked on the house then. First I earthed the water lines, because, as I expected, there was geopathic stress. There almost always is when there is spirit activity. Then I worked on the energy. They thanked me profusely.

'Just one thing,' I said. 'Don't go telling all the neighbours about this. There are a lot of sceptics around. You'll only be opening yourself up for ridicule. They'll think you're mad.'

'So, Joe Cassidy, you're telling us that people think you're mad?'

I laughed. 'Some do, yes. But I'm used to it now. I grew up with it and have worked with it. And I believe your young boy. I think he was seeing what he told you he was seeing. But if you spread word around, people will stop sending their children here to play.'

'And we'll be known in the area for living in a haunted house.' Jane shuddered.

'Exactly,' I said. 'And that could come into the equation when you try to sell it. For what it's worth, I do believe you've seen the last of that young spirit.'

Normally it takes a while for a house healing to work. People might sense a slight lifting of the atmosphere straight away, but it can be a week or so before they really notice the difference. But Jane McKenna rang me just two days later.

'I was coming back from shopping yesterday,' she said. 'My mind was everywhere. I was struggling with my keys and my bags, and you, Mr Cassidy, were the last person on my mind.' She laughed. 'I mean, I wasn't thinking about all the problems we've had with this house. I was just concentrating on getting the shopping in and getting it packed away. But the minute I got through the front door …'

'Yes?'

'I mean, before I even got as far as the kitchen, I noticed it. The whole feeling in the house had changed. It was different.'

'Better?'

'Oh yes!'

'And the lad?'

'Jake slept through last night. And the room has lost that chill. He looked so good this morning. Really rested. I can't thank you enough.'

That wasn't the end of the story. Not quite. I felt that the McKennas might soon learn more about that girl spirit.

'I feel you will hear facts which back up all that I have told you. I feel you'll know it's the truth.'

A number of weeks passed and this time it was James McKenna who rang me.

'You won't believe this, Joe.'

'What?'

'Things have been great here, thank God. Not a sign of that spirit. But we were unexpectedly invited to a christening last weekend. Some neighbours had invited us. And, don't worry, we weren't regaling them all with spooky stories. But I was introduced to this old gentleman. He was a lovely man but very old, one of the oldest men living in the area, and I got chatting to him. He said, "You live in that house down by the crossroads, don't you? The one old Mrs O'Connor used to own?" I said we did and he said, "I don't remember myself, but I often heard my parents talking about that house. There was a couple living there and they had one daughter, and she died." I asked him when that would have been, and he said, "Ask the priest. He'll know."'

So one thing led to another. The McKennas came clean to the priest and said they'd had a diviner in the house and told him what I'd said. The priest checked his records and he told the McKennas that I was spot on. The girl had died the exact year that I had said.

When I'm asked to a house some distance away, I'll occasionally stay overnight. More often, though, I'll make a day of it. Sometimes we'll make it an outing, and Jean will come too. We'll share the driving. There have been times when the whole family has come along, especially when the children were younger.

We enjoy an outing. We always have. I was brought up to love them, the Sunday drive. My father *loved* to go off on a Sunday, to somewhere not too far away. We'd all be thrown into the back of the van and often went to the hills around Wicklow. Glendalough, in particular, was my father's paradise.

So when, one day, a woman called Jennifer Byrne rang me from Mayo and asked me to check her house out for spirits, I agreed that I would. She was having problems with her daughter, who said a spirit was keeping her awake at night. I got the distinct impression that the woman felt there was more to it and that her daughter was perhaps being bullied, or that she was stressed for other reasons, and it was the stress that made her see these things.

The girl suffered from asthma, and this had been particularly bad in recent months. Jennifer worried that her daughter wasn't getting the sleep she needed, and when she heard about me through a friend, she decided it would be worth a try.

We arrived in good time. Jean dropped me at the front door and said she'd go and find the nearest coffee shop so that she could sit down and read her book. Jean is a great one for reading. She always has a book on the go. Jennifer's husband answered the door. He was friendly, but perhaps not as open as his wife.

I spoke to the couple for a while. When they mentioned the asthma I thought that perhaps the house had geopathic stress. Then I met their daughter. I asked her what she saw.

'This spirit comes and wakes me,' she said.

'What does she say?'

'She tells me my bedroom's not good for me. She says I shouldn't be sleeping there.'

Her father looked uncomfortable. 'When she first started saying that, we thought it was an excuse for her to keep coming down to the sitting room,' he said.

I felt sorry for the child. For a while nobody had believed her. Her mother began to listen to her first, but her father found the situation hard to talk about. I can understand that. It's hard for a father. All he wants is to protect his child. He can normally fix things for her, and in this situation he felt powerless.

'It's OK.' I smiled at him and put my hand on the girl's shoulder. 'I believe you. Tell me, does this spirit scare you?'

'No,' she said, and grinned. 'But she gets me into terrible trouble!'

I laughed. 'Then I'd better have a word with her, hadn't I? Let me check out the house and your room in particular, and see what I come up with.'

So I took myself around the house. I checked for geopathic stress and, though there was some, I didn't feel it was significant. I believed the girl. I saw no reason why she would make it up. I spent a long time in her room, and though I felt there might be a spirit presence, it didn't make itself known to me and I couldn't understand why it would keep disturbing the child.

I was baffled. So I went outside and sat down on this big pile of granite for a cigarette and a think. Work had been done recently on the house, and this granite had been left there by the builders. It was directly underneath the young girl's bedroom window.

As I sat there, I was saying to the universe, 'What's the problem here? I've come a long way, and I don't want to go home without solving this.'

And this spirit came to me, and said, through telepathy, 'You're sitting on the problem.'

I jumped up. 'What?'

'The granite is the problem. I'm trying to warn that little girl not to sleep close to it.'

I was astonished. I went back in to the family, and we sat round the kitchen table.

'You know that pile of granite?'

'Oh yeah. We've been meaning to move that for ages.'

'Well, you will need to move it now. Or at least as soon as you can get the manpower.'

'Why?'

'I believe the spirit was warning your daughter that the properties in the granite could harm her. If you move it, I believe your problems will be over.'

I remember the sense of relief the family felt when I explained about the granite. The father seemed keen to make it up to me. He wasn't a demonstrative man, he wasn't the type to throw his arms round me; but you knew by his whole demeanour, from the look in his eyes, that he was really grateful.

They insisted that I had some lunch with them, and as we ate, I explained, as best I could, what I knew of the spirit world. In my business you have to be careful how you give people news. Some healers can be very dramatic, and that can frighten people. I'm very conscious that what I do in my work is not part of normal life. And even though a problem exists, when you're dealing with a child, and with her dad, it's important to put them at their ease.

I told the child, 'This spirit isn't something to be feared. This is like your guardian angel, trying to protect you.' That made the child happy, and her dad too. He was relieved that he hadn't a poltergeist, or anything else that was wishing them harm.

'Thank you!' said Jennifer, and there were tears in her eyes. As for the little girl, she just grinned. From looking pale with worry, she now seemed carefree. She ran off to play.

The message from the spirit was so clear on this occasion that I was very confident in telling the family that they wouldn't be bothered by the spirit any more. And when Jean called back for me, they asked her in for a cup of tea.

I like it when the personal combines with the professional. I remember them talking to Jean and asking her what it was like being married to a healer. And she told them. She said that sometimes it was amazing, and that she could get a healing whenever she needed one, but that being married to me didn't always make for the easiest life.

'Joe knows what I mean,' she said, laughing. And indeed I did.

I *do* know it's hard for Jean sometimes. People often turn up at our door without an appointment – sometimes when we're in the middle of dinner – and if they've driven a long way, I don't feel I can turn them away. And if the washing machine breaks down, and the engineer comes to fix it, you can almost guarantee he will have a child who needs healing, or a dog maybe. It's my life. I'm used to it, but it gets a bit much for Jean sometimes. We don't have our private space.

I had set my fee with the Byrnes on the telephone, and they were more than happy to pay it. Amazingly, though, Jennifer offered us something more. When we'd finished our tea she said, 'Come on now. I want to show you around the town.' Now in truth, that's the last thing we wanted. Our aim was to get into the car and get back onto the road. We didn't want to arrive home too late. But there was no refusing

Jennifer Byrne. So we followed her down, and she brought us to a woollen mill. She told us to look round, and after we had done so she handed me a voucher. I looked at it and felt it was for far too much.

'Take it,' she said. 'It's because I appreciate so much what you have done for my family. And it's not just sorting the problem. It's the way you believed my daughter and spoke to her, and made her feel that what she saw and heard was valid. That, for me and my husband, was as valuable as anything else.'

Thanks to her, before I left that town I was fitted out with a new jacket and a new pair of trousers.

She rang me a couple of weeks later. She said they had moved the granite, and her daughter was now sleeping peacefully all and every night. And they never saw that spirit again.

While there are a lot of sceptics in the world, people who categorically don't believe spirit activity exists, there are others who are all too ready to believe it. Over the years there have been times when I've been called to a house, and a spirit isn't there. These people, and I have to say they've always been women, want to believe a spirit is there. They convince themselves of it, and then they call me.

I blame those programmes on television that are based in haunted houses. If someone stays up half the night watching a programme like that, they want to believe that the same thing is playing out in their house. It doesn't happen often – it's occurred maybe six times in my career – but it is an aspect of my job I am both aware and wary of.

16. Healing Houses

I never advertise. And I never suggest to people that they should see me. I feel that when people come to me, it is meant to be. They hear about me in all kinds of ways. One day I was called out to work on a house by an old lady. I'll call her Mrs Kelly.

She hadn't told me any details on the phone, just that she wanted the house worked on; but when I arrived I noticed she had terrible arthritis. Her fingers, in particular, looked very stiff. She offered me some coffee, but had to ask me to open the jar for her.

'I've tried everything for this wretched arthritis,' she said. 'I'm seeing a herbalist for it right now. In fact, he was the one who suggested that I call you. He feels the problem might be the house and that maybe a diviner could help.'

It was a lovely house. It wasn't modern. I'd say it hadn't had much done to it since the 1950s, but it was cosy and had a lot of knick-knacks around. And Mrs Kelly was a really lovely woman. The problem, I felt, was geopathic stress. I was about to check the house when this old man came through the back door from the garden.

'Tom, this is Joe Cassidy,' said Mrs Kelly. 'Remember, I told you he was coming?'

He didn't look too pleased to see me. He didn't shake my hand, but to be fair, he couldn't, because his hands were covered in soil, and he went to wash them at the sink. Glancing over his shoulder at me, he said, 'My wife asked you here. But really, what can you do that all the doctors and practitioners can't?'

I began to explain about geopathic stress and the effect it can have on people, but I was wasting my breath. He went back out to the garden.

I checked the house and, sure enough, the geopathic stress was quite bad. There were a good number of water lines, and the worst thing was that they were crossing over each other. This can cause a very negative atmosphere. But I did feel I'd be able to help, and I told Mrs Kelly so.

I remember it was a beautiful summer's day, and I was whistling while I worked. The garden was lovely and very well kept. There was a frame with climbing roses and there wasn't a weed in sight. Meanwhile, Mr Kelly was working around me in stony silence. He was clearly a keen gardener, but it didn't seem to be making him very happy. He was trying his best, it seemed to me, to make me feel uncomfortable.

After a while he decided to make his presence felt: every time I went to work on a patch of land, I found myself blocked by his wheelbarrow. It always seemed to be in the way. Now, I'm a patient man, but there was only so much of this that I could take. So after half an hour of this, I said, 'Have you a problem with me being here?'

He scowled. And the next thing, I saw Mrs Kelly looking out of the kitchen window. A minute later she was in the garden asking if there was a problem. Her husband didn't answer. He just concentrated on heaping manure onto a flower bed, his back to me.

'Look,' I said to her, 'with all due respect, you contacted me, and you asked me to come and survey the house.'

'Yes. I did.'

'Well, I feel there is a problem here. This man, your husband, is obviously living here with you, and he's making my life very awkward. Tell me, do I work here, when he so obviously doesn't want me to, or shall I leave and will you think about it? Because I have to carry out this work if I'm to sort out the problem.'

Mrs Kelly turned to her husband. 'Tom?'

He sighed. 'Well, explain a bit about what you're doing.'

So I explained. And he said, 'But I haven't got arthritis.'

People find it difficult to understand, but you can get all kinds of illnesses and conditions with geopathic stress, and it can also affect your mood. The contrary display he was showing me could well have been his way of suffering. Still, it was his house, his garden; I didn't want to be telling him what to do. They had reared their family there and had lived there for years. I said, in as gentle a way as I could, 'Maybe you've been affected in another way.'

He grunted, and didn't otherwise comment. Then he said, 'Well, I suppose you had better carry on then.'

So I did, and he stayed out of my way. But he still didn't seem too happy to have me there.

A few weeks passed, and the phone rang. It was this same gentleman, Mr Kelly. He said, 'Mr Cassidy?'

'Yes.'

'Herself,' he said, 'she's not in as much pain as before.'

'That's good.' I paused, then risked saying, 'How about you?'

'What do you mean?'

'Have you noticed any difference? I know you told me you weren't suffering from arthritis.'

'That's one of the reasons I'm ringing you.'

'Oh?'

'I don't have arthritis. But I feel maybe the geo whatsit ...'

'Geopathic?'

'Yes, the geopathic stress. Maybe that *has* been affecting me.'

'You think so?'

'Yes. I've been rearing my family, but I've been contrary. One of my sons ...'

'Yes?'

'I've fallen out with him. That is, I fell out with him years ago. And we never really patched it up. He lives abroad now.'

'That's a shame.'

'It is.'

I wondered where this was going.

'I feel I've been happier since you treated the house.'

A few weeks after this, his son came home on a trip. He and his father were able to sit down and have a good old chat, and he apologized to his son for the way he had been. They seemed to be back on speaking terms.

I thought that story was interesting. We had a man who had been awkward. He'd been awkward since shortly after he moved into the house. He was awkward with me. I was asked to that house because the lady wanted me there for her arthritis, but maybe the reason she was suffering was linked to her husband in some way. She'd been living with this man for thirty-seven years, and he was never easy.

Not everyone is affected by geopathic stress, and it can affect you at different times. Say you'd lived in an affected house for twenty-six years and you were fine. Then you went to hospital for an operation, and when you went back to the house your system was a bit low. That's when the geopathic stress can kick in.

I would say that Mr Kelly's contrariness did not help the way Mrs Kelly was feeling. And while she wasn't magically cured, seeing her husband change over the few weeks and openly admit that there might be something to this certainly helped her. She got relief from the pain, and relief from seeing her husband become happier in himself and make up with their son.

Some people know they are ill, but don't really want to admit it. My friend Anne's uncle was a case in point. A bachelor with a passion for horse racing and football, he was loved around the area. One winter a neighbour rang Anne and asked her if the old man was all right. He hadn't been seen out and about. When Anne had visited him recently, he'd said he was fine, but she wondered if perhaps something had been not quite right after all.

Anne went to visit him, and at first she thought all was well. He was wearing a big heavy overcoat though, and he seemed reluctant to take it off, even though the day was mild. Anne couldn't understand why. She worried about him, but when she suggested he see a doctor, he insisted there was nothing wrong with him.

A few weeks later, the old man collapsed and was brought into hospital. He had tests, and it was discovered that he had bowel cancer. He didn't seem at all surprised. Anne felt he'd known what he had all along, and had probably thought, *Sure, it's going to kill me anyway.* She realized that he'd worn that coat to hide all the weight he had lost.

Now the sad thing was that if he had gone to a doctor in good time, something could have been done about it; he could have been treated and cured. Now, though, it was too late. The doctor gave him a year. Anne nursed him through his illness, and eventually he died.

After his death, Anne was in charge of his estate and she

put the house on the market. This was at the height of the housing boom, and the estate agents expected it to sell immediately. But for some reason, it hung around. There was no lack of potential buyers. Lots of people went to view it and they seemed to love the house.

It went to auction and several people were interested in it. It was on a main street and would have made a good commercial property. It sold for a good price there, but then the buyers pulled out. It went on the market again, and one of the buyers who had been outbid at the auction put in a good offer. It was accepted and they put down a deposit. But again, for no apparent reason, they pulled out after a few weeks. This happened several times, and it was frustrating for Anne.

She asked me to check the house for negative energy. I didn't find geopathic stress, and although I did get a sense of the old man who had lived there, I didn't find a reason for the house not selling. I was puzzled.

Then one morning I woke up and I had been dreaming about that house. The dream was telling me that there was money hidden in the house, and that the man who had died wanted Anne to have this money. This was what I felt was delaying the sale of the house.

I told Anne this, and she asked me where the money was hidden. I told her that it was in the attic.

'That can't be right. We cleared out the attic before the auction,' she said. 'There was a load of junk up there, but now it's completely empty.'

'Could you take me to the house again?' I asked her.

'I could, but I'm telling you, it's empty.'

We went up to the house the next morning. She showed me the attic. It was above a back kitchen that the man had built onto the house. I clambered up and had a good look around, but Anne was right. There was nothing there at all.

'I told you.'

'Do you mind if I have a look round the house again?' I asked.

'Be my guest.'

I went up the stairs and looked around. And over in the corner of one of the bedrooms I saw a little trapdoor going into another attic.

'Can I have a look up here?'

'There isn't even room to get up there,' she said. 'It's a tiny space.' But she went to fetch a stepladder, put it up and climbed it. It was a tiny trapdoor. I wouldn't have been able to get my shoulders through, but she managed it. She found a painting, and handed that to me.

'Look for a tin now,' I said. Because in my dream there had been a picture and a biscuit tin. And sure enough she found one. She opened the tin and, lo and behold, there were big piles of banknotes inside, secured with rubber bands. She was amazed – especially when she counted the money and found eight thousand euro.

'Wow! Thank you, Joe,' she said. Then she offered me the picture.

In truth, I didn't really want it. It was of a Roman emperor, not really the kind of thing you would want on your wall, but I thanked her. I didn't say it to her, but I thought, *That's going into the bin tomorrow.*

Later that day I had it propped up in the hall, ready to put out. Jean and I were having our tea, and the next thing there was this almighty crash. We went out to see what had happened. It was very strange: the picture was still leaning against the wall, but there was glass all over the floor.

It was when I was putting the picture in the bin that I noticed there was another picture underneath it. It was a print of Dante and Beatrice on the Santa Trinita Bridge in Florence. It was a print, but probably quite an early one. I love that picture. It's still on my wall today.

17. Healing Land

Sometimes, when people call me in for one problem, I end up working on more than the one. That was the case with Shane Murphy. He'd bought some land, about twelve acres, in a lovely situation. Now he was a young man in his twenties when I met him. He worked hard and saved all he could. He wasn't a drinker or a smoker. He'd set his heart on building the house of his dreams for himself and his partner. It was to be a family house for when children came along. But he'd been turned down for planning permission because of a water issue. So when he rang me, it was because he knew I was a water diviner.

I walked the land with him and asked why he'd been turned down. He took me to an area where some holes had been dug to check the land was suitable for a septic tank. It needed to be good for percolation, but the holes were full of water.

'Can you help?'

'I'll have a look and let you know.'

'Fair enough.' He sighed. 'This land has brought me nothing but trouble from the minute I bought it, so I could do with a bit of good news.'

'What do you mean?'

'Nothing's gone right. When I started fencing it, I had problems getting the posts in.'

'Tell me, what happened?'

'Well, the machine I use to make the holes kept breaking. And the strange thing was, when I took it in to get it repaired the guys told me there wasn't a thing wrong with it.'

'That's strange.'

'It was. And then I broke a sledgehammer trying to get the posts in place. No, a correction: I broke two sledgehammers.'

'That's not good.'

'And then there were the dogs.'

'What about them?'

'You know I breed them? Normally it's straightforward enough, but I've had a spate of problems there too. The bitches have been aborting pups. I tell you, it's heartbreaking. If there is bad luck to be had, you can be sure I am having it.'

As I had a good look round, I realized the land needed more than just water divining. It needed healing too, and I believed that a greater source wanted the land healed. I picked up on the history of the land and I had a vision that there had been a feud over it – or certainly some family trouble. *This is going to be a long job*, I thought. I would have to work on it continuously for a few weeks.

When I felt the land was healed I asked Shane to have two more test holes dug, and to dig them close to where the other holes had been. He looked at me as if I had two heads.

'Sure, why would I be doing that? Haven't they already turned me down? Isn't that just throwing good money after bad?'

'You're not listening,' I said. 'Dig the test holes.'

He agreed to, but he went away scratching his head. I didn't hear from him for a week or two. When he did ring me he sounded in the best of spirits.

'Joe Cassidy,' he said. 'I don't know what you did. And when you told me to dig more holes, I have to admit, I was convinced I was wasting my time. You'll never believe it.'

'What won't I believe?'

'I had those holes dug like you said, and I waited the

allotted time to allow for rain and seepage. Then I contacted the man from the council and, would you believe, the same representative came again. You know, the one who had turned me down.'

'Right.'

'And he's standing over these two new holes, and there's not a drop of water in either of them. Not a drop.'

'That's good then.'

'It is. This man agreed that I can now build my house and have my septic tank. He's saying the percolation is suitable, and this is the same man that refused me the last time he was there because in his professional opinion it wasn't suitable. And now, in his professional opinion, it is. What do you make of that?'

I laughed. 'I'm used to that kind of thing. My life is not about logic.'

And it made that man very happy. He built his dream house and, as far as I know, he lives there with his family still.

If the land owned by Shane Murphy had a troubled history, it was nothing to what I found one day in Kilkenny. A lady rang one winter's day saying that the cottage her daughter was renovating seemed to be haunted. A family uncle had lived there, and something odd appeared to be going on.

They were doing some tiling. If they put the tools down and went back out for something, some tools would go missing. They felt sure this was the uncle playing tricks on them. He'd been a real joker when he was alive. They'd just sigh, and go, 'Oh, it's just himself.' It wasn't frightening. But the longer it went on, the more irritating and disturbing it got. They began to wish he wouldn't make his presence felt.

The daughter was at work the day I went to the cottage.

Her father, Ben, let me in, and I looked around. Sure enough, this spirit was making his presence felt, but I could tell there was more to this one. I felt the spirit wanted me to explore the land. I was about to say this to Ben, but he beat me to it.

'I'd like to show you around the fields,' he said. 'I'd be interested to know what you pick up and if it has anything to do with the history of the area.'

I found this strange. I'd been asked to come about the cottage, but that seemed to be the last thing on this man's mind; Ben seemed much more interested in the land. It was almost as if I was on trial. But I walked around the land with him. First he took me across a field to an area where there were ditches and some grassland, with a lot of trees nearby.

'There was something here, in the past,' I said, though there was no sign of any buildings.

'What are you picking up?'

'I think some kind of business was run here. Would I be right?'

'You would. There was a sawmill. It closed down in the twenties or thirties I believe.'

Next he walked me across another field. It was a wonderful day for a walk. The frost lingered on the fields and made lacy patterns in the hedgerows. But I wasn't there to enjoy myself. At the edge of the field, I felt the presence of another spirit. I stopped dead in my tracks. Ben turned and looked at me.

'Well? What are you picking up here?'

I felt uneasy. I was sure that Ben knew something sinister about this land, but I realized it was a sensitive subject.

'What's this about?' I asked him.

'What?' he said, looking distracted.

'Well, I'm getting that there's a lot of sadness here about a young person.'

Ben nodded, but he didn't make any comment.

'Am I right in thinking that someone has been killed in this area?'

'You are.'

'And it was a violent death?'

'That's what I heard.'

'You've heard stories?'

He said he had, and that the stories dated back to the time of the Black and Tans. The locals had heard that the Black and Tans were in the area one night checking up on people, and a few of the young lads decided to lay an ambush. The story was that they felled a tree somewhere near the sawmill, and when the Black and Tans stopped, they jumped on them. Most had got away, but they had caught this one Black and Tan and killed him.

They were, of course, worried that they'd be found out. They knew the man's disappearance would be reported straight away. So they took his body to the sawmill, where they cut it up and put it in sacks. They hid those sacks in the sawmill until they felt it was safe enough to bury them. At the time the local police were out in the area, but they could find no trace of the man. And nobody spoke out about it, though many of the locals must have known.

I know that terrible atrocities were carried out on both sides in that black time of Ireland's history, but it made me so sad. There I was standing in the place where this man had been killed, a man who had had a horrific death. He was dead and gone, and most of the people who loved him were probably dead and gone too. And they never knew what happened to him. Nobody had been able to properly mourn his death.

He'd never had a funeral. And Ben just wanted, in some way, to check that the story was true. I said a few prayers for the man and for those who must once have mourned him. I felt someone should recognize that a horrific crime had been committed here.

It had nothing to do with Ben, but it did have something to do with the generations who came before him. In rural Ireland it wasn't done to squeal, and when it came to the Black and Tans, the locals would be sure to support each other. The story had been handed from generation to generation. It was part of history, but it remained a local secret. The story never got out to the wider world. Ben knew the story, and he'd wanted to have it confirmed.

As for the uncle, I felt that he *was* involved in some way. Maybe he was directly involved, or perhaps he knew the lads who killed the man. I thought it was likely he felt guilty that he had never told the authorities, and now he was dead he wanted to make sure that this was put right. This was why his spirit was uneasy.

'I think he wants that young man's death marked,' I said to Ben. 'I think, then, his spirit will be at peace.'

'How can I do that?'

'Perhaps you could plant a tree in his honour.'

'Would that stop all the trouble at the house?'

'I'd say so.'

'Then that's what I'll do.'

He was true to his word, and his daughter was no longer bothered by the spirit of the old man.

18. More Land Stories

In the height of the boom, a syndicate of wealthy people bought a stud farm, with the aim of turning it into a state-of-the-art equestrian centre. They were hoping it would attract high-end foreign tourists. They had put a few million into the scheme and were planning to build some exclusive houses on the land too. Anyone who bought a house would have automatic use of the facilities.

They bought some valuable horses, but when they put the horses into the main field beside the avenue, they refused to graze. Not only that, they wouldn't settle. Those horses were going hysterical. They tried to jump out of the field and break through the fence. One or two of them had cut themselves. It had now reached the point where the best field in the place couldn't be used at all.

One of the syndicate rang to ask if I was a diviner, and I said that yes, I was.

'I don't know, but I think there might be a way that you can help us,' he said. He told me what had happened, and I said I'd have to call in.

So off I went to meet the whole syndicate. I remember distinctly that one of the men who met me was a complete and total sceptic. It's difficult dealing with a group of people who have different opinions. The man who rang me was a gentleman, and he explained the problem with the land. But this other man clearly didn't want me there, and felt that there had to be a logical reason why the horses were behaving the way they were. He never met my eye.

These men were running a business. At that moment they had money, or easy access to it. It was the time of the Celtic Tiger. I was running a business too, and I could have made a lot of money here, but I had still not developed my business sense. If I had been a businessman I would have said, 'I can fix this for you. I know that some of you don't believe I can. I will, but it's going to take time and have a price.' Or I might have asked how much the land was worth to them, named a high price and told them to take it or leave it. Instead of that, I said, 'Go to your meeting room, and I guarantee you will be able to bring any horse out when I'm finished. And he'll graze this field.'

I worked on the land. I tapped into its history. A famous battle had been fought many years ago in that area, which lies between two archaeologically important sites in the county, and I was picking up that a lot of men had died in that very field. Even though this had happened many years ago, the negative energy lingered on. Men were killed, and where they were killed they were buried. I listened to the story of the land. I got a vision of it, and I felt the roar of the battlefield and the pain of the men who were buried in the ground below me.

Horses are very sensitive animals. I got the feeling that horses hadn't grazed on that land for a number of years before the lads bought it. But I don't know for sure. It might have been the case that other animals grazed there, but failed to thrive. All I know for certain is that at the time the lads bought the land, no horse would graze in that field.

I cleared the energy from the field. I found a spot that I felt was especially vulnerable, and to my amazement, the universe was telling me that to solve this problem I had to eat a bit of the soil from the land. I had never done anything like that before, and I will probably never do it again, but I took the story through my body.

When I'd finished my work, I went up to the stable yard and called the men out.

The sceptic said, 'Well, what do you think?' There was a challenge in his eyes.

I stared at him and said, 'I know you think this is the biggest bit of codswallop ever, but with all due respect I've been asked here. You could have said you didn't want me to come. I've been asked to do a job, and I've done it.'

'What have you done?'

'Get a horse,' I said, 'and put it on the land. You can bring any horse out there. Bring the wildest horse in the yard. It's fine.'

So they brought a horse down and they all came to watch. As they opened the gate, I felt the sceptic's eyes on my back. I felt he was willing me to fail.

The horse walked in through the gate. It looked around, walked gently towards some luscious-looking grass and started to graze.

'That's amazing!' The gentleman who'd rung me shook my hand warmly. 'Thank you, Joe.'

As for the sceptic, he looked flabbergasted but he didn't say anything. I've seen very few sceptics relent when they are proved wrong. I think the ego gets in the way. He just walked away and was the first back up to the office. He probably went straight onto his computer to make some more money.

Sometimes people ring me on behalf of someone else. They say, 'I really think this friend of mine should see you. Could

I arrange an appointment for them, please?' And I explain that it's much better if the person rings me themselves.

This happened with Larry, a farmer from Longford, some years ago. His wife rang me first and I told her, 'Fine. But get him to ring me, will you?' And when he *did* ring, he sounded hesitant. I sensed a reluctance on his part. He didn't seem keen to talk, and this reluctance continued when we met.

When Larry walked through my door, I got the impression that he was an old man. He looked as if he was about seventy. He was a lovely man, but one of very few words, and he was very unwell. He'd lost weight and was complaining of stomach trouble; he said he wasn't eating too well. I gave him a healing, but I felt there was something he wasn't telling me. I couldn't get him to open up.

I suggested that perhaps his farm was getting him down. I said, 'I feel your land comes into this. I think maybe I should take a look at it.'

But he didn't want to discuss it. He said that he wanted to come for another healing, so I made another appointment for him. But Larry stayed on my mind. He puzzled me.

Seven nights later, Larry was due to come again. And when at six o'clock he walked through the door, I thought, *Who's this? Do I have someone else booked in?* I looked again and it was Larry, but he looked so much younger. I can safely say he looked twenty years younger than he had the week before, and during the healing he told me that he was around fifty.

The healing had had a dramatic effect on him. His stomach was now fine and he felt well again. He told me he had met people who had said, 'Jesus, but you look well. I was really worried about you.' And this change had occurred in only seven days.

I gave Larry a second healing, but I was still concerned

that his problem came from his land. This is what I was picking up. So I said, 'To get to the bottom of this, you know and I know that I have to work on your land.'

He looked at me. Then he looked away and said quietly, 'Yeah, it's like no matter what I do at home at the moment, no matter what I touch, it turns to disaster.'

'Why do you think this is?'

There was a pause. He really was reluctant to speak.

'I don't seem to have any interest in the place,' he said. 'I know I haven't been well, but I feel everything is connected. The animals are failing to thrive on the land.'

'Would you like me to visit?'

He agreed, though he still sounded reluctant. So I drove there. I was astonished when I drove into his yard. There was no sign he'd lost interest in the farm. The place was immaculately kept. The fields looked well tended, the fencing was intact, and as for the house and the yard, they were beautiful. You couldn't see so much as a lollipop stick lying around the place. I remember thinking that if he had lost interest in his animals, it could have been only in the last while. It looked like he had been very much on top of things until recently.

It's a strange thing with land. It can happen that you have good luck with it for thirty or forty years, and then suddenly everything changes. No doubt about it. Larry's bad fortune had been recent.

I went out and walked his land. It was a hilly area. I was reading the land, but I wasn't picking up anything much. And I was distracted: I kept being drawn away from his land. There was a house – it must have been a mile and a half away – stuck up in the hills. I kept being pulled towards it.

I walked on, still trying to pick up the energy from Larry's land, but it was no good. I was still being drawn to that house, miles away. I found that strange. I spent some time out there, then I went back up to Larry. I was in the kitchen with him, having a cup of tea, when I said, 'I have to say this straight. Do you understand? I have to go with what I get.'

'Yes?'

'Well, I was going around your place. And the problem ... well, I'm getting that the problem is in the distance, out beyond your farm.'

He said, 'Where?' And he looked me in the eye for the first time. From his reaction, I knew I was onto something.

I took him to the window and said, 'See that house over there?' It was fairly easy to identify. It was painted a sandy colour and showed up clearly on the horizon. 'I'm being drawn to that house all the time.'

'Right,' he said, and I could sense a kind of excitement in him. But there was more than that: he seemed uncomfortable too. I wondered why.

I said, 'It's like trying to get water from a stone with you. Since I met you it's been that way.'

He looked down and concentrated on stirring sugar into his tea.

'You're looking a lot better since we met. You say you're feeling a lot better. If you want this farm to thrive again, you're going to have to come clean with me. What's the story here?'

'Are you picking up any more? More than there's something about that house?'

'Well, I'm picking up that you're not getting any good wishes from that house over on the hill.'

So then, slowly and reluctantly, he told his story. He and his wife had been friends with the couple in the house on the hill. They'd go out for a few drinks together, and then maybe back to one or other house for more drinks, until the small hours. After a while of this, his wife said, 'You know something? That Síle?'

'What about her?'

'She fancies you.'

'Go away with that.'

Larry was a modest man. I believe him when he said that he really hadn't noticed anything. But as the weeks went on, he finally copped on. He had to admit that yes, his neighbour did seem to be flirting with him.

Now, he could have taken advantage. He could have had a bit on the side, and no one would have been the wiser. But that didn't occur to Larry. He drew a line under the whole thing. He and his wife started to distance themselves from their friends. But that, in a small community, isn't easy.

One night they met at a neighbour's party. It was Christmas time and a lot of drink was taken. Síle made a deliberate play for Larry. It was obvious to everyone, and he had to put a stop to it.

There was a row. Síle implied that Larry had led her on. Larry's wife didn't let her get away with that. She staunchly defended Larry, and threw some accusations Síle's way. Síle's husband naturally sided with her, and it all blew up. Larry hadn't been on speaking terms with the couple since.

So Síle was turned down by a man, and turned down publicly. She'd made herself the victim of gossip; and her house overlooked Larry's farm. She had been looking down over the farm with good feelings, but now that she was a woman scorned, she was looking down with venom. She was sending bad energy.

I picked up on the story and I was right. Larry was so modest, he found the story hard to tell. It was hard for him, to say, 'Another woman fancied me. And me just an ordinary farmer.'

Now that I'd got accurate information from Larry, information which confirmed what I had picked up, I got a vision of Síle. I said to Larry, 'She has short blonde hair? She's about five foot five, and she has blue eyes?'

He confirmed all this.

I then looked up at the house and focused. I sent Síle back the energy. I blocked the bad energy coming down, and I sent Síle healing. I delivered the message that by sending down bad energy, she wasn't doing herself any favours.

I was wishing her well, because she needed to deal with her demons. There must have been something negative going on in her life in the first place for her to make a play for a man like Larry, who wasn't interested.

Larry said, 'It wouldn't have happened if drink hadn't been involved.' He said they were friends through alcohol. Maybe that was Síle's problem. Anyway I blocked the energy, and Larry's land went back to the way it had been before his problems began.

19. Tapping into the Afterlife

Sometimes I read of a tragedy in the newspaper or maybe see it on the television news, and I know for sure that I will be hearing from a person concerned with the case. And when I read of a mother whose son had died in tragic circumstances in America, I knew I'd be hearing from her.

This boy had been drowned suddenly. He had been caught by a freak wave, and it was especially sad because his mother had wanted to treat her child to a holiday of a lifetime after the marriage separation she had just been through. You can imagine her panic and absolute horror – and perhaps the guilt, even though there was nothing she could have done to save him.

As soon as she rang me, I knew at once, from her first word, that she was the boy's mother, even though she didn't mention her son on the phone. She simply said, 'Please can I come? I'd like some healing.' When she arrived, though, it was clear that she had come more for my psychic powers than for healing. She wanted to contact her son in the afterlife.

I said, 'My heart goes out to you, but I'm not going to do a psychic reading on you.'

Her face fell.

'I do hands-on healing. That's the important thing. But if your son decides to come from the other side, and if he gives me some information for you, then that's another story.'

'Does that happen sometimes?'

I nodded. I started giving the woman healing, beginning

as usual on her head, and after a while the spirit of the boy did come to me, and he was saying, 'Tell Mum. Tell her I'll never forget those days in the orchard.' Through him I could see the orchard. I could see a wall in there, and I had a vision of the two of them picking strawberries and apples.

'Are you ready for this?' I asked the woman. 'Are you sure you want to hear it?'

She looked at me and started crying. I handed her a tissue. When she had composed herself, she said quietly, 'Yes. Yes, please.'

'He's telling me about the happy days you had in the orchard. He says that one day you were pushing him in the wheelbarrow. And you slipped and he went over, but he wasn't hurt.'

'I remember. And we laughed. We laughed so much.'

She continued coming to me after that first time, and I gave her more healing. At the end of it, she said she felt better in herself and more able to cope. She said she felt comforted to think that there was something for us in the afterlife.

I remember that about a year and a half later I was visiting the town where the lady lived. I knew, before I saw her, that I would meet her that day – that would have been the spirit of her son making a connection with me. I saw her as I walked into a shopping centre, and she looked a lot better in herself. I felt her son was letting me know she was coping.

I remember another woman who hoped for a psychic reading. I'll call her Fiona. The thing about Fiona was that she would ring and make an appointment, she'd book in. And then she'd cancel. This happened a good few times before finally, one day, she arrived for a healing.

I told her to take off her shoes and lie on the plinth, just like I tell all my clients. I explained I would do a healing, and if a spirit came, it would come. She agreed to that.

The story here was that Fiona's father had died, and she just could not come to terms with it. She was a married woman and she had children, but for all that, she felt that her life was over. This feeling had been going on for months.

'What is your greatest problem, Fiona?'

'I don't know what's happened to him now. I've never really questioned if there's an afterlife. I've never needed to. But every time I think of my father, I visualize him as bones in the ground. I can't imagine an afterlife. So I feel that maybe there is no God. Maybe there's nothing.'

I worked away on the healing, but Fiona wouldn't relax.

'No disrespect to you, Mr Cassidy, but I don't know if I want to be here. I mean, how can I expect you to prove to me that there's an afterlife?'

'Well, I know one thing.'

'What's that?'

'I can definitely tell you that your dad isn't just a bag of bones.'

'How?'

'Because he's here with you in this room. He's talking to me now.'

She sat bolt upright. 'He is?' She was scanning the room with her eyes. 'What is he saying?'

'He's asking, Fiona, why you have got his handkerchief in your handbag.'

Fiona started to laugh. The laugh turned to a choke and then to a sob, and she began to cry noisily. I handed her a tissue, and when she'd composed herself, she said, 'When I was leaving the house this morning, something made me go and take one of his hankies with me. It seemed crazy, but I thought it might help me to connect with him. Did he say anything else to me?'

'He did. He begs you to get over your grief and to get on with your life. He's worried that if you don't, it could lead to some problems with your marriage.'

Fiona thanked me and went home saying she now felt she would be able to move on with her life.

Often the people who come for a healing don't really know why they are there. Often, I feel that the spirit of a loved one has pushed them into it. Sometimes the spirits appear to me, but I don't always tell the person. At other times, if I feel it would help the person to know, I will tell them.

I feel that what most people call coincidence could be the work of a spirit. There are those times when you think of someone you may not have contacted for a long time, and the next moment they're calling you on the phone. I believe an outside influence has made you think of that person.

20. Seeing Others with My Gift

Young children are more susceptible to the spirit world than adults are. They are more open to it. Many go round talking to an imaginary friend. I know that most people dismiss the idea of imaginary friends and think they're fanciful, but I believe that the friend is often a manifestation of the spirit of someone who has gone before.

It's not long before children become self-conscious. If they sense something, adults usually tell them not to be stupid and not to play with their imaginary friend. So they stop talking about it. As they grow and become involved in school, friendships and the complexities of life, more often than not they leave this phase of their life behind.

Through my work I've met many children who have communicated with a spirit in their house, but it's rare to find one with a strong gift. One day a woman asked me out to her house. It was an old house near the centre of a town and was in a well-to-do area. The couple were renovating the house, but they had encountered problems: builders kept letting them down.

Now, it wasn't the money. They had agreed a price. The builders would arrive in the morning, but if the woman left to do errands or a bit of shopping, she'd come home and they'd be gone. At first she thought nothing of it, thinking that maybe they were going off to work on another job, but one day it came to a head.

Only the carpenter was working there that morning. He

was hanging a door. She went out to buy him a bun to have with his coffee, and told him that was where she was going. But when she got home, just ten minutes later, he was gone. The door was left half hung, and his tools were scattered around the place. She couldn't make any sense of it.

The carpenter didn't appear the following day as planned, and she hadn't managed to reach him on the phone. She started thinking there must be a story behind it, that maybe the carpenter and the other builders disliked working in the house for some reason. And that's when she called me.

I arrived in the afternoon, and the woman showed me around the house. We were chatting in the kitchen and I was about to go round the house by myself, to see what I could pick up, when this young girl burst in, in her school uniform. She ran up to the woman and gave her a hug.

'Joe, this is my daughter, Sophie. Sophie, say hello to Mr Cassidy.'

Sophie was busy hanging her jacket on the back of a chair. She was a beautiful little girl, with long blonde hair and bright blue eyes. What I really noticed, though, was that she had this extraordinary aura. Waves of positive energy were coming from her. You couldn't miss it.

She came and shook my hand, smiling shyly. Then she said, 'Mammy, this is the man who's going to fix the house.'

'No, love. Mr Cassidy isn't a builder.'

'I *know* that! I mean really fix it. So that the builders will come back.'

Her mother didn't say anything, she just gave Sophie a glass of milk and a biscuit, and told her to go through to the lounge to turn on the television.

'You told her I was coming?'

'No, I didn't. Sure, I didn't know you were coming. I only rang you this morning.'

'That's true.' I thought I was hearing things, but the woman didn't seem surprised. 'But you heard what I heard?' I asked her. 'How would Sophie have known what I do?'

She shrugged her shoulders. 'Sophie is a strange child,' she said. 'She says she's been seeing things in the house. And talking to someone.'

'Don't tell me any more. Not until I pick up what's here myself,' I said.

'OK. But she's been saying these things and we've been dismissing her. But then, when the builders started letting us down and seeming so uneasy when they were here, we decided it was time to do something about it.'

'So you called me in.'

'Exactly.'

As I started walking round the house, I felt that there was a spirit presence here. It was a woman, and she seemed troubled. As I walked, I noticed from the corner of my eye that Sophie was following me, and this wasn't just a curious girl wanting to chat and get in the way. She was silent and watchful. It was as if she was challenging me, and I found it unsettling.

When I got to the bedroom where the carpenter had been hanging the door, she came and stood in front of me. She didn't say a thing. She just looked into my eyes, intently. It felt as if she and I were in this bubble. And the disconcerting thing was that I, Joe Cassidy, a known healer and diviner, was not in charge. Sophie was. If I had wanted to get out of her bubble of power, I don't think I would have been able to. Sophie, an eight-year-old girl, had the stronger gift.

Sophie was telling me, by telepathy, about the woman

spirit who was in the house. The nearest I can get to describing it is to say that it was like working with a horse or a dog, when you also use telepathy. She was standing there, and I knew she was reading my thoughts. She was in control. And she was saying to me, by telepathy, 'Do you see the woman that I see? Do you see what she looks like?'

And I *was* seeing the spirit. She was a strong presence. She was a large woman, with broad shoulders. She was wearing one of those overalls made out of material with a small flower pattern.

I was picking up that the woman had been in an abusive marriage. Her husband had been an alcoholic. He had been a street angel and a house devil.

I was getting a picture of this from the start, but it was much stronger when the girl was standing there, in front of me. When I pick up on things, it's like a vision. It's like a reel in my head. I see scenes of everyday life, and I can feel the emotions. I certainly felt that this woman had been in a very awkward relationship.

After a while, Sophie walked away and went back to watch the TV, and I walked round the rest of the bedrooms. But I was feeling shaken. And when I went back into the kitchen, before I told Sophie's mother what I had picked up, I asked her more about her daughter.

'I hope Sophie wasn't bothering you,' she said. 'I hadn't realized she'd left the lounge.'

'It's not that. She's a lovely girl. But tell me more about her. What have you noticed about her that might be different?'

'Well, there was one instance.'

'Yes?'

'A few weeks ago a good friend was calling here to see me. She'd never been to the house, so obviously we were giving her directions. I remember she rang when she got into the town. She wanted to check exactly where the house was. She was ringing from outside the shopping centre, and I told her she'd be with us in three minutes. I said I'd stand at the gate, so she'd see me, and I turned to Sophie and asked her to come out with me. But she wouldn't move.'

'Did she say why?'

'No real reason, except she was busy playing. But when we tried to persuade her to come outside, and reminded her that Linda, who was her godmother, had a present for her, she looked me straight in the eye and said, "I know that. And I know what it is. It's a rag doll and it's got pink hair." I told her not to be silly, and in the end she did come out to say hello.'

'And was she right? About the present?'

'Well, that's the thing. Yes, she was. We nearly fainted when she pulled it out of the bag.'

'I'll bet you did!'

'And there's no way she could possibly have known that. None of us knew. But now, tell me what you found in the house.'

I told her all that I knew. And then she told me exactly what had happened with the carpenter.

'Well, it happened as I told you before. I went out for ten minutes and told the carpenter I was coming back with a bun for him. I know he heard me, so I couldn't understand it when he just vanished.'

'And did you get to the bottom of that particular scenario?'

'I did in the end. I'd left message after message with the man, but finally I got hold of him. This was after I'd spoken to you, Mr Cassidy. I have to say, he didn't sound too thrilled to hear my voice!'

'What did he say?'

'Well, I asked him if he was coming tomorrow. I pointed out that he'd left the door just hanging there. I said I felt it was dangerous. I mean, it was!'

'And he said?'

'He said, "Maybe." Then he asked me if I would be there. So I asked him whether it mattered if I was or wasn't. I said, "Is there a problem?" And that's when he told me.'

'Told you?'

'What the problem was. He said, "You'll be working away on the house and the next thing there are noises."'

'All the builders noticed this? Or was it just the carpenter?'

'It was all of them. They'd think someone was there, but there'd be nobody else in the house. But it was the carpenter who experienced it the most. He said, "I've never encountered anything like this before, but I kept getting an eerie feeling like somebody was there." He said he'd put down his hammer, and when he went to look for it he'd find it somewhere stupid – it was hanging out of his coat pocket once – somewhere he would never in a million years have put it. He was a bit freaked.'

'I'd say he was.'

'And then that day, the day he ran off.'

'Yes?'

'That day, as he was hanging the door, he saw his tools move.'

'He did?'

She nodded. 'He was a bit embarrassed to admit this. Well, he was a bit embarrassed to admit any of it. But that day he saw his hammer being picked off the floor. Then the stepladder creaked, and his hammer was put down at the top of it.'

'No wonder he ran!'

'So you can see, I really do need to get rid of this spirit.'

'Or have it put at peace.'

She laughed. 'Whatever! Anything that will give me back *my* peace!'

That woman's spirit wouldn't have always been in the house. The previous owners were probably never aware of her. I expect the energy had been stagnant for years. But when the couple came in and started the renovation, that could have disturbed things. They were building an extension, and digging foundations in particular can change the natural order of things. It changes the whole energy of a place.

To heal the house, I connected with the spirit of the woman, tapping into the events that had gone on. I picked up that when she'd lived in the house with her husband, bad energy had been created there. She wanted the energy cleared for this couple, who were making the house into their family home. My job was to clear the negative energy and to help her to move on.

I thought afterwards that maybe there was another reason I was sent to that house. Maybe it was to help Sophie. Before I arrived, her parents doubted her word. Then, when they suspected she had a gift, they were freaked out by it, especially Sophie's father. But when I told them that Sophie's gift was strong, and showed them how a gift like that could be used, Sophie's father had to accept that his daughter has this gift. That means Sophie can talk to her parents about anything strange that she sees. And when she grows up, she and they will have accepted her as the person she is. They will have accepted that she is different. She won't have to go through all the self-doubt, worries and illness that can emerge when you suppress the strange things you can see and do.

21. Curses and the Occult

In my time as a healer I've often been called to heal a sick animal, but when Mrs Devine rang to tell me she wanted me to stop her animals dying, I sensed at once that this was an unusual case.

'I'm finding an animal dead most mornings,' she said. 'Sometimes it's a chicken, other times a duck. But worst of all, my pot-bellied pig has died.'

I went over to her small farm in Offaly and asked her more about the deaths.

'There was a cat dead one day too. I found the poor devil in my shed.'

'I assume a vet has been involved?'

'Oh yes. When this kept happening, I had some autopsies done in Dublin. But the reports couldn't find any good reason for the deaths. It's so strange. I mean, it's not like it's just one type of animal.'

As I walked around the yard, I had a sense that someone wished her bad luck.

'This will sound extremely strange,' I said. 'But could there be anyone who might hold ill wishes towards you, maybe someone who has been to your house?'

'I don't think so.' Her brow furrowed in thought. Then she called over to her husband, who was busy doing some whitewashing across the yard, and asked if he could think of anyone.

He said, 'Remember that incident at the party?'

She put her hand on her forehead and said, 'Oh! Of course!'

'There *is* someone?'

She nodded. 'We had a party. This was just a few weeks ago. We invited all the neighbours, but there was one we'd rather not have invited. When she gets drunk she isn't the easiest, but what could we do? If we didn't invite her she'd hold a grudge and we'd never be allowed to forget about it.'

'So you did ask her?'

'Against our better judgement. We thought that if we didn't, she might turn up anyway.'

'And did she create a scene?'

'She did. It was a shame. The plan was to have her for a couple of hours and then offer to take her home. And she was fine for the first while. The trouble was, when we offered her a lift, she wouldn't be shifted. She had a lot of alcohol on board by then.

'It was getting late, and apart from this lady all our duty guests had gone. Just our close friends remained. The fellows were moving from beer onto whiskey and vodka, and someone was getting out a fiddle, so we could have a sing-song. And no way did this lady want to miss out on all of that!'

'So what happened?'

'She got right awkward, and I insisted she go. She muttered, "You invite me and you kick me out. Who do you think you are? You and your fecking animals!" I managed to push her towards the door then. But as she left, she shouted over her shoulder, "And may all your animals die."'

She looked at me, wide-eyed. 'I didn't think anything of it at the time. I mean you don't, do you? I was sure it was just the drink talking.' She paused. 'Could it *really* have been her?'

'It fits,' I said. 'I don't think when she went to your party she had the intention of wishing you bad luck, but then she got jarred.'

When people wish someone bad luck, usually nothing will happen. But in some cases certain ancestral connections can cause a person's ill will to be detrimental to others. Maybe that lady herself didn't know that. I don't feel that in the sober light of day she'd have meant to do what she did.

In that scenario, I worked on the atmosphere. I enhanced the energy that the curse had stifled, and the animals stopped dying.

Sometimes the land fights back. What I'm talking about here is when you get a sacred area of land, or a fairy tree, which someone tries to tamper with. To give an example: a man from County Meath came to me for healings. He had a sore shoulder and wanted hands-on healing to help with it. He was a property developer, and he told me that he seemed to be having a terrible run of luck. At the time I was treating him, the Celtic Tiger was still roaring. But while most developers were continually successful, this man was always encountering problems.

I asked him if he'd had to interfere with a sacred place in his line of work.

'Not in my work, no. But there was a time years ago ...'

'Yes.'

'I'm talking ten years ago. More maybe. There was this bush at the side of the road that locals were always going on about. It was supposed to have sacred powers.'

'Go on.'

'There'd been strange happenings there, hundreds of years ago. There are lots of stories about it, stories that have been passed down through the generations. Spirits are supposed to linger there, and they say you mustn't interfere with the bush.'

I nodded. I knew about sacred areas. I'd been brought up knowing to respect bushes like that, and I'd heard the stories about those who hadn't respected them. I believed the stories.

'Well, I didn't believe there was anything in it. But that bush, it was always left untouched. The authorities would cut the hedge round it; this bush wasn't ever cut. Not ever. They said that anyone who interfered with it could have bad luck afterwards. And one night, a friend and I went on the lash. And we decided to cut down the bush.'

'And did you cut it down?'

'We tried all right. We hacked away at it, but it wasn't too easy. We ended up with scratches all over our hands, arms and faces until finally we gave up. You understand, we had had more than a few. We kept falling over.'

'And did anything happen?'

'I woke the next morning and I couldn't remember if we'd managed to cut the bush down. Now that I was sober, I really hoped we hadn't. So I drove out to the bush to check the damage when … well, this surely has to be a coincidence, but my friend was out driving to work in his van, in the opposite direction. I didn't see him. But it seems we crashed into each other, head on.'

'Was it bad?'

'Put it this way: the next thing I remember is being cut out of my car. And, get this, the crash happened right opposite the bush. I'll tell you one thing, coincidence or not, I'm never trying that one again.'

'And you feel the bad luck you've been having could be connected?'

'It did occur to me, yes.'

I removed the negative energy from the man, and his luck began to improve.

I heard another story about that same bush. It's said a couple went to an auction and bought a grandfather clock. This was madness really, because the clock wasn't in working order and there was no guarantee it could be fixed. They put the clock in the back of their estate car and drove home. At the very moment they passed that bush, the clock chimed. They nearly jumped out of their skin with fright. They got home to find the clock in perfect working order.

Eddie Mooney made his living by driving machinery. He was getting plenty of work, so he borrowed money to buy new machinery. He was doing work for a property developer and for the first few weeks he was paid regularly and there was no problem.

Then, one day, he was asked to dig up a piece of land. When the developer pointed the land out to him, Eddie noticed that it had a fairy ring on it. He mentioned this and the man made it clear that this wasn't a request, it was an order, and that if Eddie refused to do the job he would not get his final payment, which included money he had already earned.

Now, Eddie was a country man. He knew that such sacred land should never be tampered with. He knew that if he did so, he would be inviting bad luck. But he needed the money. Nevertheless, he said, 'I can't touch that land. I won't. Under no circumstances.'

The property developer went red with anger. 'It's up to you. If you don't do it, you won't get paid. End of story.' And he walked off.

Eddie walked round, deep in thought. He wondered how he would go home and tell his wife there was no money. How would he explain it to the hire purchase company?

'I was put in this terrible position,' he told me. 'I drove my machine to the fairy ring and dug the bucket down into the earth, then I had second thoughts. I decided to think it over during the night, so I left the site. That's all I remember.'

'Why? What happened?'

'Well, I was still thinking about my dilemma as I was driving home. I thought, *I'm in a fair predicament here.* And the next thing I remember I woke up in hospital.'

'In hospital? Whatever happened?'

'I ended up in a ditch. I don't know how – I don't remember. I was found at nine that night by a passer-by.'

Eddie was badly injured and spent a long time in hospital, so there was no money coming in anyway.

'When I eventually came out of hospital, I went down to collect my machine. I knocked on the property developer's front door, and he answered. He'd obviously been made aware I'd had an accident. When I told him that I was there to collect my machine, he said, "I've bad news for you." "What do you mean?" I asked him.'

'And what did he mean?'

'Well, he told me that the evening I'd left there, the evening I'd had that crash, I'd not been long gone when he smelt smoke. He looked out of the window of his house and saw that my machine was on fire.'

'I don't believe it! Hadn't you enough bad luck already?'

'Hadn't I. The machine was destroyed – and there was no reason for it that I could see. It hadn't been doused with petrol and it hadn't ever given trouble before. I'm just glad I went with my gut feeling and didn't do any further digging that day.'

I believe that if you have been given the gift of divining and healing, you have a responsibility *never* to misuse it. It's not about finding wealth or guessing lotto numbers, and in the same way you have to be careful never to use your powers to the bad.

Years ago, near the start of my career as a healer, I was approached by a man who had driven across Ireland to see me because his wife had gone off with another fellow. I thought he'd come to me for healing for himself, but he asked me to wish bad luck on his wife and her new partner. He held out a fistful of money. I shook my head and pushed his hand away.

'There's a lot more where that came from,' he said.

'I'm sorry. You've approached the wrong person here.'

'I just want to get back at them for what they've done,' he said. 'You can understand that, surely?'

I explained again that I could give him a healing, and that I felt he needed a healing. 'But I won't use my gifts for bad intentions,' I said. I wouldn't then, and I certainly wouldn't today.

22. Relationship Problems

In my work, I often encounter women who are suffering from stress in their lives. These women don't generally come until the stress is causing other problems: perhaps they're not sleeping, or maybe they have back pain or constant headaches. Very often the stress starts because of a problem within their marriage.

Seven years ago I had a call from Rachel. She'd heard about me from a neighbour, and she asked me to call in because of a problem with her house. I didn't ask for any details, and I arranged to go the following Thursday. I had a vision of what the house would look like, and it was as I'd imagined: a lovely detached house in a nice area.

The minute Rachel answered the door and led me to the kitchen I could sense that the energy in the house was out of sync. I sensed too that the reason for this was a relationship that wasn't going right, and that this had happened in this same house before.

I don't know if a client notices, but from the moment I hear from someone, I start tuning into them – and I start working as soon as I cross the house's threshold. Rachel might have thought we were just sitting in the kitchen, drinking tea and chatting about everyday things, but I was busy at work. I was picking up on Rachel and picking up on the house. I didn't say any of this to her while we were sitting exchanging pleasantries though, and I didn't say anything about the problem until she had shown me round the house and then left me to wander around by myself. In fact it wasn't until I was back in the kitchen again that I said my first meaningful words.

'How long is he gone?' I asked her.

She jumped. 'How did you …' Then she composed herself. 'My husband left about two, no maybe three months ago.'

'I see.' I felt that there was no other woman involved; I sensed that the man had left because of a problem within himself. But I didn't say that to her until I had heard what she had to say.

'Do you know what's going on?'

She shrugged. 'I wish I *did* know. It's a weird one. I'm convinced he hasn't got another woman. If he had, I don't imagine he'd be so miserable.'

'He's not happy?'

She shook her head. 'It's like he's changed. Like he's boxed himself away. He's not the person I know.'

'You're not living here too long?'

'No.'

'You've done a lot with the house, I feel?'

'Yes. It was a long-held dream to buy a house like this. We've both worked hard and life has been good to us. We were happy enough where we were before, but we wanted the extra space.'

'You've three children?'

'Yes. Well, two are teenagers now, and that was the point. We wanted them to have a bedroom each and for there to be enough space for them to bring their friends back for the odd night. It was something we both wanted, very much indeed.'

'But it hasn't worked?'

'Well, for the children it has. I mean, it was wonderful having the bigger garden. I love this kitchen too.'

Looking round, I thought that anyone would. It was fresh and modern, and had a sitting-room area at one end.

'And the money hasn't been a problem,' she continued. 'I mean, the larger mortgage is easy to manage with our combined salaries.'

'But your husband didn't settle?'

'No, he didn't. I don't understand it. I know he was keen to move in here. We all were. But I think it was when we moved here that he started to change.' She sighed. 'I don't know if you can believe this, but it was as if I was living with another man. And frankly, not the easiest of men. I'm sorry,' she said. 'You don't want to hear all of this.'

I reassured her. I said, 'You needn't be afraid to talk. I think there's a reason for all this.'

'You do?'

'Yes. I'll explain it all in a minute.'

'My husband has always been a confident man, sociable too, and he always saw the good in life. But now …'

'Yes?'

'Well, I confess I'm really worried about him. I've been worried for some time. I even heard him sobbing once.' She looked at me, as if to gauge my reaction. 'Actually sobbing. This was before he went to sleep.'

'Did he say why?'

'He said he didn't know, that he couldn't explain it. How can anyone be so sad and not know the reason why?'

'Did he never say?'

'Well, one day he started to get really agitated. That's not like him either! And he said – well, he shouted it actually – "This bloody house! I don't know why but I can't settle in this bloody house."'

'Where is he living now, your husband?'

'He's up the town. We own a house on the main street. It's normally let out, so he was lucky.'

'Do you see him at all?'

'Well, yes. It's strange. He's moved out, but that doesn't mean he never spends time here. He's here every morning.'

'Why is that?'

'He brings the paper up here every morning before work. He sits and has a cup of coffee, and says hi to the kids. Then he goes again. He still calls this "that bloody house", and he still insists he was right to move out. He says it was the only way he could clear his head.'

I told her then what I'd been feeling in the house.

'There is definitely negative energy here,' I said. 'And it has, I believe, to do with relationship problems. I believe other couples who have lived here have had their difficulties too.'

She smiled. 'I think you could be right,' she said.

That surprised me. I'd expected her to question me more about it, because although this sort of thing is normal to me, I'd thought it would have been a strange thing for her to hear.

'Let me explain,' she said. 'You didn't ask me how I got your number, and that in itself is a strange story.'

She told me she'd been going out to her car a couple of weeks earlier when she saw her neighbour in her garden.

'I'd seen this lady around the place, but we'd never met, so I called out "good morning" to her and she came over to introduce herself. She was a bit uneasy though, and I wondered why.'

'In what way?'

'She seemed to be frightened I'd take offence. She started by saying, "If you don't mind me saying – I don't want to sound like a nosy neighbour – but has your husband left the house?"'

I laughed. 'That's nosy all right!'

'Yeah, and I *was* a bit taken aback, but she told me she was asking for a reason.'

'And what might that be?'

'She said she wanted to help. She said, "I've lived in this area almost since the first houses were built. And I have to tell you that you're not the first couple to move into that house and suddenly split up." Then she said, "You're the seventh." I couldn't believe what I was hearing.'

'Was that it?' I asked her.

It turns out that it wasn't. The neighbour told Rachel that soon after they had moved in, she had been pulling the curtains back one day when she couldn't help noticing Rachel's husband walking out to his Jeep. She said she'd got the shock of her life. Although she knew a new family had moved in, everything about Rachel's husband seemed familiar.

'She said it was like looking at the man who had lived in the house two families before us – at least who had lived there until they split up. She said that his demeanour, everything about him, was identical.'

'That's a bit strange all right.'

'It is. And I was wondering why this woman was bothering to tell me all this. I couldn't see how it was going to help.'

'And that's when she gave you my number?'

Rachel laughed. 'How did you guess? She handed over your number and said I was to be sure to ring you.'

That sounds bizarre, but it's often the way. I'm constantly surprised at how people hear about me, and who from.

I worked on that house and cleared away the negative energy. She thanked me and asked what she should do next.

I must stress again that I was certain no other woman was involved and that this man still loved his wife and wanted to live with her and his children. So I said to her, 'I think you should play this one gently.'

'What do you mean?'

'Don't just tell him the house is OK now. He probably wouldn't believe you anyway.'

'Well, that's true enough.'

'You were saying he has been coming up here every day for a cup of coffee.'

'That's right.'

'Well, say nothing. Just watch him. See what happens.'

When I've done a healing on a house, the first seven days are the most important. That's when the energy is changing in the house. And for the first four or five days, Rachel's husband came to visit as usual. He'd throw the paper down on the kitchen worktop, have a cup of coffee and chat to her. At first it was like it had been before: he would stay for thirty minutes or, at the most, forty, and then he would leave. He would be getting edgy and a bit hyper. It was as if he just could not settle.

Come the fifth day, and the sixth, Rachel noticed a change in her husband. After they had finished their coffee he didn't rush off. So she unloaded the clothes from the machine and hung them out on the line. An hour passed. Then an hour and a half. He was still in the kitchen.

The following week, when he'd finished reading the paper, he picked up the house phone and started organizing his working day. This was unusual even when he had been living in the house. He was still there and it was almost lunchtime; in fact she needed to go out. Finally she said, 'What are you doing?'

He looked up. 'What do you mean?'

'You're still here. You're usually gone by now.'

He looked at her for a long time. *Really* looked at her. And she realized that he hadn't done that in ages. For the last while he'd been unable to look her in the eye.

'It's the house.'

'What about it?'

'It feels normal. I'd like to live here. That is, if you'll have me back.'

She threw her arms round his neck and said that of course she would, and that she'd never wanted him to move out in the first place. Then she told him that she'd called me in. She explained about the neighbour and the other couples, and about how I had healed the house.

He broke down. He said, 'I knew I was acting out of control. It wasn't me. Do you remember me saying ...'

'Yes,' she says, 'I do remember. You kept saying, "This bloody house." You were always saying it.'

They *did* get back together again, and as far as I'm aware they are still together today and still living in that same house. I don't know how that bad energy got into the house in the first place; it may have been created when the house was first built. All I know is that the energy had lingered from couple to couple. It had probably got stronger with each couple who moved in there. And now, that bad energy has gone.

I heard from Rachel's husband not long after they had got back together. He rang to thank me, and he wanted to say it in person. So I went round to their house and had coffee with them both. It was great to see them both looking so happy and relaxed.

23. Working with Children

One evening I was working in the garden, throwing weeds into a wheelbarrow, when I heard a car coming up our drive. It was the crunch of the gravel that alerted me. The car was coming at speed, and then there was a screech of brakes.

I remember being a bit startled. It certainly wasn't the first time somebody had come looking for me without an appointment, but it doesn't happen every day. I came round from the side of the house in time to see a neighbour sitting in the driving seat, with something between her knees.

Peering into the car, I saw that the tiny thing she was holding had a head of black hair. *Jesus, Mary and Joseph*, I thought, *what is my neighbour Janine doing with that monkey?* Then I heard the 'monkey' screaming fit to burst, and realized my mistake. Opening the car door, I saw she had a small baby clutched between her knees. It can't have been more than three weeks old, but I've never seen such a shock of black hair on a newborn.

'Janine! I didn't even know you were pregnant.'

She threw me a look.

'Is it colic?'

'Ah Jesus, Joe, can you help us? This fellow hasn't stopped crying since the moment he was born. I can't get a moment's peace.'

She looked wrecked, and she must have been in a state to drive over to me with the baby on her knee. Sure, she'd have known it wasn't the thing to do, especially when the infant carrier was securely installed in the back of her car.

I felt sorry for her. This was her first baby, and I could still remember what it felt like to have a child with colic. I've never forgotten how bad it felt being kept up night after night when Laura suffered with it, all those years ago.

She brought the baby in.

'Hop up on the plinth, will you, and we'll put the little fellow lying back against you,' I said. I took him from her and handed him back, once she was settled. He was still screaming.

I started the healing, and the baby became calmer. Janine, though, kept talking. She was trying to get across to me that this child had barely stopped screaming its whole life. Then, after a while, as she held the baby, she became calmer too.

This often happens when you give a baby, or more particularly a child, a healing. It's like you give good energy to the mother through the child. Even if a mother is just sitting in the room with the child, you can see her sense of calm and that she's fighting sleep. Often she does nod off; that's very common.

Janine closed her eyes. She smiled. 'I think I'll stay here all night, and you can keep your hand on him,' she said.

I laughed. 'We won't do that. But you can bring him back for another healing.'

'When?'

'I usually say a week, but you may need to come a bit sooner.'

Janine walked calmly back to her car, with the baby, who was now sleepy, lying contentedly in her arms. She carefully strapped him into his carrier. He nestled there, and still didn't cry. Then, yawning, Janine thanked me.

She contacted me two days later, saying the baby was much better and so was she.

'I'd forgotten what sleep felt like,' she said. They came for one more healing, and the problem seemed to be solved.

It's a strange thing. If one baby comes with colic, I often get a few more. And it's not that one mother rings another. It's the same with bad backs or with asthma: I often notice that cases of the same condition follow one another in any given week.

I see babies on a regular basis, and once I saw twins. They'd come with their mother from quite a distance away, and they both had colic. I remember that day because of the screams. I worked on one baby and it calmed, but the mother and I couldn't hear ourselves think for the screams of the other one. I ended up going from child to child, healing them in tandem. I've never done that before or since. I remember that woman had been driven almost demented; she said she had had no rest from it. In that case the healing helped, too – as it does almost every time.

I see the cycle of life as a healer. Pregnant women come to me for morning sickness. A huge amount of them have had benefit from a healing. I've used distance healing for morning sickness, too; to do this the pregnant woman sends me a photograph and I send a healing. I don't think it's ever failed. They always ring to let me know the sickness is gone.

Very often when a woman comes to me when she's pregnant, an energy begins. It makes no difference whether she has come for morning sickness or just energy healing to help the pregnancy go well, that same woman often comes back to me with the same child. I treat the child, as it grows, for various ailments – psoriasis or eczema, for example. And the nice thing is that the children who have been coming to me since they were babies commonly ask to have a healing when they are older, perhaps when they're revising for their Junior Certificate and they feel stressed out. They ask their parents if they can come and see me; the parents don't instigate it. That always gives me a lump in my throat. And the parents love it too.

People usually ring for a booking a day or two in advance. Sometimes, though, I'm asked to give a healing with very little notice. One day, I remember, I was going to Kilcullen to meet someone for lunch. I was rushing out the door of my clinic, when my phone rang. It was another friend, Greg, who I'd not seen for some time.

'Where are you, Joe?' he said. 'Are you working today?'

'I have been, yeah. I'm just on my way out now. I'm meeting someone for lunch.'

'Oh.' He sounded disappointed.

'Why, what is it?'

'A relation of mine just rang me. Her daughter is very sick. She's been in Our Lady's Hospital for Sick Children in Crumlin, and she's heading home with her family right now.'

'What's the problem?'

'It's cancer. She's been in hospital a while. She's had the chemo, and now she's going home. They're all in a bit of a state. I feel a healing just might help.'

'Where were they ringing you from? Where are they now?'

He told me, and it wasn't far from me.

I said, 'Tell you what. Get her to give me a ring. If she wants me to see the child I'll cancel my lunch.'

I rang to cancel, and in about ten minutes the family arrived. They were a young couple, and the child was eight or

nine. She didn't look well at all. She'd no hair from the chemotherapy, and she was very thin and weak. She needed help to
get up onto the plinth.

For a split second, I thought, *What am I doing?* The child
had been through so much, and her parents seemed so young.
They were distraught. They'd had to watch her suffer with the
tubes and the blood tests and the injections and the terrible
sickness, and now they'd been told there was no guarantee
that the chemotherapy had worked. And here was I, giving
her yet another treatment. But then I stopped thinking that
way. I was the healer. This was what I did. It wasn't my first
time. I had to concentrate on working with the energy.

So I did the treatment with the child. It wasn't easy. She
was vomiting, I remember, from the chemo, and I had to
give her a little bowl. I finished the treatment, and the mother
took the child out to the car.

Something told me I should ask to see that child every day
for a while. But was it fair to ask them to bring her to me
when she was so sick and weak?

'My heart goes out to you,' I said to her father. 'I can't
promise you that I can do anything here, but I feel that I
want to see your child for the next few days. Think about it.
I'll leave it with you. If you feel the child is well enough, and
if you think she's had some benefit from this first treatment,
then let me know and I'll see her any time.'

He rang the next day and said they'd like to come. He said
she'd had a better night than usual and that he'd do anything
for his daughter if it gave her some relief, both from the cancer
and from the effects of the treatment. The chemotherapy had
only seemed to make her sicker. They brought her a few times
and she seemed to get huge relief from the healings. Now,
whether it was the chemo or my healing, or a combination of

the two, it's not for me to say, but that child recovered and she is still alive today.

Two years later I was going to do some work in the same county where the child lived, and as often happens with me her parents rang me just a few days before, to tell me all was still well. I asked her mother where exactly she lived, and she told me.

'I'm down your way this week, doing some work,' I said. I mentioned a village. 'Is this near you?'

'It's half a mile from me. You will really have to call in.'

So I went to visit them on my way to the other job. I remember going in through the back door, and there in the kitchen was this beautiful ten- or eleven-year-old girl. She had long, glossy hair and perfect skin. The last time I'd seen her she'd been skin and bone. She grinned at me, came over and shyly shook my hand. She'd made me some fairy cakes, I remember. As we sat at the table and ate, she told me about her life.

I'd seen a pony in a field outside and I asked her if it was hers. She said that it was, that she was horse riding again. She said she loved it. I've never forgotten that girl.

24. Illness Stories

Many of the people who come to me for healing have tried a lot of other treatments first. By the time they come to me, they may be desperate. Their attitude is, 'Sure, healing can't do any harm,' and the vast majority do get relief of some sort. Often they need a full course of six healings, but some improve significantly after just one or two. One lady, in particular, I will never forget.

Mrs Hardy had a problem with her foot. I'm not sure exactly what the diagnosis was, but her doctor had said her condition was as rare as hen's teeth and he didn't know how to help her. Now, it wasn't just the pain that was getting to her, though certainly that was bad at times. The real problem was that she had difficulty getting around.

This was a lady who loved her independence. She was a widow, but she was very happy living alone. She loved her house. She could no longer manage the stairs, however, and it looked as if she might have to move into her son's house. She didn't like that idea at all! She was sociable and was used to having her friends around whenever she wanted.

'I'm well,' she told me. 'I don't feel old. But because of this thing that's wrong with my foot, which the doctors say they can't treat, I'm to be moved out to the granny flat, to be looked after until the end of time.' To her, this was a real tragedy.

When she came for a healing, I remember that she had trouble getting out of her car. It took a while for her to organize her crutches. But I did the healing and she said she felt very relaxed. We made a booking for the following week, and she went off, happily enough.

The following week, I was in the kitchen, finishing my lunch, when Jean, who was reading her book in the next room, called out to tell me that someone had arrived for me. I went outside and it was Mrs Hardy. She was nearly running across the yard as she approached me. There wasn't a sign of those crutches, and she had a grin from ear to ear.

'Ah,' she said, 'hello, Joe. I'm better now. I don't need to have my treatment.'

'I can see that. But look, there was no need for you to come back. You could have rung me.'

'Ah no,' she said. 'I wanted to thank you.'

She gave me a ten-pound note, then she hugged me.

'You've made an old woman very happy!' she said.

When she gave me that ten-pound note it was like she was giving me ten thousand pounds. I had such respect for that lady. She had driven a good sixty or seventy miles to give me that ten-pound note, and I really appreciated it.

When I came back in, Jean asked me who the lady was.

'Mrs Hardy,' I told her. 'She was the woman who was here at the same time last week.'

'Not the woman on crutches?'

'That's the one. She's better now.'

Jean just couldn't believe it. She has met a number of my clients over the years, and she has rarely seen such a rapid transformation as she saw in that lady that day.

It's so good when you can help someone like Mrs Hardy, and it's even better when they show such appreciation. She now had her independence back and she could live her life the way she always had before.

*

I had another client with a bad ankle, but this time it was because of arthritis. An old injury had set the arthritis off, and the woman, who was in her early seventies, was in terrible pain. When she came to me, she was already booked into hospital for an operation. She'd had a scan and been told that there was nothing else for it.

I asked her what she wanted from me.

'Relief from the pain,' she said. 'The ankle has given me trouble for years, but the pain is really bad now. Someone just gave me your number and I thought it was worth a try.'

I gave her a healing, and as I was finishing, she said, 'Would you like to know how I got my injury?'

I smiled. 'I think I already know. I had a vision of it.'

'Tell me then.'

'You were cycling along a country road on a bike that was too big for you. You had to stand up to pedal, because the seat was too high. Am I right?'

She smiled. 'It was my sister's bike. I'd taken it because mine had a puncture.'

'You were wearing a dress, and you hit a pothole and crashed down.'

She still smiled.

'Your main concern at the time wasn't the pain in your ankle, although I think it hurt a lot. You were more worried about telling your mother. You knew she'd react badly, because it was the first time you'd worn that dress, and the dress was torn. You were upset about it. You'd felt like a queen in it.'

She looked at me in total shock.

'You're absolutely right. Right on every detail. It's funny. I remember that day so clearly: the sun, the smell of newly cut hay, the sense of freedom. And then, after I fell off the bike, all that pleasure was replaced by worry and guilt!'

I booked her in for the following week; the operation was scheduled for a week after that. When she came for that second appointment, she said the first one had brought her great relief. It had really helped. I gave her the second healing and I wished her luck for the operation, which was going ahead on the following Thursday.

A few days later, she rang me, sounding agitated.

'Joe. I don't know what to do. I'm down to have this operation. The scan showed I needed it, but now I feel that I don't. The ankle feels perfect.'

'If I were you, I'd be going for a second opinion,' I said.

She rang the hospital, but she couldn't get anyone to listen to her. The doctors believed that the scan couldn't lie. The scanner couldn't lie. They probably felt the lady was nervous about the operation and was trying to get out of it.

She drove to the hospital and badgered the consultant's secretary, insisting that the scan be repeated. And when they repeated it, it was quite evident that the problem had gone. The doctors were amazed. As for the woman, she was simply delighted.

I can never guarantee a perfect result, and I would never tell someone not to go for an operation. I leave it in the hands of the universe. But when I get a result like that, it makes my whole job worthwhile.

One night a man was brought in for a healing by his wife and his best friend. He needed them both to help him walk into my clinic. I remember him clearly, though this was some time ago. He was six foot five or six tall and a fine-looking man, but things were bad for him. He had a tumour on his brain, and walking wasn't his only problem. He also had trouble getting his words out. He had come, he explained in his halting speech, to get some relief from his pain.

'That's all I want,' he said. 'The pain in my head – I just can't bear it.'

I gave him a healing, and the pain did seem to lift a little. He said he wanted to come again. Usually, if I'm giving someone a course of healing, I'll see them once a week. But in this case I felt the man would benefit from coming to me every day. I could see how ill he was, and how tortured he was by the pain. I was going by my instinct here.

'Would you like to come every night for the next week?' I asked him. 'I feel that would be best for you.'

'Anything. Anything that helps this pain.'

The next night, when his wife and his best friend brought him in again, he didn't look any better. And the third night there was still only a limited improvement. So I was surprised when, later that night, I got a phone call from his wife.

'Joe, you'll never guess what happened tonight. Never in a month of Sundays.' She sounded so excited that her words were running into each other.

They had gone home after the treatment. The man's best friend had stayed for tea. After they'd eaten, they'd stayed at the table for a while, as they had on the two previous nights.

'But something happened,' she said.

'What was that?'

'He got up from the table. He wasn't thinking about it. He just got up, walked across the kitchen and switched on the kettle.'

'That's amazing.'

'It really was.'

He drove himself for his next three healings. Then I said goodbye and wished him well.

Two months later, I was locking up for the night. The last client had gone, and I was blowing out the candles and tidying up. But when I went outside, I sensed somebody standing behind me. It gave me a fright.

'What the f**k happened here?'

It was that tall, good-looking man standing there, looking confused.

'I'm sorry? What do you mean?'

'It's unbelievable what you did for me.'

I was thinking, *Well, aren't you happy then? You look much better.* And of course he was. He'd come to thank me. It's just that he had got more from me than he was expecting, so he was confused too. When you've been very ill, and suddenly you're not, it can be a shock. He was having to deal with a new reality, and it was taking him some time and adjustment to do that.

Sometimes, when someone is very sick, there is nothing I can do to help them – at least not physically. But I still feel there's a reason they come to me; that I am there to help them in some other way. Let me explain.

About ten years ago my phone rang. It was a farmer. I'll call him Tom.

'You'll remember me, Joe,' he said. 'I saw you last year. I came for some treatment with you. I'm fine now, but I'd love you to see a good friend of mine.'

I didn't immediately remember this man, but when he said he lived in County Sligo, it all came back to me.

'Oh yeah, I remember you now. When does your friend want to come?'

'Well, the thing is, I have to bring him. Could you fit us in on Saturday?'

Now, I don't normally do healings on a Saturday. I try to keep the weekends free for my family. But in this instance, I agreed.

'Sure. Bring him along then. I'll see you at eleven o'clock.'

The Jeep arrived on the dot of eleven. Tom jumped out and shook my hand. Then he opened the passenger door and introduced me to his friend, Paddy, who was slowly clambering out. He was an elderly gentleman. He walked with a stick and he looked frail. I took him into my treatment room and asked him to remove his shoes and his jacket, and to get up onto the plinth.

Paddy struck me as a lovely man. He was a real gentleman, with that old-fashioned courtesy and charm. I felt an affinity with him. My sense of him was that he was a man of the land. I like that in a person.

I explained what I was going to do, and then I put my hand on his forehead. Within sixty seconds I had such a powerful reaction that I felt I was stuck to the floor. I was getting a strong message, and it wasn't a good one. I was picking up that this man was not well and was not going to get better. In fact, he was going to be dead within ten days.

Now, I was there with my hand on this man's head. And I'm a healer. And I was saying to myself, and to God, or the greater source, *Why has this man come to me when I can't help him? Why has he come all this way if he's going to be dead in ten days?*

Then I realized it wasn't my healing power that this man needed. What he needed was my sixth sense, and that was in full flow. I was getting a strong message that this man's son was in Canada, and that he must be warned to come home and see his father before it was too late.

173

Now, this man knew there was something wrong with him. That's why he came to me. He'd been to see his doctor, but he hadn't yet got a diagnosis, so he didn't know that he was dying. At this time, nobody knew that – not his family and not his doctor. He hadn't got a clue. This made it very awkward for me. When I'd finished the treatment, the man seemed very relaxed. He said he'd enjoyed it.

'Can I come back and see you in a week, Joe?'

I hesitated, trying to work out what I could say.

'I've to go up to the hospital for a test – my doctor organized that – but can I come back and see you as well?'

'Paddy, tell you what. You go back to the hospital for what you have to do, then when you're free again, I'll see you whenever you want me to see you.'

'Thank you, Joe. That's good of you.'

I couldn't tell Paddy the bad news. How could I? I'm not a doctor. I hadn't done a scan. I was only using my intuition. But I knew, without doubt, that this man would be dead and buried within ten days. So what was I going to do about it? And how could I make sure that his son came home in time? It was a hard one. I decided I'd have to talk to Tom.

When I finished the healing, Paddy said he needed the loo. The second he'd gone, I rang Jean and explained the situation.

'Jean, could you please offer Paddy a cup of tea? Maybe a sandwich. I need to talk to his friend.'

When Paddy reappeared, I said to him, 'Sure, go in and have a cup of tea and a sandwich with Jean. You've a long drive.' But it was hard to persuade him. Paddy had impeccable manners.

'Ah no!' he said.

'Sure, go on. We'll be with you in a minute,' I reassured him.

When he had left the room, I turned to Tom. 'Do you mind if I ask you a few questions?' I said.

'Fire away.'

'Has this man been told he's very ill?'

Tom looked startled. 'What are you saying? No. No, he hasn't.'

'I believe he is. And the strange thing is – I don't know how to say this – but I believe he's going to be dead in ten days. Has he got a son who lives in Canada?'

'He has. Actually, he's my best friend.'

'Well, if he's your best friend, can you contact him and get him home?'

'You're sure of this?'

I nodded. I was completely sure.

There's one thing I will never forget. Before Paddy left my house that day, he was admiring the hedge marking the boundary. He took a few snips off it and said he was going to pot them. I liked that. I was thinking, *This man is dying, but he's taking new life with him.*

A few days after I saw Paddy, he went to the hospital for tests. Tom rang to say that he'd been diagnosed with terminal cancer. The doctors said there was nothing that they could do. They kept him in hospital. And by the Tuesday week he was dead.

Tom, true to his word, had rung his best friend and explained the situation, and Paddy's son had arrived the Saturday before his father died. So I had done all that I was meant to do.

25. Depression Stories

Sean was a successful businessman. His company had started small, but it had got bigger and bigger and now he employed a lot of people. The money coming in was great, but his work was stressful. At the end of the day he'd thank God for another day over. He'd tell his colleagues, 'I'm going for a few pints. I deserve it, after all the hours I've worked.' But then drinking became a habit.

Sean's personal assistant had worked for him through all the good times and he trusted her implicitly. But he didn't examine the bank balances too closely. When times are good, it's easy not to.

This woman had her own problems, however. And she had started dipping into the till. She was probably thinking, *Well, this fellow is drinking every day of the week. He's not going to notice.* And for a long time Sean didn't notice. This had been going on for years.

It was when the downturn happened that Sean became alert to what she'd been doing. It was a difficult time for his business, and this discovery made things even worse. He was shocked and he felt betrayed. He'd liked the woman and had always thought that they had a good working relationship. Obviously he had to let her go, but he found this hard to do. When he came to see me, he told me he was depressed.

His main problem, though, was that he was drinking too much. For a long time he hadn't seen this as a problem, because he was a man who could consume a lot of alcohol and not appear to be drunk.

'I can drink eight or ten pints in the bar. I can get up from the bar, go to my car and drive home. I don't feel the effects, though obviously if I were stopped the Gardai would have me up for drink-driving.'

'You're a family man?'

'I am, yes. I know I shouldn't drink and drive, but I feel I drive safely with alcohol on board. In fact, just the other day my wife remarked on it. She said it was scary how much I could put away without showing that I'd had even a drop.'

'Do you feel your drinking is a problem?'

'Well, there is one thing bothers me.'

'And what would that be?'

'I don't think I can do without the drink. I seem to need it in my body. And another thing.'

'Yes?'

'I know I should stop. But if I do, I feel the stress of my work might get to me. The alcohol helps me to deal with things.'

He got up onto the plinth and I started the healing. I'd only just begun when he started to groan. It was a weird sound, like a low scream. And then he got himself off the plinth and went over to the corner of the room. Now, this was a strong man. He was tall and broad across the shoulders. And he crouched down in the corner of the room, making this strange, primal noise.

To be truthful with you, it was a bit frightening. He was almost in a foetal position, as if he was going back to the womb. So whatever healing was going on, it had connected with him at a very deep level.

After a few minutes the sounds stopped and Sean started to cry.

I said, 'You're fine.'

And when he'd composed himself, he told me he could never remember crying before, ever, in his life. He got back up on the plinth, looking extremely embarrassed.

'I came here tonight because somebody recommended you. And, forgive me saying this, I came here to pacify my wife, to keep her off my back. I was thinking probably this was the biggest load of bullshit I was putting myself through, but I'd go ahead with it. I don't know what happened when you put your hand on me.' He looked at me then. 'I don't know what happened, why I acted the way I did. But I cried.'

'You needed to cry.'

'I know I did.'

Sean got dramatic healing from that session. He'd tried to sort out his drinking before that time, he told me, but he felt the healing was the greatest help. He came back to me a few times, and said he was feeling much better about his life. This man had been to treatment centres in the past to deal with his alcohol intake, but he still continued to drink. And though, when he'd seen me, he didn't give up alcohol completely, he certainly got his intake under control.

When people come to me for healing, I talk to them as well. Now, I'm the first person to say I haven't had training, but there is something I ask people to try if they are concerned about their alcohol consumption. I call it charging the alcohol.

Usually, when a person has a problem with alcohol, he tends to treat it as a liquid that will numb the way he is feeling. It helps him while the alcohol is in his system. He knows he'll feel no better in the morning, he knows he can expect a hangover, but meanwhile he can escape his problems for a few hours. He sees alcohol as a drug.

I suggest that when someone goes to a bar or a restaurant and has a glass of beer, whiskey or wine, they should pause a while. They should place their hand around the glass, they should hold it there for a while, and they should connect with it.

If you think about the ingredients of the drink, and realize that this is the produce of the earth, you should be able to feel the energy of it. If you can do that, and think of the grape or the barley, instead of mindlessly chucking the drink down you, I think you can enjoy it and it can be good for you. You will enjoy it in moderation. It's when you lash two bottles in a night that wine is bad for you. If you connect with it, you can stay right. You can say to yourself, 'It took yeast, water and barley to make this pint of Guinness. It's a product of God or the universe's being and I want to treat it with respect. I'm going to drink it knowing it came from the earth. It's going through my body and out to the earth.'

I've discussed this method with many of the people who have come to see me, and they have told me that when they follow it, they have more control over their intake.

There are many people in Ireland who are suffering because of the way people behaved in the past. We have the scandals of the church; we have the scandals of our institutions. There are the paedophiles, and the fathers who abuse, but there is another can of worms out there, one that's not often spoken about. And that's abusive mothers.

Often people come to me for a healing because they have a physical problem, but when you dig, you find their troubles stem back to their childhood. I don't know what went on with some mothers in the past. Maybe they were frustrated because they couldn't express who they were, or perhaps they suffered at the hands of their husbands and took it out on their children. But I often meet well-to-do women who seem to have a perfect life but in fact are haunted by their childhood.

Agnes came to see me one day. She was a married woman with two children, and from the outside her life appeared good. But she was depressed. It was, she said, because she couldn't get her mother's unkindness out of her mind.

'My mother used to beat me a lot,' she told me on her first visit.

'Was it just you, or did she hit your brothers and sisters too?'

'I don't think she loved any of us, if that's what you mean. There was a fair bit of psychological torture going on with us all. But I was the one who was beaten.'

'Did it happen a lot?'

'All the time. Do you want an example?'

'If you like.'

'The school bus used to pull up at the bottom of the driveway. I'd be going out to catch it, with my brother and sisters. One day, well, this happened more than once, but this day, as I was going through the door, my mother called me back.'

'Why was that?'

'She said, "Agnes, I forgot to put something in your lunch box." I went back in and she kicked me hard in the stomach.' There were tears in Agnes's eyes as she told me this. 'Then she kicked me out of the door. And no, before you ask, she didn't touch my lunch box. It would be that kind of thing.' She sighed. 'That day, she shouted out to the bus driver as I was running to catch it.'

'What did she say?'

'"Agnes is an awful devil. She's always forgetting something on me." And Joe, I swear the bus driver suspected what was going on. Why couldn't he do something about it?'

'I don't know. I really don't.'

'Do you know something, Joe? The first time I sat down for Christmas dinner after I married, and I was sitting at home just with my husband, I started crying and I simply couldn't stop. It was overwhelming.'

Her husband had been horrified and had asked her what was wrong.

She had told him, 'This is the first Christmas dinner I can remember that hasn't been poisoned with cold tea leaves.'

He was appalled. She hadn't told him half of what had gone on in her house. Agnes then opened up to him and told him about her experience of Christmas when she was a child. She repeated it to me that day. It's a story I have never got out of my head.

At a very young age Agnes was like the Cinderella in the family. She had to cook a lot and even had to look after her older brother. Her mother was a real tyrant towards her. And though her father, she is sure, knew what was going on, he didn't stand up to his wife, although he made small efforts to protect her, saying, 'Agnes, don't rush home from school today. Take your time.'

Christmas, Agnes said, was the worst time of all. She'd be the one preparing the dinner on Christmas Day, and then she'd have to give out the plates. As she came to the end, her mother would say, 'Agnes, don't forget your own dinner.' And she'd do a plate for herself. But she wouldn't be joining the other children at the table; she'd be left sitting on her own. And every Christmas, Agnes said, her mother would tell her father she was going to check on Agnes, and she'd get the cold tea leaves and shove the lot into Agnes's dinner, stirring it all around into a black mess. Then she'd say, 'If you don't eat all of that, you're in for it.'

Agnes couldn't wait to get married and leave home. She remembers her wedding day vividly. Everyone appeared to be happy: Agnes has a photograph of the family group, and her mother is smiling beside her. But five minutes before that happy picture was taken, Agnes's mother had pulled her aside and said, 'May you never have a day's luck in your marriage, and may you be cursed.'

Agnes was happy in her marriage, but her self-esteem had suffered from all that battering it had got as a child. And she couldn't forget her mother. How could she, when she still lived in the same town.

Sometimes she'd meet her mother in the grocery store, and she'd always have a nasty dig at Agnes. Her mother was a big strong woman, she didn't need looking after; but if she saw Agnes, she'd turn to the woman behind the counter and say, 'Look at this one, here. I, her mother, could be dying up there and she wouldn't lift a finger. It's all about her.' And the other woman would nod, as if in agreement. After all, Agnes's mother was a pillar of the community and a woman of the church.

Agnes couldn't let go of that childhood. It kept playing in her mind. She ended up confiding in her local priest, telling him part of the story. He said he felt her mother was evil – he used that word – and it was the priest who had suggested she come to me. Another of his parishioners had been talking about me, it seems.

Agnes's case was extreme, but it wasn't, unfortunately, so unusual. With someone like Agnes, who had all these bottled memories, I would still give a traditional hands-on healing. During the healing, I would work from the top of her head down to the bottom of her feet, because the body is one big energy. I would be trying to release the block and therefore to release the energy, and that, in turn, would allow Agnes to release her memories.

Agnes had spent years wondering what she had done wrong. Her stomach was in a complete knot. I worked a lot on the stomach area, so it helped her physically. The healing also helped her see that she'd done nothing wrong in life. She'd just been born in the wrong place – or rather, to the wrong person.

I'm not a counsellor, and what I do is not counselling. But I do end up listening. My father had a good way of listening, and my brother Pat too. So I get that from them.

Agnes was especially fond of her brother. He'd known what Agnes had gone through, but he'd married and gone to America. He had been there for a number of years, and he had his first child. One time he came back to visit and stayed with Agnes. But while he was there, he felt he'd better go and see his mother, so he drove there in Agnes's car.

He hoped his mother might be a little bit pleased to see him, and he wanted to show her his baby. He thought, *She never showed much affection to me, but surely she will turn round and pay attention to an infant?*

His mother was feeding the chickens when he arrived, and she walked over to him.

'What are you doing here?'

'I'm home. I'm up with Agnes.'

'Oh. It's with Agnes, is it?'

She didn't ask him in, but he followed her into the kitchen. He hoped she'd ask to hold the child, her own grandson, but she didn't even make eye contact with the child. Eventually he decided enough was enough, and began to walk away. She called him back, and he thought she was going to say hello to the child, so he turned round and said, 'Yes?'

'You're going back to America?'

'In a few days, yes.'

'Well, if I drop dead when you've gone, don't come back for my funeral.' She glowered at him. 'Cos I'll haunt you for the rest of your life if you do.'

I wanted to see Agnes's mother to try to understand her better. I wanted to pick up on what was wrong with her, on why she'd treat her own children so badly. I visualized what she would look like. One day I travelled down to Agnes's hometown and I saw her mother working in her yard. She didn't know I could see her. She looked exactly as I had visualized. I remember that her face was lined into a frown.

I picked up that she was a woman who resented being married and that she wasn't too happy with her husband. I felt that she didn't get out of life what she pretended she had, or what she wanted. Her own childhood hadn't been too good, but I knew that she had to deal with whatever was tormenting her, and not put it onto other people.

I stayed in contact with Agnes for a number of years after I met her. She did get on well with her life, and she kept in contact with her mother – she felt she had to, although her children hated their grandmother. They didn't know the extent of what their grandmother had done to their mother when she was a child, but they didn't like the way she treated Agnes as an adult. They had wanted a granny they could treasure, but with Agnes's mother, that was not to be.

26. Finding Missing Animals and Objects

Occasionally, when someone rings to ask if I can do some work for them, I get the feeling they doubt that I can help. They'd do anything; they contact me because they are desperate and a friend has told them that if anyone can help, then I can. So they ask me for my services, but all along they're saying to themselves, 'I'll try this man here, but I'm going to catch him out.' This is what I felt when I had a call from a cattle farmer one day.

The minute this man, Eoin, rang me, telling me he'd had some cattle stolen, I began to get a picture of where those cows were. But when I started asking him a few questions, I knew for certain he just wasn't listening to me. I felt that he needed proof before he handed over his money. I could have told Eoin all he needed to know without meeting him, but he was saying, 'You have to come over. You have to see where the cattle were stolen from.' That wasn't really necessary, but there was no talking to him. He said he'd come and collect me, and take me to the place.

He arrived the next morning, and we headed off in his Jeep. Now, this man was clearly desperate. He'd lost some of his livestock, his way of making a living; he was like a workman who had lost his tools. But for some strange reason he needed to check if I knew what I was talking about too.

On the whole journey over, as he was chatting, I sensed this man was doubting me. Before I left home I had a good idea where his stolen cattle were, but Eoin wasn't engaging with me. He didn't seem to want to know. I was thinking, *Jesus, this man is hard work.*

We got to an area I recognized through my sixth sense, and I thought, *That's strange, that's the vision I had of where he kept his cattle when he was talking to me on the phone.* But Eoin drove past it and kept on going down the road, chatting about nothing in particular. I realized that he was testing me, trying to catch me out. So I said to him, 'Do you not think you should be turning back?'

'What do you mean?'

'Well, where were the cattle stolen from?'

'Why?'

'Well, I feel it's back up the road.'

And he said casually, as if it had just occurred to him, 'Oh, you're right.'

'OK. So bring me back to where they were taken from.'

He did a three-point turn and headed back. We went into the yard. Now, he'd never told me how many cows had been stolen, but standing in that yard I got a vision. It was coming to me that there had been panic there, that some lads had reversed in with trailers. They were getting the cows into the trailers as quickly as they could. I was getting that there were two trailers and that it was night-time.

'Were there thirteen taken?' I asked.

He looked startled. 'There were.'

'Now, I don't want to alarm you,' I said, 'but I think you're going to have to act very fast.'

'Do you know where they are?'

'I'm getting that they're in a small townland.' I mentioned the name of a place. 'I haven't a clue where it is, but strangely enough, I think you have a friend lives in the locality.'

'What? A friend is involved?'

'Ah no. The friend has nothing to do with the theft of the cattle, but he might be able to help.'

'Do you have any idea where this townland is?'

'It's near the border. The border with Northern Ireland.'

He nodded. 'You're right. I know a farmer in those parts. I'll give him a ring.'

'And I stress, you'll have to act quickly here, or it will be too late.'

He rang his friend and asked if there was a townland near him with the name I'd given him. And there was.

'How will I find the cattle?'

I drew him a picture, showing everything I could see in my mind. It included a picture of a warehouse.

'Now, this place,' I said, handing him the piece of paper, 'you may go scouring the roads to find it. It doesn't look like a normal cattle shed; it's more of an industrial unit. But I guarantee your cattle are in it.'

Two days later, Eoin rang me. He said he had driven around the area for a couple of hours and was about to give up when he found what seemed to be an industrial unit. He walked up to the place, only to find it was locked up. But he managed to climb up to a gap where he could see in. And yes, his cows were there. He was convinced of it.

He was able to prove they were his cows from the tags, and he got them back. If he'd left it any later, a lorry would have come across the border, the cows would have been up the ramp, and they would have vanished.

I don't just find large animals for people. I work with smaller ones too. And one morning this lady rang me in a terrible state. She had been taking care of her relations' dog while they were on holiday. Now, this was a much-loved family dog. It was treated like a child. The owners couldn't bear the thought of sending it to kennels, so they asked her to care for it for the two weeks, knowing the dog would be happier with someone it knew.

It was a beautiful dog: a Samoyed, which is a bit like a husky with a thick white coat. At first everything had gone well. The dog settled into his temporary home. But then, one day, when she'd gone to fetch him in from the garden, there was no sign of him. She found a hole that he had dug; it looked like he had crawled under a wire fence.

'He can't have been gone long when I found he'd escaped,' she said. 'I'd checked him just ten minutes before. We called him and called him, and searched up and down the road, but there wasn't a sign of him.'

'And when did he escape?'

'It was yesterday afternoon. He's been missing overnight.' I could hear the panic in her voice. 'A friend gave me your number,' she said. 'Can you help, Mr Cassidy?'

All the time she'd been talking to me, I had been getting a vision of the woman and where she lived. I said to her, 'I understand you're in an awful state, but don't tell me any more now. I just want you to answer the questions I put to you.'

She said she would.

'Do you live in a bungalow out in the country?' I asked.

'Yes.'

'Is the house painted cream, with a blue front door? And is the garden gate newly painted?'

'Yes. Yes to all of that . . .'

'If you come out of your gate and turn left, is there a crossroads?'

'Yes, there is.'

'Well, I feel that the dog is up that road. I advise you to get into your car and go up there.'

'I've already looked. I've looked so many times. I'm afraid he's dead.'

'No,' I said. 'That dog is alive. And it's nearby. You have to find a house that has a boat in the back garden.'

I remember her automatic reaction was, 'God, I don't know anyone with a boat.'

'This boat has been there for a long, long time,' I said. 'It doesn't get used. I'm getting a strong feeling the dog is there.'

'OK.' She sounded doubtful.

'Will you do that, and ring me back?'

She said she would. And a little over an hour later the same woman rang me again to thank me. I could hear the relief in her voice.

She had driven up the road, looking for a boat, but, as she'd expected, there was no sign of one. She came across a sheep farmer repairing a wire fence. She knew him, so she stopped the car and told him about the dog that was missing. He said that he hadn't seen him.

'Do you mind me asking you if there's a house along here that has a boat out the back?' she said.

'Oh,' he said, 'there is. The boat must've been in the garden for the last thirty years. It hasn't been moved.'

She went down to the house and rang the doorbell. A woman came to answer the door.

'I'm just going around the area,' the lady with the missing Samoyed said. 'I've lost a dog. It doesn't even belong to me. Have you seen one?'

'A white fluffy dog?'

'That's right.'

'Oh, thank God! This dog appeared here yesterday. He

THE DIVINER

was in a complete panic. We didn't recognize him from around. We thought he had been dumped. I was worried that he'd be killed by a tractor on the road, so I took him in. Come with me.'

They walked around the side of the house, and the dog was tied to the boat. Needless to say, when the dog saw the lady, he started jumping up and down with excitement. As soon as the lady got home, she rang me.

'That was amazing,' she said. 'I'm so grateful. I don't know what I'd have done if I hadn't found that dog. He's the most important thing in that family. They'd have been heartbroken if anything had happened to him.' She was almost crying with relief.

It's not only animals that I find for people; I find valuable objects too. And one time a woman rang to tell me she'd lost her ring. She was moving house and couldn't find it anywhere.

'I've searched high and low,' she said. 'I don't know how much it's worth, but it's so very pretty, and to me it has great value. It belonged to my grandmother, then my own mother. I've admired it all my life, and when I go, I want to pass it on to the next generation.' Somebody had given her my number. 'They said you're a diviner,' she told me. 'Can you help me to find it, Mr Cassidy?'

This wasn't the first time I've been asked to find jewellery. 'OK,' I said, 'stay on the phone, but I'm not going to talk for a minute or two. I want to zone in on your house. I want to get a vision of it.' Less than sixty seconds passed. Then I said, 'Do you live in an old farmhouse?'

'I do.'

'Is there a room where they'd have kept cheese in years ago? A cool room or a pantry?'

'There is.'

'And you have a freezer in there at the moment. A big chest freezer.'

'Yes.'

'The ring is behind the freezer.'

'No, no it's not. I already looked. We moved the freezer out, and it's not there.'

'I'm getting it's there. Behind the base of it.'

'Well, I can't move it again at the moment.'

'Sure. But when you can.'

I was picking up that she was an elderly lady and that she wouldn't be able to move that freezer herself. She would have to wait for her son to come and visit.

'Ring me,' I said, 'when you've been able to take a good look. I'd like to hear.'

And later on that evening, she did.

'My son came in. We moved the freezer, but when we looked the ring wasn't there. I began to doubt you, Mr Cassidy. But then ...'

'Yes?'

'When we started to push the freezer in again, the ring fell off one of the freezer's legs. So thanks very much.'

It's nice when someone calls to tell me what happened, because sometimes I never hear the outcome. Very often, I only learn I was successful when a friend of the person rings me to ask me to find something for them. They'll tell me that their friend said it was amazing the way I had found their bracelet or their earring or pendant or watch.

27. Sixth Sense

We all have a touch of the sixth sense, but most of us don't acknowledge it. Most people call it coincidence. You think of someone you haven't thought of for a while, and then you hear from them. Or maybe someone has been on your mind a lot, and then you hear that they're not well. I believe we should all act on our instinct. If you think of someone, call them. Don't put it off.

One day I was working on a house for a friend. She had recently started a relationship with a man from South Africa, and her house needed some work done for geopathic stress. Her partner happened to be staying in her house as I was working on it. He was very keen to get me on his own, and I knew he wanted to test me to see how well I could use my sixth sense. He invited me to have lunch with him in the coffee shop next door. He questioned me about the history of the house his partner was living in. He knew a bit about its history and my information seemed to satisfy him. However, he went on to ask me if I could get a sense of what his own house looked like in South Africa. I concentrated and got an image of it.

'Is it a large, two-storey house? Is there a sloping lawn? Does it have a wonderful view across a lake, which stems from natural springs?'

'Yes. Yes, it does.'

I continued describing the house to him, and he agreed that everything I saw in my vision was the truth.

This man had an engineering background, and I had had the distinct feeling that he was a sceptic and he thought my work was a load of nonsense. Maybe he thought his partner was wasting her money when she hired me; I don't know. But I saw his reaction when I'd finished talking to him. He was clearly thinking, *This is incredible!*

People come to see me from all around Ireland. I'm always amazed by the distances they will travel. They've come from West Cork, from Kerry and from Donegal, and they would do this before the motorway made travelling so much faster. There are times, however, when people would like healing, but they're not able to get to me. Maybe they are too sick. Maybe they live abroad. This is where distance healing comes in handy. I need to use my sixth sense in order to distance heal, but it can be extremely effective.

A number of years ago, my phone rang at night. It was someone ringing from Italy. Luckily, she had very good English. I've no idea how she heard about me, but she said, 'My friend has just had some bad news. She's very ill. Is it true that you do distance healing?'

I said that I did, and I asked her to send a photo of her friend. She said that she would, and I gave her my address.

'Is your friend with you now?' I asked.

'Yes, she is here.'

'Then could you please sit down beside her?'

'OK.' There was a pause. 'I'm sitting beside her now. I'm holding her hand.'

'That's good.'

I was building up a picture of her friend. It was like looking at a photo. I focused, and a picture of her came to me.

'Your friend, is she about fifty?'

'She is.'

'Does she have dark, shoulder-length hair?'

'Yes, that's right.'

'I'm picking up that she's tall. About five foot eight? And she has beautiful brown eyes. People say they are her best feature.'

'How do you know that? Yes, that's all correct. I don't think you need a photo!'

'Is she a lawyer? A solicitor, perhaps?'

'Right again.'

'I would still like the photograph,' I said. 'Then I can connect better with your friend and give her a healing.'

The photo arrived no more than a week after we spoke. The woman rang again three weeks later to say that her friend's treatment had been cancelled. She was now well again.

Another time, a lady rang me from Wales. She wanted to come over especially for a healing. She said she could come over on the ferry.

'That may not be necessary,' I said. 'Would you not send me a photograph first? We can take it from there.'

'But I'd like to come,' she said. 'I'm in unbearable pain with my arthritis, and I've tried so many treatments. I've heard such good things about you, Mr Cassidy.'

She sent the photo, I worked with it, and the woman rang to say it had brought her wonderful relief. In a case like that, I have a picture of the person in my mind from the moment I hear their voice. And the stronger the picture is, the more success I will have. It shows the whole energy is working.

Distance healing also has a dramatic effect on leg ulcers. I've worked on a lot of those. I was doing a distance healing for a girl's mother just recently. The daughter rang, but it was the mother I had the vision of. The daughter sent the photo, and I was able to work with this. Now, of course, technology has made the whole system easier. If someone can't get to me, or if they have a horse or a cow or a dog that is ill, they can simply take a photo with their phone and send it straight over to me.

My sixth sense can work in other ways too. One time, a long while ago, I saw a scene on the nine o'clock news on TV that stuck with me. The story had been running all day and I'd first heard it on the radio: a distinguished man had signed some documents he shouldn't have, and now he was in difficulties. It was nothing too serious, but the media were making a field day of it. They were hounding him. I'd gone out to make some coffee, and when I walked back into the sitting room I saw this lady on TV closing the gate of her home. I realized it was the man's wife.

I stopped and just watched. I knew for certain that the lady would be contacting me for a healing. When this feeling happens, everything goes into slow motion. The first thing that came into my head was, *This poor lady*. Her husband wasn't a bad man. He had just signed something off and now it had come back to haunt him.

He was a country man, and before this he didn't have a very high profile. He and his wife were private people who kept themselves to themselves, and now the media were gathered outside their home. She wasn't used to that and it hurt her. You could see it in the way she closed that gate.

A day or two later, I was driving along when my phone rang. I pulled over to answer it, and the minute this lady said hello, I knew it was the man's wife. I knew before she said her name, and the vision of her closing her gate came into my mind again.

She said, 'Mr Cassidy? Might I make an appointment to see you?'

She came two days later, and I remember she was so upset. She said, 'My husband is not a bad person and now he's a broken man.'

I gave that woman some healings. I worked on her energy, and it helped her to cope. She was such a gentle lady. She said her husband was just sitting in the house. She felt he was depressed, and this was taking a toll on her. It was a sorrow and a worry.

She asked me to work on her house too. The media intrusion, and the bad will they felt towards this woman's husband, had affected the house's energy. It no longer seemed like a place of refuge to her. She wanted to protect her husband and her family. I worked on the house, and she got some relief from that.

I enjoy going to the races, and in past years I've been over to Cheltenham for the racing week there. One year I was booked to go, and night after night before I was due to go I had a recurring dream: four men were on the ferry, and one of those men came home in a coffin. Now, I don't go around worrying about life. But this dream kept coming. I was sure it was a message for me, and I was thinking, *What is the dream trying to tell me here?* I knew my own life was not in danger. I was travelling with two other men, so the number four couldn't refer to us. But I was intrigued to understand what this dream was all about. This went on every night for about a fortnight.

It never crossed my mind to cancel my trip, and off I went with my two friends. We enjoyed the few days. We stayed in this beautiful English village near Cheltenham where there was a duck pond and lovely walks. We even won a few bob, and we had a great couple of days' racing. I hadn't been thinking about that dream very much while we were there, but once or twice I stopped and thought to myself, *I wonder what that was all about.*

We headed back on the ferry with not a bother on us. I was drinking a Club Orange when a representative from the ferry company came over clutching a big Manila folder and sat down beside a couple who were sitting next to me. He started talking to the young woman.

I overheard the conversation. On the way to Wales a week earlier, a group of young guys had been harassing this girl and she had told them to get lost. Her boyfriend had appeared, and one of the young lads had thrown a punch at him. At this point, some security men came on the scene. They contacted the police in Wales, and when the ferry arrived, the ringleader had been arrested and the other lads let go. As far as I could ascertain, the couple had made a complaint against the lad who had thrown the punch and they wanted him taken to court in Ireland. The man from the ferry company was explaining the difficulties of this. He was saying, 'Look. That's what happened. We dealt with it as best we could. The police in Wales arrested the guy.'

'Yes,' she said, 'but it's not good enough. They didn't press charges. Now I'll have to follow it up with the guards in Ireland.'

The rep said, 'I know. Those lads were totally out of control. For what it's worth, one of those lads died over there. He drank himself to death. He inhaled his own vomit.'

'Oh,' she said, 'my God! I wouldn't wish that on anyone!'

'I know,' he said, 'and actually, his coffin is on this ferry with us.'

When he said those words, I almost choked on my Club Orange. I realized it was those lads I'd been dreaming about. Those were the four lads going away, and one of them was coming back in a coffin. There was my dream.

Sometimes, living with a highly tuned sixth sense can be a lonely experience. You can't always share your instincts with others. Sensing what is ahead for people can be difficult, especially when it's someone who is close to me.

I don't share what I can see with others. It's like with my healing. Unless someone asks me specifically, I'll keep my views to myself – though I do, of course, share any concerns I have with Jean.

It's very painful for me knowing when a member of my family is facing death, and particularly so when I know there is nothing I can do for them. Their fate has been mapped out for them. But there is a good side to this. When someone close to me is very ill, and I sense that this is not their time to depart this world, I find that very comforting.

I'm not a well-organized person. I put it down to my dyslexia. A few weeks ago, Jean was tidying up old receipts in my wallet when a piece of paper fell to the ground. She picked it up and looked at it.

'Joe, do you still need this phone number?'

'Show me.' I took a look at the name and number. 'God, I haven't heard from that woman in about three or four years.'

It was the number of a lady I've done a lot of work for on various occasions. I've given her healings and I've worked with other people in her family as well. I'd become friends with her over the years.

'I'll keep that number, I might give her a call sometime.'

Jean smiled. 'I'd say you'll be hearing from her first.'

Jean is used to living with me, and she knows how these things tend to work. And, lo and behold, the following morning my phone rang. When I answered, it was that very lady. She started off just chatting, and asking me how things were, but I knew by the tone of her voice that something was wrong. And sure enough, she was upset: her sister wasn't well. She was worried about her and wanted to book some healings.

Her sister, it turned out, may have needed surgery on her neck and had been told she would most likely need chemotherapy after that. She came to me for healing before her appointment with the doctor. She had a biopsy taken, but it was inconclusive. I continued giving her healing until the biopsy was repeated, and that time it was clear. The surgeon said there wasn't a trace of anything. So that was a good outcome for her.

28. When My Sixth Sense Saved Me

I often see pictures of things that have already happened, and of course I get visions of things that will happen in the future. Sometimes it's an advantage to others, and occasionally it's a benefit to myself. Once it even saved my life.

A few years ago, I wasn't well. I cancelled my afternoon appointments and lay down on the sofa to rest. I didn't know what was wrong. This was by far the sickest I'd felt since all that trouble before I became a healer.

I remember we had a cat at the time. We called her Daisy. She jumped onto me and started scratching furiously at my chest. I pushed her away, but she jumped up again. She seemed really agitated, almost angry. I didn't think much about it at the time.

I went into the shower, had a wash and was about to go to the doctor, when Jean arrived home early from work. She had some shopping and she was putting everything away.

'I'm off then,' I said to her.

'Off? Where are you going?'

'I'm going to the doctor.'

She was in the middle of stacking milk and yogurt into the fridge, and she turned round then, pausing. 'Why? Why are you going in there?'

'I don't feel well.'

'Since when? What's wrong?'

'I've got a pain in my chest.'

'I'll drive you.'

'No, I'm fine. You sit down and have your tea.'

I didn't want her worrying, so I drove myself in and the doctor checked me over. He took my blood pressure and looked a bit worried.

'I'm going to get an ambulance, Joe.'

'Oh?'

'Yeah. I'm getting you into hospital.'

It arrived fairly swiftly, and I was taken up to Dublin. As usual, the staff in the A&E department were rushed off their feet, but because I'd arrived in an ambulance I was high priority. So it wasn't too long before a doctor came and examined me. He listened to my heart and took my blood pressure.

'That's up,' he said. I could tell he was concerned about me. Well, I was concerned about myself. I felt extremely unwell, and if anything, I seemed to be getting worse. After a while, there was a change of staff. Before he went off duty, the doctor came over to say goodbye. He put his hand on my arm and said, 'Mr Cassidy, I hope everything works out for you. And just one thing. Don't be afraid to emphasize your concerns about yourself.'

'I'll do that. Thanks very much.'

That doctor was a gentleman. I trusted him and felt safe while he was there. When the new team came on duty, though, I felt there was a change of atmosphere in the place. Now, I don't like complaining about doctors. That's not my place. But it felt to me that unlike the previous team of medical staff who were looking after me, this lot didn't think there was much wrong with me. And that made me ill at ease.

I was admitted onto the ward, and nurses would come in and check my pulse and my blood pressure. They seemed to think I was fine. Yet I'd never felt as sick in my life.

One doctor commented on my slow heart rate, but he said

it was a positive thing, telling me it was a sign that I'd been fit in my day. I *was* indeed fit as a boy, when I was playing tennis and Gaelic football, and soccer, but that was hardly the case any more. I felt extremely unwell. When I needed to go to the loo, I had to walk down to the other end of the ward. It was a terrible struggle. I was gasping for breath, and there was tightness across my chest. Not only that, but sweat was pouring off me. My pyjamas and the sheets were wringing wet. And when I got back from the loo, it was like someone had tipped a bucket of water over me. Yet, for some reason, the staff felt I wasn't particularly sick.

After two days, a nurse came over to me. She was going off duty for the weekend and she asked me how I was.

I said, 'I don't feel well at all.'

She said, 'To tell you the truth there's nothing showing on the monitor, only that you have a bad flu. But would you like a room on your own?'

I was in a public hospital on a six-bed ward, and it didn't bother me, but I was feeling very bad, so I said, 'Please. Because I feel so unwell, I'd love to be in a room with an en suite.'

She got the room for me, which was a relief. That night I felt really ill. I could not catch my breath. I was nearly frightened to go to sleep in case I never woke up, that was how bad I felt. So at 2.30 a.m. I pressed the buzzer and a nurse came to me.

I said, 'Could you get me a doctor, please. I don't feel well at all.' I could hardly get the words out, I was so short of breath.

She stood and she said to me, 'Mr Cassidy, you're in a heart unit. There's nothing wrong with you, only a bad flu. You're taking up a bed.'

There was no doctor for me until the next morning. When

he was doing his rounds, he came in to me and said, 'We've checked everything. We've done your bloods, we've done an ECG, you took the stress test and we've taken X-rays. All the test results are fine. You'll be going home tomorrow.'

Jean wasn't too worried. She's so used to me having strange symptoms. As a healer, I often seem to pick up the symptoms of the people I'm treating. It seems to be part of their healing process. I knew in my heart though that this was something more.

My intuition, my sixth sense, made me stand up for myself. I knew I wasn't well. I said, 'No, doctor. I'll go when you do a procedure to prove there's nothing wrong with me.'

'What's that?'

'I want you to do an angiogram on me.' An angiogram is an X-ray test that uses a special dye and camera to take pictures of the blood flow in an artery. I felt strongly that I needed this procedure done, and that if I had one, something was going to show up. The doctor clearly didn't feel the same way.

'No. There's nothing wrong with you. You're going home.'

I asked him to sign a piece of paper saying that he had refused to do that particular test. He wasn't keen to do that. And later on he came back in to me and said he was going to arrange to get the angiogram done.

'But really, Mr Cassidy, there's no need for it.'

'So you say.'

'And you'll be going home straight after it.'

For various reasons I had to go to the Blackrock Clinic to get the angiogram done. Two nights before I went, before I had persuaded the doctor to arrange it, I had a dream. I was in a large room, and there were these murals on the walls. I had the same dream the next night too. The dream was vivid.

Anyway, at around seven o'clock the next morning, these two men came up to the ward, put me in a wheelchair and wheeled me down to an ambulance. It was a father-and-son team, and I warmed to them immediately. As I climbed out of the wheelchair to get into the ambulance, buckets of sweat began to pour off me again.

I was able to lie down in the ambulance, and I found that a relief. The older man began to examine me, checking my pulse and blood pressure.

'How long were you in the hospital?'

'I've been in five days now.'

'And how long have you been experiencing these symptoms?'

I told him they had come on the day I went to the hospital.

I felt safer in that ambulance than I'd felt at any time since that first doctor had gone off duty in A&E. It seemed like this man was taking better care of me and was observing and listening more to me than any doctor or nurse had in the past five days.

He said, 'I don't want to frighten you, but I feel we should get you to the Blackrock Clinic sooner rather than later.'

We arrived at the hospital, and as I was brought into the waiting area for the angiogram, I noticed the murals on the walls. They were of flowers and grass, and beautiful scenery. It was exactly as I had seen in my dream. This was the room I had seen for the past two nights, and now I was lying on a trolley, looking at it.

A nurse appeared just then and asked the ambulance men for my file. It was clear that there was a queue and I was at the end of it. She put out her hand to take the file, but the older ambulance man clung onto it more tightly. This made her angry.

'You've done your job,' she said. 'It's over to us now.'

'I know that. But please can you get the doctor to come out and examine Mr Cassidy?'

'I can't do that.'

'Well, I'm not handing him over until you do.'

She sighed one enormous sigh. 'Well! It will be on your head if he rears up.'

The doctor came out to examine me and straight away he asked for my trolley to be brought in for the procedure. He was a gentleman and apologized to the patients in front of me, explaining that this was an emergency.

When you have an angiogram, a small tube, or catheter, is inserted into your groin and pushed up, to see if there's a problem with your artery. It all shows up on a screen. We were not long into the procedure when the doctor said, 'We have a problem.'

'It's me with the problem, isn't it?'

He laughed. 'Yes, but I have a problem too.'

'What's that?'

'You need work done. Immediately.'

'Will it work?'

'It should do. If it doesn't, you're going to need a triple bypass.' He was talking about a stent. This is a small mesh tube that supports the artery, to prevent it from narrowing. They insert it through the fine tube used in the angiogram.

The doctor began trying to get the stent in. The patient would usually be well prepared for this procedure, but he said that he needed to get it done as quickly as he could. I told him I was a healer and so maybe could help. He listened and agreed.

'I feel I need time to relax,' I said. 'And when I say go for it, go for it.' I explained that I wasn't just panicking and that

I trusted him absolutely. I asked for quiet in the room and then I asked him to explain what the procedure was. He showed me on the screen what he needed to do.

'See here,' he said, pointing. 'These two arteries have narrowed. You could have had this condition since birth.'

There was absolute quiet in the room. I relaxed. And when I felt the time was right, I told him to do what he had to do. And it worked. The tension in the room dropped at once. The consultant looked relieved.

'Good man,' he said, smiling at me. 'That's done the trick now.'

I got the impression from everyone's demeanour that I was one lucky man. I was wheeled into recovery.

A few hours later, the consultant was back to check how I was. He asked me how long I'd been feeling that way, and I told him of my experiences in the other hospital.

'They had you walking to the bathroom?' He sounded incredulous.

'They did. Until I got my own room.'

He shook his head in disbelief.

'You do realize,' he said, 'that doing that, you could have dropped down dead with a heart attack! You are one fortunate man.'

I agreed that I was. This was a time when my sixth sense had, possibly, saved my life. It had been a fight to be heard, but it was a fight worth having. It was then that I remembered my cat Daisy's reaction and the way she had been scratching at my chest. I realized she had known, with her animal instinct, that something was seriously wrong with my heart.

'I'm going to ring that hospital,' he said. 'I'm going to give out to them. You, Mr Cassidy, should have been seen earlier.'

I had to go back to the other hospital to be disch..
While the consultant was on the phone, he said, 'I assun.
you have a bed for Mr Cassidy.' And they said they hadn't.
Now, this man wasn't going to accept this. He reared up and
let them have it. And suddenly they found one.

When I got back to the other hospital, I was once again
wheeled up to the ward. The first person I saw, as I was being
wheeled along the corridor, was the nurse I'd called in the
night, the nurse who had told me, categorically, that there
was nothing wrong with me and that I was taking up a bed.

I'm sure she saw me. I saw the colour rise on her face, but
she didn't acknowledge me as I was wheeled by.

'What's up with her?' asked the porter, as she bustled by.
We went on chatting. He'd heard about my procedure, and
said, as we reached my bed, 'You are one lucky man!'

I was still thinking about that nurse. I was annoyed that
she hadn't the grace to acknowledge me, let alone to say she
was sorry. God forgive me, but I wasn't letting her get away
with that. I turned to the porter, and said, 'Could you please
take me back down to the nurses' station?' I knew he had to
go there anyway to drop my file off for the doctors.

'OK. You're the boss!' He turned the chair round and we
set off. There was the nurse, writing in a logbook.

She looked up and blushed.

'When you have time,' I said, 'perhaps you'd like to read
my notes. They will explain to you that I haven't got a dose
of the flu and I hadn't last week either. They will explain to
you that I didn't needlessly take up a bed on the ward. Perhaps in future you might listen to a patient in distress.'

I don't know if she took it on board. She still didn't
acknowledge me. But it made me feel a bit better. I told the
porter to take me back to my bed.

PART III

29. Siobhan's Story

Sometimes, people come to me for a session or course of healing, they get relief and I never see them again. It's often that way with houses, too. People call me to check for geopathic stress, to deal with a spirit or to divine their land. They're happy with my work, and that's it. Often they give their friends my number, but they never have a need to see me again.

Then there are the others, the people who come to me time and again for help in different areas of their lives. I see them, and I also see other people in their family. One such person is Siobhan. I asked her, for the purposes of this book, to talk about the help I've been able to give her over the years. Here she tells the story.

I first met Joe through his wife. I came across Jean in my work, and we hit it off at once. We'd meet for coffee and for lunch now and again. Joe was sick at the time. He was in and out of hospital having various tests. I remember being very conscious of that. I also remember how it stressed Jean, especially as they could never find out what was wrong. It was such a difficult situation for her, with two small children and Joe so unwell. I used to wonder how I would have coped if I were her. I'm not sure I could have kept it all going as she did.

The first time I remember being aware that Joe was a healer was at a party in their village. This was before he had set himself up as a healer, and they were trying to work out if he could make a career out of it. I really felt he should, but I'm not sure if I said so at the time.

He has a way about him. He's a gentle person who has something extra, the sort of person you'd trust with your life.

I'm slow to believe in these alternative things. I'm a little doubting maybe, but something about Joe just rang true. It was funny. For a long time I knew in the back of my mind that I'd be going to Joe for a healing, but I didn't go until he'd been in practice a year or two. There was no particular reason to. Or at least, there was nothing specific to latch on to – to be a strong enough reason to take me there.

In the end, I went with a bad shoulder. I had strained it in some way, and it was very painful. There was no sign of it clearing up. So I decided that was the time, that was my opportunity to go to Joe. Maybe he could do something for my shoulder, and maybe he could do something to help me through what was a very difficult time for me.

My marriage was breaking up, so things were very tough at home. I had a little girl, and I was trying to decide what was best to do for her sake. It was hard to know which direction to take.

Joe was working from his house when I first saw him. I went for a full course of six healings. The main thing I remember is the calm and relaxing environment. You go into this softly lit room with soothing music playing in the background, you take your shoes off and then get onto the couch.

Joe explained what he was going to do and was careful to make sure I was OK with it. He did his thing, working his way around what were obviously key areas. Placing his hand on my head, my heart area, my stomach and my feet, he then concentrated on my shoulder. I remember the heat of his hand and feeling a strange sensation in my shoulder; it was as though he was reaching right into the joint. I remember thinking at the time that this had to be where the problem was.

The whole thing was very easy and relaxing. Those first few times, I said very little. Joe talked a bit, but you could see him focus on the healing, closing his eyes from time to time, in concentration I presume. I felt he read my character well. It was as though he was in total tune with when I wanted to talk and when I didn't. There was definitely no pressure to talk about things I wasn't quite ready to discuss.

I'd usually be tired and sleep like a baby after a session with Joe. My shoulder didn't make a dramatic recovery, but there was some improvement. I certainly never thought of stopping the treatments. I felt they were giving me more than just the focus on my shoulder; they were helping me with the emotional upheaval I was going through.

There is one incident from that course of healings that I will never forget. I turned up one day for an appointment, and the battery had gone on my watch. My watch had stopped the day before, but I still had it on. Every time I looked at my wrist I thought, I really must go and get that new battery.

It had stopped at four o'clock, and when I came out of my appointment with Joe, it said ten past four. It was going again! I couldn't believe it. And it kept going. It was a good nine months or maybe even a year before I needed a new battery again. Next time I visited Joe I mentioned this. He just laughed.

When my marriage finally broke up, my husband left home. I stayed on in the house, with our daughter. This was a difficult thing as my husband's family had lived there for some time before we got married. I very much felt the house belonged to his family and was uneasy about staying on there. But I felt I had to for the sake of my daughter. Knowing about Joe's work with energies, I decided to ask him to come out and do a job on it. I asked him to clear the house, to get rid of any bad energy that might be around. Jean would have talked about Joe's work with houses so I was conscious of his ability to lift the air in a place. I felt I had nothing to lose and maybe he could make a difference.

So Joe came out one afternoon. He went into all the different rooms while I stayed in the kitchen. I remember feeling restless as I listened to him moving from room to room. After about half an hour, he came into the kitchen and I made us both a cup of coffee.

Joe talked a lot about the energy he had found in the house. He said a lot of things. But three things in particular have stayed in my mind.

'There's a basket up on the landing,' he said.

'Yes, there are three up there.'

'I mean the largest of the three. You should get rid of it.'

My first reaction was one of surprise. But then shivers ran down my spine. That basket had come to the house in the form of a Christmas hamper, one of those big ostentatious hampers packed with chocolates and whiskey and Christmas pudding and relish. And lots of things that somehow you never get around to eating. I didn't much like where the hamper had come from, in fact I had serious suspicions about it. Looking back, I wonder why I'd even kept the basket. I'm not sure of the full story behind that hamper's arrival in our house, but as Joe's attention was drawn to it like that, it makes me think my suspicions were well founded.

The second thing I remember is that he said there was a woman in the sitting room looking out of the window. It was like she was waiting for something or someone. I've never been able to figure out what that one meant. But the third one really rang bells.

'There are conversations going on in that room off the hall. Strange ones.'

'But we haven't spent time in there. Not for years.' It was one of those rooms we dumped things in.

I couldn't work it out. Until I remembered the computer. It was sitting on an old table in the corner of that room, and I knew my husband had been doing all kinds of things on it. Joe let me work this out for myself.

I'm not sure how much he knew or didn't know. I don't know how much he kept back. There's only so much I wanted to know and have confirmed at any one time, and I think Joe recognized that. He tells you bits to help you understand but not so much to overwhelm you.

Joe worked on the house to get rid of the energy. A few days later he came back and checked it for geopathic stress. I threw out the basket and got rid of the computer's hard drive. After that, I felt a lot more at ease in the house.

Everyone suffers when a marriage ends. I did, and I suspect my husband did too. But the person I was most concerned about was my daughter.

I was worried about her. Worried about what we had put her through. She was having trouble with her sinuses. We just couldn't seem to clear them. So I brought her to Joe, hoping he could help. I wondered if the sinus problem was related to the emotional turmoil that had been going on for her at the time. Surprisingly, given the cynicism of teens, she was happy to have a full course of six sessions with Joe. By the end of those sessions the sinus problem was greatly improved. Maybe she was also feeling a lot better in herself.

Over the years I've kept in regular contact with Jean, and on one occasion when we met for a chat she told me she'd seen this lovely house. It wasn't officially on the market, but she'd heard the owners were open to a good offer. She wanted to buy it. I laughed. I thought, OK, here we go, Joe and Jean on the move again. *They had the house in Two Mile House on the market. This was the height of the boom, but for some reason they couldn't sell it. It simply didn't budge. Jean was devastated. She'd really wanted that house. But she resigned herself to staying put for the time being.*

Around this time, the matter of continuing to live in the house, with all its history, was becoming a real issue for me. I really wanted to move to somewhere that would be truly my own. But I worried about moving my daughter. How could I ask her to move from her home, the house she loved? It really wouldn't be fair to do that. I felt I was tied to the house for some years to come, really until she had finished her education. It was all taking its toll.

I remember talking to Joe about it one day. It is one of those things about him: after being in his company, the situation always seems clearer.

Possibilities seem to present themselves. Over the coming weeks I began to think that maybe a move would be the right thing to do. Maybe my daughter would be OK with it. I talked to her about the idea of a move and while she was not too keen on the idea, she said she would go along with it.

Joe can't have known how much of a part he would play in making this move happen. That summer, a house came on the market. I walked past it and thought, Maybe that will suit me. *I made an appointment to view it, and I really liked it. It was in a lovely area and had a good-sized garden. It needed work done but I felt excited about it. Mind you, others thought I was mad, as the house was in need of some modernizing. But I could see what it could look like, how it could be a real home.*

After I'd viewed the house, I felt the need to talk to Joe. As is so often the case with him, he appears just as you are thinking you need to make contact. As I walked up the town, who should I bump into but Joe himself. We went for coffee and Jean joined us just as I was broaching the subject of the house I'd seen.

'I've seen a house and I think maybe it's the right one for me. But I'd love your opinion on it.'

'Where is it?'

As I described the location, Joe and Jean burst out laughing. It was the house they'd been hoping to buy. My immediate thought was, Oh no, how can I take what was supposed to be their house? *But they encouraged me to go ahead. It all seemed to be part of this connection, whatever it is, that Joe has, this gift of helping things to move on another step.*

That wasn't the end of the story, or the end of Joe's involvement either. I'd put my house on the market and got an offer on it pretty well straight away, but the buyers were being indecisive. They had made the offer and asked me to take it off the market, but three months later they still hadn't committed.

I'd bought the other house at this stage. It's not like me to be so impulsive! With two mortgages on the go, I was getting close to the end of my ability to service both loans. Along with this, the Celtic Tiger was dying a death and prices were on the slide. I was becoming worried and getting close to giving my buyers an ultimatum, but the auctioneer advised me strongly against this.

By a strange chance it turned out my buyers were renting a house from a friend of Joe's. The people concerned had given notice they were moving as they were purchasing a house, but then came back to Joe's friend making an offer on his house. Joe, in conversation with his friend, came to the realization that his tenants and my buyers were one and the same people. What a coincidence. On hearing this, I followed through on the ultimatum: pay the deposit or the house goes back on the market.

All's well that ends well. The sale went through and I'm now happily ensconced in my new house, along with my daughter.

I've been to Joe so often, and for so many reasons, that I can't even remember them all. I'm so grateful to him, for all the doors he's opened for me. It's like he's been able to unstick things at critical times and get things moving again. Joe hasn't only helped me, he's done wonders for my mother too.

Four years ago my mother was unwell. She'd been diagnosed with shingles, but it wasn't clearing up. I asked her if she'd like me to give her photograph to Joe so he could give her a distance healing. I'm not sure what she really thought, though I know my father is a complete sceptic. Still, although she didn't have a clear picture of exactly what Joe did, she agreed to give it a go. She said, 'I suppose I've nothing to lose.'

So I gave Joe the photograph. A week later he rang me and said, 'Tell me this. What is wrong with your mother's neck?'

I said, 'God, I don't know. But I'll ask her.'

I did, and she was vague about it. She said, 'Oh, I've had various falls over the years. It's probably something to do with that.'

I passed that message on to Joe, but we never followed it up. Six months later she got quite sick and eventually ended up in hospital. While she was there they diagnosed her with two forms of cancer. It started with a lump on her neck. That's where they took the biopsy from. They said she had two types of lymphoma: Hodgkin's and non-Hodgkin's. The odds were stacked against her.

She went through all the chemo and everything, and Joe gave her some healings alongside. She got over the cancer, but as a result of the chemotherapy her heart became damaged. It was really bad. She had just 27 per cent function when it was first diagnosed. Joe gave her healings for that, too. And today she is doing really well, without doubt a star 'pupil' as far as we are concerned, and I think even more so from the hospital's point of view.

She is back to her gardening and more. The other day I went over to see her, and found her out clearing cuttings from the wood. It's quite amazing how well she has recovered, she's terrific. The medical team did their thing, but she is pretty convinced that Joe's healings were what made the difference. Certainly the healings helped her on the way.

It's hard to rationalize what Joe does. It's difficult to explain it to friends. There have been many times when I've been convinced he could help a person. I might say, 'I know this healer. I reckon he might be able to help you. Would you think of going to him?' But when they ask me what he does, it's hard to describe it. People like to hear something tangible, something concrete. Joe's work is not very tangible.

He's helped me by easing my way through life's ups and downs. I feel he carries an energy within him, and he passes on that energy, acting as a catalyst for something positive to happen.

30. Fun, Frustration and Pain

Being a healer can bring me down at times. It can be tough. But, now and again, I use my gift to have a bit of fun. A few years ago I went out for a drink in my local bar, and there were some young lads there. They were members of a local soccer team, and they were there having a post-practice pint.

I enjoy the company of young people – I have a good connection with them – and we were chatting away about this and that. They all know what I do for a living; it's well known locally. And one of these lads turned round and said to me, 'Ah Joe. Would you do something for us?'

Now I'm not like Derren Brown or Keith Barry. I don't usually work in front of a crowd; that's not what I'm about. But on the odd occasion I'll go along with a request like that. And I felt if I didn't agree, they would only keep on at me, and not let me enjoy my pint in peace. So I said, 'Right, lads.'

'Yeah?' There were five or six of them there.

'Why don't you turn off your mobile phones.'

'Put them to silent, you mean?'

'No. Switch them right off, would you?'

There was a lot of laughter about this, because one of the lads was hoping some girl would ring him. But they did turn the phones off, and the barman, who had been listening to all this, asked for the phones and checked that they *were* all off.

'What do we do now?'

'Give it a minute,' I said. 'One of the mobile phones will

219

ring. And' – I put my hand on one lad's shoulder – 'it'll be yours.'

'Will it be his girlfriend?'

I laughed. 'It won't be anybody. There'll be nobody on the other end, obviously.'

So they were sitting there, forgetting their pints and just staring at their phones. The bar went silent. A minute is a long time when you're waiting. And the amazing thing was that when, after a minute, the lad's phone *did* ring, they all ran out of the bar with fright. The barman burst out laughing.

'That's enough of that, Joe,' he said. 'I don't want you frightening all my customers away.'

A couple of minutes later, the lads slunk back.

'How did you do that? How did you know?'

'I don't know.'

They kept on badgering me, but I honestly didn't know. As I say, I'm not into that line of work. I didn't know when I went into the bar that night that I would be performing a trick. And I didn't know, until I was asked, what I would be doing. It's like with a healing. It's all quite spontaneous.

I just do it. I wasn't frightened that night that the phone might not ring. I take each day at a time. I'm a healer. Other things come into that, of course they do. Maybe having fun like that is what keeps me sane.

One day a friend was collecting me from home and driving me out for lunch. He didn't tell me where we were going, and I asked him not to. That morning, before he arrived, I was in the kitchen having a second cup of coffee, and I drew two cars. These were old, vintage-type cars. I remember one was red, and the other was green. They were distinctive. The wheels had spokes, and the doors opened from back to front.

When I drew those cars, I could see the road, the mountains, the whole lot. I knew exactly where I would be going. And I was right. My friend collected me, and we set off. Twenty minutes later we were crossing the Wicklow Gap. We came to a lay-by, and I asked him to pull in. This was instinctive. And he did. Then I handed him the piece of paper with my drawing on, but I had folded the page in two. He took it and I asked him to open it up. He looked at me curiously, but did as I asked.

He frowned. 'Joe, what's this?'

'Look! Look what's coming up the hill.'

He looked, and there coming towards us were two vintage cars. One green and one red. They were exactly as I had drawn them on the piece of paper. My friend sat there, too stunned to speak. He looked at the cars, he looked at me and he looked at my drawing. His mouth was hanging open.

'How did you do that?'

'I don't know,' I said. 'It just came to me.'

I don't know why I drew those cars that day. Maybe it was just for a bit of fun. Or maybe I felt my friend was something of a sceptic, and needed reminding that I was who I say I am.

It's a strange thing, but people seem to sense I'm a healer. If someone has problems, their troubles will attach themselves to me like a magnet. I don't know why, because I always carry around positive energy, but trouble seems to attract the likes of me.

If I go into a shopping centre and sit down to relax – and this happened a lot when the kids were younger – some old lady would be sure to come over and sit down beside me. She'd open up her heart to me and tell me her woes. And often, when she had finished, and that could be half an hour later, she would turn round, look at me in surprise and say, 'I don't know why I told you about that.'

It happened all the time, and it still does. In a similar way, it happens in the pub too. I'll be sitting there, minding my own business, and, whether it's alcohol fuelled or whatever, some lad will focus on me. And I'll sense that I shouldn't be there, that there's going to be trouble.

In a case like that, I try not to make any contact with the guys. I don't meet their eye or try to talk to them. It makes no difference. I seem to draw them. They probably need healing or there's something wrong with them.

I remember being in a bar one night during the rugby season about five or six years ago. I was at the bar, chatting to a few of the locals, and one of the men, who was there for a match, had had more than a few. I knew this man was in a round. He'd been out all day and his money was running low. I saw him putting his hand in his pocket and start rooting around. He was worried. He didn't think he had enough money to buy another round, but he wanted another drink.

His biggest problem was pride. He was frightened of being thought a skinflint. If he was thinking straight and not panicking, he would have emptied out his pockets and probably found enough there to buy two rounds. But he was in too much of a state for that. I was just sitting there quietly, but he started to verbally abuse me.

'Oh, there he is. There's Joe Cassidy. The healer. The great fellow, or at least he thinks he is.' And he went on. And on. 'Who do ye think ye are? Healer? Psychic? Are ye for real?'

That lad wasn't in the bar often, but one of the others would have pointed me out. He was just looking for a fight, just being disrespectful. As I raised my pint to my mouth, he gave my arm a nudge, as if he was really getting ready for a fight. My beer spilt, but only a little.

The bar went quiet with tension. The man I was drinking with said, 'Cassidy, how do you get yourself out of *this* one?'

'Just give me a minute now.'

I didn't know what was going to happen next. And all the while the young lad was getting more and more agitated. I didn't plan it, but I turned round slowly and looked him squarely in the eye. Something triggered. He looked straight back at me. You could feel the agitation leave him. You could hear a quietness come into the bar, because I had said, 'Just give me a minute.' A calmness seemed to come over him. He put his hand up to call the barman and he ordered a pint. For me. The barman poured the pint, gave it to me and the lad paid for it. And all this just two minutes after he'd been slagging me.

'Thanks very much,' I said.

The other lads were watching in amazement. The barman just gave me a wink. The next moment, it was like the lad came to. He looked at me, then at my pint, and then at his friends, who were silently watching him. He was wondering what had made him buy me a drink. He slunk off to the Gents without a word.

There's another strange thing that happens to me sometimes when I'm healing someone. I can take on the symptoms of their illness. It seems to be part of the process. But when it comes to members of my close family, it can happen even before I am aware that they are having problems.

I woke up one morning just recently, and I wasn't able to turn over in the bed. I had excruciatingly bad pain in my hip and my back. This got worse when I tried to push myself up.

Eventually, I managed to sit on the side of the bed, but I wasn't able to stand up. I waited for a while, and after a few minutes I managed to pull myself up and stand. I used the wall and the furniture to help me to walk slowly out of the room. I felt like a very old man, and I reckon I looked like one too. My neighbour called that morning. He was very concerned for me, and wanted to take me to a doctor. Nowadays, however, my first reaction is not to go to my doctor immediately. I've become more aware of the effects that my work can have on me.

I was confined to the house all that day, as I wasn't able to drive. I tried to think which of my clients who was currently coming to me for healing, or who had spoken to me on the phone, might be associated with this pain, but I couldn't think of anyone.

When Jean came home from work, she was surprised that I was still in the state she'd seen me in that morning. She was heading into Naas that evening, so I decided to go with her. We called to see my mother. There was no answer at her house and we were just getting back into the car when the front door opened.

'You took your time!' I said, then I noticed that she was using two walking sticks to keep herself propped up. 'What's wrong with you?'

'It's my back,' she said. 'I can hardly walk, and the pain of it is killing me.'

I didn't know whether to laugh or cry. *Well, thank God for that*, I thought. I now knew the reason for my stiffness and pain.

Even though my mother is a great source of strength for me, she doesn't regularly ask me for healing, and I would never suggest she came to me. But I was *not* prepared to hold on to her pain for a minute longer than I needed to, so I planted a question in her head, and waited. And sure enough, she said, 'Would you be able to do anything for me, Joe, do you think?'

'I could give you healing for the pain,' I replied.

'That would be great,' she said. Then added, 'Sure, it won't do me any harm.'

I did the healing there and then. My own pain went almost immediately. It took a bit longer for my mother to get relief. I now give her healings regularly for pain.

Sometimes, when I'm working on a difficult case and I want to verify that what I am getting is correct, I deliberately look for a sign. I put it out to the universe. In one particular instance, when I did this, the figure three kept coming to me. It was like someone was saying, 'You will witness something three times, and then you'll know you are right.'

Jean and I had booked a trip to Amsterdam for a few days. The first night we walked down to the main square to get something to eat, and, rounding a corner, we bumped into a man who was pushing a bicycle. He apologized and said, 'Excuse me.'

'You're fine,' we said, and walked on. We didn't think any more about it. But the next night, we were going out at a different time, taking a different route, when I stumbled and bumped against someone. I said sorry, then did a double take. It was the same man, though this time he didn't have his bike with him. Then, two days later, we were walking through Amsterdam when we bumped into this same man. Yet again. He was startled and stood there in front of us, rubbing his chin.

He pointed at us and said, 'What the ... you? Why?'

And I said, 'Don't worry. It's fine. The message is for me.'

He looked at me with wild eyes. 'Three times! We've bumped into each other three times! In different places and at different times. What are the chances of that?'

I said, 'Believe you me, the message is for me.'

I felt happy, but that poor man seemed freaked by it. He was standing looking at me, still rubbing his chin in thought, until we turned the corner out of sight.

31. Things Happen for a Reason

When unexpected things happen in life, when we lose our car keys, miss a flight or get delayed by a ringing phone, I believe it's meant to be. Our plans are changed for a reason. This has been borne out to me in my life, time and time again.

Jean and I were attending a function in Newbridge. We'd been invited to the afters of a wedding, but had arranged to meet friends for a drink in a pub first. The pub was in Naas. We had two rounds, but when the bill came, I felt my pockets and they were empty. I'd left my wallet at home.

Our friends paid for the drinks, but I needed my wallet for the afters. I suggested that Jean go on to the wedding with our friends, and I'd go back home, fetch the wallet and then go and join them. So, instead of taking the road towards Newbridge, I had to go on the back road towards home. A couple of miles outside Naas, I noticed all these cars were parked up. There were a lot of people standing on the road; others were standing up on the bank. They were all staring in the same direction.

A man tapped on my window. 'There's been an accident,' he said. 'The road is blocked. Your best bet is to turn round and find another way through.'

I wasn't about to do that. The moment I saw the cars backed up, I knew why I'd left my wallet at home. A voice in my head was saying that this was meant to be. I got out of my car and I saw that a car had skidded and gone off the road. It was on its side in the field beyond. That's what everyone was looking at.

'What happened here?' I asked.

'There's a car in the field. A man is trapped inside. It looks bad!' shouted one man. I instinctively started walking towards the car. Another man tried to bar my way.

'The ambulance is on the way,' he said. 'I rang for it myself. There's nothing can be done for the guy now.'

I took no notice, but climbed over the ditch and saw the car on its side. The passenger door was facing the sky. I could see this man lying there at an odd angle.

'I told you.' The man had followed me into the field. 'The man is dead,' he said, though how he could be sure of that is anybody's guess. 'You don't want to see it,' he said, and I realized he was shaken.

'I want to check for myself,' I said. And he helped me to manoeuvre up and over the car a little. The top of the window was open. I reached my arm through it, and the window dropped right down. I thought, *If this man is dead, I can at least give him a prayer.* I put my left hand on his head. I didn't think about it, I just did it. I remember there was blood on him – at least there was blood on my hand when I took it away.

Tools were strewn all over the place, and there was a tobacco tin and papers scattered around. I reckoned this man worked in the building trade. I remember thinking, *Let this man live. He's somebody's son, somebody's partner. His family need him.*

Two minutes later he moved. *Thank God,* I thought, *he's alive.* But his feet were caught under the pedals.

He groaned. 'I want to get out of here.'

'Can you hold on? The ambulance will be here soon.' I was worried he might damage himself. Perhaps his spine was broken? But he was in a panic; he seemed hyper. He kept wriggling his leg, frantically trying to set his feet free. He was desperate to get out of the vehicle. I think perhaps he was frightened that it might go up in flames.

'Look,' I said, 'I can even hear the ambulance.' And I could. It was obviously on its way from Naas.

'I have to get out,' he said. 'I have to get out.'

There was no stopping him. He managed to nudge himself up, and put his hand up on the window. And with my help, he pulled himself out of the car. He was unsteady and dazed. We insisted he sit down. He had blood on his ear. We found a jacket to put under him. When the ambulance crew arrived and came to work on the man, I left him and walked away, back to my car. I noticed this chap had decapitated a hefty tree. I remember being aware that this crowd of people, who were still standing there, still watching the accident, were staring at me, open-mouthed.

Now, I'm not saying that man was ever dead. The onlookers had just assumed that, because at first glance, lying there unconscious with his arms flung out, he did look it. But the thing is, nobody had checked. People had just left him alone. And even if he had been dead, and therefore beyond help, nobody deserves that. I find that when I come across an accident, my first reaction is always to go straight to the victim.

He deserved a prayer said over him at the very least. I'd do that, rather than walk away. I'm sure the people who loved that man, like his family, would like to think someone took the trouble.

There was another night when I came across an accident at the Kildare–Offaly border. It was a wet winter's evening and my friend was driving along on a country road that I had seldom been on. When we turned the corner we came across a car crash. It had only just happened. A man was lying on the road; he'd evidently been thrown out of his car. We were the second car on the scene, and it was teeming with rain.

When we got out, the man in front of us said he had rung for an ambulance. My friend's concern was to get someone to flash the oncoming cars. I said to my friend, 'I'll go over and see if I can do anything for this man.' So I went over. It was a young man. I picked up a sense of panic. When I knelt down, he grabbed my hand very tightly and asked me to pass on a message. I asked him what it was.

'I want you to tell my mother that I love her,' he said.

'You're not from these parts, are you?' I wanted to keep him talking.

'I'm from Wales. I'm here working with the Forestry. Will you please tell my mother that I love her.'

I said, 'Hold on here. This might sound strange to you, but I'm a healer. Do you mind if I put my hand on you and give you a healing?'

'No,' he said, 'that's fine.'

He looked very weak. I put my hand on his head, but there was no way he'd let go of my other hand. I will never forget his fear. I was talking to someone who truly believed they were going to die.

I said, 'Don't be thinking like that. You'll be meeting your mother again. You'll be fine.'

'I don't think so.'

'Well, I do. Just hang on, will you? Hang on.'

I remember I was soaked, crouching there on the side of the road. My friend had got a jacket from the boot to cover the young guy.

Eventually the ambulance arrived. As they were working on the guy, putting him on a stretcher and into the ambulance, I heard one of them say, 'Things don't look too good for him.'

My friend dropped me home and he texted me later, asking if I was OK. He wrote, 'Wasn't that a dreadful night? A terrible experience.' He'd asked the ambulance men if he could follow up to see how the man was, and they said he could ring the hospital. He did that and there was no news.

He rang the hospital again the next day and was told that the lad was fine.

'He was sitting up having his breakfast,' they said. 'And he'll be going home this morning.'

I do know that not everybody can be healed. But I know I was meant to meet that man from Wales that night.

I never met the Welshman again, but then I wouldn't expect to see someone from an accident scene again. But there was one time I remember. We were driving through a small village, and a group of motorcyclists passed us. They were driving incredibly irresponsibly and one of them did a wheelie on the road. Liam was about twelve at the time, and even *he* thought it was foolish.

When we were about two miles outside the village, we could see a commotion up ahead. There had been a crash. Two motorcyclists had collided. One was getting to his feet, but the other was lying on the road.

I got out of the car, telling Jean and the children to stay there, and went to that biker. His clothes were torn, and his bike had skidded up the road ahead of him, then landed in a ditch. It was a hot day, and the tarmac was sticky. I remember the biker had a pebble lodged in his chin. He wasn't wearing a helmet. He was conscious, but he was groaning with pain. It looked to me as if he had broken a leg.

I put my hand on his head and told him to relax. I remember his eyes just looking at me. Then, once the ambulance had arrived, I got back into my car and we drove home.

About two weeks later, I was taking Liam to see Eminem in Punchestown. We often went to concerts and music festivals together. He loved that when he was a kid. We'd gone to buy some burgers, and on our way back, Liam nudged me.

'Look!' he said.

And I saw the biker from the accident making his way slowly towards us. He was on crutches. I didn't try to stop him, or talk to him. But as he passed me, he stopped suddenly and stared at me. I knew from his puzzled expression that he was thinking, *No, it couldn't surely be him. Not that man from the accident!* I didn't make him any the wiser, but my hope is that he learned from that experience.

Earlier this year I was in the clinic, having just finished working with a client, when the phone rang. It was the girl who was booked in at seven o'clock. It was almost six when she rang.

'I'm sorry, Joe,' she said. 'I'm sorry to ring with such short notice, but I can't make my appointment tonight.'

I don't charge people for missed appointments. It wouldn't occur to me to do that. My philosophy is that things happen for a reason. So I said, 'No problem. Thanks for letting me know.' And we rearranged her appointment for another day. Now, my next appointment was at eight o'clock. At the time we were not living in our own house as we were having work done on it. We were renting a house a mile or two down the road. So I decided to go home and have a cup of coffee.

My son, Liam, who is nineteen, was there before me. He does some healing too. He works mainly with animals. I didn't know that he had a woman calling to the house with a dog that night. When he told me, this voice in my head immediately said, 'There will be someone who needs your healing out of this.' That might sound odd, but it's what happens in my life all the time.

As I was boiling the kettle, the doorbell rang and this lady came in with a terrier. I took one look at her and knew my gut feeling had been right. I thought, *This is why the young girl cancelled. I'm meant to meet this lady tonight.* I didn't say anything, and Liam took the dog outside to work on him. We chatted until he asked her to come outside so that he could explain the dog's condition. When she came back in again, she looked distracted.

'Was that all right?' I said.

'Well, your son ...' she began.

'Yes?'

'He's very perceptive.'

The woman had brought the dog because his paws were yellowed and peeling. She assumed he had a skin infection. But Liam said there was nothing at all wrong with the dog – not physically, anyway.

'He said my dog is stressed,' said the lady. 'And he asked me if there might be a reason for this.'

'And is there?'

'Oh yes! My husband isn't well. He's been unwell for years, but he's particularly bad at the moment.'

I nodded, and took a sip of coffee.

'And the dog has taken to sleeping on top of him. I think it's my husband who needs the healing, not the dog at all!'

This was just idle chat. She didn't realize she was talking to another healer. She went on to say how worried she was about her husband, and how conventional medicine didn't seem to be helping. And I realized she was here because her husband was meant to see me. I didn't make a big deal of it. I just said, 'Liam works mainly healing dogs, and I work mainly healing people.'

'Oh, *you're* a healer too? A friend of mine had healing done recently.' She mentioned the name. 'And she's better now. Was that you?'

It was. Though in that case it had been distance healing.

Then she blanched and laughed. 'He's Liam Cassidy,' she said, 'so you must be Joe Cassidy.'

'That's me.'

'But that's mad,' she said. 'I know all about you. I was given your name years ago. I always meant to come to you. I'm sorry. I just hadn't made the connection.'

Before that lady left, she made an appointment for her husband. She was amazed by the coincidence, but that's the way life works. We turn right at the crossroads instead of left; we think it was a mistake, but it was probably meant to be. We should learn to go with the flow.

I am very lucky that my philosophy in life has been shared by Jean and my children. This is not to say that it has always been plain sailing. Sometimes the decisions we make, based on the philosophy that things happen for a reason, have left us exposed to ridicule. We understand that others usually think they have our best interests at heart. And I'm sure they have.

People were very surprised when Laura took time out from her course in Trinity College to start writing full time, but we supported her decision. She went with her instincts, and it has paid off for her. The teenage fiction she writes is now published by Puffin.

When it got to the point that Liam felt he had no other option but to leave school, we supported him in that decision. It was a very difficult time for him and he felt different from his friends, because he was the only one not going to school. The hardest thing for Jean and me was trying to explain that decision to our friends and family. It was a tough decision, but it has proved to be for the best.

32. Liam Cassidy's Story

When I was in primary school there was a reading one day from the Bible. It was about a water diviner. I put up my hand.

'Yes, Liam?'

'My dad's a water diviner,' I said.

I remember there was a lot of interest. And a few days later I took in water-divining rods and showed people how it all worked.

Joe, my dad, has been a water diviner and healer almost since I can remember. I've always accepted it. But Joe has had trouble acknowledging that he's passed his gift on to me.

When I was young, about nine or ten, I often talked to this older man. I'd be playing with my PlayStation, and he'd be there with me. I'd tell him stuff about my life. He was like an older version of Joe. I enjoyed talking to him.

Later on, I realized that man was Joe's father, my grandfather, who died before I was born. It didn't seem strange to me, because I knew Joe saw spirits too. Joe realized what I was doing.

I think Joe was aware that I was like him, but he was hoping that I wasn't. I remember one time he drove me past this house. He said, 'My father drove me past this house when I was your age. One day I'll tell you the story about it. Look, there it is.' He pointed to this derelict house. And suddenly I was in one of the rooms. The first thing I saw was a dress on the bed. Then I saw a wardrobe. The room was painted cream. As I was leaving the house I could see this downstairs room. It was a black, dark room and it gave me a bad feeling. The whole thing scared me. My body was in the car, but I wasn't. I had no clue what was going on. I was only twelve.

When I was back in the car, I said, 'Oh my God.'

Joe said later that only thirty seconds had passed, but to me it felt much longer. When I got home, I drew the inside of the house and told Joe about the cream room. He was impressed. I'd seen something in that house that he hadn't. I'd seen it as it was in the past. I realized I was good at what Joe did.

I have always been interested in Joe's work. I enjoyed going in the car with him when he was working on a house. I'd sit in the car, waiting. I found it all exciting. I loved earwigging when he was talking to Jean about the stories.

I worried about Joe sometimes though. He worked so hard. I'd hear him on the phone trying to please everyone. I'd say, 'Relax! You don't have to see them immediately. They can hardly get another diviner from the Golden Pages. They'll wait.'

There was another incident, when I was young. It was when Joe had his clinic at one end of our house and our computer was there too. I was sitting at the computer one day when I noticed movement in the corner of my eye. I turned round and there was a man standing beside the counter. He was wearing a robe and holding a child's woollen hat in his hands. He was staring at it, and when I stood up from the computer he smiled at me.

'Oh. You must be here for Joe,' I said.

I walked round to the main part of the house and told Joe this man was waiting for him.

'I don't have anyone booked in,' Joe said.

'Well, there's a man waiting for you in the clinic.'

Joe went up but was back five minutes later.

'There's nobody there,' he said.

'Well, there was someone there. He was looking at the child's woollen hat that you have up there.'

Joe looked at me strangely.

I shrugged my shoulders. 'He must have gone.'

Joe just looked a bit puzzled. But I knew someone was there.

Later, Joe told me that he was doing distance healings on a very sick boy who was in hospital. His parents had given Joe one of his favourite hats so that Joe could use it to send healing to the child. I believe this man was there to help with the healing.

Even though these things had happened, I didn't think much about them. It was when I reached my teens that it started to impact on my life. In secondary school I would be in class and then I would find myself worrying unnecessarily about things, like if Joe was sick or if Joe and Jean were splitting up. I knew there was no substance to these worries, but I would feel nauseous and constantly distracted.

I also seemed to attract the attention of a number of teachers who would get agitated with me for no particular reason. I tried to ignore these situations and even moved school to see if things would improve, but it just got worse. I eventually left school and I was very upset about this. Jean encouraged me to talk to Joe's friend, Dr Michael Corry. He was a psychiatrist and a psychotherapist, but he had a very open mind, and Joe felt sure, as a friend, he would help me. And he was brilliant.

He accepted me for who I am. He explained that people like me are very sensitive to the energies around us, and that when I am in the company of other people I am very susceptible to picking up on their concerns and worries. He made me see I didn't have to be a diviner in the same way that Joe was, but that I could train as a psychiatrist or a psychologist, and use my gift in my profession.

I found it easy to talk to him. I remember he told me a story about a shaman who was over from America. They had dinner together, and this man said he had a wolf guide.

I have had a wolf guide since I was thirteen, but I had never spoken to anyone about it. It was great to be able to tell Michael. He said, 'A wolf is one of the most powerful animal guides a person can have.'

I explained to him that Joe had helped me to find my animal guide some time before. I had to close my eyes and imagine I was in a forest.

Joe said an animal would come strongly into my mind. And the animal that came to me was a wolf.

When I was leaving the room, Michael Corry hugged me and he howled — like a wolf. I got a kick out of this. He was the first adult, apart from Joe, Jean and Laura, who I felt respected me. When he passed away in 2010, I felt a sense of loss. The first person who had really helped me had gone.

Up until I was seventeen Joe didn't want to accept that I might be a diviner. He certainly didn't want to push me in that direction. He didn't want the doubting comments and the ridicule he has had over the years directed at me. It was a bit like an actor who doesn't want to encourage a family member to work in his field, because he knows what an insecure, difficult life it can be.

When I was young it was fun being like Joe. But at nineteen it can be a pain. When I pick up on people, I'm taking on a lot. At school I was feeling down without getting any benefit, and I realized it was because I wasn't using the gift I had.

I decided to try some healing. When I said that, Joe said he would teach me. He was telling me to start with the head, then go to the chest, then the stomach, then the feet. I tried doing that, but it didn't feel natural to me. I wanted to do it my own way. It caused friction between us.

I started by healing people. I put out the word, and people who were open to it came to me. People said they found the healing very relaxing. Often they would fall asleep as I was giving it to them.

I didn't find it easy though. One woman cried about her broken marriage; I was only eighteen, the same age as her daughter, and although I was telling her things, I realized that if I told her everything I sensed, I'd upset her more. I had to censor what I said. I found that difficult.

I'm very aware that when people look at me and see a teenager talking to them, they don't always like it. Especially if the truth is hard. Because of that, and because I wanted to feel free to do things my own way, I decided to work with animals. To be different from Joe, who works mainly with large farm animals, I decided to concentrate on dogs.

Joe has a friend who breeds dogs. I worked on the bitches and helped them to get into pup. It was really effective. Nearly all of them got into pup. There was one dog this man owned who was extremely ill. He had lost a lot of weight. You could see his ribs when I first worked on him, and he came good. We own him now.

When I heal — whether it's a person or an animal — I put my hand on their head, and I imagine blue and orange on my arm. I don't know how it works.

Animals seem to trust me. When I'm healing them they just sit there. They are so calm. I remember, just the other day, a woman brought her dog to me. It saw me and came with me to the treatment room. She was amazed. She said that dog would never go with anyone.

I don't see myself ending up as a traditional healer. I don't want to see animals or people day after day, the way Joe does. He loves nothing better than to spend lots of time with people, but I have more of a business brain.

One thing I do know. I don't want to end up like some people do, performing on a stage. There's much more to being a diviner than that.

I've already done some corporate work. I've done a bit of that with Joe. We would sit round the table trying to name a price, they would make an offer, and I would come back with a counter offer. Joe would be kicking me under the table. He would be ready to agree to the first figure they thought of. He couldn't understand that I'd keep going.

I know my work is worth it. I've proved that it is. I worked one time for a company who wanted to sink a well. They knew water charges were coming in, so they wanted a private source of water in order to save money. I told them where to drill for a well and how far down they would have to drill to find an excellent source of water.

Then there was another man. He owned a ton of properties, and after the crash his business was down. He wasn't getting the rents in. He called me in to cleanse the energy of the buildings. I did that, and business went up again.

I can do distance healing too. When I was younger, Joe would test my skills. He would give me a photograph of someone and ask me what I was picking up. I would always be able to tell him what their problem was. Like one time, he gave me a photograph of a middle-aged woman and I said, 'She hasn't got a problem. It's her husband.' And Joe said I was right.

I'm back in college now. I'm doing music production and sound engineering in Temple Bar. I'm enjoying all of it. But there is a very big downside to being a diviner. I'm nineteen. It's a time for going out, having a drink and having a good time with friends, and there are times when it's hard to do that. I'll be in the pub, and I'll pick up on the energy. Sometimes it gets too much. I can't enjoy myself, sensing the way the night will pan out, so I end up just going home.

I was at the music festival Oxegen a couple of years ago. For the first two days I had a great time. I blocked out the energy. The third day I went home for a shower. I was going to head out again, but I got this sick feeling. I knew it was a sign that I shouldn't go back, so I didn't. It turned out that a group of young lads were picking fights with various groups, and that night they ended up causing trouble around the tents where my friends were staying. I'd sensed it was going to happen.

I've accepted my gift, and I'm going along with it. There's not a lot else I can do. I'm confident now. But I'm still learning. Joe has accepted that I am like him, and that I have my own way of doing things. He's relaxed about it, and supportive. Jean has always been supportive; she's known Joe since he was a kid, so she's always said that it's just like life repeating itself.

Epilogue

Many things interest me, but I am fascinated by the concept of time. As human beings we're conditioned about time from a very young age. Whether our days are spent in the crèche or school or work, time controls our lives. Everything revolves around our schedule.

We concentrate only on the realm of time that we live in. Sometimes, when I go into houses, I can tune into the past. I can also tune into the future. I can see what happened or what is going to happen, as if I'm watching a reel of film. Occasionally things can get caught in time.

There's a place in Wales where some hillwalkers have had the same experience over the years. They are walking along, enjoying the countryside, and the next moment they hear a plane in distress. The plane crashes and they run to the rescue. They see a pilot trying to get out, but then everything disappears in front of them. They are still standing there, but the plane has gone. Lots of people have witnessed this scenario in the very same spot. A plane crashed there during the Second World War and there haven't been any accidents since, yet people continue to report seeing the plane.

I can go into a house and pick up on an energy, I can communicate with somebody who used to live there over eighty-four years ago. It's not like they've been waiting around for eighty-four years until Joe Cassidy arrives. They are on the other side, and they can zone in and out when they want to. Eighty-four years on the other side is probably just a drop in the ocean. Life here is very short, even if you live a long life.

I have had to describe myself as psychic in the past, when I was at my wits' end, but I don't think of myself as psychic. I just have an ability, a sixth sense. Take animals, for instance. I like to say that the animal instinct is in all of us. After all, we came from the forest. During the tsunami, despite all the technology we have, thousands of people died. But lots of the animals survived. I watched coverage on TV of dogs, monkeys and many other animals moving up to the top of a hill, to protect themselves from the water before it approached. Their senses kicked in; they knew what was coming, and all that mattered was survival. The elephant that had never acted up before in the zoo broke his chains and walked to the top of the mountain. He could sense danger before it arrived. He used an innate instinct. That's an ability that animals have – a sense that we haven't got, or maybe we do, but we don't tap into it. When a human says they are using their sixth sense, some people can have a problem with it.

Nothing is black and white. I like to call myself a philosopher. If somebody comes along and offers a view on something, I might not agree with them, but I will give that person respect and hear them out. Recently I was crossing the Ha'penny Bridge in Dublin when I saw a young man begging. He wasn't actually asking for money, he just held a cup in front of him. I was standing at the river wall when another man came along in work clothes. He looked like an electrician. He seemed to know the young man, and he bent down and said, 'I'm really sorry, I didn't know it had got this bad for you.'

'Sure what can I do, I lost my job. Sure what can I do, only keep hope up.'

The electrician asked the young man if he had anywhere to stay that night, and he said that he had. The electrician was shocked because he knew this young man and now he was sitting on the Ha'penny Bridge.

Most people walking past probably thought, *Look at him, I expect he's shoving needles into his arm*. Even if he was, there are all kinds of reasons why people end up like this young man, begging on the street.

I am a people person. I don't believe you should label somebody because they have a different way of life from you, or because they come from a different race. I remember years ago I was out pushing Laura in the buggy. She had her bottle but I had no drink of water with me. It was a scorching hot day. Travellers were parked on the side of the road, and a woman was cleaning her caravan. I spotted a child going over to this big milk churn and taking water out of it with a glass.

A lot of people were giving out at the time about the travellers being parked there, and were giving them abuse. Many people wouldn't have even dared to stop. But I asked the woman if I could have some water and she said, 'Certainly, no problem,' and we chatted for a few minutes. She didn't say, 'Feck off, you're from the settled community and you give out about me.' Don't judge a book by its cover. Listen to other people.

A lot of people live for their summer holiday and spend a lot of time thinking about it. Or they spend the week looking forward to their weekend. They do not live in the moment. When you get up in the morning and go outside there's probably a tree to the right or the left of you, or something else

244

of beauty. Lots of people don't even notice, but when I walk out into the garden, I see everything. We should appreciate what's in front of us every day. We are conditioned to believe that we must get away to relax, that we must take that break away from home. But imagine if you found a way to relax every day of the week. If you appreciate nature, if you take a moment each day to really see it, it will enhance your life and your well-being. Live in the present, not in the future.

We spend a lot of time thinking about the future, and much of this time is spent worrying about it. What's the point in worrying? It is not worth putting your energy into worrying about something that you have no control over. It is better to put your energy into what you are trying to achieve that day.

At the moment, people are finding it hard to pay their mortgage. But if you're sitting in your house, then you still have your house. You should keep saying, 'I still have my house, and I will always have it,' rather than thinking, *When are the banks going to come in and take it off me?* You should always be mindful of the message you are putting out to the universe. It's like the saying goes, 'Be careful what you wish for because it might come true.' Think positive.

There is a lot of negativity when money is tight for people. It is a big change for us not to be able to buy as we please. Plenty of money gives us plenty of opportunities. Maybe it's actually a positive that we all had to slow down. I spoke to a man recently who had dropped his son off at school for the first time in eleven years. The young lad was chatting to him on the way over, he was so excited that his daddy was dropping him off at school. He got out of the car and gave his dad a kiss on the cheek, and the man cried the whole way back home. He realized that he hadn't talked to his son before

6 p.m. in the last eleven years. He had always gone to work before his son got up for school.

A lot of the time you can find a positive in even the most negative situations. Of course, this doesn't apply to everything. I'm the first to say that if you're dealing with something like a sick child, it's very hard to be positive. Or when somebody close to us dies, it is hard for us to see the positive things in our lives. We mourn their death instead of also celebrating their life.

We're all going to die. It's ahead of us all, so when somebody passes away we should look at what they did when they were here, what they got out of life. And we should appreciate the other positive things in our own lives.

I loved my father, and I had a great relationship with him. I watched him worrying about money, and that put a lot of pressure on him, but he had a happy life. And I firmly believe that if my father hadn't died, I wouldn't have written this book. I would have probably worked alongside him, and I might have been happy, but I wouldn't have been completely myself.

Of course, I wish he and my brother Pat were still alive, but I have to look at all the positive things in my life, all the people I've met and am going to meet, all the stories I've been part of and will be part of in the future. I'm very grateful to be called the diviner.

Acknowledgements

Thanks to my agent Faith O'Grady, my editor Patricia Deevy and everyone at Penguin Ireland for the opportunity to tell my story. Thanks also to the fantastic people who have allowed me to be part of their stories, some of whom are now my very good friends. Thanks to my parents, brothers and sisters for creating a happy childhood, and to my parents-in-law for all their support. Thanks to Derek for encouraging me to be myself; and to Heidi for the healings that energize me. Thanks to Barry and Caroline for their genuine friendship, and to Siobhan for telling her story. Thanks to the greater force that chose this path for me, that sent Sue Leonard my way to listen to my story in the beautiful setting of Glendalough Hotel, and who in turn used her exceptional skills to structure this book with me. Finally, thanks to my daughter Laura for looking out for me and for her help in making this book possible; my son Liam for keeping me strong through his strength of mind and great sense of humour; and to Jean for being the best story of my life.